A

Thousand

More

A NOVEL

K. S. Lynn

Praise for

A *Thousand* More

"*A Thousand More* takes readers on a harrowing journey across decades of love, loss, lies, deceit, sorrow, and redemption. The unexpected twists and turns keep readers wondering what will happen next with their beloved characters. It's a story of the power of love and forgiveness. This debut novel is one readers won't want to put down."

— LISA A. KING,
author of *Just Do You, Leadership, Authenticity, and Your Personal Brand*

"This heartfelt story about family, identity, and the secrets we carry pulled me in from the first page. I eagerly followed the lives of these characters, and at the end, I was wiping away tears."

— SUE MULLER HACKING,
best-selling author of *Heels to Hiking Boots: Exploring the World to Find the Way Home*

"*A Thousand More* begins with a heartless choice that haunts us through this wonderfully complex story of friendship, romance, tragedy, and betrayal, leading us to love some characters while hating others. Characters are the heart of any good story, and K. S. Lynn delivers."

— JOHN S. MALNOR,
author of *Killers Keepers and Scars of Justice*

Cover Design by Keegan Evans
Interior design by K. S. Lynn

Published in the United States by Twenty Years Publishing, LLC.
Owego, New York
First Edition

Library of Congress Control Number: 2025911020

ISBN 979-8-9989217-1-1 (Print Assigned)
ISBN 979-8-9989217-0-4 (eBook Assigned)
ISBN 979-8-9989217-2-8 (Audiobook Assigned)

To Carol, Sharon, and Kathy

Your absences are felt daily and deeply.

Cherish the presence of loved ones, for one day you will feel their absence and realize the new reality of your present.

~K. S. Lynn

Content Warning

This is a work of fiction. While the story and characters are a product of the author's imagination, the book explores themes of adoption, miscarriage, infidelity, sex, death, and adult language. These themes may be triggering for some readers. The author has approached these topics with care and respect, aiming to shed light on complex human experiences. However, individual reactions may vary, and reader discretion is advised. If you or someone you know is affected by similar issues, please seek support from a trusted professional or helpline.

CHAPTER 1

Manassas, Virginia
June 30, 1982

Ann Carrington never dreamed the recklessness of two seventeen-year-olds would be the answer to her prayers. At thirty-three years old, she had built a successful career in real estate, married a man who adored her, and lived an affluent lifestyle. But her failure to bear children overshadowed it all. After three miscarriages in as many years, the adoption of the teens' identical twins would end the deep yearning for a child that had held her captive for as long as she could remember.

Ann stood in the doorway, breathing in the scent of lavender, while admiring the completed nursery. Everything was in order. The custom mahogany cribs adorned with white silk sheets were thoughtfully placed against a mural of blush pink roses. She hired and befriended Martha, the perfect nanny, and in two months, her daughters would fill the elaborate cribs.

She closed her eyes, and the smile fell from her lips, hearing Seth's voice in her head. *Ann, why must you fret over every detail? It's much too soon to be worrying yourself with the nursery.* She released a heavy sigh, then ran her fingers down the light switch, leaving only the dim glow of a nightlight in the nursery.

Ann walked down the hall to the main bedroom and settled under the plush duvet of their king-size four-poster bed and turned off the table lamp. When she closed her eyes, she imagined Seth cradling their daughters, completely captivated by them, bringing a smile back to her lips. No longer would she be plagued by loneliness when business deals pulled her husband away, as Martha and the twins would fill her days and nights with the companionship she craved. Her family at last would be complete.

She reached over and laid her hand on Seth's pillow. "You won't be able to leave them as easily as you do me," she whispered to the empty bed beside her.

Ann moved restlessly in her sleep, her eyes darting side to side behind closed lids as if she were following the intense rally of a tennis match.

She opened the nursery door to find a young woman sitting in the rocking chair, cradling two infants and talking softly to them. "Mommy and Daddy love you. No one will ever take our baby girls from us."

A young man appeared before her, trying to push her out of the nursery, and shouted, "You can't have them!"

She heard the telephone ring, ran to her bedroom, picked up the receiver, and cried, "Seth, they took our girls, Seth?"

"Mrs. Carrington, this is Ms. Phillips of Loving Hearts. I'm sorry to inform you that the biological parents have changed their minds."

NO! PLEASE! NO! she screamed as tears spilled down her cheeks.

She turned around and was standing in an empty nursery, the mural of roses now a dull gray wall. The cribs, changing table, rocking chair, even the floor-to-ceiling drapes—gone. Everything was gone.

The telephone rang for the third time, causing Ann's heart to race as her hand searched the bedside table in the dark. Her fingers traced the handset, lifting it from the base, finally ending the incessant ring. Half asleep and startled, she raised her head from the pillow and answered timidly. "Hello?"

"Mrs. Carrington, this is Ms. Phillips..."

Ann sat on the side of her bed, wide awake, holding the receiver to her ear, the nightmare still fresh in her mind. She trembled, waiting ring after tortuous ring for her call to be answered as the clock on her bedside table stared back at her, reaching 2:00 a.m.

A weary voice finally responded. "Hello?"

"Martha, they are here. The twins are here. Ms. Phillips of Loving Hearts called, and Seth is out of town. I don't know what to do," she rambled.

"Oh, my goodness. Ann, I'll meet you at the hospital."

"Thank you, thank you. Oh, Martha, I had the most horri—"

Martha interrupted her. "Ann, listen to me."

"Okay," she said, and closed her eyes, telling herself it was only a nightmare. It wasn't real.

"Ann, take a deep breath and let it out slowly."

Ann nodded. "I will. Thank you, Martha." Then she abruptly hung up the handset and ran to her walk-in closet.

She grabbed a pair of black slacks, a white silk blouse, and her pink stilettos, then stopped in the doorway. "What are you thinking? You're not showing a house, Ann. It's the birth of your daughters." She turned around and placed the heels back on the wall of footwear, then grabbed her black leather penny loafers and a light pink cardigan. "There, much more practical."

She threw the clothes on the bed and did as Martha told her, took a deep breath, and let it out slowly. With Seth out of town, she was grateful that Martha would be at the hospital with her. But even with the news of the twins' early arrival, she still felt a deep sadness.

"Seth, our daughters are here. If only you were. Why must they always send you so far from me?"

The two women stood peering through the glass barrier. Compassion and fear covered Ann's deep brown eyes. The neonatal intensive care unit (NICU) seemed such a cold, sterile environment with so many monitors and wires that snaked over the twins' tiny bodies. Ann was desperate to cradle her newborn daughters in her arms.

At two and a half pounds, Danielle's imperfect heart was monitored closely, and with any luck, she would not require surgery to repair the small hole. Michelle was stronger, stable, and two pounds more than her identical twin sister.

Ann's voice cracked. "It's too soon. They weren't supposed to come until August."

She felt Martha's arm wrap around her. "They are in excellent hands, dear."

Sadness lingered in Ann's eyes. Was the universe once again telling her she was not meant to be a mother?

One Month Earlier

Martha Kirkwood sat in the Carrington's formal living room, admiring their stately home. At forty-five years old, she would start over once again. When the children she reared aged out, she moved on to the next family, caring for their most precious members.

It had been nearly a decade since she cared for an infant, but she always cherished creating a special bond with 'her little loves,' as she referred to them. Unable to have children of her own, Martha needed the families as much as they needed her.

It was her mother's untimely death that led her down the path of nurturing and caring for children. A week before her sixteenth birthday, Martha was forced to drop out of school to become the caretaker of her four younger siblings. After seeing her brothers and sisters off to school, she took on yet another role of her mother's; cleaning the homes of Virginia's upper class.

Martha had learned that affluent societies had little compassion for the personal matters of their hired staff. They were essential, but easily replaceable. A handful of her mother's employers took pity on her, offering only a fraction of what they paid her mother. She accepted graciously, as any extra money would help her father pay the household expenses and feed the large family.

Martha became intrigued by the upper class, watching their mannerisms and how they carried themselves. Their slightly southern accent took on a sophisticated life of its own when they spoke. At night, she would stand in front of the mirror trying to 'correct' her Southern-Scottish meld and mimic the conversations she eavesdropped on while busying herself in the adjacent room of her employer's stately home. It wasn't long before the roll of her "r's" disappeared. She spoke and carried herself with confidence and class as she emulated the affluent dialect.

Her father remarried almost two years to the day of her mother's death. The woman, a widow herself, brought along two young sons, adding to the already crowded home. Martha no longer needed to run her family's household, and upon her eighteenth birthday, she was expected to leave her family home and forge a life of her own. The wages she earned from cleaning estates would no longer belong to her family but become her livelihood.

Of her mother's many clients, Mrs. Gladwell was the first who allowed Martha to take over her mother's housekeeping services.

Martha gathered her supplies, preparing to leave for the day, and approached the foyer where Mrs. Gladwell stood. "Mrs. Gladwell, can I do anything else for you?" she asked.

"Martha, I've noticed that you carry yourself confidently and are well spoken."

Martha stood taller with a glow of pride. "Yes, ma'am, I suppose I do."

"It seems I am in need of a nanny. I assume your siblings no longer require your supervision. Is that correct?"

"Yes, Mrs. Gladwell, that is correct." She knew the wealthy had a furtive way of gathering information, particularly if it benefited them.

"Perfect. Your room will be down the hall from the children. You may bring your belongings on Sunday evening. Monday morning, the children will need to be woken at 7:00 a.m. sharp."

"Thank you, Mrs. Gladwell. It will be my pleasure to care for your children." Martha nodded, and so began her lifelong career.

Ann entered the room and sat on an identical sofa, pulling Martha from her daydream. A large ornate coffee table served as a polite barrier between them. Ann was a radiant woman, Martha guessed, in her early thirties, with strawberry blonde hair that sat neatly on her shoulders, framing her delicate, attractive features. She looked like a polished professional but appeared nervous and unsure about the paramount vetting of someone who would be her newborn's nanny. But it was the loneliness in Ann's eyes that made Martha curious.

Martha realized that her confident, soothing tone must have eased her potential employer's nerves when Ann walked over and settled beside her only a few minutes into the interview. Ann shared that after trying for years to conceive and being devastated by false hopes and miscarriages, she threw herself into her real estate business.

Martha smiled politely and tried to get a word in, but Ann rambled on about her husband, Seth. He was a corporate lawyer who, with his charm and Robert Redford resemblance, swept her off her feet, marrying her only after six months. They had lived all over the world and finally put down roots in Virginia. He was fiercely protective of her and would do anything to see her with a child of her own.

Ann paused to take a breath, allowing Martha to finally ask, "So, when are you expecting the twins, dear?"

Ann's face brightened. "August, the end of August. Seth is responsible for setting the adoption in motion, and I am eternally grateful to him." Ann leaned forward and took Martha's hand in hers. "He's entrusted me with finding the perfect nanny, and I know we've only just met, but I believe I have found her."

Martha's eyes widened. This nervous, soon-to-be mother of twins appeared to need more than just a nanny. Although there was only a little over a decade between them, she felt an overwhelming maternal protection for Ann. Martha couldn't explain it, but knew this was where she was supposed to be.

Her eyes softened, then she laid her hand on Ann's. "I would be honored to be your twins' nanny."

July 30th

The neonatologist entered her office, shut the door, and sat at her desk.

"Good evening, Mr. and Mrs. Carrington. Thank you for coming to the hospital on such short notice." Her tone was soft, but she held a sober demeanor. "Danielle's vitals are currently stable; however, she presented with arrhythmia earlier, and I'm afraid her breathing has become compromised as well."

Seth glanced at his wife's tear-filled eyes and grasped her hand, then looked back at the doctor. "I'm assuming she'll require surgery to repair her heart?"

The doctor tilted her head. "I had hoped to avoid surgery; however, with the recent events, yes, it is necessary."

Ann squeezed her husband's forearm. "Oh, dear."

Seth stood and extended his hand. "Thank you, doctor. Whatever she needs, we fully support your recommendations."

Ann sat quietly in the passenger seat, praying Danielle would survive the surgery.

Seth took his right hand off the steering wheel and placed it on Ann's. "Darling, the doctors will take excellent care of her."

Ann glanced at him with tears in her eyes and nodded.

Seth pulled his hand away and placed it back on the steering wheel. "Ann, I will be taking a position overseas."

"When? How long have you known about this?"

A crease appeared between his brows. "I was in discussions when you called me about the twins. We need to be settled in France by the end of October."

Ann turned in her seat to face Seth. "If the twins aren't ready to leave the hospital by then, what will we do? We can't leave them, not after finally..."

Seth tightened his jaw and gave Ann a disappointed glance. "Are you suggesting I refuse this opportunity?"

Ann's shoulders dropped as she leaned back in her seat. Her voice was apologetic but filled with deep sadness. "Of course not. I just ..."

Seth softened his tone. "Maybe this isn't our time."

Ann shot a panicked glare at him. "We've adopted them. They are our daughters. What are you saying, Seth?"

He kept his eyes on the road, looking straight ahead. "Circumstances change. Anything can be revoked."

Ann sat speechless and stared in disbelief at the words that so easily left her husband's lips. How could the man who claimed to adore her threaten to take away the one thing he knew she desperately wanted?

Seth glanced at her. "Darling, everything will work out as it should. I'll make sure of it."

September 1st

Ann's hands trembled as she tried to quickly change an irritated two-month-old Michelle into her preemie ensemble for her arrival home.

"You're doing fine," Martha said, reassuring Ann.

She glanced at Martha with a look of doubt while offering a polite smile. "I was so hoping we would bring them home together, but it seems Michelle is all I'm able to handle at the moment."

Martha tilted her head. "You're going to be a wonderful mother to both of your girls."

Trying to calm her daughter, Ann leaned in closer and whispered in a soothing tone, "Your sister is trying to overcome many obstacles, but she's strong. You'll be together soon, my love."

Martha caressed Ann's shoulder. "You'll be a family of four before you know it."

October 1st

"Hello, Loving Heart Associates, this is Ms. Phillips."

Ann's tone was sad and solemn. "Hello, Ms. Phillips, this is Ann Carrington."

"Good morning, Mrs. Carrington, how are you? How are the twins doing?"

"It's only Michelle, home with us."

"Oh, I didn't realize."

"Danielle has required heart surgery, and … well, the doctors are doing their best."

"Oh dear, I'm so sorry. I hope Danielle improves. What can I do for you today?"

"We…" Ann paused and began to weep.

"Are you okay, Mrs. Carrington?"

"We are moving out of the States for two years." Ann paused again. "Danielle is not stable enough to move with us, and it would be much too difficult to travel back and forth."

"I'm sorry to hear that."

"Seth—I mean, we—have made the difficult decision to renounce the adoption of our dau … of Danielle."

"I see. Do you understand what this means? If the court agrees and she survives, you will lose all legal rights, and she will be placed into the foster system."

Ann tried to speak but could only weep into the phone.

"I understand this is extremely difficult for you. Take your time."

"I'm sorry. I just…," Ann muttered.

"Are you completely sure about this?" she asked, but there was silence on the other end. "Mrs. Carrington, are you still—"

"Ms. Phillips, this is Seth Carrington," he said sharply.

Her eyes widened. "Oh, hello, Mr. Carrington."

"If you have further questions, you can discuss them with our lawyer. He will contact you later today."

"I understand. I will wait for his call. Goodbye." She hung up the phone, stunned by the Carrington's decision. Danielle, now an orphan, was to fight for her life alone and unwanted.

Martha sat in bed and looked around her room. This was by far the most luxurious quarters she had ever received, complete with a large sitting area, en suite, and private balcony. It was Ann, undoubtedly, who spared no expense in making her feel at home and comfortable. When Ann told her of their move, selfishly, the thought of living in France excited her, but it was what Ann also shared that shook her to her core. They were asking too much of her.

Martha stood in the foyer and held the front door open as Ann kissed Seth goodbye and wished him safe travels. Martha noticed the sadness in Ann's eyes, as Seth's work always took precedence over everything else in their lives. She watched Ann walk into the formal living room and stand in front of the fireplace.

She approached the archway of the room. "Ann, may we talk?"

Ann didn't turn around but nodded her head yes.

Martha sighed, then walked in and stood beside her. "I want you to know that over the short time I have been here, I've come to consider you family."

Ann looked up from the flames and met Martha's eyes.

"I realize you are my employer, and it is not my place to question your decisions. I'm sorry to overstep, but abandoning Danielle is something I don't think I can be a part of; it's not right."

Ann's eyes filled with tears as she took Martha's hands. A hint of desperation lingered in her voice. "Martha? Are you leaving us?"

"Ann, please help me understand why we must leave now when

Danielle is so vulnerable. Why are you not waiting for her?"

"Seth said we must be in France by the end of October."

"Ann, you and I could stay here in Virginia. Then, when Danielle has recovered, we meet Seth in France."

Ann closed her eyes and shook her head. "No. I need to be with my husband. Michelle needs to be with her father. He won't leave without us."

Martha placed her hand on Ann's arm, this time, her tone conveying a hint of disappointment. "They are identical twins. How can you separate them?"

Ann's brows drew together, and she pulled away. "I have no choice. Besides, Seth has ensured that Danielle's medical expenses will be taken care of and..." She took a deep breath. "Her adoption expenses, too," she whined, then covered her face with her hands and wept.

Tears pooled in Martha's eyes as she wrapped her arms around Ann. "Ann, this doesn't feel right."

Ann clung to her and whispered, "But I need you. Michelle and I need you."

As the words left Martha's lips, she questioned whether she was letting her emotions take over her sense of morality. "I won't abandon you, Ann."

"Thank you, Martha. Thank you."

Paris, France
October 30th

Ann cradled her daughter, rocking her to sleep in the lavishly decorated nursery. "My precious girl, I can't believe you are four months old already. Your sister was so frail. The doctor did her best, but..." She sighed and rested her head against the back of the rocker as a tear rolled down her cheek. "It was so difficult to leave." She looked down and ran her finger across the wisps of hair on Michelle's forehead. "Please forgive us."

From Martha's bedroom window, the Eiffel Tower shimmered in the distance against the dark sky. She had never traveled out of the state of Virginia, let alone the country, and for the next two years, she would call France home. Though it was beautiful, her heart was heavy. *How did I agree to something so unforgivable?* she asked herself. No one had forced her to make this decision. She chose to remain with the Carringtons and to never speak of Danielle again. Tears filled her eyes as an image of the tiny infant came to her mind, wondering if she would ever be free of guilt.

Manassas, Virginia
November 1st

"How does someone adopt a baby then abandon them, a twin no less?" Liza asked the head nurse in the NICU. "I thought they were good people. They seemed so attentive and caring toward the twins."

"I don't know, Liza. I heard the husband got a new job out of the country. It is sad that she's going into the foster system, if the sweet little angel makes it."

Liza ran her finger across Danielle's forehead. "She'll make it. I'll see to it. I talk to her every day and tell her how strong she is and that she'll do wonderful things in her life."

"Liza, you are becoming too attached to this one. You'll be a mess if she doesn't make it or when they place her in the system," she said, pulling off her medical gloves. "I'm heading to break. Do you want anything?"

Liza didn't look up and continued to stroke Danielle's forehead. "No, I'm fine. See you in fifteen." Her eyes radiated with compassion. "You have a long road ahead of you, little one, but you've got this. You are strong and loved."

"Patrick Jones, are you serious?" Liza glared at her husband, her hands propped firmly on her hips.

"I know we decided not to have children, but what those people did, Liza, is truly despicable. You said it yourself. We can't let her go into the foster system."

"Are you sure, Patrick?" Liza's heart raced at the realization of her husband's suggestion. For the last decade, the preemies in the NICU were "her babies" until their attentive, loving parents took them home. But Danielle no longer had attentive, loving parents or the intimate bond of her identical twin.

Patrick rested his hands on his wife's shoulders. "She's all you ever talk about. Your love for that little girl is why she's pulled through."

November 30th

A wide grin overtook Ms. Phillips's face. "Congratulations, Mr. and Mrs. Jones. You are Shelby Renee's legal parents."

Liza beamed as she rocked the five-month-old sleeping peacefully in her carrier. Then, a quiet panic came over her. She knew how to care for Shelby as a nurse, but caring for her now as her daughter suddenly terrified her.

"All of Shelby's medical expenses and adoption fees have been taken care of."

Liza's eyes widened. "Oh, my heavens, was it the Car—?"

Ms. Phillips raised her eyebrows. "I'm sorry, that information is confidential." Then she gave Liza a wink. "Here is Shelby's new birth certificate with her name change, declaring you and Patrick as her parents."

Patrick stood and extended his hand. "Thank you for everything."

Ms. Phillips shook his hand and smiled. "I know she had a rough start, but she is blessed to be wanted by a loving couple."

Liza grabbed the carrier handle and turned to Ms. Phillips. "Thank you so much for all your help with the adoption."

"You are welcome. Take care and safe travels."

They had no intention of ever telling Shelby the circumstances that led to her adoption. The fact that the original adoptive parents chose to separate identical twins and abandon Shelby at the most critical time in her life justified their decision. They both agreed that Shelby would never know of her twin sister.

The Joneses walked out of the adoption agency, ready to start their new life as a family of three. They would set down roots in Boston, Massachusetts, to avoid Shelby ever meeting her sister. It was not nearly as far away from Virginia as Liza wanted, but Patrick's job only allowed him to transfer along the East Coast.

They settled into their modest suburban home, and a week later, Liza walked into the Neonatal Intensive Care Unit in the children's hospital to start her shift. She continued to care for the vulnerable premature patients, and when "her babies" left the hospital in their parents' loving care, the memory of the Carrington's unimaginable decision returned to her. She was grateful, though, that their decision brought Shelby into her and Patrick's lives, but Michelle was never far from her mind.

CHAPTER 2

Short Hills, New Jersey
1985

Seth informed Ann that their time in France was coming to an end, and they would be returning to the States by Michelle's third birthday. As an experienced realtor, Ann closed a deal on a five-bedroom colonial estate in the affluent suburbs of Short Hills, New Jersey, in a neighborhood of young families.

A long doorbell chime echoed through the foyer. Martha opened the large, ornate mahogany door and glanced down. "Well, hello there."

The little boy looked up at her and displayed a wide smile. "Hi, neighba!"

Martha leaned forward and scanned the grounds, then placed her hands on her knees, meeting him at his eye level. "It's lovely to meet you." She raised her eyebrows. "Does your mother know you are here?"

A young woman jogged up the brick-paved driveway to the front steps.

"Bradley!" she said through labored breath. "I'm so sorry. Hello, I'm Jennifer Cole, Bradley's mother and your next-door neighbor." She smiled and rested her hands on her son's shoulders.

Martha chuckled. "Nice to meet you."

Michelle came into the foyer and grasped Martha's dress.

Martha glanced down and rested her hand on Michelle's shoulder. "This is Michelle."

She smiled shyly, then reached for Bradley's hand and led him inside, beginning their lifelong friendship.

August 1993

Michelle gently shook the globe, mesmerized by the falling snow on the quaint little village, a memento of her father's travels. She drifted off into a wondrous world away from her New Jersey hometown. Laughter outside pulled her from her daydream and drew her to the bedroom window. She looked over at the neighbor's yard and waved furiously.

"Mom! Mom! Can I go to Brad's, please?" she yelled, running down the marble staircase to the foyer, nearly colliding with her mother and Martha.

"Yes. I need to leave to show a house, though. Don't overstay your welcome. Your father should be home around six o'clock, so be home for dinner. Martha will expect you."

Ann looked lovingly at her daughter, then brushed the light brown bangs across Michelle's forehead. "You need a haircut so we can see those beautiful ocean eyes."

She appeased her mother with a smile and a thank you, waved to Martha, then darted out the front door, ran down the long brick driveway, then around the tall wooden fence that lined the two properties.

A tree fort sat next to the Cole's side of the fence, the top allowing an impressive view of the second floor of the Carrington's house and most of the neighborhood. On many summer nights, a flashlight show of secret signals was exchanged from Brad's tree fort to Michelle's bedroom window.

Bradley James Cole was like a brother to Michelle; his presence filled an emptiness she couldn't quite explain; she felt closer to him than anyone else. The interaction she witnessed between her girlfriends who had brothers made her curious, though. Most of them claimed to hate their brothers because they were annoying and gross, and she agreed most were. But she never found Brad irritating or gross, at least most of the time. He was a boy, after all, but in her eyes, he was the perfect brother and friend; she could never imagine hating him.

At eleven years old, Brad was already a mirror image of his father. With the same facial features, brown hair, and dark blue eyes, he would be athletic like him too, sharing a love of football and baseball. As soon as he saw Michelle come around the fence, he dropped the football and ran over to her.

They settled in the tree fort and soon heard someone climbing the ladder.

Brad's mother appeared, shaking her head. "Phew, I think this ladder gets longer every time I climb it."

"Oh, thanks, Mom!" Brad grabbed the bag of pretzels and drinks from her and handed Michelle a juice box.

"Thanks, Momma C-ta." Michelle smiled, having given Brad's mother an endearing nickname. Jennifer was like her second mother and always made her feel a part of their family.

Jennifer chuckled. "You're welcome, sweetie. You two have fun." Then she disappeared down the ladder.

"Liam wants to play baseball later. You in?" Brad asked as pretzel crumbs fell from his mouth.

"Yeah, we'll crush 'em this time."

"Hey, is your bike fixed yet?" Brad asked.

Michelle scrunched her nose. "No."

"You can ride my bike to the field, and I'll run next to you," he offered. He always thought of Michelle first, emulating his father's considerate affection toward his mother.

"That's okay, I can walk."

"I don't mind. Besides, I like to run. It gets me ready for the game. You know I can steal any base."

She raised her eyebrows. "Yeah, you're almost as fast as me."

He threw a pretzel at her. "You wish."

She threw the pretzel back at him and smirked. "Well, I guess you're faster than Liam."

Liam Grant was their classmate and baseball rival. He ignited a competitive spark in Michelle, but there was something about him she felt drawn to, and she hated it. Maybe it was the way he looked at her that made her curiously uncomfortable, but she would never reveal that to Brad.

He laughed, then shoved the pretzel in his mouth. "Try not to let him get to you."

She rolled her eyes. "I know. He just thinks he's all that." Then she took a long sip from her juice box.

"And a bag of chips!" Brad shot back.

She coughed and choked, shooting juice out of her nose.

Brad rolled onto his side, laughing so hard that the sound could not escape his gaping mouth.

Her cheeks burned with embarrassment as she wiped her nose with her shirt. *Who was the gross one now?* she thought to herself, then laughed along with him.

Clumps of grass made their permanence known through the years of neglect on the baseball field as faded chalk lines etched their way to each base. The pitcher's mound was all but worn flat except for a large divot that every neighborhood kid loved to grind their toe in as if they were the next Major League pitcher ready to throw the game-winning strike.

Liam stood on the pitcher's mound, throwing the ball into his mitt, waiting for Brad and Michelle. He never saw one without the other and hated that it still made him jealous. He first noticed Michelle in kindergarten. She and Brad were always together, so he thought they were siblings. When he found out otherwise, it drew out his competitiveness. Even at five years old, he often fought for Michelle's attention on the playground.

The fact that she was a tomboy made her even more intriguing. Michelle's toughness and beauty captivated him. She often pulled back her shoulder-length, light brown hair in a braid away from her face, and her long, dark eyelashes peeked through her bangs, highlighting her blue-green eyes that drew him in whenever their eyes met.

Michelle and Brad entered the park and walked toward the ball field.

An outfielder yelled, "Finally, we can start the game!"

"We're up to bat first! Chelle, you're leadoff." Brad handed her his bat.

An outfielder on Liam's team yelled, "Easy out, easy out!"

His first pitch whizzed past Michelle's helmet, making her jolt her head back.

"Hey!" Michelle squinted. "What's a matter, Liam, intimidated by a girl?"

He pursed his lips. "You're the first out, Carrington." Then he wound up to throw the next pitch.

The first baseman leaned forward and smacked a fist into his glove. "If she wants to play with the boys, she has to take the heat."

Liam sent the next pitch to the plate.

Crack!

He ducked, nearly falling to the ground. When he looked up, Michelle was already rounding second base, running as fast as she could toward third.

Brad and the rest of the team were yelling from the dugout. "Go to third, go to third!"

An outfielder finally threw Liam the ball, and when he looked over at third base, Michelle stood with her hands on her hips, panting with a wide smile.

She smirked and glared at him. "How'd you like that first out?"

The dugout was still hooting and howling, pleased with the game's start as Brad took his batter's stance at the plate.

Liam glanced at Michelle. "You'll never make it home, Carrington." He held the ball and glove above his head and stared Brad down. "You got what it takes to get her home?"

Brad circled the bat above his head with confidence. "Bring it."

"Strike one!" yelled the catcher.

Michelle inched off third base. "Come on, Brad. Hit it over the fence. Bring me home!"

Liam glared at Brad, then looked back at Michelle and threatened a throw to third base.

She quickly pivoted and dove back into the bag.

"Keep yapping, Carrington. You WILL be my first out," he warned.

"Just throw the ball," Brad shouted.

Liam's eyes shifted between third base and home plate. He wound up and threw the pitch, confident it would be a second strike. Michelle was already halfway to home plate when the ball left his hand.

Brad pulled the bat and bunted, causing the ball to land between the pitcher's mound and first base.

"Liam, get it! Throw it to me, throw it to me!" the catcher screamed.

Out of the corner of his eye, he saw Michelle slide into home, so he scooped the ball in his glove, lunged, and tagged Brad.

The first base coach yelled, "You're out!"

Liam walked back to the pitcher's mound, hearing the other team go wild as they ran to Michelle, patting her on the shoulders and helmet. He watched Brad walk back toward the team with a big grin and give Michelle a high five.

"Why don't you give her a kiss, lover boy?" Liam shouted, smacking his lips.

Michelle threw her helmet to the ground and marched toward the pitcher's mound.

Liam's eyes widened. He had seen that look before; she was ready to pummel him, but Brad stepped between them.

"Shut up, Liam!" Brad barked.

Liam's teammates yelled, "Fight, fight, fight!"

"Aw, come on, let's just play the game," the players from the dugout yelled.

"I can't stand him. Why didn't you let me clock him?"

"Because I don't want you to hurt your hand. We need you to catch." He knew Michelle could hold her own against any of the boys, but he was her voice of reason. He always stood up for her and had a way of calming her down.

Liam grinned as he watched Michelle and Brad walk back to the dugout. He was quite happy with himself for irritating them.

The sun soon blanketed the field with an orange glow, telling them that dusk was close behind and they needed to end the game. Brad's team was ahead by one run, and Liam's team already had two outs.

Liam gripped the bat and glared at Brad. "Let's see what you got, Cole."

Michelle squatted behind Liam in her catcher's gear, glove open and ready for Brad's pitch. "Bradley James Cole, strike him out!"

Michelle's banter made Liam eager to hit a home run, and if it impressed Michelle, that would be a bonus.

The ball smacked into her catcher's mitt. "Strike one!" she shouted. "Come on, he's an easy out!"

Liam watched Brad give Michelle a smirk and wind up for the next pitch.

The ball smacked into the center of her mitt again. "Strike Two! Your mamma needs to take you to get glasses."

He circled the bat above his head. "Watch this, Carrington. You'll be eating my dust."

The dugout was yelling and jumping up and down, cheering Liam on.

Liam thrust his jaw forward as Brad nodded, giving Michelle the signal for the next pitch. Liam knew the signal. A curveball was coming.

Crack!

The bat broke in half, sending the head of the bat into the fence behind home plate. There was dead silence until the only sound to be heard was Liam panting as he rounded first base, then second base. Finally, a blast of cheers erupted, making him determined to reach home plate.

The dugout shouted, "Run, Liam, run!"

He ran as fast as he could and barreled into home plate, knocking Michelle to the ground with a hard thud and landing on top of her. A cloud of dust billowed around them, and for a split second, Michelle stared into his crystal-blue eyes, making her blush.

Neither realized that the outfielder had caught the ball, making the last out. The game was over, and Brad's team won.

"Get off me, jerk!" she yelled, pushing Liam off her.

"Sorry, Chelle, are you okay?" He stood and put his hand out to help her up.

Brad appeared beside Liam and also extended his hand to her.

Liam watched her eyes dart between him and Brad, but she took Brad's hand. He saw tears in her eyes as she brushed the dirt off and grabbed the catcher's mask off the ground. When Michelle walked away, he noticed her limping and a cut on her right elbow, where a trail of blood ran down the back of her forearm, making him feel even worse. He never meant to hurt her.

Heat flooded Liam's cheeks. "Next game, Bradley James Cole."

For a split second, she stared into his eyes, but it wasn't enough. She chose Brad, and he had a feeling that would never change.

Michelle tried to ignore the throbbing in her knee and the sting of the dirt-covered cut on her elbow, but she couldn't stop the tears from welling up in her eyes.

Brad walked alongside his bike. "You okay?" He knew that she wouldn't admit it if she weren't, but her silence told him she was trying to be tough, to be one of the boys.

"Yeah." She kept thinking about the way Liam looked at her after falling on top of her. When they both offered their hands, she had to take Brad's. He was her best friend, and she trusted him. He would never hurt her or make her cry. But for a split second, Liam captivated her, which made her hate him even more.

Michelle eventually had to accept that Brad and Liam had formed a new friendship in middle school. They were a dynamic duo on the football and baseball fields, becoming teammates instead of rivals and eventually close friends. At the risk of being replaced as Brad's best friend, she tolerated Liam and hated to admit that, over time, she came to consider him a good friend.

Although Michelle and Brad remained close throughout middle school, they still were not an official couple, so Liam took this as a sign that he might win her over. But he was torn, feeling loyalty to Brad, but wanting more than friendship with Michelle. It could cost him both their friendships, and he wasn't sure he wanted to take the risk, at least for now.

May 1997

Liam had grown into an outrageous flirt throughout their freshman year of high school. With his dark hair, crystal-blue eyes, and charming smile, he had all the girls swooning over him, except Michelle. He knew that flirting with her was a lost cause. Instead, he continued to treat her like one of the boys, teasing and bantering to get her attention. And when Michelle caught him staring at her from across the classroom, he quickly looked away, feeling his cheeks burn. He could never quite read her. Sometimes, she would pick on him, and other times, ignore him. His attraction to her was exciting, confusing, and trying all at the same time. He wondered if he would ever be free from the spell she had over him.

Greyhound buses lined New Jersey's Six Flags Great Adventure parking lot. The Short Hills freshman class scattered out of the buses like an army of cockroaches racing each other to the park entrance to secure their place in line for their favorite thrill ride.

Brad, Michelle, and Liam rushed to the roller coaster first. The line snaked back as far as the eye could see. The screams of excitement and terror filled the air as a train of passengers rushed overhead, forcing the line of impatient victims to witness their fate four stories high.

Liam looked up, and a rush of nerves ran through him. He loved the thrill of the ride, but his stomach not so much. Michelle would never let him live it down if he backed out now. So, he told himself, *suck it up and just be cool.*

At last, they were next in line and ushered like cattle between stalls. The train pulled into the station and released its wary riders. The dazed, intoxicated bodies weaved their way to the exit, their faces drained of color.

"I bet five bucks you puke, Carrington!" Liam barked.

Michelle squinted her eyes at him. "If it hits you in the face, Grant, it will be worth it!"

A burst of laughter exploded as the next group placed themselves in the coaster's grip. The harnesses dropped in unison over their heads, locking them in place.

Liam took a deep breath, released it slowly, then looked over at his classmate, Hannah, who motioned the sign of the cross, gripped the handlebars, and closed her eyes. "Oh shit," he whispered.

The train car's acceleration from 0 to 128 mph forced them back into their seats. The 90-degree ascension to the heavens led them plummeting down into a corkscrew of dizziness and finished them off with a 129-foot camel hump before discarding them back at the station. Their hour-long wait was over in fifty seconds.

As soon as the harnesses released, Liam bolted down the ramp, holding his hand over his mouth, his face a pale green. He found the closest garbage can and released all the contents of his stomach, or so he thought.

"Looks like you owe me five bucks, Grant!" Michelle yelled.

Liam glanced over at Michelle and raised his middle finger at her, then leaned over the garbage can a second time.

When he glanced up again, he saw Brad and Michelle standing a safe distance away, but their noses scrunched from the stench of vomit and sunbaked garbage. They walked over to a nearby bench and sat down.

After finally emptying his stomach, he walked over, sat at the end of the bench, and put his head in his hands. He opened his eyes and peered between his fingers, seeing Brad's sneakers in front of him.

"Do you want us to wait for you?"

He kept his face buried in his hands. "No, just go."

Michelle put a water bottle in front of his face. "Here."

He grabbed the water bottle, then glanced at her. "Thanks."

"Are you sure you don't want us to wait?" Brad asked again.

"No."

Brad shrugged his shoulders. "Okay, we'll see you on the bus then."

Michelle gave him a sympathetic expression. "Hope you feel better."

He had flipped her off, and still she showed him kindness. He couldn't figure her out.

The sun lowered in the sky, leading herds of students back to the parking lot. They piled back onto the buses, sunburnt and exhausted but chatty, bragging about the number of times they had endured a plethora of nausea-inducing rides.

Michelle's face peeked between the tall, velvety seats in front of her. "How's your stomach?"

Liam sighed. "Okay."

"Sucks you didn't get to go on any more rides."

"Yeah." He liked the fact that she asked how he was doing. He'd take it even if it were out of pity.

As darkness set in, the bus became quiet and lulled its weary passengers to sleep. A few hours later, the bus came to a sudden halt.

The interior lights popped on, triggering groans and yawns through-out the cabin as students stood and stretched. They grabbed their belongings and filed out of the bus into a sea of parents waiting in the school parking lot.

Liam glanced over his seat. Michelle looked so peaceful and pretty. Her long lashes lay delicately on her sunburnt cheeks, and her lips were a rosy pink. He glanced down and saw her fingers woven between Brad's and felt jealousy stir inside him. "Wake up, lovers, we're home."

Startled awake, they quickly released their hands and sat up in their seats. He saw the embarrassment on their faces. If they liked each other so much, they should just be a couple. Then he could move on and get over his stupid crush.

CHAPTER 3

Boston, Massachusetts
December 1983

Patrick wrapped his arm around Liza's shoulder as they watched eighteen-month-old Shelby sleep in her crib.

Liza whispered, "Our little girl is absolutely perfect."

Patrick smiled, squeezed his wife, and whispered back, "Yes, she is. You'd never know she had heart surgery. Her scar has all but disappeared with that magic salve of yours."

They tiptoed out of the nursery and closed the door. Liza turned to her husband. "Thank you."

Patrick tilted his head and pinched his brows. "For what?"

"For knowing what I needed. What Shelby needed. Uprooting our lives." She shook her head as tears pooled in her eyes. "I always imagined it would be just you and me. And I was content with that. But..."

He placed his hands on Liza's arms and looked into her eyes. "The first time I held that baby girl, I knew she was *our* daughter." He rested his forehead on his wife's. "But there is one thing I miss from our childless years."

A hint of worry appeared in Liza's eyes. "What?"

"Sleep."

July 1989

Patrick pulled two mugs from the cabinet and filled them with coffee and a dash of creamer when he heard the front door open and close. He turned around with a smile at the sight of his wife, his hands clasped around each mug. The smile instantly fell from his lips when he saw that Liza's eyes were tired, puffy, and bloodshot.

"Patrick," Liza's voice squeaked.

He set the mugs on the kitchen table and wrapped his arms around her. "Oh, honey, did you lose a patient last night?"

Liza wept in his arms and shook her head no.

"You're shaking. What is it that has you so upset?"

"I was leaving pediatrics and ran into Sarah's parents." She took a deep breath and closed her eyes. "Oh, Patrick, Sarah passed away."

He stepped back and rested his hands on Liza's shoulders. "How? What happened? Shelby was with her yesterday."

"Secondary drowning." Her hands trembled as she drew a tissue from her scrubs' pocket.

Patrick tilted his head and narrowed his eyes.

Liza blew her nose and sighed. "Apparently, Sarah and her brother went swimming after dinner. Sarah fell off a raft, and they thought she had just swallowed some water when she came up gasping and coughing, but..." Liza's eyes filled with tears. "She seemed fine and went to bed. A few hours later, Mary checked on her." Liza sniffled and shook her head. "Sarah was blue and unresponsive. They couldn't revive her," she cried, covering her face with her hands. "She's only seven years old."

Patrick took Liza in his arms again and saw Shelby out of the corner of his eye, standing frozen in the kitchen, her eyes wide with fear and confusion.

"Shelby, honey." He released Liza, then went over and knelt in front of his daughter, resting his hands on her arms.

Shelby looked at her mother. "Mommy?" Then she looked into her father's tear-filled eyes. "Sarah died, Daddy?"

Liza kneeled next to Patrick and rested her hand on Shelby's cheek. "I'm so sorry, sweetheart. Yes, she did."

She stared at her parents, watching tears spill from their heartbroken eyes. Her heart and mind raced. *They were lying. She saw Sarah just yesterday, laughing, picking on her annoying brother, throwing popcorn in the air, catching it in her wide-open mouth, and shooting soda out of her nose when her dog ran past them with her brother's underwear. No! They were lying!* Tears pooled in her eyes, and her chest tightened, trying to steal her breath.

Liza reached out to hug Shelby, but she pulled away. "No! Sarah isn't dead!" she screamed, and ran upstairs to her room, slamming her bedroom door.

Shelby gripped her mother's hand as her father walked close behind them. She wished they could turn around and go home. Sarah's house was the last place she wanted to be.

Sarah's father opened the front door, gave Liza and Patrick a sad smile, and welcomed the three of them inside. "Hi Shelby, thank you for coming."

Shelby looked around. She had never seen so many people in Sarah's house. Adults and children filled the living room and adjoining dining room, talking in hushed tones.

In front of a picture window, a long table held several flower arrangements. A poster-size collage of pictures showcased Sarah, along with some of her favorite books, toys, and games.

Shelby stared at the display of memories. Her eyes filled with tears when she spotted a picture of her and Sarah in kindergarten with their arms wrapped around each other.

Thumping from under the table made her jump and her eyes widen. She stepped back and found Bailey lying underneath the table. Her expression softened when she met the deep brown, sad eyes staring back at her.

Shelby dropped to her knees, cupped her hands over Bailey's silky black ears, and rested their foreheads together. A long pink tongue licked the stream of tears that ran down Shelby's cheek. Bailey's tail thumped faster when Sarah's brother knelt under the table and ran his hand down the length of her long back.

"I gave her Sarah's favorite sweatshirt so she wouldn't forget her."

Shelby glanced at the purple sweatshirt buried under the sixty-pound black Labrador—Sarah's two favorite things in the entire world. Then she looked at Sarah's brother, said nothing, but nodded in agreement.

It wasn't fair. She wanted Sarah back, wanted the deep sadness to disappear. Then Sarah could skip out of her room and say, "I tricked you all! I was hiding!" She wanted the pain in her heart and the tears to stop. She wanted her best friend back.

August 1990

It had been a little over a year, but Sarah's death was still fresh in their hearts and minds. Liza closed Shelby's bedroom door and sighed. She hated that Shelby had experienced the loss of a friend at such a young age. She walked downstairs and spotted Patrick sitting in his recliner, reading the newspaper.

He rolled the corner toward him and peeked over at his wife. "How is she?"

"She said she wants to quit swimming lessons. She's afraid she'll drown like Sarah."

Patrick frowned. "I'll talk to her." He went upstairs to Shelby's room, knocked on the door, and then heard a muffled "Come in."

"Hey honey, your mother told me you want to quit swimming lessons."

Shelby had her face buried in her pillow but nodded yes.

Patrick sat on the side of Shelby's bed and rubbed her back. "I know that what happened to Sarah last summer was scary and very sad. But the reason we signed you up for lessons was to help you become confident in the water."

Shelby rolled onto her back and wiped her cheek with her hand. "But what if I swallow water like Sarah did and die, Dad?"

Patrick tilted his head. "Honey, that was a terrible accident. Sometimes, things happen that we have no control over. I'm so sorry you lost your friend. I understand that you are scared, but it's important that you learn how to swim to help you get over that fear."

Shelby stared at the ceiling, then met her father's eyes and sighed. "Okay. I'll give swimming lessons one more try." She sniffled. "I'll do it for Sarah."

Patrick smiled. "I think Sarah would be proud of you."

Shelby sat up and hugged her father.

Patrick squeezed her tight. "Your mother and I are proud of you, too, kiddo."

December 1993

Shelby pulled her homework out of her backpack and set it on the desk, eager to start math class.

Everyone stopped to look when a pale, head-to-toe, freckled

redhead with green eyes entered Mrs. King's sixth-grade classroom.

"Class, I would like to introduce Samantha Wright. She moved here from Texas. Can everyone say hello?"

Sam's face turned bright red, camouflaging her freckles. She glared at Mrs. King. "It's Sam."

The class yelled hello and sat in their seats. Shelby's eyes widened as Mrs. King walked Sam over to her desk. "Shelby, could you show Samantha around today?"

Her face brightened. "Sure, Mrs. King!" Then she noticed Sam give their teacher a side-eye.

Mrs. King corrected, "Sam." Then she added, "You can have the desk next to Shelby right here."

Sam sat down and threw her backpack on the floor beside her chair.

Shelby leaned toward Sam's desk and whispered, "How do you like Massachusetts? A lot colder than Texas, huh? Mrs. King is a really nice teacher."

Sam faced straight ahead but gave Shelby the same side-eye. "How are you so perky this early in the morning?"

Shelby shrugged her shoulders. "I guess I'm just a morning person."

Sam released a drawn-out yawn. "Great."

Shelby had a strange feeling about Sam, as if she had come into her life for a reason, possibly a kindred friendship. First though, she needed to get Sam through her first day at a new school. Shelby feared it would be a challenge with Sam's less-than-enthusiastic personality.

By the end of middle school, Shelby and Sam had built a close friendship and bond. Sam cheered Shelby on at the fall swim meets, and in the spring, Shelby helped with the players' stats for the junior varsity softball team and kept Sam's fiery temper in check as the team's catcher.

As close as they were, their views of their male classmates were at opposite poles. Shelby was shy and found the middle school boys immature and annoying. Sam's snarky personality, on the other hand, drew the attention of the boys, even if they were the targets of her remarks. Shelby merely wanted to avoid the drama that Sam seemed to thrive on, having a new boyfriend every other week, always keeping her options open.

Sam sat on the floor, leaning against Shelby's bed. "I had to break up with him. Don't want to be tied down over summer break. I'm sooo done with middle school."

Shelby rolled her eyes. "Well, at least you'll be busy with travel ball while I'm at swim camp for the next two weeks."

Sam displayed a sly grin. "Yeah, and think of all the high school guys we'll have to choose from in a few months."

"You mean *you'll* have to choose from. I'm staying out of all that drama."

"Oh, come on, Shel. We could double-date, and I bet the guys are way more mature in high school."

"You're hopeless." Shelby rolled her eyes again.

"Yeah, a hopeless romantic." Sam glanced at Shelby, waiting for her reaction, then they both burst out laughing.

May 1997

Shelby ran down the stairs. "Mom, Mom!"

"Oh, my heavens, what is it, Shelby?" Liza gulped the last of her coffee. "I'm going to be late. What do you need?"

"Did you sign my permission slip for our freshman class trip? It's due today!"

Liza moved a pile of papers around the kitchen counter, frantically searching for the form she had signed the night before.

"I found it!" she shouted, raising it above her head like a prize-winning ribbon. "Here. Now you're going to miss the bus. Have a good day. I love you." She kissed Shelby's cheek and marched her to the front door.

"Bye, Dad!"

Patrick peered over the top of his newspaper. "See ya, kiddo. Have a good day!"

The school bus stopped at the end of the Joneses' driveway and flung open the narrow double doors. The smell of exhaust and worn leather filled Shelby's nostrils, causing her to wrinkle her nose as she climbed the steps. She walked down the narrow aisle and took her seat with Sam in the middle of the bus.

"Ugh, one more dreaded day before the class trip. I can't wait to miss a full day of school," Sam groaned.

Shelby rolled her eyes. "Same."

"I can't wait until we get our licenses. I hate riding the bus," Sam complained.

Shelby adjusted her backpack on her lap. "Well, at least it doesn't smell like puke today."

Sam lifted her chin and glanced toward the front of the bus. "Give it time. Puker Parker is our next stop."

Shelby wrinkled her nose again. "Great." Then she turned excitedly toward Sam. "Hey, are you still helping your aunt at her flower shop this weekend?"

"Ugh, yes. Why? Do you want to come with?"

"Yeah, it will be fun."

"Fun? The place makes me sneeze. I think I'm allergic to flowers."

Shelby bumped her shoulder into Sam. "More like allergic to work."

"Ha. Ha. You're so funny. I'll let my aunt know you're coming." Sam yawned. "She'll be thrilled."

Liza opened Shelby's bedroom door and turned off the alarm. Both girls were still sound asleep. She rubbed Shelby's shoulder. "Honey. I made breakfast. You need to get ready to go to the flower shop."

Shelby rolled over, wiped the sleep from her eyes, and smiled.

Liza chuckled. "You always wake up with a smile, silly. Wake Sam up and come downstairs."

Liza left Shelby's bedroom door open, allowing the hallway light to illuminate her room. The aroma of bacon, eggs, and toast made Shelby moan, "Mmm." Then she stretched her aching legs from walking miles in the amusement park the day before.

Sam lay on her stomach deep under the covers as strands of her red wavy locks snaked up the pillowcase.

"Sam," Shelby whispered loudly.

"Hmm?" Sam groaned.

Shelby shook Sam's arm. "Come on, my mom made us breakfast."

"I'm not hungry. Just let me sleep."

"Your aunt's flower shop, remember?"

"You go. I'll stay and sleep," Sam mumbled.

Shelby hopped out of bed and pulled the covers off Sam. "Come on, the flowers are waiting."

Sam gritted her teeth. "I hate you."

Shelby laughed. "I love you too."

Sam dozed in the car while Shelby sat wide awake, smiling in anticipation of the day ahead at the floral shop.

Liza pulled into the parking lot. "Okay, your father will pick you two up around lunchtime. Have fun!"

Shelby ran to the florist shop entrance while Sam slogged behind. Shelby opened the door to Aunt B's Bouquets, setting off the bell, making her smile at its high-pitched greeting.

"Hi Shelby, I'm so glad you came with Sam this morning."

She glanced at her niece. "Oh dear, Sam, you're really dragging. Too many roller coasters yesterday?"

"Hi, Aunt Becky."

"Sam, we'll have you sit in the back and trim some stems."

Sam gave her a thumbs up, then trudged to the back room.

"Shelby, I could use your help with a couple of orders. Are you ready for Floral Arrangements 101?"

Shelby's face lit up. "Absolutely!"

"Now that's enthusiasm I like to see."

Becky brought Shelby in the back to observe the entire process of completing an order. She clipped stems, arranged the flowers and greens, and rearranged them until she felt they were perfect. Then she finished it with a bow and plastic card holder. "And that's how it's done," Becky said, placing her hands on her hips.

Shelby's eyes brightened. "Wow, that's beautiful!"

Becky handed Shelby an order slip. "Okay, here you go."

"Really?"

Becky raised her eyebrows. "Show me what you got." Then she left Shelby on her own.

Shelby read the order slip twice, followed Becky's process, adding a step of her own by first sniffing each flower before placing it in the vase, and half an hour later, crafted a floral arrangement worthy of the cover of "Flower Magazine."

Becky came into the backroom and gave Shelby an approving smile. "Well done. I think you've discovered your gift, my dear."

Shelby beamed with pride. "Thank you! I loved every second."

"Talk with your parents first, but if you want a job a few hours a week, you have it."

"I'd love that! Thank you, Aunt Becky!" Shelby squealed, wrapping her arms around her.

Patrick arrived as scheduled and dropped Sam off at her house.

"I'll call you tomorrow!" Shelby yelled out the car window, then leaned toward the driver's seat. "Dad, Sam's aunt said I have a job if I want it."

"She did?"

"Yeah, isn't that cool?"

"How will you have time, Shelby, with finals coming up and summer swim camp starting?"

"It's only a few hours a week, Dad, and school is almost done. I could get rides from my friend's parents after practices," she pleaded.

"We'll see what your mother has to say."

Shelby flopped back in her seat, crossed her arms, and glared out the window, already knowing what her mother was going to say. She had three more years of high school. At some point, her parents would have to let her work at the florist shop.

May/June 2000

Liza placed her hands on her hips. "Shelby, stop fidgeting."

"Ugh, my feet are killing me already," she complained, glancing down at her three-inch heels.

"Well, you're the one who picked them out, young lady."

"I can't believe I let Sam talk me into going to the prom."

Liza tilted her head. "You'll have fun, honey."

"The limo and Sam's parents are here," Patrick yelled up the staircase.

Sam and two male classmates exited the limo and walked up the Joneses' driveway. After several pictures were taken, the four entered the limo and left for their formal dining.

A few hours later, they arrived at their high school and separated into their sports groups. Shelby went with the swimmers, Sam with the varsity softball seniors, and their dates joined their soccer teammates.

After dancing and mingling with their classmates late into the night, the DJ played the last slow song of the evening.

Shelby's date slipped a piece of gum in his mouth and asked her to dance.

They swayed awkwardly to the song "Faithfully" and occasionally made eye contact.

"You look really pretty."

Shelby blushed and lowered her eyes. "Thank you."

After an excruciating four minutes and fifteen seconds, the song was over, ending their embrace. The bright lights came on, and the DJ wished everyone safe travels home.

Shelby and her date walked out of the school and stood under a large oak tree, waiting for their rides to arrive.

He tilted his head. "I hope you had fun."

"I did, thanks." Shelby smiled, then hugged him.

He held her in his arms, pulled his head back, stared into her eyes, then leaned in and kissed her.

Shelby closed her eyes, and her stomach fluttered. His lips were soft and minty, and she thought to herself, *this is nice*. Then, like a bolt of lightning, he shot his tongue and, unintentionally, the piece of gum into her mouth.

She pulled away and spat the gum out. "Eww, gross!"

His eyes widened. "Oh, sorry," he said, as heat flooded his cheeks. "Um, my ride is here."

She watched him disappear into the crowd of classmates, guessing her reaction mortified him. She shook her head and coughed, "Ugh." Then she heard Sam yell her name and wave for her to come over to the sidewalk.

"So how was your first kiss?" Sam smirked.

Shelby looked away and blushed. "It was okay until he tried to shove his gum down my throat."

"Don't you mean his tongue?" Sam laughed.

"No!" Shelby wrinkled her nose. "He put his gum in my mouth!"

Sam bit her bottom lip, then burst out laughing. "Well, at least you'll never forget your first kiss."

Sam sat on Shelby's bed, tossing a stuffed bear in the air.

Shelby widened her eyes. "Can you believe we only have two weeks left of our senior year?"

Sam gave Shelby her signature side-eye. "Finally!"

"I'm so excited to swim for UConn." Shelby looked at Sam and frowned. "But I'm going to miss you."

"I can't believe you want to do four more years of school. Two years at Berkshire Community and working a few hours a week with Aunt Becky is all I'm signing up for."

Shelby laughed.

Sam glanced at her. "But I'll miss you too. Who knows, Shel, maybe you'll find the love of your life at UConn."

"I'll be so busy with classes and swimming, I'll be lucky to find sleep, let alone love."

Sam smirked. "Well, let him know what flavor gum you like."

Shelby narrowed her eyes. "Real funny, and your love life is all the drama I need."

"What can I say? I attract 'em, just can't keep 'em."

Shelby rolled her eyes.

Sam threw the stuffed bear across the room, hitting Shelby in the head.

"Hey!" Shelby laughed.

"Well, when you find the love of your life, don't forget about me, okay?"

Shelby noticed Sam's eyes misting over. "How could I ever forget you? You're my best friend. You will always be in my life, even when we're miles apart."

Sam looked away. "I know."

"Hey, I'll come home on breaks when I can, so we can hang out." Shelby threw the stuffed bear back at Sam. "Don't worry, Sam, you're stuck with me whether you like it or not. Nothing could ever change our friendship."

CHAPTER 4

Short Hills
September 1999

Michelle lay on her bed while Hannah sat at the window seat, looking over at the Cole's house.

Hannah played with a flashlight, turning it on and off. "When will you and Brad finally admit you love each other and become a couple? Everybody knows you guys are into each other."

Michelle rolled her eyes. "Not everyone knows. What if it got weird between us and ruined our friendship? Besides, he might not feel the same."

"Seriously, girl, are you blind?" she barked, pointing the flashlight into Michelle's eyes.

Michelle blushed, got up from her bed, and grabbed the flashlight from her.

Hannah laughed and stood up from the window seat. "We killed it at camp. I mean, I've never seen you so aggressive on the court. I think you broke that girl's nose."

Michelle gritted her teeth. "I feel bad. Kinda." Then she smirked. "Her face got in my way when I went for the layup."

"Well, she had it coming after tripping you. She could have ended your season."

"Yeah, seriously."

"How's your knee?"

"It's okay now."

Hannah raised her arms and motioned a free throw shot to an imaginary basketball hoop. "Anyway, I bet we go to States this year."

"Definitely."

"Hey, I gotta run. Think about what I said. It's our last year of high school. Don't miss your chance at true love." Hannah held closed fists under her chin and batted her eyelashes.

Michelle laughed and threw a pillow at Hannah as she walked out of the bedroom.

Hannah wasn't entirely wrong. The friendship between her and Brad had grown stronger over the years, and he was the first person she wanted to see after returning home from basketball camp. But being a couple would be a whole new dynamic in their nearly two-decade-long friendship.

With camp over, she had a few days left of summer vacation to enjoy before the start of her senior year. Football practices were in full swing, and Brad was on the field more than he was at home, so when she peered out her bedroom window and saw his car in his driveway, she had to see him.

She walked around the fence and saw the hose snaked across the grass and a bucket of suds in the driveway. A well-toned figure popped up from behind the car's hood and brushed the dark-brown hair away from his eyes. The sun glistened on his bare bronze torso, outlining a six-pack. His deep blue eyes greeted her, along with a broad smile and a friendly wave. A flush crept up her face; this wasn't the Brad she had left five weeks ago.

"Hey, Chelle, how was camp?"

Her eyes followed the curves of each well-defined muscle of this new physique walking toward her. She caught herself staring, but couldn't look away.

Brad hugged her tight, his firm pecs pressing into her breasts, causing the pit of her stomach to flutter. His skin was warm from the sun, and he smelled of Coppertone.

She pulled away from their embrace, uncomfortable with the way her body reacted to his touch, and looked down at the ground. "Camp was good."

"Can you believe it's our senior year? Did you finally decide where you're going—Boston or UConn with me?" He grinned, then snapped the shammy at her leg.

"Ouch!" she squealed and grabbed for the shammy.

Brad pulled it behind his back and arched his eyebrow at her. "Oh, think you can get it, huh?"

Brad's father walked over to them and interrupted their flirtation. "Hey Michelle, how's it going? How are your parents?"

"Hi, Mr. Cole!" she said, giving him a hug. "They're good. They should be home tomorrow from their cruise."

"So, I heard Brad ask you what school you decided on."

"Yeah, probably UConn. I like the basketball coach and their program."

"You'll both be Huskies then." Tim winked.

She glanced at Brad. "I guess so."

Tim walked back toward the house and looked over his shoulder. "Can you do me a favor and inspect Bradley's work? He missed a few spots."

"Yes, I'd be happy to," she said, giving Brad a smirk.

From the corner of her eye, Michelle saw Brad's mother appear in the driveway with outstretched arms.

"Oh, I've missed you, sweetie," Jennifer said and kissed Michelle's cheek. "You're staying for dinner. I won't take no for an answer. Tim told me you've decided on UConn. I'm so happy for you, and I'm sure Bradley is too," she said, giving her son a wink. "I'll call you when dinner is ready. You're staying for the bonfire too," Jennifer ordered.

"Okay, thank you, Momma C-ta."

Brad snapped the shammy in her direction again. "I think she loves you more than she loves me."

Michelle tilted her head. "I've always been her favorite. You should know that by now." She picked up the basketball lying in the grass and shot a layup on her way to the car. "Excuse me, but I have a job to do," she quipped, flashing a confident grin.

She ran her finger along the car's hood and raised a brow. "Missed a spot." Her eyes widened as she watched Brad pick up the hose and send a blast of icy water at her. "Shit, that's cold!"

Brad gave her a devilish grin and threatened another blast. "Look what you made me do. Now we have to dry the car off again."

She narrowed her eyes at him. "You're an ass."

A car horn blared, drawing their attention to the road as a white convertible pulled into the Cole's driveway. A petite blonde in a cheerleading uniform hopped out of the car, bounced over to Brad, and stretched up on her toes to hug him.

"Hi, Claire." Brad looked at Michelle with an awkward smile while hugging Claire back.

She ignored Michelle, giving Brad her undivided attention. Claire Whitaker was a junior on the varsity cheerleading squad and daughter of the Short Hills Varsity football coach. Her family moved to New Jersey from South Carolina when Claire was in eighth grade. Her southern twang charmed and mesmerized the pubescent middle school boys. By ninth grade, her full figure, plump lips, doe eyes, and flowy blonde waves were a magnet in the testosterone-filled hallways of the high school. Taking full advantage of her assets, Claire dated several football players who were privy to her promiscuous reputation, and this year, she had her sights set on Brad.

Michelle knew Brad wouldn't do anything to jeopardize his full scholarship to UConn by dating the coach's daughter, and to Michelle's relief, it was a risk he wasn't willing to take.

Claire tilted her head and batted her lashes at Brad. "A few of us are going to the movies. Do you want to go?"

"Thanks, but I've got this thing with my parents, you know, something I can't get out of," he lied.

Brad glanced at Michelle as she mocked Claire. He laughed and caught himself. Claire whirled around to see Michelle shaking her hands with invisible pom-poms. Michelle froze, drew her lips in, and tried not to laugh.

Claire glared at Michelle, then turned back to Brad with a sweet smile. "Well, if you change your mind, the movie starts at nine." She stretched up on her toes again and kissed Brad on the cheek.

It wasn't the first time Michelle had witnessed other girls flirting with Brad. But something was different this time; jealousy flared inside her.

Claire sauntered down the driveway, the pleats of her skirt swinging side to side with the sway of her hips. She turned and waved to Brad.

Michelle faked a smile and waved back. "You better get your sweet ass in that convertible and drive right on out of here."

Brad laughed, then threw her a shammy.

She grabbed it out of the air, then began drying the car, and became lost in her thoughts. *Ugh, I can't stand her. She's not even his type.* Then, her mind jumped to her conversation with Hannah. *Brad's like a brother and he's my best friend. But he looks so good. Should I listen to Hannah? What if he doesn't feel the same? Would it make things awkward between us?*

Brad glanced at her. "You're quiet all of a sudden."

Her face reddened as if she had broadcast her innermost thoughts. "I take my job seriously. No need to inspect *my* work."

"Dinner's ready," Jennifer yelled from the kitchen window.

Michelle exhaled a sigh of relief.

Brad grinned and raised his eyebrows. "Looks like you got a little wet. You might want to dry off for dinner."

She narrowed her eyes at him. "Yeah, thanks."

The more Brad flirted with her, the more flustered she became. That little voice inside spoke again. *Get a grip, Chelle. He's a guy. That's what guys do. They flirt.* But she liked it. Who was she kidding? She loved it.

CHAPTER 5

May 2000

Bursts of cheers echoed throughout Short Hills High as promposals became a daily ritual. Michelle found them annoying and ridiculous.

Trying to outdo each other with elaborate proposals, the seniors put their prospective dates on the spot in front of as many classmates as possible while anticipating a "yes" and a round of applause.

Michelle found a note taped to her locker, directing her to the gym, and found it strange. It wasn't unusual for Brad to slide a note into her locker, asking her to meet up with him.

She entered the gym slowly, looking around for Brad. The cheer squad stood in a circle, their pom-poms covering something. One by one, each girl spun around and yelled out a word written on a basketball held in one hand while shaking their pom-poms in the other. They took a knee in unison, revealing Liam kneeling with a single rose and an adoring smile.

She looked around as crowds of students peered into the gym, watching in anticipation. Her face turned scarlet red, and her first thought was, *oh shit.* Then her second thought was, *I can't embarrass Liam.* After all the teasing and bantering over the years, he had become a good friend. *But what about Brad? She assumed they would go together; no stupid promposal needed.*

She gave him an awkward smile. "Yes?"

Liam walked up to her, handed her the rose, and hugged her. Cheers and clapping echoed throughout the gym as she stepped back.

She glanced across the gymnasium and saw Hannah with her mouth gaping open, and Brad clapping with a look of disappointment.

Ann clasped the diamond necklace and turned Michelle around, studying her daughter's silky brown hair that flowed around the back of her neck and cascaded down her shoulder.

The shimmering, floor-length red dress hugged Michelle's curves, causing her to adjust the sweetheart neckline that showcased her breasts.

"Michelle, stop fidgeting."

"These heels are killing my feet already," she complained.

Ann placed her hands on Michelle's arms and gushed. "Well, you look beautiful, darling, doesn't she, Seth?"

Her father kissed her cheek. "You are picture-perfect, sweetheart."

"Thank you, Dad. Okay, Mom, we have to go. Mrs. Cole asked me to come over so she could take pictures, too. Liam should be at Brad's soon." She checked herself in the foyer mirror one last time and released a heavy sigh. "Okay, I'm ready."

Michelle took her mother's arm and carefully descended their front steps one at a time, wishing she had practiced walking in heels.

Jennifer was adjusting Brad's tie in their driveway when he heard a clicking sound on the blacktop. He turned his head, and his body tightened.

Michelle met his gaze, making her blush and her heart race.

Brad's eyes widened. "Chelle, you are stunning."

Jennifer gasped. "Oh, sweetie, you are gorgeous!" Then she pushed them together. "Let me get a picture of you two."

Michelle smiled shyly. "You don't look half bad yourself."

He rested his hand on her hip and held her tight against him, making her stomach flutter with his touch.

A white stretch limo pulled into the driveway, drawing their eyes away from each other. They watched Liam step out and walk toward them, holding a small container of flowers.

Michelle couldn't deny that Liam also looked handsome in his tux, but it was Brad she wished to be with.

Liam gave a suggestive arch of his brows, causing her to blush again. He reached for her hand, taking her from Brad's embrace, and spun her around. "Wow."

She scrunched her nose. "Can't wait to get these heels off."

When she glanced at Brad, his face told her he truly regretted his procrastination.

Liam placed the corsage on Michelle's wrist, then handed her the boutonniere.

Michelle struggled to pin it onto Liam's lapel and glanced at her mother, her eyes asking for help.

Ann tilted her head. "Can I help you, honey?"

She handed the boutonniere and pin to her mother and smiled at Liam.

Ann placed the boutonniere on Liam's lapel and patted his shoulder. "There, all set."

"Thank you, Mrs. Carrington."

"Can we get a picture of the three of you?" Jennifer asked.

Brad and Liam each wrapped an arm around Michelle's waist. She felt like she was in a silent testosterone tug-of-war as they gently pulled her closer to themselves.

"Oh, you all look so gorgeous!" Jennifer gushed. "We'll follow the limo to Hannah's for more pictures. Bradley, your father and I will drop your car off at the school so you can drive home after the prom."

"Thanks, Mom."

The three of them finally piled into the limo, drove a few blocks, and pulled into the driveway of a modest home, where Hannah stood in the front yard with her parents.

The same day Liam asked Michelle to prom, Hannah informed Brad that he was taking her, knowing the four would double date. Having no interest in Brad, her only goal was to get Michelle and Brad to admit they wanted to be more than friends.

Hannah's parents, giddy with excitement, introduced themselves and took several pictures of the foursome. Brad was cordial, but Hannah noticed he couldn't stop staring at Michelle. It only confirmed what Hannah already knew; Brad was definitely into Michelle, and if Michelle hadn't seen it by now, she *was* blind.

Michelle and Liam sat across from Brad and Hannah in the limo. Brad glanced down and noticed Michelle's toenails painted red to match her dress. He'd never seen her toenails painted before; no doubt that was her mother's doing. His eyes then followed the long slit of her dress that revealed her shapely, athletic thigh.

Michelle could feel Brad's eyes on her as she looked out the window. She enjoyed his attention without acknowledging him. After all, this was his fault. He allowed Liam to swoop in and ask her to the prom.

The limo stopped in front of the Brickville Inn, and the chauffeur opened the door to help Michelle and Hannah step out. The four joined the mob of prom guests who lined the sidewalk, chatting and adjusting their formal wear before making their grand entrance into the restaurant. As the promenade marched through the dining room, patrons paused to watch.

The host stopped at a round table in the center of the restaurant and pulled Michelle's chair out between Brad and Liam, then went around the table and pulled out Hannah's chair. He laid a menu in front of each of them and informed them that Brittney would be their server.

Liam, with his usual flirtatious charm, had Brittney laughing and blushing even though she was five years his senior.

Michelle rolled her eyes. Liam easily attracted women. He was handsome and charismatic, but a player. She didn't understand why he had asked her to the prom. He could have asked any number of girls who fell under the spell of his crystal-blue eyes and charm.

The formal atmosphere made her uncomfortable, and she guessed it made Brad uncomfortable, too, when she saw him study the fine silverware.

Brad leaned toward her. "Which fork do I use first?"

She widened her eyes and shrugged her shoulders, causing Brad to laugh. She should have paid attention to Martha all those years ago during her lessons in table manners.

A server placed a basket of warm bread in the center of the table, and four white-sleeved arms simultaneously set a salad in front of them.

Hannah whispered, "It's the first fork on the left; work your way from the outside in." Proudly sharing her knowledge of proper dining etiquette.

The trio nodded back, thankful that Hannah was discreet in a room full of sophistication. However, the formal etiquette was short-lived as Hannah struggled to poke a cherry tomato with her fork. She gave it one last stab, catapulting it off her plate. It landed, then rolled next to a finely polished Oxford.

Hannah's mouth gaped open as her face turned several shades of red.

The trio froze wide-eyed, unsure how to react until they could no longer contain themselves, and broke out into quiet laughter.

Hannah squirmed in her chair, wishing she could disappear underneath the table.

They looked over at the gentleman, who glanced down at the tomato beside his shoe. Then he looked at their table and gave Hannah a wink.

The girls excused themselves to the calm refuge of the ladies' room, where Hannah returned to her pale complexion. She released a heavy sigh and then covered her face with her hands and laughed.

An older woman entered the ladies' room and complimented the girls on their dresses. She leaned close to Michelle and whispered, "The eyes of every male in this restaurant followed you when you walked through the dining room in that red dress."

Michelle blushed and smiled self-consciously.

"Enjoy it, dear. Before you know it, you'll look in the mirror and ask who that wrinkly old woman is looking back at you." She chuckled and patted Michelle's arm. "Enjoy your evening, young ladies."

They were all relieved when their four-course dinner ended without further mishap. As they stood on the sidewalk waiting for the limo to take them to the high school, the night air had cooled, covering Michelle in goosebumps. Liam took off his jacket and placed it around her shoulders.

He knew how to be a gentleman; she would give him that. "Thank you."

"You're welcome," he said, his arm lingering on her shoulder until she glanced at him again, and he removed it.

Thirty minutes later, they entered the Hollywood-themed Short Hills High prom. Several classmates pulled Hannah away while a group of football teammates exchanged wisecracks with Liam and Brad.

The DJ played "Faithfully," sending a wave of couples to the dance floor. Liam grabbed Michelle's hand and led her through a sea of swaying bodies, pulled her close, and rested his hands on her waist. "Did I tell you how beautiful you look tonight?"

She nodded and blushed. "Yes." Then she glanced around and spotted Brad and Hannah awkwardly rocking from side to side on the dance floor.

"You know we should hang out and go on a date sometime."

She scrunched her nose. "An actual date?"

"You and Brad aren't a real couple, right? I mean, you guys are always together, but not like a couple together."

"I guess," she replied in an annoyed tone.

She was relieved when the song ended and pulled away from Liam's embrace.

The bass of "Just Dance" reverberated under their feet, sending a new crowd of students to the dance floor. A group of cheerleaders crowded around Liam, pulling him into their circle, so Michelle made her way through the gyrating bodies, and spotted Brad and Hannah standing by themselves.

Brad's eyes lit up as she approached them, then he noticed her irritated expression. "You okay, Chelle?"

"Yeah," she lied. "You guys having fun?"

Hannah gave her a sly smile. "I'm going to get a drink."

She knew Hannah had left them so they could be alone. She could feel Brad's eyes on her, making her uncomfortable but intrigued. Once they began talking, they fell back into the rhythm of close friends; it was easy and natural.

As the prom came to an end, the DJ announced the last slow dance of the evening. Brad turned to her. "Well?" She nodded, then he took her hand and led her to the dance floor.

Her stomach fluttered again with his touch. She placed her arms around his neck, losing herself in his deep blue eyes. Holding him this close was new and exciting. Maybe Hannah was right; he felt the same way, making her smile inside.

Brad rested his arms around her waist, pulled her close, then brushed his cheek against hers and whispered, "I'm such an idiot."

She placed her hand on the back of his head and whispered in his ear, "I know." Making him laugh.

Liam looked around for Michelle and saw her in Brad's arms on the dance floor. The chemistry between the two of them was undeniable. She may have agreed to be his date, but once again, her choice was clear. It was Brad; it would always be Brad.

The bright fluorescent lights popped on, signaling that the prom was over. The guys carried their jackets and ties on their shoulders, while the girls carried their stilettos, walking their blistered, bare feet down the sidewalk to a parade of weary parents waiting to bring them home.

Liam walked up to Brad and Michelle. "You ready, Chelle?"

"Um, Brad's giving me a ride home since I live next door, and Hannah left already."

It's not how Liam thought their night would end, but he wouldn't let Michelle see his disappointment.

"Okay. Well, thanks for being my date." He leaned in and kissed her cheek. A female classmate called his name, drawing his attention away from her. He told himself that if Michelle didn't want him, he had plenty of other options.

"Thank you, Liam," Michelle yelled as he trotted away toward a group of girls.

Brad turned off the headlights as he pulled into his driveway so he wouldn't wake his parents.

Michelle threw her high heels in the grass, grabbed the long skirt of her dress in her arm, and climbed the tree fort ladder.

Brad kicked off his shoes and socks, threw his tuxedo jacket on the hood of his car, and followed her. He laughed and struggled to get comfortable as he settled against the fort wall. Michelle turned her back to him, allowing him to guide her hips between his legs, then leaned into him, resting her head on his shoulder.

"I can't believe we fit up here," she giggled.

"Let's hope it doesn't collapse," he laughed.

He rested his arm across her chest and breathed in the scent of her hair.

She stroked his arm with her fingers. "I always loved coming up here with you."

He placed his lips next to her ear. "You took my breath away tonight."

Michelle smiled, closed her eyes and relaxed into his arms, loving the feel of his embrace.

A bright flash of light startled them.

Brad looked over the fort wall and saw a figure walking across the driveway. "Hello?"

"What are you two doing up there? It's one o'clock in the morning," Brad's father yelled.

"Sorry to wake you, Dad, we'll be down in a minute."

"Walk Michelle home and grab your things from the lawn," Tim grumbled.

Brad raised an eyebrow at Michelle, and they giggled like children.

As they walked around the fence and up her long driveway, he took her hand and wove his fingers through hers.

When they reached the top of the stairs on the Carrington's front porch, Michelle turned to him. "Well, thanks for walking me home, Mr. Cole." A nervous rush ran through her, and her face sobered when their eyes met.

Brad's heart pounded in his chest as he stared into her eyes. He took her face in his hands and kissed her deeply.

All the years of longing to kiss her, the taste of her lips, her body pressed against his, had his head spinning and his body tightening. Kissing Michelle was better than he could have imagined.

A rush of electricity ran through her body, not wanting their kiss or the feeling to end.

They placed their foreheads together and smiled.

"That was nice," she whispered.

"I know I screwed up, but I won't ever let you down again."

She placed her hand on his shoulder. "I'm holding you to that." Then she sauntered to her front door and glanced over her shoulder, giving him a coy smile.

Brad knew in that moment that their relationship would never be the same. Michelle wasn't just his best friend; she was his forever.

CHAPTER 6

Summer/Fall 2000

Michelle's parents whisked her away on their private yacht the week after graduation for a month-long cruise. It was their graduation gift to their daughter, and they insisted she spend the summer with them before heading to college.

It was only the second time Michelle had accompanied her parents, as seasickness had cut her maiden voyage short. Armed with wristbands and Dramamine, Michelle had to give it another try, but being away from home made her miss Brad more each day.

The Coles also took every opportunity to spend as much time as possible with Brad before he left for UConn. Jennifer stared out the kitchen window, watching her husband and son looking under the hood of Brad's car, going over the proper maintenance before taking it to college. Not that long ago, it seemed, Brad was in elementary school. A favorite memory popped into her head as she glanced at the Carrington's estate.

A seven-year-old Brad sat working intently as papers and a rainbow of crayons lay scattered across the dining table.

"What are you making, Bradley?"

"Chelle's happy birthday card," he said, the tip of his tongue peeking from the corner of his mouth. "Did you know, Mom, that infinity goes on forever and ever and ever? It never stops."

"Yes. I did know that." Then she glanced over his shoulder and read, 'love you 1,000 x infnte' written inside a heart. She smiled, not correcting his misspelling, ran her hand down his thick brown hair, and kissed the top of his head. "Michelle is going to love the card."

Tim pulled the oil dipstick from the car and showed it to his son. Brad tried to listen to his father's instructions, but his mind wandered. As much as he loved his parents, he longed to be alone with Michelle. He knew he wouldn't be able to see her before heading to UConn for football camp, and the two-month wait intensified his desire to have her close to him again.

Mansfield, Connecticut
UConn Campus 2000

The UConn campus was buzzing with the start of the fall semester. Michelle finally settled into her dorm room, while Brad and Liam had been on campus since the beginning of August, preparing for the football season.

With football practice over and having a few hours of free time, Brad made his way to Michelle's dorm. As he reached the top of the stairwell, he saw Liam in his doorway kissing a blonde in skin-tight hip-hugger jeans and a half-shirt. Brad knew his friend all too well. His dark hair, crystal-blue eyes, and 5'11 stature were as magnetic on the college campus as they were in high school. Liam took full advantage of his captivating charm, attracting women, and the UConn campus had no shortage of prospects.

The blonde passed him on the stairs, giving him the once-over. When he reached Michelle's room on the next floor, a petite girl with long, black, silky hair rushed out the door and ran into him.

"Oh, sorry, Brad, I'm late," Lucy blurted.

"Hey, Lucy. See ya."

He first met Lucy when he helped Michelle move into her dorm. She was a quirky brainiac whose housekeeping was a stark contrast to her attention to detail. A calendar hung above Lucy's desk. Each day planned down to the hour, while piles of clothes, textbooks, and bags of trail mix covered her twin bed.

But it was Lucy's cheerful demeanor that made her the ideal roommate. Michelle was thankful and looked past the disaster that was Lucy's bed after hearing horror stories of roommates from hell.

"Chelle?" Brad called out, not seeing her in the room.

"Be out in a few. I'm just getting in the shower."

Brad just sat down on her bed when she yelled to him.

"Oh damn, could you grab me a towel?"

He rolled his eyes and stood up from the bed.

"I forgot it before I got in the shower. It's in the closet on the shelf."

Brad knocked on the door and announced that he was coming in. "Here you go," he said, throwing the towel over the shower bar.

"Thanks."

"Want to grab something to eat when you're done?" he asked.

"Sure."

Steam engulfed the room, and beads of sweat formed on his forehead. The moist air was strangling him, so he turned to leave when he heard a smack and felt a sting as hot water soaked the back of his shirt.

"What the hell?" he barked, twisting his body to assess the attack.

She peeked around the shower curtain and held her hand over her mouth. "Oops, did I get you wet?"

Brad scanned the bathroom, found a cup on the sink, and quickly filled it.

"What are you doing? Don't you dare!"

She let out a screech as an ice-cold waterfall poured down her back. "You're such an ass!"

He raised his eyebrows. "Oh, I'm the ass? Who started it?"

She giggled, then her heart skipped a beat, realizing Brad's proximity to her naked body.

He stood silent for a moment, his heart beating in his chest, and stared at her silhouette behind the shower curtain. After months of waiting, they were finally alone. This was what he had fantasized about. But he turned to leave.

Michelle peeked around the shower curtain again. "Wait. Don't go."

He looked over his shoulder, met her ocean eyes, and closed the bathroom door.

Her breathing quickened as he removed his shirt and kicked off his shoes.

He opened the curtain and gave her an admiring once-over. "You're so beautiful," he whispered.

She blushed with nervous excitement, then slid her fingers into the waistband of his jeans and pulled him into the shower. "You're getting your jeans wet," she said playfully.

His dark blue eyes looked at her with intensity. "So, take them off." He leaned into her and breathed in the lavender scent of her shampooed hair while sucking the warm water from her lips. Her warm breasts pressed into his chest, causing his body to tighten as she unbuttoned and unzipped his jeans.

She bit her bottom lip as he removed his water-soaked pants, taking notice of every defined muscle and of every aroused inch of him. She had never craved something so intensely, needing to feel his body against hers, and pulled him close again.

He kissed her tenderly, savoring the desire that radiated between them. "God, Chelle," he whispered as his hands explored her curves.

She turned off the shower and gazed at him. "Let's take this to my bed."

The moonlight reached through the slats of the window blinds, casting shadows in the dorm room as their bare bodies lay intertwined on the twin-size bed.

"Lucy won't be back until Monday."

He kissed her neck. "Lucy who?"

She shook her head and giggled.

He ran his fingers over her golden skin, following the curve of her hip and narrow waist, counting each rib. Then he traced the fullness of her breast and placed his hand on her chin, sliding his thumb across her bottom lip. "Are you okay?"

She bit her lower lip and nodded. "I never felt so close to you. It was better than I imagined."

He tucked a strand of hair behind her ear with his finger. "Why did we wait so long? I've known you were the one my entire life."

"Maybe we were afraid?"

He tilted his head. "Afraid of what?"

"That our friendship might be ruined if it didn't work out." Tears filled her eyes. "I couldn't handle it if things changed or got weird between us."

He kissed her and stared at her with his deep blue eyes. "Chelle, our bond is too strong; nothing could change us. Remember," giving her a warm smile. "I love you a thousand times, infinity."

She smiled back at him and traced the curve of his ear, then combed her fingers through his hair, remembering the handwritten birthday card he made for her, professing his love at seven years old. "You are my heart and soul, Bradley James Cole. I love you a thousand more."

The morning sun lit Michelle's dorm room with a warm glow. Towels and clothing still lay in piles on the bathroom floor. Slamming doors and chatter in the hallway woke them.

"Good morning, beautiful." He smiled and kissed her softly.

She stretched her legs, drew her shoulders up, and smiled with her eyes closed.

"Do you always wake up with a smile?" he teased.

"Mmm," she moaned, then opened her eyes. "I could get used to waking up to those baby blues every morning."

He grinned, ran his fingers through her hair, and kissed her. "I can arrange that."

"What would Lucy say?"

"Her face will be stuck in her books, and she's always running late. She wouldn't even notice me."

She raised her eyebrows. "Well, she may notice you coming out of the shower."

"Let her admire this chiseled physique," he boasted, flexing his bicep.

Michelle rolled her eyes, grabbed the sheet, and jumped up from the bed, wrapping a toga around herself. "I'm starving. Let's get breakfast."

"Oh yeah, we never grabbed something to eat last night." He grinned.

She looked over her shoulder with a flirty smile. "I'm jumping in the shower. Want to conserve water?"

He leaped up from the bed and followed her with a broad smile. "All in the name of conservation, of course."

Shelby walked into her dorm room and collapsed on her twin bed. Five minutes later, her roommate, Ashley, walked in and followed suit. The two lay on their beds and yawned, followed by a simultaneous groan.

Shelby ran her hands down her face. "College swim practice is a beast."

Ashley yawned again and nodded her head in agreement.

"I'm so hungry, but don't have the energy to walk to the dining hall," Shelby whined.

Ashley reached into her sweatshirt pocket and threw a granola bar across the room, hitting Shelby in the face. "Ow."

"Sorry."

"Thanks," Shelby laughed. "I can't believe it's October already, and our first meet is in two days," she groaned.

"How'd you like the announcement that our test is on the same day as our first meet?" Ashley asked.

Shelby rolled her eyes. "I swear they do it on purpose to stress us out."

"No doubt." Ashley rolled onto her side and rested her head in her hand. "Hey, are you lifeguarding in the spring?"

"Yeah, and hopefully over the summer too at my high school, along with working at the flower shop."

"Geez, girl, do you ever give yourself any downtime?"

Shelby chuckled. "You sound like my best friend, Sam."

UConn Campus
March 2002

The charged atmosphere had the crowd cheering and standing in their seats with only ten seconds left in the game. The women's basketball team was on its way to an undefeated season, but this game proved to be a challenge, and they were trailing by two points.

Michelle read the pass between her opponents, stole the ball, and dribbled down the court. Halting at the three-point line, she jumped and released the ball, floating it over her defender's out-stretched arms. The cheers from the fans fell silent as they watched the ball arc and swish into the basket. The crowd went wild, but Michelle's excitement was short-lived. As soon as her feet landed, she crumbled to the court, writhing in pain, holding her right knee. Her basket won the game, but a torn ACL would end her season with the Huskies.

Brad sat on the side of the hospital bed, joking with Michelle, trying to ease her nerves. The IV stung, but the fluid running through her veins warmed her as she became more relaxed. Her eyelids became heavy as she focused on Brad in a drunk-like stupor.

Ann leaned over, kissed her daughter's forehead, and whispered, "I love you."

Seth placed his hand on Michelle's shoulder. "We'll be here, sweetheart, when you get out of surgery."

Brad leaned in and kissed her cheek. "Good luck, babe."

Michelle put her hand to her lips and threw Brad a kiss as a nurse wheeled her away. "That's my boyfriend, isn't he handsome?" she slurred.

Michelle pushed herself to return to the competitive level before her injury, expecting to take her position back during the 2002-2003 season. She was free from the crutches, the knee brace, and months of physical therapy and thought the nine-inch scar on her right knee would be the only thing left that revealed what she had been through, but it wasn't.

Soon after her injury, a teammate stepped up and showcased her own talents, leading the Huskies to the year-end tournaments and playoffs. Although completely healed, Michelle failed to regain her starting position, as her teammate permanently replaced her.

Brad was lying on his side in the twin bed, his head resting in his hand. Michelle lay on her back next to him, her knees bent and her hands tugging on her hoodie strings.

She glanced at her knee. "It's an ugly reminder of what I lost."

"I get it, babe. It sucks. But you're still on the team. Some people never get to play again." He ran his fingers over her scar. "It's not ugly, it's badass."

She rolled her eyes.

"It's your badge of honor. It shows your strength and perseverance," he teased.

She raised her eyebrows. "I'll show you strength and perseverance." She straightened her legs and pulled him onto her, then wrapped her legs tightly around his waist.

He groaned, then grinned with a playful spark in his eyes. "I like badass Chelle."

May 2003

Shelby climbed down from the lifeguard chair and noticed her swimming and diving coach walking toward her. "Hi, Shelby."

"Hi, Coach!"

"So, I know you'll be starting your last year in the fall, but I have an opportunity for you after graduation," Coach said and raised her eyebrows. "That is, if you are interested."

Shelby tilted her head. "An opportunity?"

"We will be losing our assistant coach after the 2003-2004 season, and I'd like you to interview for the position."

Shelby's lower jaw dropped.

"Why do you look so surprised, Shelby? You've stepped in when we needed help and have taken the underclassmen under your wing. You've earned the respect of many people here, and you deserve the opportunity."

"I just never expected this. Thank you, Coach." Shelby smiled.

"We'll talk more in the fall and next spring. Enjoy your summer."

Brad and Michelle packed their belongings and left for New Jersey, ready to enjoy summer break before starting their last year at UConn. Liam left for New York City, so they wouldn't see him until he returned to campus in August.

Brad's mother consumed much of their time when they were home, so they had to take advantage of any opportunity to spend a moment alone.

Michelle's mother knocked on her bedroom door. "Honey, I'm off to an open house. I'll be a few hours, and Martha left to shop for the week's meals."

"Okay." Michelle knew it was her mother's subtle way of letting her know she had the house to herself, but only briefly.

She heard the front door shut and made a quick call, knowing that a few minutes after her mother's car left the driveway, Brad would enter through the back door to sneak upstairs to her room.

She heard a knock on her bedroom door. "I received a request for a booty call."

She came out of her en suite wearing a men's dress shirt and saw Brad standing with his arms outstretched in the doorway.

"We have less than two hours. I suggest you close the door behind you," she ordered, pulling him into her room.

"Nice shirt." He grinned. "I wondered where it went."

She ran her finger along the band of his gym shorts and batted her ocean eyes at him. "It found its way onto my body."

"Not for long," he said slowly, unbuttoning the shirt while staring into her eyes. He kneeled and opened the last button, running his hand up the back of her thigh, kissing her stomach, and squeezing her cheek in his hand.

Michelle closed her eyes and ran her fingers through his hair, her body tightening with his touch. She placed her forefinger under his chin and guided him to his feet. "I suggest you get naked because I plan on taking advantage of every second alone with you." Then she slid the dress shirt down her arms and let it fall to the floor.

His eyebrow shot up. "Yes, ma'am."

From their first kiss, Michelle knew their feelings for each other were beyond a teenage crush. When his dark blue eyes looked into hers, she simply could not imagine her life without him.

CHAPTER 7

UConn Campus
May 10, 2004

Brad stood in Liam's dorm room, holding a small black velvet box open.

Liam's eyes widened. "Hell, any girl would say yes to that rock."

Brad admired the ring and smiled to himself. "It was my grandmother's. I'm going to ask Michelle tonight, and if my interview goes well, we'll have two things to celebrate." He looked at Liam and lifted an eyebrow. "Hey, I have something to ask you."

Liam placed both hands on his cheeks. "Oh, yes, yes, I'll marry you, Bradley James Cole!" he said in a high-pitched voice, then extended his left hand.

Brad laughed and swatted Liam's hand away. "Shut up. I'm serious—will you be my best man?"

"Hell, yes. I thought you'd never ask."

"Thanks. And listen, if anything happens to me, promise me you'll look out for Michelle."

Liam scowled. "What are you talking about? If anything happens to you?"

Brad's expression sobered. "I mean it, Liam. Promise me."

"Yes, of course I will. But nothing's going to happen to you, dude. You're in your prime," Liam said, hitting Brad in the stomach with the back of his hand.

Liam had accepted that Michelle and Brad were in it for the long haul. Michelle would always hold a piece of his heart, but he was truly happy for his childhood friends.

Brad wrapped his arms around Michelle's waist. "Two weeks to graduation, and if I get this job, we're shacking up, Carrington."

Michelle laughed, then kissed him. "Good luck, babe."

"Okay, I gotta go. I don't want to be late for my first real interview."

Liam slapped Brad on the shoulder. "Good luck, but you won't need it. I bet they hire you on the spot."

Liam rested his arm around Michelle's shoulder as the two watched Brad walk away.

"Did you tell him about your job offer with your mother's real estate agency?"

Michelle sighed. "No. He was so excited about this interview, I couldn't."

"You know he'd follow you anywhere."

"I know, but..."

The screaming of a motorcycle's open throttle echoed through the UConn campus.

Michelle felt an uneasiness wash over her. She whispered, "Something doesn't feel right." Then she yelled out to Brad.

He turned and waved as he stepped off the curb to cross the street to the parking lot.

The squeal of rubber on the pavement drew students' eyes to the road. Time slowed as Brad's body cartwheeled through the air and landed in the middle of the road with a heavy thud. Within seconds, the smell of gasoline and burnt rubber filled the air.

"Brad!" Michelle screamed.

"Call 911, and stay here," Liam told her, then ran to Brad.

Her heart pounded in her chest, and her lungs burned as adrenaline fueled her body, running behind Liam.

Liam turned around and grabbed her by the shoulders. "No. Michelle, it's bad. Let me help him."

She pulled free from his grasp and pushed him away. "Let go of me, Liam!"

She kneeled next to Brad, and her eyes darted frantically as blood pooled around his head and crept across the pavement. His right leg bent at a 90-degree angle at the knee, and his left arm hung dislocated and limp.

"Brad, look at me, stay awake," she said calmly, stroking his face.

His eyes opened wide with fear, then shifted and focused on her. "Ahhh, Che...," he moaned, then closed his eyes.

"No, no. Keep your eyes open. Stay awake; help is on the way. Stay focused on my voice," she pleaded.

As blood trickled from the corner of his mouth and nose, he struggled to speak but was able to whisper, "Cold."

Liam kneeled beside Michelle and placed his hand on Brad's leg. "They're almost here."

"Please, Brad, hold on, stay awake," Michelle cried.

Campus security pushed bystanders back as the ambulances approached the accident scene. An EMT knelt next to Brad. "Hey, buddy, what's your name?"

Michelle's body trembled as she replied. "It's Brad. Brad Cole."

"Chelle, we'll follow the ambulance to the hospital. Come on," Liam said, taking her arm to help her up.

She yanked her arm free. "No! I'm riding in the ambulance with him."

"Miss, I'm sorry we don't have room. Please ride with your friend. We'll take good care of him."

The EMTs loaded Brad into one ambulance and the motorcyclist into the other. She stared at the puddle of blood, frozen in shock as both ambulances sped away, their sirens echoing through the campus. The crowds dispersed, and then Liam placed his hand on her arm. Michelle pulled away again, giving him an expressionless look.

"Chelle," Liam said softly. "Chelle, come on, let's go."

She stared out the car window as a tear ran down her cheek.

He placed his hand on her knee. "They'll help him. He'll be okay."

This time, she didn't recoil at his touch. She took his hand and held it tight.

CHAPTER 8

Boston
May 14, 2004

Shelby walked in the front door, holding a large garbage bag of dirty clothes. "Mom, Dad, I'm home."

Patrick appeared in the foyer and kissed her cheek. "Let me take that."

"Thanks, Dad."

"The first load is in the car?" he asked.

"Yep, I'll bring the rest home after graduation."

"Oh, Shelby, I'm so glad you made it home safely," Liza said, wrapping her arms around her daughter. "I was so worried about you after you told us about that horrible accident on campus. Those poor young men—so heartbreaking."

"I'm fine, Mom, but it was awful. I heard that his girlfriend and best friend saw it happen."

"Oh, that's terrible."

"It's weird. I didn't know them, but I felt a deep sadness. My heart actually ached when I heard about it." Shelby shook her head. "It was so strange."

"Well, I wish I had better news for you here, but you should go see Sam's Aunt Becky today. She asked if you could stop by the shop next time you were home." Liza tilted her head.

"Oh no, Mom."

"I know, sweetie. You should go today."

Aunt Becky threw her hands up. "Shelby! Welcome home!"

Shelby carefully wrapped her arms around Aunt Becky, discovering every bone in her frail stature. "How are you feeling? Are you taking it easy?"

"Oh, don't you worry about me," she said, patting Shelby's hand. "Tell me, what are your plans after graduation?"

"Well, I hope I still have my job here for the next few months before I leave for—"

Becky interrupted. "Of course, of course. It will be nice to see you more often instead of only on your school breaks." Then her eyes filled with tears.

Shelby tilted her head and took Becky's hand. "Aunt Becky, what is it?"

"Come sit with me, honey. We need to talk."

"Okay." Shelby knew Becky would be lucky to see the end of summer. Sam's aunt hardly looked like the same vibrant woman from eight years ago when Shelby first stepped into the floral shop. She hated that Becky's illness had ravaged her body so quickly, but was grateful it didn't touch her mind or spirit.

"You know I don't have any children, and Sam has always been like a daughter to me, but..."

"Yes." Shelby nodded.

"Sam has no interest in taking over the business, and I don't have much longer on this Earth."

Shelby drew her lips together as tears filled her eyes, then she whispered, "Aunt Becky."

"No. Now it's alright. I've accepted it, and I'm not afraid," she said, giving Shelby a tearful smile. "I want you to know that I have left Aunt B's Bouquets to you in my Will. She's yours, Shelby."

Shelby's eyes grew wide, and her mouth parted, but her words fell short.

"I know you'll take great care of her. You'll make her better than I could ever dream."

Shelby took Becky's hand as a tear ran down her cheek. "I don't know what to say."

Becky laid her hand on Shelby's. "You don't have to say anything. You have a gift. Now, share it with the world."

Shelby wiped a tear from her cheek and sniffled. "Thank you. I will make you proud."

"Oh, honey, you did the first day you stepped foot in this place."

CHAPTER 9

Short Hills
May 14, 2004

Michelle stared at the shell of herself in the mirror as warm water ran over her numb hands.

A whisper came from one of the bathroom stalls. "I heard it's a closed casket because the injuries were so bad."

Two stall doors swung open. "Oh. Michelle. We're so sorry about Brad. How are you doing?" one girl asked.

Michelle's face remained expressionless. "Well, at least it's a closed casket, right?"

The girls looked at one another, their faces burned with embarrassment.

Michelle released a heavy sigh and walked out of the restroom.

She went to the large greeting area, where the overwhelming aroma from dozens of floral arrangements filled the room and stung her nose. The vibrant colors were a stark contrast to the dark apparel worn by so many paying their respects.

She sat beside her parents and watched the procession of condolences pass by the closed casket and noticed that Brad's mother stood close to his father, needing him as physical support. Each new face reared Jennifer and Tim's heart-wrenching grief. Tear-soaked tissues were permanently fixed in Jennifer's hands, and her shoulder-length brown hair was pulled back in a loose bun, revealing bags and dark circles under her glazed brown eyes.

Michelle couldn't endure another minute of their grief and turned to her mother. "Why do people say the flowers are beautiful at a wake?"

Ann tilted her head with a puzzled look, then put her arm around her daughter. "It's a kind gesture to bring beauty to a dark time, honey."

"Flowers are supposed to be for happy occasions like birthdays, weddings, anniversaries, or to say I love you." Her tone was filled with bitterness and anger. "Brad will never have any of those—no more birthdays, no wedding, no anniversaries, no Father's Day, nothing."

A sudden feeling of nausea crept into her throat, forcing her to put her hand to her mouth and run to the restroom.

Ann glanced at her husband, then followed her daughter. "Michelle, honey."

Michelle lay on her bed, exhausted but unable to sleep. The wake was excruciating, and the funeral tomorrow would be unbearable.

Ann sat on the side of the bed and brushed the hair from her daughter's face. "I wish I could take all your pain away, my love."

"How do I go on without him? He's a part of me. I don't know a life without him." Michelle buried her face in her pillow and sobbed while clutching Brad's dress shirt, which still carried his scent.

She felt her mother's arms cradle her. But it was Brad's arms she begged to hold her. The grief ran so deep that every inch of her ached for him.

May 15

A sunbeam reached across the bedroom and lit the wooden picture frame that sat on Jennifer's dresser of a twelve-year-old Bradley, grinning from ear to ear while holding a football trophy.

Today was the day to say goodbye—a tribute to a life taken much too soon.

Tim sat on the side of their bed and gently stroked Jennifer's arm. "Honey, can I help you to the shower?"

"How could we lose both of them? How? What did I do that both my boys should be taken from me?" Jennifer looked to her husband for an answer as tears streamed down her face.

"You did nothing wrong, Jen. It doesn't work like that. You are the perfect mother and wife. You are a saint. Brad adored you, and Brayden..." Tim paused as Jennifer closed her eyes.

He helped his wife sit up and wrapped his arms around her. "Sweetheart, we have to get ready."

He walked to the bathroom and felt the urge to crumble to the floor and yell with everything inside him, but he knew he needed every ounce of strength to carry them both through this unimaginable day. Tim looked in the mirror, not recognizing the man who stared back at him. He took a deep breath, then turned the shower on for his wife.

Jennifer leaned against the bathroom sink and opened the prescription bottle, slowly placing the pill between her lips. She too stared at the stranger in the mirror, who looked old, broken and withered.

Today, they would bury their son.

The organ echoed through the church as a sea of black flowed in and filled the pews.

Jennifer stood with her hand on Brad's casket, her eyes filled with tears, oblivious to the crowd behind her.

Tim wrapped his arm around her. "Honey, the service will be starting in a few minutes." Then he guided her toward the first pew.

She locked eyes with Michelle and extended her arms. "Oh, sweetie."

Michelle stood and melted into Jennifer as they both sobbed. Tim placed his hand on his wife's back, and she reluctantly ended their embrace. She sat down and settled under her husband's arm. The Prozac took over, and Jennifer sat with glazed eyes as the sermon and hymns melded into one long tone. When Liam walked to the altar, she came out of her trance.

Liam gripped the sides of the pulpit to keep his hands from shaking. He took a deep breath as his voice squeaked through his tears.

"Brad." He cleared his throat and apologized. "I've known Brad for what seems like my entire life. We both loved the competitiveness of football and baseball. Eventually, being called the dynamic duo." He paused for a second and locked eyes with Michelle. "I found out quickly that as much as he loved sports, his one true love was Michelle. If you saw one, you'd see the other." A trail of polite laughter gave him a slight reprieve from the deafening silence.

He recounted his favorite stories with his best friend, then finally released a heavy sigh and ended with a prayer. *"Lord God of hope, we come to you today in deepest grief and with such sadness of heart at the sudden death of such a beloved friend. He was snatched away from us in such a tragic way. Lord, we know that our time is in your hands. The shock and sadness that the life of this precious person was cut short fill our hearts with deep pain and sorrow. Be our comfort in this time of loss."*

As Liam spoke, Michelle stared at the large picture of Brad displayed on the easel next to his casket. Liam's words were drowned out by her heartbeat pulsating in her ears. She felt nauseous as a cold sweat came over her. She closed her eyes and heard Brad's voice. *You're okay; you can do this. Breathe, babe.* She opened her eyes and saw the minister at the pulpit asking guests to join them at the cemetery.

It was over.

She watched as Liam joined the other pallbearers, carrying the love of her life down the long aisle of the church.

The mile-long procession followed the hearse to Brad's final resting place. Headstones of various sizes were carved into the cemetery's landscape like dominos. Rows of folding chairs sat parallel to the suspended casket.

The minister blessed Brad one last time, and the casket adorned with flowers was lowered into the ground.

Liam stared at Michelle as she sat expressionless. Her mother leaned over and whispered something to her. Michelle turned and glared at her mother. He had never seen her look so angry and was taken aback when she directed that anger at her mother.

"Alright? I'll never be alright! Nothing will ever be alright, Mother!" she barked as quietly as she could, but it drew the attention of those seated within earshot. Michelle closed her eyes, shook her head, then walked away toward the procession of limos.

He wanted to go after her, wrap his arms around her, and take her pain away, but he stayed seated and watched her disappear into the limo. A few minutes later, Brad's parents walked to the Carrington's limo, and he saw the back window open slowly. Michelle reached out and took Jennifer's hand.

He stood to leave when he heard Brad's voice in his head. *Promise me you'll take care of her.* It was only a short time ago that Brad had made him promise, and he thought it a strange thing to ask, given they were weeks away from college graduation and had their whole lives ahead of them. Then he wondered if Brad sensed that his life would be cut short.

It sent a chill down his spine, then he glanced at the limo one last time. Michelle had no idea that Brad had planned to propose the night of the accident, and he wouldn't be the one to tell her, at least not yet. But he would keep his promise no matter where the rest of their lives took them. He would be there for her if all Michelle wanted from him was a shoulder to cry on. The thought of being anything more was purely selfish.

CHAPTER 10

Michelle collapsed onto her bed and eventually drifted off to sleep. When she opened her eyes, the room was pitch black. She went to the window seat filled with plush pillows and stuffed animals, and looked over at the Coles' house. Not a single light was on; it was dark and lifeless.

She leaned back, felt something hard poke her back, and pulled a flashlight from behind the pillow. It surprised her that the flashlight still worked after being hidden for years. Tears rolled down her cheeks as she rested her head against the window. She sent a beam of light at the tree fort and flashed an SOS signal. Flashes of light answered her back. She sat up, and her breath caught. *Did she really see that?* The flashes repeated.

"Brad?" she said desperately, then instantly felt foolish for saying his name out loud.

She ran outside and made her way to the tree fort, afraid of what or whom she might find.

She stopped at the foot of the ladder and shone her flashlight at the top of the fort. "Who's there? What are you doing up there?"

A soft voice answered. "It's just me, honey."

"Mom C?"

"Yes."

She climbed the ladder to find Jennifer wrapped in a blanket, holding a flashlight and Brad's high school football jersey.

"I'm sorry if I scared you, honey."

"I thought I was seeing things."

Jennifer extended her arm, and Michelle sat down and settled into her embrace.

"It doesn't seem real, like it's a bad dream, Mom," she whispered.

"I know, honey. It feels like I'm just going through the motions; I'm numb." She sighed. "You know, I used to watch the two of you sending your flashlight signals back and forth; it was so cute."

Michelle bit her bottom lip, trying to hold back her tears. The flashlight slipped from her hand and rolled onto the wooden slats, revealing something carved into the fort's sidewall.

"What's that say?" She leaned forward, grabbed the flashlight, and pointed it at the wall. Carved inside a heart were crude letters that spelled out Brad **+** Chelle.

"I don't remember ever seeing that in all the time we spent up here."

"He loved you so much, honey." Tears pooled in Jennifer's eyes. "When he was five years old, he told me you were his best friend and wanted you to live with us." She gave a soft chuckle.

"Mom, how are we going to do this? Go on without him?"

Jennifer placed her hand on Michelle's cheek. "We have to. He would want us to live our lives and be happy."

"I don't know how I'll ever be happy again."

The two held each other for hours. They laughed, cried, questioned why, stared at the stars above, and talked out loud to Brad.

Jennifer placed her hand on Michelle's arm. "I'm going inside now, honey. Will you come back tomorrow? I want to show you something."

"Sure." Michelle rested her hand on Jennifer's. "I love you and will always be here for the both of you."

"I know, honey. We've always thought of you as our daughter." Jennifer kissed Michelle's forehead, then made her way down the ladder. "Stay as long as you want; I'll see you tomorrow."

Michelle wrapped the blanket tight around her, tilted her head back, and looked to the heavens. "I love you a thousand times infinity, Bradley James Cole. You are my heart and soul."

"Chelle! Catch!" a young Brad yelled.

She reached for the football, but it fell through her hands.

"Nice try. You'll get the next one. Go long, I'll throw a spiral."

She watched him run away from her, holding the football tight to his side.

"Brad? Wait, come back!"

"Go long, go long!" he yelled.

She looked up as a spiraling football came at her.

Michelle jolted awake, disoriented. As she lay in bed, she stared at the sun reaching through her window, becoming more aware of her new reality. Tears filled her eyes until a tapping drew her attention to the window. A bright red cardinal was pecking at the glass.

When she sat down at the window seat, she was surprised it didn't fly away.

"Is it you saying hello?" she said, placing her hand on the window. The cardinal gave one last peck and flew away. She thought back to her and Brad in her dorm room, feeling foolish for complaining about what she had lost after her knee injury. *If only I had known what actual loss was.* She sighed and looked over at the Cole's house. *What was Jennifer going to show her? Would she be able to hold it together?*

Tim opened the front door and hugged Michelle. "Come in, honey. Jennifer's in the kitchen."

Walking through her second home gave her an overwhelming sense of sadness. Brad was in every part of it, but she could feel his absence. She hated that feeling.

"Hi, honey." Jennifer wrapped her arm around her. "Come," she said, leading her down the hallway.

Opening Brad's bedroom door felt like an invasion of privacy, but being around his belongings brought her comfort at the same time. Everything was as he had left it before leaving for UConn. Little League and high school trophies adorned a three-tier shelf above his desk. Major League and NFL posters covered most of one wall. A picture of them at their high school graduation sat on his nightstand, and next to it was a small black velvet box.

Jennifer took a plaid decorative box off Brad's desk and sat on the bed, patting the spot next to her. "Come sit, honey."

When Michelle sat down on Brad's bed, a flood of memories rushed through her—the two of them as children, then teenagers, and intimate stolen moments during college breaks, making her cheeks burn in the presence of his mother.

"I never thought I would have to talk about this, but I feel compelled to tell you. I don't know why; I just need to." Jennifer opened the plaid box, pulling out a black-and-white sonogram picture.

Michelle glanced at the image and back at Jennifer. "Is that Brad's sonogram?"

"Yes, but it's also his brother's."

She gave Jennifer a puzzled expression.

"There are two babies, Bradley and Brayden," Jennifer said, pointing at the picture.

"Brad had a twin? How did—"

"I was six months along when I started going into labor. The boys were fraternal twins, and when my water broke, Tim rushed me to the hospital. I delivered Brayden, but he was too little; it was too early. By God's grace, the doctors were able to stop the contractions. I was on bed rest for the remainder of my pregnancy and was able to deliver Bradley to full term."

"I'm so sorry. But Brad never said anything about a brother."

"We never told him. I couldn't bear to talk about Brayden. I know it was wrong. Tim never pushed me, even though he thought we should tell Bradley when he got older. But there never seemed to be a right time." Her voice cracked as tears filled her eyes. "They are together, my dear sweet boys are together now." She held a tissue to her nose. "I don't think Bradley ever felt his brother's absence because you filled it. You two had a deep connection from the first time you met as toddlers."

Michelle stared at the floor. "It was always easy with him. It felt right." She shook her head. "We talked about traveling around the world together when we were kids. We had so many plans."

"Oh, he adored your snow globe collection. He told me all about each one, where your father brought it back from, and the little towns inside. He couldn't wait to visit all those places with you someday." Then Jennifer's smile faded as she took the black velvet box off the nightstand and stroked the top with her thumb.

Michelle's eyes widened when Jennifer placed it in her hand.

"This was my mother's ring. Brad asked me for it a month ago." Jennifer could barely speak. "Oh, honey." She took a quick breath. "He was going to pro ... pose." Jennifer covered her mouth and tried not to sob.

Michelle opened the small box. A single solitaire diamond sparkled against the black velvet. Her hands trembled as she cried, then she closed it. "I can't..."

"Please keep the ring, honey. He wanted you to have it. I want you to have it."

Tears rolled down Michelle's cheeks as she whispered, "Thank you." *How could she not accept it? It was a symbol of Brad's love for her. A symbol of his commitment to her. A symbol of a lifetime together, they both were denied.*

CHAPTER 11

UConn Campus
May 15, 2004

Shelby's heart felt as if it would beat out of her chest as she knocked on the coach's door. This would be her last week on campus.

"Shelby!"

"Hi Coach, I'm sorry to bother you, but I need to talk to you."

"Sure, come on in. Are you all set for graduation? The staff is eager to welcome you aboard. I knew you'd get the assistant coaching position."

Shelby lowered her head, exhaled, then met her coach's curious expression. "Coach, I feel awful and appreciate the opportunity, but..."

"But?"

Shelby's heart sank, and tears pooled in her eyes as the words left her lips. "I can't take the job."

Boston
Sunday, May 23, 2004

Mourners and elaborate floral arrangements filled the reception hall. A dozen large round tables with bright-colored linens displayed pictures of a happy and successful life. Becky was adored by her family, friends, and the many patrons who had received Aunt B's Bouquets of condolences, congratulations, and happy birthdays over several decades.

This was Shelby's first celebration of life memorial. Aunt Becky was adamant about not having a funeral. She wanted her loved ones to celebrate the beautiful life she had been privileged to enjoy for as long as she was allowed.

It was also the first time Shelby saw Sam weep; ever. Although Sam may have complained about working at the floral shop, she had a close relationship with her only aunt and was devastated when Becky lost her battle.

Only a handful of people knew Shelby would be the new owner. She was nervous, grateful, and honored that Aunt Becky had left her pride and joy to a young business college graduate with whom she saw so much potential. Becky's staff and the community would expect a smooth transition and business as usual, so she refused to fail. This was more than just a job; it would be her lifelong tribute to a beautiful soul taken much too soon.

Shelby looked across the reception hall and saw Sam sitting alone. She walked over and sat beside her best friend at the large round table. "Hey, how ya doing?"

"Okay."

"The celebration was nice. Your dedication was beautiful." Shelby leaned over and bumped her shoulder into Sam's. "I'm proud of you for having the confidence to get up in front of everyone. Who knew you were such a good public speaker?"

Sam stared at the floor. "Apparently not Aunt Becky."

Shelby turned in her chair and faced Sam. "What do you mean?"

Sam looked up and locked eyes with Shelby. "Why didn't you tell me she left you the floral shop?"

"Sam." Shelby sighed.

"When did you find out it was yours?"

Shelby looked down. "A couple of weeks ago."

"You didn't tell her you were starting a job at UConn as the assistant swim coach?"

"How was I supposed to say no? I thought she would have told you. I'm sorry."

"Well, it's obvious she didn't have the confidence in me to run it, so good luck. I know *you* won't let her down."

"Sam, that's not true."

Sam stood up from the table. "Well, I guess I should be happy you are staying in Boston. It all works out. My best friend is staying in town, and I won't have to quit my job at the spa now. What does a massage therapist know about the flower business, anyway? Right?" Sam scoffed and walked away.

"Sam, wait." Shelby sighed and stayed seated, knowing better than to follow her.

She knew Sam wasn't happy about her taking a job in Connecticut, and the more she thought about their conversation, the more irritated Shelby became. *Did Sam honestly expect Aunt Becky to leave the business to her after all the years of complaining about working there? Does Sam even care about what I gave up and the people I disappointed to honor her aunt's dying wish?*

Shelby closed her eyes and exhaled, praying that their friendship would survive this. She couldn't imagine her life without her best friend.

CHAPTER 12

Short Hills
Sunday, May 23, 2004

Liam rang the doorbell to the Carrington estate and glanced over at the Cole's house. It still didn't seem real that Brad was gone.

Martha opened the large, ornate mahogany door. "Hello, Liam, come in. Michelle is in the kitchen." She led him down the hallway, where a gallery of fine art adorned the wall, catching his eye. Anytime he had been to Michelle's house, the decor displayed the latest trend.

Michelle sat at the large island, picking at a plate of salad.

Liam had never seen her look this disheveled. Her hair sat in a messy pile on top of her head, and her T-shirt and sweats swallowed her as they hung loosely on her thin frame.

She slid off the bar stool and hugged him. He could tell it took everything in her not to cry.

"Hey, Chelle. How are you holding up?"

"Just trying to get through one day at a time." She sat back down on the bar stool and picked through her salad again.

"A few of us are going to a bonfire tonight. Want to go for a little while?"

"I don't know."

Martha chimed in. "It will do you good to get out of this house, dear."

"Maybe." She sighed.

"I'll pick you up at eight, okay?" He hugged her again and glanced at Martha with a hopeful expression.

Martha walked him to the foyer and rested her hand on his arm. "Thank you. She needs this. She's fortunate to have you in her life. See you tonight."

Liam figured Michelle would back out, but he rang the Carrington's doorbell at eight on the dot. Michelle opened the front door, holding her sweatshirt. Her face was forlorn, but her blue jeans, fitted T-shirt, and brushed hair told him she would go.

He gave her a smile. "Hey, I am glad you decided to come with me."

Michelle waved to Martha as she entered the foyer.

"Drive safely."

He didn't push her to talk in the car. It was enough that she came with him. They pulled onto a long dirt driveway and parked in an open field. A small group gathered around the large fire pit, drinking and laughing. Nestled in the trees, string lights framed the roofline of a small cabin. People ran in and out of the entrance, while others sat on the front porch and on the steps.

They sat down on a large tree trunk next to the fire pit. Liam offered Michelle a beer as she stared at the fire.

She threw her head back, drank half of the bottle, and blotted her lips with her hand. "I had a dream about him."

"You did?"

"I dreamt we were kids, and he was throwing a football to me, telling me to go long." She closed her eyes and sighed. "It's been two weeks, and it still doesn't feel real." She finished her beer and asked Liam for another one.

"Whoa, you might want to slow down."

Michelle glared at him. "Who are you, the beer police?" Then she opened the cooler and grabbed another bottle.

"I'm just saying." He pulled a bag of pretzels from the side pocket of the cooler and handed it to her. "Here, you should eat something."

She took the bag, grabbed a handful, and looked at him, placing a pretzel in her mouth. "Happy?"

He returned his gaze to the fire and sipped his beer. She could give him her worst, and he'd still care for her. But he understood her anger. He, too, was mad at the world for taking his best friend from them.

They sat and stared at the fire, not saying a word for almost an hour. Michelle opened her third bottle of beer as Liam finished his second. He got up from the log. "I'm gonna say hi to the guys. Do you want to come?"

"No."

"I'll be right back," he said, hesitant to leave her alone.

She waved him away. "Go on."

"Don't drink all my beer, okay?" he said jokingly, but he was serious.

She rolled her eyes and shoved another pretzel into her mouth. "Don't worry. I won't drink all your beer."

Half an-hour later, after her fourth beer, she weaved her way to the cabin.

"Oh, hey, Michelle."

Michelle scowled, trying to focus her eyes on the blonde standing in line for the bathroom.

"It's Claire." She smiled.

Michelle stepped back and placed her hand on the wall to steady herself. She never expected to see her least favorite person from high school. "Claire? What the hell are you doing here?"

"I came home for Brad's funeral. I'm so sorry. He was such a great guy. So many people were there; I guess you didn't see me."

Michelle scowled again. "No. I guess not. What the hell is taking so long?"

"Do you want to go ahead of me?" Claire asked.

She didn't have it in her to accept Claire's kindness. "Why are you being so nice to me now? Because Brad is dead? All you wanted in high school was to make him one of your conquests."

Claire's eyes grew wide, and her cheeks turned bright pink as people turned to watch Michelle berate her.

She was angry at the world, and Claire's mere presence was more than she could handle. "Screw it," Michelle barked, then weaved her way out of the cabin.

Liam had watched her from a distance, but after a few female classmates distracted him, he glanced at the log and saw she was gone.

He looked around, and as he walked back toward the bonfire, he saw someone in the woods.

"Chelle? Is that you?" As he drew closer, he saw her pants around her ankles while she squatted and held onto a small tree to steady herself.

"What are you doing?"

"The line was too damn long!"

"Geez, let me help you." He reached for her arm to help her balance.

"I'm fine! Let go!" she snapped, jerking her arm away and falling backward. "Dammit, Liam! What the hell! I'm all dirty now!" She rolled onto her hands and knees and tried to stand.

He helped her to her feet and steadied her as he pulled up her jeans. "Come on, let's get you home and cleaned up." He placed her arm around his neck, then wrapped his arm around her waist.

As they approached his car, she stopped. "Wait, wait! I'm going to be sick!"

He held her hair and rubbed her back. "Okay, get it all out."

"I'm sorry," she whined.

"It's alright. Let's get you home." He helped her into the passenger seat and buckled her in.

"If you're going to be sick again, tell me, and I'll pull over. Don't puke in my car, okay?"

She rested her head back and gave him a thumbs-up. "Don't take me home." Her eyes stayed closed as her head rocked from side to side. "Please take me anywhere but home."

He let out an irritated sigh. "I'll take you to my house. My parents are out of town. You can crash there tonight."

"Thank you, Liam." Then, her limp hand ran down his arm. "You're such a good friend," she slurred.

Twenty minutes later, he pulled into the three-car garage, carried her into the guest room, and set her on the en suite floor. He left, then returned and knelt in front of her.

"Chelle, open your eyes. Here's some water. Drink it," he said, placing the glass in her hand.

"Yes, sir." She raised her right hand to her forehead and saluted him, then took a gulp of water.

He shook his head. "You have pine needles and leaves in your hair." He attempted to pick them out when she slapped his hand away.

"Well, if you didn't push me down, I wouldn't be all dirty. I can clean myself. I'm a big girl." She tried to stand, but lost her footing and fell into him.

"Whoa, sit here." He placed her on the commode, turned the shower on, and removed her sneakers and socks. He glanced at her arm and brushed the dirt from it, running his thumb over the heart-shaped scar on her right elbow, courtesy of him, from their home plate collision as kids. Not the kind of imprint he wanted to leave on her. He would much rather have left an imprint on her heart. But it wasn't meant to be, and he had forgotten about that day until now.

"Sit on the bench in the shower so you don't fall. Here's a towel. I'll be right outside the door if you need me." He sat on the floor against the bathroom door and could hear her struggling to remove her clothes. "You okay in there?"

"All good. All naked now," she giggled.

He closed his eyes and tried to erase the image of her naked body only feet away. The white noise of the shower lulled him to sleep until she opened the door, causing him to sit up abruptly.

Michelle stood in the doorway wrapped in a bath towel, her hair wet and tousled. "Hey, do you have some clothes I could borrow?"

He got up from the floor and pointed. "I put them on the bed."

"Thanks." She shuffled to the bed, grabbed the pile of clothes, and weaved her way back to the bathroom, leaving the door open a crack.

He heard her gargle with the mouthwash he had left for her. His job was done. Now, he could finally crawl into his own bed.

"Liam?"

"Yeah?"

"I'm sorry. You know I don't usually drink like that."

"I know. It's been two weeks from hell; I get it. Don't worry about it. I'm heading to bed. Good night."

"Wait," she said, resting her head against the doorframe. "Can you sit with me until I fall asleep?"

He closed his eyes and sighed. "Sure."

She crawled onto the bed and slid over, making room for him.

He pulled the comforter over her, propped up the pillows, and sat beside her on top of the comforter.

She laid her head on his lap and began to cry. "Why'd he have to die? Why him?"

"I don't know, Chelle. It's not fair. I miss him too." He moved the wet strands of hair from her face, then rested his hand on her shoulder. "I will always be here for you, Chelle, whatever you need."

"You're too good to me," she said, then she sat up, leaned into him, and kissed his cheek.

Liam looked deep into her aching eyes. "I better go, Chelle."

"Please don't. I don't want to sleep alone. Please, just lie next to me."

He released a heavy sigh. "Okay, just for a little while."

He turned off the lamp on the bedside table and rested his head back on the headboard. The room was dark except for a narrow slit of light that peeked from under the bathroom door.

She laid her head on his shoulder. "The room is spinning."

"Just breathe."

She took a couple of slow breaths, and within minutes, they both fell asleep. Liam began to dream when Michelle's body twitched, startling them both awake.

"Jesus, you scared me. You okay?"

"Sorry," she giggled.

"What's so funny?" he said in an annoyed tone.

"I scared you." She covered her mouth with her hand and laughed harder.

"Yeah, real funny." He gently pushed her off his shoulder.

He sat up to leave the bed when she pulled the covers off her and straddled him, still giggling. She laid her head on his chest and let out a heavy sigh. She kissed his neck, then his cheek, stopping at his lips.

"Chelle," he whispered. He loved the feel of her and had wanted to kiss her for as long as he could remember. But this wasn't what Brad meant when he asked him to take care of her.

She rested her forehead on his and whispered, "Please, I need to feel normal for a while. I need to feel anything but broken."

"Chelle. You're drunk."

She leaned back and removed the oversized T-shirt. "I'm not drunk. I know what I want."

~ 97 ~

The light from the bathroom door allowed him to see her silhouette. His eyes burned with desire, and his heart thudded in his chest. She was perfect. His mind told him to leave, but every inch of his body told him to stay.

"Chelle, I—"

She placed her finger on his lips. "Shut up."

The next morning, Michelle was still sound asleep, so Liam set a glass of water, two pills, and a note—*Take these, then come to the kitchen*—on the bedside table. He guessed it was her first full night of sleep in days.

He set a coffee mug and plate on the kitchen island and saw Michelle walking down the hall toward the front door.

"Hey, did you see my note? I made you some coffee and toast."

She stopped in the hallway, keeping her back to him. "Thank you, but could you just take me home?"

He stared at her and sighed. "Sure."

He had imagined a different scenario. She would thank him for being there for her and wrap her arms around him. But this wasn't about him. Last night was merely a distraction she needed to forget her broken heart.

He glanced at her as she stared out the passenger window.

"It's okay, Chelle, we're good."

"I shouldn't have. How could I? He's only been gone two weeks."

"Look, it was nothing," he lied. His feelings had grown even stronger for her.

"No! It's not okay, Liam!" she snapped back.

His eyes widened, and he stayed silent for the remainder of their drive. When they arrived at her house, he parked, opened his car door, and paused when she grabbed his arm.

When he faced her, her eyes were filled with tears.

"I'm sorry. You've been such a good friend, and I took advantage of that. Please don't call me. It's best if we don't see each other for a while."

"Chelle?"

"I'm sorry." She got out of the car, shut the door, and disappeared into her house.

CHAPTER 13

June 2004

Michelle sat on her bathroom floor, running a tissue across her lips. "Shit, what the hell is wrong with me?" She rested her head against the wall and heard a knock on the door.

"Michelle? Are you alright, dear?"

She released a heavy sigh. "Yeah, I'll be out in a minute, Martha." Another wave of nausea surfaced, so she leaned back against the wall and waited for it to pass.

Martha sighed. "I'll be in the kitchen if you need anything."

It had been five weeks since Brad had passed, and the sadness only grew deeper inside her. She was on autopilot, moving through life in a daze. She chalked the sudden nausea up to a stomach bug and eventually made her way to the kitchen.

Martha stood at the kitchen island, writing on a notepad. "Michelle, dear, I need your help today at the store. Your parents are having guests over for dinner, and I could use an extra set of hands with the groceries."

She sighed. "I'm not up for it today, Martha."

Martha glanced at her. "Getting some fresh air will do you good."

She went to the pantry and pulled out a box of crackers. "Maybe another day."

"No. Today. We'll leave in a few hours," Martha commanded.

Michelle opened her mouth to speak, then snapped it shut, shocked that Martha had spoken to her like a child. Couldn't Martha see she felt awful?

The click of their seat belts broke the awkward silence. "Here," Martha said, handing her a pen and a piece of paper with a long list of items. "Please read it out loud. I want to make sure I didn't forget anything."

Her eyebrows shot up when she glanced at the paper. *This is going to take hours,* she whined in her head.

"Go on now, please read me the list," Martha repeated.

While in the store, she was Martha's runner. She avoided eye contact or polite small talk with other patrons, praying she wouldn't run into anyone she knew. She couldn't take another, "I'm so sorry about Brad. How are you doing?" At least the nausea subsided, but the hour-and-a-half-long outing to the grocery store was torture. She appeased Martha and held back any complaint.

"One more stop. I need to run to the pharmacy. You can wait in the car."

Michelle rested her head back on the seat and stared out the car window, watching people go about their lives. The world didn't stop, didn't change, because Brad died—but her world, and his parents' world, did change and would never be the same.

Martha returned to the car, buckled her seat belt, and handed Michelle a small white paper bag.

Her eyes flickered with annoyance. "What is this?"

"Open it, please."

She opened the bag and pulled out a slim box. "Martha?"

"Well, it's not for me, dear."

Michelle sat on the side of her bed, staring at the box. *I can't be pregnant. It's just a stomach bug or something I ate. Martha thinks she knows me better than I know myself. She's wrong, and the test will prove it.* Michelle took a deep breath, entered her bathroom, and closed the door.

She rested her hands on the sink as her mind raced. Then she stared at herself in the mirror, feeling her heart beat faster with each passing second—her mind was reeling. *When was my last period? I think it came after the funeral, but it only lasted a day. When was the last time Brad and I were together? It was on that horrible day. No, it has to be too long. Dammit, then I was with Liam.*

She glanced at the test. *Two pink lines. Pregnant.* "Oh shit. No, no, no," she said out loud, then whispered, "It has to be wrong." Then she pulled out the second test. *It has to be a false positive,* she tried to convince herself.

She set the second test on the sink and closed her eyes, praying for a negative result. The minutes passed in slow motion. *Two pink lines. Pregnant.* She looked in the mirror again, her eyes wide with fear. Then, a sudden urge to vomit hunched her over the sink.

Michelle walked to the kitchen and leaned against the large granite island.

Martha looked up from the stove. Michelle's expression told her what she had suspected.

"I took both tests, but they have to be wrong."

Martha tilted her head, walked over to Michelle, and wrapped her arms around her.

"I can't be pregnant. I can't!" She buried her face in Martha's shoulder and cried.

It was the end of June, and Liam had honored her wishes to stay away. She sometimes missed his company, but it was for the best, especially now—at least until she knew for sure.

Michelle hugged her parents goodbye and wished them safe

travels on their annual summer cruise. She had no intention of telling them about the pregnancy tests or her doctor's appointment to confirm it. She swore Martha to secrecy, and if it was a false positive, crisis avoided. If not, she would eventually tell them.

Michelle stared at the black-and-white screen as the technician rolled the ultrasound wand over her lower abdomen. The technician turned the monitor toward Michelle and pointed to a dark oval and two tiny white peanut-sized objects. "Congratulations, you have twins!"

"Twins?" Michelle's voice squeaked.

"You're approximately five to six weeks along."

Michelle's eyes filled with tears as she stared at the monitor.

"Honey, are you okay? Do they run in your family?"

She closed her eyes, and her voice quavered. "I don't know."

Filled with guilt, anxiety, and fear, she kept repeating in her head, *This is all too much. I can't do this."*

She walked out to the waiting room, where Martha sat patiently.

"Michelle?"

"Can we just leave, please?"

They got into the car and sat in silence for a moment.

Martha turned to her. "Dear, what is it?"

Michelle cried, "I'm having twins."

CHAPTER 14

Milltown, New Jersey
September 2004

Michelle found peace and solace at her family's lake house, which held many precious memories. She and Brad would spend summer days bouncing on inner tubes across Farrington Lake, roasting marshmallows by the fire pit, and telling horror stories late into the night until they passed out in their sleeping bags on the screened-in porch.

This is where she would raise the twins.

While her parents were on their annual cruise, Martha was her confidante and support—at least until her parents came home, a day she dreaded.

Martha came out on the screened-in porch, handed Michelle a cup of tea, and sat in the rocking chair beside her.

"Liam stopped by the main house again, asking for you. He's stopped by several times over these last few months. He's worried about you."

She ignored Martha's comment, sipped her tea, and stared at the lake. "Brad and I would sleep out here and talk for hours, planning out our lives." Her arm cradled her growing figure as she continued to rock.

"Michelle, I've kept Liam away, but he will find out eventually. Then there is the matter of your parents. I do not feel right keeping this from them. They trust me, and I won't lie to them."

"Liam is living his life. He didn't ask for this. I won't ask him to give up everything because of one mistake."

"Michelle, you can't do this alone. You need to tell Liam and your parents."

"I will tell my parents eventually, but on my terms," she said sharply.

"How can you deny Liam his children, Michelle? It's not right."

She stopped rocking and replied with a tone of arrogance. "It's not your decision."

Martha stood up from her rocking chair and faced her. "After all these years, I've earned the right to express my opinion and tell you when you are wrong. Liam has a right to know about the babies. Your parents and I raised you better than that."

She stared at the lake; her mouth set in a hard line.

Martha kneeled next to her and held the rocking chair still.

"Look at me." Martha took Michelle's chin and gently turned her head to face her. "I know Brad was the love of your life, and no one will ever replace him. I'm not saying you need to marry Liam, but he needs to know."

Tears pooled in Michelle's eyes.

Martha stood and kissed her forehead. "I'm turning in. Love you, dear. I know you'll do the right thing."

Martha sat on the side of her bed, wondering why secrecy plagued this family. Michelle's parents denied her ever knowing her identical twin sister, and now Michelle was denying Liam of learning about his twins. She refused to be involved in another secret. She wouldn't let history repeat itself.

The autumn leaves fluttered to the ground as the tiny lives fluttered inside her, making their presence known. At first, Michelle found the sensation alien-like, but now it fascinated and comforted her. She knew she had to talk to Liam, and the longer she waited, the worse the conversation would be, but she kept finding excuses to avoid him, and it was obvious by her ever-growing figure that she was expecting.

Michelle ignored his calls, and when he stopped at her family home to check on her, Martha would politely tell him she was not there. He assumed Martha was lying, but he continued to ask her to relay messages to Michelle. Over four months had passed, and she hadn't made a single call to let him know she was okay. He felt he had a great deal of patience, but this was just cruel.

He rang the doorbell and waited for Martha to greet him. If Michelle were home, he wouldn't leave until she talked to him. Otherwise, he'd tell Martha that this would be his last visit.

The large mahogany door opened, and Martha gave him the same despondent expression she had given him over the last few months.

"Hello, Liam."

"Hello, Martha. You know what I will ask you, but this will be the last time. I'm moving to New York City."

She gave him a guarded look. "Michelle is not here…"

He shook his head. "Okay."

"But I will tell you where she is."

He gave Martha a puzzled expression.

"She's been living at the lake house. If you want to follow me, I'm headed there now."

"Has she been there this whole time?"

"Yes, and I believe it's time for the two of you to talk."

Liam had only been to the Carrington's lake house a few times with Brad. He understood Michelle wanted to get away, and it was peaceful there, but Martha seemed to know more than she was letting on, which made him concerned and curious.

It was as he remembered. This wasn't just a lake house set back among towering trees—it was a second home. It had all the conveniences of modern living; no roughing it here.

Martha approached Liam's car. "Please give me a minute, then come to the front door."

"Okay." *Why did Martha have to warn Michelle that he was there? It was all so bizarre,* he thought to himself.

Martha opened the large oak door of the lake house. "Michelle?"

She groaned, finding it harder to get out of the rocking chair.

Martha met Michelle in the living room and placed a hand on her shoulder. "You have a visitor."

A deep crease appeared between her brows. *Who else knew she was at the lake house besides her parents?*

"Liam is here. He's waiting in the driveway." Martha raised her eyebrows. "It's time."

Michelle's heart thumped in her chest. She stood frozen. *How could Martha tell him?*

A knock at the door made her jump, and she wished she could retreat to her rocking chair and hide away from the world and Liam, but she walked over and opened the door.

Liam's eyes met hers, bringing a smile to his face. Then he took in the full view of her.

"Chelle?"

She released a heavy sigh. "Come in, Liam."

He followed her to the living room, noticing a slight waddle in her step.

She sat at the opposite end of the large sectional and wouldn't look at him. When she tried to explain, he interrupted her.

"How far along are you? Are you seeing someone?"

"I'm due at the end of January with twins. And no, I haven't been seeing anyone." She looked at the floor and pressed her lips together.

Liam's expression was tinged with disbelief. "Twins?" Then his brows snapped together. "Wait, you weren't going to tell me?"

She tilted her head. "Liam—"

"What the hell, Michelle? Were you planning to hide here, have the babies, and keep it a secret from me? You know I would—"

She interrupted Liam this time. "You have a successful career, and you're probably with someone. When are you not? I won't ask you to take this on. Besides..." She hesitated.

"What does that mean? And take this on? They are not your sole responsibility, and I sure as hell have a right to know about them, whether or not I'm with someone."

He walked over to the stone fireplace, rested his elbow on the mantle, ran his hand through his hair, and closed his eyes. The possibility they were Brad's raced through his mind. *Would that change anything, though? He promised to take care of her.*

She saw the frustration on his face and offered a compromise. "Listen, I don't expect us to get married. We can work out visitations."

He looked at her, confused. *Either she was in denial that they could be Brad's, or she honestly believed they were his.* "I'm not going to be a weekend father. Jesus, Chelle." He took a deep breath, walked over, and sat beside her. "Look, I told you I would always be here for you, and I meant it." He glanced at her protruding stomach, then into her eyes. "Especially now."

She leaned her head back and stared at the ceiling as tears flooded her eyes. She placed her hand on his. "I'm so sorry. I was terrified. Martha is the only one who knows, and I wanted to..." She paused and put her hands over her face and cried.

He wrapped his arm around her. "Listen, I will take care of you and the babies. You don't have to worry about anything."

Michelle lowered her hands from her face, looked down, and cradled her stomach. "Liam…"

"What's wrong?"

She took his hand and placed it on her stomach.

Astonishment flickered across his face when he felt a tiny lump roll across his palm. "Whoa! Was that a foot or a hand?"

Michelle smiled and nodded.

Liam sat in amazement, waiting for another wave of motion as a flood of emotions ran through his head. *He was angry with her for keeping the pregnancy from him, but he was grateful for that one night. He was overwhelmed at the thought of being the father of twins. Then, he realized it wasn't only his promise to Brad that would keep them connected; the twins would bond him and Michelle for the rest of their lives.*

CHAPTER 15

September 2004

The waiting room was filled with a sea of women at various stages of life, with a few wide-eyed, expectant fathers sprinkled in. Liam watched the mothers interact with their young children; some were patient, and others looked like they hadn't slept in days. A two-year-old waddled over to him and handed him a little fish cracker.

Liam smiled. "Thank you."

She immediately grabbed the cracker from his hand and shoved it in her mouth.

Michelle glanced at Liam, and they both chuckled, a momentary reprieve from the awkwardness between them.

The little girl's mother gave Liam a polite smile while taking her daughter's hand and leading her back to their seats. "That's nice of you to share, but let's stay in your chair."

A nurse called out Michelle's name, drawing their attention away from the little girl, then she led them down a long hallway to the exam room. "Who do you have with you today?"

"This is Liam, the twins' father," Michelle replied shyly.

The nurse gave him the once-over. "Nice to meet you, Liam."

"Nice to meet you too, Maria."

Michelle glanced at him with a raised brow.

He mouthed, *What? It's on her badge.*

Michelle rolled her eyes and shook her head at him.

The three entered the small exam room, where Michelle took her usual spot on the exam table.

"Liam, you can have a seat if you'd like," the nurse said, trying not to let her gaze linger on him.

He sat down, then he scanned Maria from head to toe.

She took Michelle's vitals and noted them in the chart. "Dr. Allen will be in shortly. Have a nice day." The nurse glanced at Liam. "Again, it was nice to meet you," she said as she walked out the door.

"Seriously, what is it with you and women?"

He widened his eyes and shrugged his shoulders, and as he opened his mouth to answer, Dr. Allen walked into the room, so he stood and introduced himself.

Dr. Allen gave him a polite nod, shook his hand, not as charmed by him as most women, then turned to Michelle and opened her patient chart. "Your blood pressure is a little elevated today. Are you watching your sodium intake?"

"Yes, I am," she said, knowing Liam was the cause of her higher-than-normal blood pressure.

"Looks like your weight gain is right on target." Dr. Allen helped Michelle lay back on the exam table and massaged her hands across Michelle's abdomen. A line appeared between her brows. "It seems one baby may be breech. There's still time for the baby to turn, but it will be harder for them to move around as they grow, so we'll monitor it as you get closer to your due date."

Liam noticed the look of concern on Michelle's face.

"If the baby doesn't turn, will I have to have a C-section?"

"It is possible, however, let's not worry about that now. Have they been moving?"

"Yes, mostly at night."

"Good. I want you to buy a blood pressure monitor, track it a few times a week, and let me know if it continues to be high. Also, watch for swelling in your ankles," Dr. Allen instructed.

Liam stood. "We'll stop and buy the monitor on the way home. I'll make sure she takes her blood pressure. Thank you, doctor."

"Looks like you have an attentive partner," Dr. Allen said, then she helped Michelle sit up. "Okay, we'll see you at your next appointment."

Liam could feel Michelle's glare from the passenger seat of his sports car.

"So, do you plan on driving to the lake house every day to take my blood pressure?"

He kept his eyes looking straight ahead. "Well, I was thinking I should move into the lake house and stay in the guest room."

"Martha is with me, and I'm quite capable of taking my blood pressure."

He looked at her out of the corner of his eye. "I'm assuming Martha will go back to the main house when your parents return."

Michelle turned her head, looked out the passenger window, and said nothing.

"Are you going back home when Martha leaves?" he asked, then glanced at her. "I'm guessing your parents don't know yet."

"I haven't decided. And I will tell my parents when I'm ready."

He knew it wouldn't be an easy conversation, especially with her father. Then he imagined his own parents' reaction, having kept the pregnancy a secret from them as well. He noticed she was annoyed with him, so he decided to wait before bringing up moving into the lake house again. She didn't say yes, but she didn't say no either.

CHAPTER 16

Short Hills
October 2004

Michelle walked up to the front door of her childhood home. Her parents had been gone longer than usual, so seeing her would most likely shock them. If Martha hadn't brought her, she would still be hiding away at the lake house, avoiding the outside world.

She sat in the formal living room and looked around. It wasn't until she was a teenager that she was allowed to sit in this room, but only for important conversations and special occasions. Unfortunately, this was one of those important conversations, and she felt like that scared teen summoned for an interrogation. Her parents would be home at any moment, causing her heart to nearly beat out of her chest, so she closed her eyes and took a deep breath.

Martha greeted Ann and Seth at the front door while the limo driver placed their bags in the foyer. She pulled Ann aside and told her that Michelle was waiting in the front room and needed to speak with them.

Her parents stood in the archway and stared as Michelle eased herself off the elegant plush sofa. Ann finally walked over and placed her hands on Michelle's arms with tears in her eyes.

Seth stood with his hands on his hips and furrowed his brows.

Ann's face carried compassion and concern. "Michelle, darling?"

Her face reddened. "Mom, Dad, obviously, this wasn't planned."

Ann tilted her head. "Michelle, when are you due? My goodness, we haven't been gone that long, have we?"

Before Michelle could answer, Seth blurted out, "Who is the father?"

She looked at her father with wide eyes, then glanced back at her mother. "I'm due at the end of January." Then she lowered her head. "Liam Grant."

"January? Honey, you look further along. You've been seeing Liam?" Ann rattled off.

"No, we're not together. It was one night. A mistake." Michelle's face burned with embarrassment, then she sat down, feeling the weight of her body, and shame. "I'm having twins, which explains my size."

Seth's jaw tightened. "I hope Liam is stepping up and realizing his responsibility here."

"Yes, he wants to be involved, Dad."

"Twins? How long has Martha known about this?" Ann asked.

"I found out a couple of days after you left for your cruise," she lied.

"Please don't be mad at Martha. She told me I had to tell you both, and she's been between here and the lake house, so I haven't been alone. And now Liam wants to move into the lake house with me."

Ann sat next to her daughter and placed her hand on Michelle's knee. "Nonsense, dear, you'll stay here in your home."

"Mom, I need to do this on my own. I mean, Liam and I will figure this out."

"Michelle, how are you going to handle twins? Your mother and I were fortunate to have Martha's help with you."

Ann glanced at Seth as her guilt and shame, buried decades ago, resurfaced.

"You can't possibly do this alone. You'll live here and have support from us and Martha," Seth commanded.

"Dad, I'm not a teenager. I'm a grown woman."

"Is this how a responsible adult woman behaves? Gets pregnant and hides away at her parent's lake house?" Seth snapped.

Ann tilted her head. "Seth." Then she took Michelle's hand. "Your father and I are just worried about you, darling."

"Then it's decided. Martha will stay at the lake house with you. I don't want you out there alone." Seth looked to his wife. "Your mother will look for another staff member."

Ann gave Seth a surprised glance. No one could replace Martha, but their daughter needed her. "I'll start looking right away."

Michelle eased herself off the sofa and walked over to her father. "Thank you, Dad."

He sighed, placed his hands on her cheeks, and kissed her forehead. "You know I love you, but this is extremely disappointing and not what I expected for your future."

Liam waited at the lake house, knowing the conversation with her parents would be difficult. He wanted to go with her, but she insisted on telling them herself. When Martha and Michelle finally pulled into the lake house driveway, Liam noticed the expression on their faces. *That wasn't a good sign*, he thought.

He opened the driver's side door for Martha, then went to the passenger side and helped Michelle out of the car.

Martha patted his arm, then walked inside, leaving them to talk alone.

"How'd it go?"

Michelle released a heavy sigh. "My parents insisted I come back home."

"Are you going to?"

"No. I won't live under their constant scrutiny and control. I know they mean well, but I'm staying at the lake house. My father, thankfully, insisted that Martha stay here with me, though. He's so disappointed in me."

Liam was relieved that she wasn't returning home and Martha would be with her, but a small part of him hoped Michelle wouldn't accept his offer to move in. He truly wanted to be there for her, but wondered if he could give up his apartment and bachelor lifestyle to be the man she needed him to be. He promised Brad he would take care of her, and now that promise included two new lives. It was all happening so fast.

CHAPTER 17

Milltown

In mid-November, Liam placed his bags in the guest room. Michelle continued to sleep in the main bedroom, on the sectional, or anywhere else that offered a comfortable position as her figure grew.

Liam started the fireplace as Michelle settled on the sectional. He grabbed a blanket and placed it over her lap, then sat in the over-sized chair next to the fireplace, put his feet on the ottoman, and closed his eyes.

"Thank you," she said, massaging her stomach.

Liam yawned, then asked, "Are you comfortable?"

"Yes, we're fine."

He watched her lay her head on the armrest and close her eyes. This would be his life now, taking care of the woman he cared deeply for, maybe even loved, for what felt like his entire life. He would keep his promise to Brad and accept what Michelle would offer him. His eyelids grew heavy, and the glow and warmth of the fire eventually lulled them both to sleep.

The next morning, he was still in the chair and glanced at the empty sectional. One night down, a lifetime to go.

It wasn't long before a blanket of white covered the landscape. The lake house nestled in the trees continued to be their refuge from the rest of the world. It was their first Thanksgiving and Christmas without Brad. Michelle had no desire or stamina to venture into the frenzy of mad shoppers on Black Friday, or any Friday, for that matter. Instead, she asked Liam to pull out bins of Christmas decorations to distract her from the reality of many firsts without the love of her life.

Michelle never dreamed that she and Liam would live together, let alone be expecting twins. She pushed him away for months and hated to admit that his companionship and commitment were exactly what she needed.

She took an ornament from the bin and struggled to reach the upper limbs of the eight-foot Douglas fir.

"Here, let me help," he offered, taking the ornament from her and placing it on the tree.

"Thank you. I hate not being able to do simple things." Then she stood back to judge the half-decorated tree.

An hour later, Liam placed the last ornament and added a star to the top of the tree. He stepped down from the ladder, plugged in the string of lights, then stood next to Michelle and admired their work.

Michelle handed him a beer and kissed him on the cheek.

He glanced at her, surprised by her kiss, and whispered. "Beautiful."

Michelle took in the full view of the tree and smiled. "It is." Then she glanced at Liam and noticed him staring at her. "What?"

"Now I get why they say expecting mothers glow."

She felt her cheeks burn. "Stop it."

"No. I mean it, Chelle, you are beautiful." He leaned toward her, cupped her face in his hands, and kissed her softly.

If Martha had been home, he wouldn't have kissed her. But they were alone in the ambiance of the crackling fire and twinkling tree lights.

She pulled away and stared into his crystal-blue eyes as her heart beat faster. She hadn't felt a desire for him since their one-night stand. Sober and no stranger to his charm, she kissed him back.

Michelle sat under a plush blanket between Liam's legs while resting her head on his shoulder and massaged her stomach.

He ran his fingers between hers and followed the rhythm of her hands, caressing his lips with her hair. "We can do this. Make a life together, the four of us," he whispered.

She closed her eyes and released a heavy sigh. "I know this is not what our lives were supposed to look like. Brad was going to propose. His mother gave me the ring, a family heirloom." A single tear ran down her cheek. "I didn't want to take it, but I couldn't hurt her."

He removed his hands from hers. "I know. He told me he was going to propose the morning of the—"

Michelle sat up, held the blanket close, and turned to face him. "I'm sorry if talking about Brad hurts you. He will always be a part of me."

"I don't expect us to have what you and Brad had. I just think we can make this work as a family. I will always be here for you and the twins, Chelle."

"Liam, I know I have to move on without him, and I appreciate how supportive and involved you are, but I don't want you to resent me for not being able to give you the love you deserve." She saw the disappointment on his face and the hurt in his eyes.

Still, he kissed her forehead, helped her up, and walked to the guest room.

She stood wrapped in the blanket and admired Liam's taut physique as he walked away. *She couldn't deny their mutual attraction, but she loved him only as a close friend. That's all she could offer him, at least for now.*

Liam stood in the guest room shower, his ego bruised. *What more did she want from him? He didn't expect her to forget Brad. Clearly, tonight changed nothing between them. He may not be the love of her life, but he would love her for the rest of his.*

Michelle stood in the nursery doorway. "Well, expect Christmas to be all about the twins from now on. I think our mothers bought out Bloomingdale's."

Liam glanced at her as he placed the last bolt into the second crib frame. "I'm not surprised." He pushed the crib against the wall, stood back, and shook his head. "Who knew putting baby furniture together would require a full weekend and a ton of patience."

Michelle settled into the rocker and ran her hands over her stomach. "Thank you for all your help and for being here with me."

"It's all good, Chelle," he lied.

"Liam, are you scared?"

He sat on the ottoman, lifted her feet, rested them on his lap, and massaged her right foot. His eyes widened. "Scared is an understatement."

She chuckled, then closed her eyes and moaned as he massaged her left foot.

He couldn't deny that becoming a father was terrifying. He had been so distracted with holiday family gatherings and preparing the nursery that the realization hit him all at once. In a little over a month, the twins would be here, depending on him. His life would forever be changed.

A week later, Liam watched the ball drop and confetti cover New York City on the large TV screen as thousands cheered and kissed, ushering in 2005.

Michelle lay under his arm, asleep on the large sectional, oblivious to the end of 2004, the worst year of their lives.

He stared at the TV, reminiscing. Normally, he would be in the city partying in the new year with a 5'10 model in his arms. There was no denying he missed the electric atmosphere of the New Year's celebration. But the bachelor lifestyle he had become accustomed to was no longer his to enjoy. He kissed Michelle's cheek and whispered, "Happy New Year."

Liam woke up filled with anxiety after a restless night of dreaming about partying in the city, Michelle rejecting him, then nightmares about leaving the twins in a cab and desperately searching for them. He needed time away. Time to escape what would soon be a life he wasn't sure he was prepared for.

He threw the strap of his leather Coach bag over his shoulder and avoided eye contact with Michelle as she stood in the guest room doorway.

"I'll only be gone for three days."

"We'll be okay. Martha will be here with me."

"I know, but I'll call you when I get to the city." He walked to the doorway and kissed her on the cheek.

She took his hand, giving him a sincere smile. "Have a safe drive, Liam."

He looked into her eyes and resisted the urge to kiss her. "Thanks."

When he pulled out of the lake house driveway, he felt relieved and immediately felt guilty. He couldn't let resentment set in already. He told himself the drive to the city would give him time to think. The realization of being a father at twenty-two caused a sudden panic, and he wanted desperately to hold on to his bachelorhood.

As he drew closer to the city, he felt that excitement again; it made him feel alive and free. The blaring of horns and relentless traffic distracted him until he found refuge in the hotel's parking garage. He settled into his signature suite and remembered to take care of his single responsibility for the night—call Michelle.

CHAPTER 18

Milltown

Michelle sat in the nursery rocking chair, looking out the window, watching snowflakes float to the ground like a scene in one of her snow globes. She knew it wasn't easy for Liam to move out of his apartment. Becoming a father sooner than he planned had to be overwhelming. Maybe he didn't even want children. But she had come to rely on him more than she wanted to admit.

The loud ring of the landline startled her and pulled her out of her daydream.

Martha called out to her. "Michelle, Liam is on the phone, dear."

"Hey. I made it. Traffic was crazy, as always."

"I'm sure. Thanks for calling and letting me know you made it okay."

"Have a good night, Chelle."

"You too, Liam."

Michelle hung up the phone and walked over to Martha. "Do you think he can do this?"

"Liam is dedicated to you and the twins. Yes, this is a major lifestyle change for him and for you. One day at a time, my dear."

Michelle sighed. Martha was much more optimistic, only seeing the charismatic Liam—not the one look from those crystal-blue eyes that said, *"I've got you hooked, Liam."*

Michelle walked back to the nursery, sat in the rocking chair, and massaged her stomach. *Why was she surprised he ran off to New York City, his playground? What did she expect after she told him she only loved him as a friend?*

Liam went to the bar cart, poured himself a bourbon, and stared at the bustling city below him. Could he become the man Michelle needed him to be and the man Brad expected in his absence? He drank another bourbon, settled on the couch, and flipped through the TV channels, eventually drifting off to sleep.

The following morning, he awoke and groaned, feeling the effects of sleeping on the couch the entire night. The hot shower loosened his tight muscles and woke his mind as the delivery of the twins played out in his head. All the Lamaze classes should have him feeling prepared, but the imminent birthing experience terrified him.

After a full day of meetings, he ordered room service and surfed through a sea of emails.

He would drive back to New Jersey the next day, but something told him he wasn't ready; he needed a few more days of freedom—a few more days to worry about no one else but himself.

"Hey Chelle. How are you feeling? ... Good. I'm sure Martha is taking good care of you. Listen, I need to stay a couple more days. Are you sure you'll be okay? ... Alright, have a good night."

He wouldn't let himself feel guilty. He needed this. Just a few more days to be who he used to be.

A knock on his hotel room door ended the conversation in his head.

Michelle watched the other mothers in the obstetrician's waiting room. They appeared calm and prepared. Maybe they hid their fear well and were also terrified of labor—or the responsibility of keeping a tiny human alive—or, in her case, two tiny humans.

Martha leaned toward her. "You'll be a wonderful mother." Then she patted Michelle's hand. "Would you like me to go in with you, dear?"

"Sure." She sighed. *Liam should be here. He had been gone for the entire week. Was this his last hurrah? They weren't married or even sleeping in the same bed, so who was she to say what he did and who he saw? But she selfishly expected his commitment and loyalty only to her, even though she couldn't promise the same to him. She still had a full three weeks until her due date, and he could be back home in less than two hours, but did he need to be in the city this long?* She remembered her blood pressure, took a deep breath, closed her eyes, and pictured Brad's face. His memory brought her peace and heartbreak at the same time.

A nurse appeared in the waiting room doorway and called her name.

Martha followed close behind as Michelle waddled to the exam room.

She introduced Martha, then Dr. Allen helped her lay back and ran her hands over her ever-expanding stomach.

"Have you had any Braxton-Hicks?"

"A few."

"It feels like both babies are in the correct position, but your blood pressure is a little high, so try to rest as much as you can and elevate your feet. Do you have any questions?"

"No, I'm just nervous about labor."

"That's natural. Did you attend the Lamaze classes?"

"Yes, we did. It was kinda overwhelming."

"If you have any more Braxton-Hicks, that would be a perfect time to practice the breathing techniques. Also, I've had mothers bring something to focus on during labor, like a picture or a baby blanket. It helps so they're not concentrating only on the contractions."

Michelle faked a smile and nodded her head.

Michelle sat in the passenger seat, staring out the side window as her mind wandered off. *She almost forgot that today, January 10th, was Brad's birthday. He would have been a great father. They should be growing old together at the lake house. What will Brad's parents think when they find out about her, Liam, and the twins? Mom must have told them by now,* she thought.

"Martha, do you mind making a stop for me?"

"Of course, dear. Where is it you want to go?"

"The cemetery."

It was unusual to have such little snow covering the ground in January, so it was easy for them to trek, arm in arm, to Brad's gravesite.

Michelle's eyes filled with tears as she stared at his headstone: *In Loving Memory, Bradley James Cole, January 10, 1982 - May 10, 2004.* Then she glanced at the monument next to Brad's. *In Loving Memory, Brayden Timothy Cole, October 10, 1981.* She hadn't noticed it at the burial, but she hadn't even known about Brad's brother at the time. It broke her heart that his parents had to bury both their children.

"I miss him so much, Martha."

"I know, dear. I'll be right over here. Take your time."

"Happy Birthday." She closed her eyes. "It feels so long ago some days, then it feels like yesterday. A part of me died with you. Well, I'm having twins. Hmph, you probably already know that. I'm sorry. I feel like I've betrayed you." She wiped a tear from her cheek. "Liam has been great, but he's not you. No one could ever replace you. I need you so much right now. I don't know how to do this without you," she cried, placing her hands over her face.

She felt Martha's arm wrap around her. "Come, dear. Let's go to the car—you're shivering."

They walked back toward the car arm in arm until Michelle stopped and grabbed her stomach, feeling an intense cramp and a warm sensation run down her legs. "Oh, no! Martha! My water broke!"

CHAPTER 19

New York City

The 'wah' of sirens and the deep roar of fire engine horns echoed off the skyscrapers of the bustling New York City streets. Liam lay on the king-size bed, staring out a wall of windows. The winter sun was bright and warmed the room. A plush comforter draped over the edge of the bed while a white Egyptian sheet lay across his naked body. A long, shapely tan leg lay over his waist as delicate, manicured fingers combed through his hair.

"I missed you on New Year's Eve, handsome," she whispered in his ear.

"It's been a crazy few months," he said. As guilt brewed inside him, he rolled away and sat on the side of the bed. "I'm sorry, I have a meeting soon."

He felt her breasts press into his back and her arms wrap around his neck as a waterfall of silky blonde hair flowed down his chest. He kissed her arm. "You're very tempting, but I need to get in the shower."

"Well then, I'll just have to join you." She giggled.

He glanced at his phone as it vibrated on the nightstand. "I need to answer this. Hello. What? Is she okay?" He stood up from the bed. "Yes, I'll get there as soon as I can. Thank you, Martha."

"Martha?" she teased.

"Sorry, it's a family emergency. I have to go back to New Jersey."

He walked to the en suite and locked the door behind him. Normally, he would be a gentleman and walk her out, but with the news that Michelle was in labor, the only thing he cared about was getting home to her.

After a few minutes, he heard a knock on the en suite door. "Listen, I'm going to head out. I hope everything is okay. Call me next time you're in the city."

He didn't respond and heard the penthouse door shut. Steam swirled around him as he ran both hands through his wet hair, unsure if it was guilt or worry that consumed him more.

East Center Hospital in New Jersey

Martha knocked and entered the birthing room. Michelle was breathing through another contraction while the nurse placed an IV in her arm.

"I've spoken to your parents and called Liam; he's on his way."

Michelle's eyes filled with tears. "Martha, it's too early; they need more time."

The nurse placed the last piece of tape over the IV and patted Michelle's shoulder. "Dr. Allen has been notified that you were admitted. We'll take good care of you and those babies, honey."

Time moved at a snail's pace as her contractions grew closer and more intense. She was relieved when Dr. Allen and an ultrasound technician finally entered her room.

Dr. Allen placed her hand on Michelle's arm. "I didn't think we'd be seeing each other so soon."

She stood next to the technician, observed the monitor for several minutes, and turned to Michelle. "Well, it appears that we have a stubborn baby here. I had hoped they would have stayed in their positions from the last ultrasound, but sometimes they flip back around. Michelle, we need to prep you for a C-section."

Michelle's blood pressure surged with the news of surgery, sending the monitor into a light show of blinking yellow and red lights.

Her eyes filled with tears as she glanced over at Martha. "Is Liam here yet?"

"No, not yet, dear. Your mother should be here soon, though."

The nurse came in again and noted Michelle's vitals. "You're doing great. Just keep breathing through the contractions, honey. The anesthesiologist will be here soon. The epidural will help with the pain, and that should help lower your blood pressure, too."

Michelle was exhausted and dozed in between contractions. She thought she was dreaming when the anesthesiologist appeared at her bedside. Finally welcoming the effects of the epidural, she fell asleep. What felt like only minutes later, two nurses woke her when they rolled her hospital bed down a long hallway.

The operating room lights made her close her eyes, but she could still see their brightness. A sheet placed at the base of her neck blocked her view of the blue figures at her sides, while a nurse stood by her head.

"How are you doing, Michelle?" asked a familiar voice.

"Dr. Allen?"

"Yes. How are you doing?" she repeated. Then she requested a scalpel.

"Okay."

"Good. We're going to deliver these babies now. You might feel some tugging, but no pain."

She closed her eyes and tried to concentrate on her breathing as a smooth sensation slid across her lower abdomen. The nurse asked her again how she was feeling. She nodded, relaying that she was okay.

Dr. Allen ordered the Baby A team to prepare for its delivery. Michelle felt as if she was being lifted off the narrow operating table as blurs of blue floated around the room, their voices muffled behind their surgical masks. A high-pitched cry echoed throughout the room, followed by encouraging chatter.

Dr. Allen announced with a smile in her voice. "Congratulations, Michelle. You have a girl."

A nurse brought the tiny bundle next to Michelle's face. "Hello, Mommy." Then she whisked the baby away.

Dr. Allen glanced over at Michelle. "Okay, let's get this stubborn one out now."

This time, the tugging was more aggressive. The nurse watched over the blue sheet, placed her hand on Michelle's shoulder, and asked how she was doing again. She couldn't respond with words or a nod.

Dr. Allen's voice stayed calm but became authoritative as the blue figures darted around the room.

Michelle could sense something was wrong; she felt weak and could hear the monitor beeping faster and many voices speaking all at once until she lost consciousness.

A wave of affection filled her as Brad cradled the twins in a rocking chair. His face showed so much love and pride. Her heart was whole again as the love of her life held the tiny lives she brought into the world.

Liam sat next to Michelle's hospital bed and gently brushed the hair from her face as she tried to open her eyes.

"Hey, you did it. They are perfect," he whispered.

Michelle turned her head and smiled. "Brad."

"Chelle, it's Liam." It was as if she had twisted a knife into his heart, but he deserved it.

She tried to open her eyes. "Liam?"

He squeezed her hand. "Chelle, we have a boy and a girl. I saw them. They are little but strong."

Her voice strained as she spoke. "We have a boy, too?"

"Yes, Dr. Allen said he was stubborn and didn't want to come out."

"But only one baby cried," she whispered.

"Chelle, your blood pressure dropped, and you passed out during the C-section. I'm so sorry I wasn't here to help you through all this."

She didn't acknowledge his apology but looked at him through sleepy eyes. "I want to see them."

"They are monitoring them for the next twenty-four hours, but I'll ask the nurse if we can wheel you down later. Just get some rest now."

"Okay," she mumbled, then dozed off.

Liam watched her sleep. He was grateful she and the twins were safe, but he was filled with guilt. How could he be so selfish? He promised her then and there that he'd never betray her again.

He fell asleep in the chair next to her bed and woke up the next morning to Michelle staring at him.

She whispered. "Hey."

"Hey, good morning," he whispered back. He sat up, took her hand, and kissed it. "It looks like they brought your breakfast. Are you hungry?"

"A little."

He raised the hospital bed and noticed Michelle wince. He had never seen her so weak and in so much pain with the slightest movement. She told him Martha was with her when her water broke and that they were at the cemetery visiting Brad's grave.

He had no right to be hurt, and Brad would be so disappointed in him. Not only did he miss the birth of the twins, but he wasn't there for Michelle when she needed him the most. She told him it was okay, but he saw the disappointment on her face and heard it in her voice. He truly was selfish.

A few hours later, a nurse came into the room with a wheelchair. "Ready to see your babies?"

Liam took Michelle's arm, helping the nurse set her into the wheelchair. Hearing her moan and trying to breathe through the pain made him realize how much she had been through.

A short ride down the hallway led them to the nursery. "Here they are." The nurse stopped in front of two clear bassinets. "They are doing great, Mom and Dad."

They glanced at each other with wide-eyed wonder; it was official—they were parents.

"Do you have names for them?" the nurse asked.

Michelle smiled. "I want to see them first."

She winced as Liam helped her up from the wheelchair. They both reached into the first bassinet and stroked the tiny pink hat.

"You look like a Chloe," Michelle said and glanced at Liam.

He nodded. "Definitely, Chloe."

"Chloe Taylor Grant, meet your daddy, Liam Taylor Grant."

He was taken aback. If he had had any doubts before, he knew she truly cared for him now. He helped her to the other bassinet, and again, they reached in, and this time stroked a tiny blue hat.

"You look like a Benjamin," they said simultaneously, then looked at each other and smiled in agreement.

Michelle tilted her head. "But what will your middle name be?"

Liam stroked the tiny blue hat again. "How about James after Brad?"

Michelle's eyes filled with tears. "Benjamin James. It's perfect."

He took her hand. "Well, the twins share his birthday, January 10th. It's only fitting."

She tilted her head. "You remembered? Thank you, Liam."

He did remember. It was the best way he knew to honor his best friend. "I know he's smiling down on them, Chelle. We're both so proud of you."

Liam pulled into the lake house driveway as Martha waited on the front porch, wrapped in her winter coat, braving the January cold. He brought the twins inside one at a time, leaving them in Martha's capable hands, then helped Michelle out of the car.

"Doctor said no stairs."

She rolled her eyes. "I can try." Then she quickly realized that the two inches she could lift her foot off the ground wouldn't get her halfway up the seven-inch step. "Oof," she moaned.

"Here, put your arm around my shoulder." He gently lifted her in his arms, carried her up the stairs, and set her down next to the kitchen island where the twins were snuggled in their carriers.

The two stood admiring the tiny lives for which they were now responsible. Liam rested his hand on the small of her back. "If you want to lie down, we'll be able to handle things here," he offered.

Martha nodded. "Yes, that is a good idea. Sleep when the twins sleep."

"Okay, if you're both sure."

"Go, Martha and I have got this." He was eternally grateful for Martha. Had she not been with them, Michelle would have seen what a nervous wreck he really was.

He sat at the kitchen island, watching the twins sleep, mesmerized by them. They were so tiny and perfect. He vowed to be there for them always, to be the father they needed and the partner their mother deserved.

Michelle eased onto the bed and stared out the window. She felt grateful that the twins were healthy and that the three of them were finally home. A single tear hit the pillow as she whispered, "Thank you for keeping us safe. I felt you with me." She closed her eyes, saw Brad's face, remembered the feel of his touch, and drifted off to sleep.

A little brown-haired boy waved his arms in the air. "Grandpa, Grandpa, throw me a pass."

A strawberry-blonde young girl sat high on her father's shoulders, resting her hands on the top of his head. His hands gripped tight around her ankles.

Michelle wrapped her arm around Brad's waist and rested her head on his shoulder.

"Nice catch, Ben!" a gray-haired Tim Cole yelled.

The little girl clapped her hands with excitement.

"Hey, nice throw, Grandpa!" Brad turned to her and smiled with pride.

Tim shouted back, "He's a natural, just like his dad!"

Muffled cries pulled her out of her dream. Confused about where she was, she blinked her eyes open and sat up, but was jolted by a sharp pain and grabbed her stomach. Her heart sank, realizing it had only been a dream. The cries became louder as she shuffled her way to the living room.

Martha handed Liam a bottle and returned to the kitchen.

Michelle settled on the sectional, and a minute later, Martha returned and handed her Chloe and a bottle.

Liam held Ben out in front of him, his tiny head cradled in his father's large hand.

Ben's eyes focused on Liam's voice as he carried on a conversation with him.

Michelle watched them and chuckled.

"Do you hear that? Mommy is laughing at us. The Super Bowl *is* a big deal."

She looked down at Chloe and pictured the little girl from her dream. *Would the twins look like the children she dreamt about? She glanced back at Liam. He looked so natural holding Ben. If he was terrified, he hid it well. Maybe Liam could be a good father, not the player she knew him to be. And possibly one day, she would allow herself to open her heart to him. Maybe one day.*

The Super Bowl was an excuse to have a small gathering and for Michelle and Liam's parents to visit their one-month-old grandchildren. Even with Martha's help, Michelle and Liam's exhaustion was apparent, and having their parents fuss over the twins allowed them a welcome reprieve.

Ann was cuddling her granddaughter when Michelle caught her mother's attention. As they entered the nursery, Michelle took Chloe from her and laid her on the changing table.

"What is it, honey? Everything okay?" Ann asked.

"I had a dream about Brad after we came home from the hospital," she said, as tears pooled in her eyes. "Mom, it was so real. When I woke up, I thought..."

Her mother wrapped her arm around her. "Honey, I know you miss him. We all do."

Michelle closed her eyes. "Have you told his parents about the twins?"

"I haven't. We've spoken only briefly on the phone. We were out of town, and I've been so busy with work. I feel awful that I haven't reached out to Jennifer in such a long time."

Michelle smiled at Chloe through her tears. "I need to be the one to tell them. I owe them that much."

"Why don't you freshen up, honey? I'll take care of Chloe." Ann kissed Michelle's cheek, then whispered to Chloe, "How's my beautiful granddaughter?"

Michelle went to the main bedroom, leaned against the en suite door, covered her face with her hands, and cried. *She had to pull herself together. It wasn't fair to Liam that she still longed for Brad nearly a year later. First, grief, then the birth of twins, and now exhaustion. How much more could she take?*

CHAPTER 20

Milltown
May 2005

Michelle stood in the shower and closed her eyes as the hot water fused with her tears. *They lied. The pain doesn't get easier with time.* She knew she had to let Brad go and focus on her life with Liam and the twins, but her heart ached for him, especially today.

She went to the living room, sat by the picture window, and watched the sunrise. At least Chloe and Ben would distract her. But before she could push the grief deep down inside, she would have to talk to the one person who understood more than anyone. She would call Brad's mother today.

The Coles already knew about the twins. Ann confessed she had told Jennifer after running into her at a department store with a handful of baby clothes. Michelle felt awful that Brad's parents hadn't heard it from her, but she hoped that talking to Jennifer about Chloe and Ben would bring some light to this dark day.

Liam walked out to the kitchen, yawned, and ran his hand through his hair. They were successfully navigating their lives as parents of twins, working as a team, and growing closer. Whether on the sectional or on top of the bedcovers, they often fell asleep in each other's arms, exhausted. It may not have been the intimacy he desired, but he loved she found comfort in his embrace.

He looked toward the living room and saw Michelle curled up in the plush armchair by the picture window. Today, May 10th, was

Brad's one-year anniversary. He hated this day too. It was a reminder of losing his best friend and Michelle losing the love of her life, something he would never be to her.

He kneeled in front of the chair and stroked her hand with his thumb. "Hey, you okay?"

Michelle turned to him with tears in her eyes. "I just want to forget. The image of him lying in the road, the blood. It's burned into my..." She took a deep breath and looked out the window again as tears spilled down her cheeks.

"Hey, look at me," he whispered, guiding her chin toward him.

Her eyes carried so much pain and grief that he tried to fight back his own tears.

"We're not going to remember him like that," he said, taking her hand.

She stared into his eyes, hanging on his every word.

"Remember his kindness, his laugh." The corner of his mouth lifted. "And that beach-bum hair."

A slight smile crossed her lips.

"That's how we remember him, okay?"

She nodded and wiped the tears from her face.

He stood, kissed her forehead, and without hesitation, whispered, "I love you."

She looked at him with wide, tear-soaked eyes, but said nothing.

He never meant to say it out loud. The words fell from his lips as easily as saying hello. It felt honest and natural. Part of him wished he could take it back and save it for when he thought it would be reciprocated, but Michelle couldn't unhear it. "I'm sor..." he started to say, then walked away.

It was the last day of June, and Michelle's parents would soon be on their annual excursion. But not before they celebrated her birthday.

This year, though, was more than just the usual birthday luncheon. The twins would meet the woman who held a special place in their mother's heart.

Michelle entered the living room of her family home, first with Chloe, followed by Martha with Ben.

Jennifer stood up from the armchair, her eyes filled with tears, as she wrapped her arms around Michelle. "I've missed you so much."

Michelle melted into Jennifer's embrace, her perfume a familiar and soothing nostalgia. "I've missed you too."

Jennifer leaned over, admiring the now five-month-old twins in their carriers. "Oh, Michelle, they are absolutely precious."

Ann came over and wrapped her arm around her daughter. "Happy Birthday, darling. We prepared all your favorites."

"Thank you, Mom."

Michelle looked at Jennifer. "Would you like to hold them?"

Jennifer's face lit up as she settled back into the armchair.

"Here is Chloe Taylor," Michelle said, placing her in Jennifer's arm, then she took Ben from Martha. "And here is Benjamin James."

Jennifer glanced at Michelle. "James?"

"Yes, Liam insisted."

"Oh, look at them. I haven't held a baby in forever." She beamed.

Michelle snapped a few pictures, admiring how content Jennifer looked holding the twins. She was impressed by how they nestled into Brad's mother without a fuss, as if they felt a natural connection to her.

"Oh, will you please send me a picture?" Jennifer asked.

"Of course." Michelle smiled, but her heart broke for Jennifer, being denied grandchildren and that special bond.

A few hours later, Jennifer approached Ann and Michelle. "Ann, thank you so much for inviting me today. Michelle, please don't be a stranger. You are always welcome to visit." Jennifer hugged her and kissed her cheek. "Happy Birthday. I love you, honey."

Michelle didn't want to let go; it was like holding a part of Brad. But Ben cried out and ended their embrace.

"I'm coming, my little man." She placed her hand on Jennifer's arm. "I love you too."

Michelle settled Ben and turned to Martha. "Martha, can you watch the twins for a minute?"

"Yes, of course, dear."

She walked upstairs and opened the door to her childhood bedroom. A memory flashed before her eyes of her and Brad throwing a stuffed bear back and forth, roaring with laughter. A smile grew across her lips, then a deep sadness draped over her like a weighted blanket.

She opened her desk drawer and pulled out a handwritten card. *Happy Birthday! love you 1000 x infnte, Bradley.* "Another birthday without you," she whispered. Behind the card was Brad's funeral program, along with her handwritten note to him inside after he died. Tears filled her eyes, but she wouldn't let her mind go to that day.

She folded the birthday card, program, and note, placing them in her jacket pocket. Then she spotted the small black velvet box, shoved it into her other pocket, and released a heavy sigh.

She wondered if she would ever allow herself to love another man. Liam loved her as a close friend, but the way he said, *I love you* on the anniversary of that terrible day. She knew it was more than just a sentiment between friends. It was a profession of his true feelings.

They collapsed onto the king-size bed, exhausted. The twins were down for their morning nap, which gave them a moment of peace.

"Who told Martha she could have the weekend off?" Liam sighed.

Michelle yawned and laid her forearm over her eyes. "You did."

He dragged his hands down his face. "No more time off for Martha."

Michelle rolled onto her side to face him. "I think we should have the twins baptized."

"Where did that come from?" He gave her a confused look. "We've never really talked about it, and the last time we were in a church was…" He paused, knowing the last time was for Brad's funeral.

"I want to ask Jennifer and Tim to be their Godparents."

"Brad's parents?"

"They were like my family growing up. I think I spent more time with them than with my own parents." She sat up and peered down at him. "Do you have a problem with it?"

Liam ran his hands over his face again and shut his eyes. "No. I don't have a problem with it. They're great people. The twins would be lucky to have them as godparents," he said with a drawn-out yawn. "Let's just sleep before they wake up. Please."

Michelle lay back down on the bed. "Glad you agree."

"Did I have a choice?" he whispered, giving in to the exhaustion.

"No," she whispered back, then closed her eyes.

Michelle pulled into the Cole's driveway. It was her first outing alone with Chloe and Ben.

Tim opened the car door, smiled, and babbled with the twins. A sight Michelle had never seen before and found quite amusing.

Jennifer held the front door open, beaming with excitement. "We were thrilled when you called and wanted to visit, honey."

"Well, this is my maiden voyage with the twins. So far, so good."

Tim took Ben, and Jennifer took Chloe. They both handled the twins carefully, grinning from ear to ear.

They sat in the living room while Brad's parents fussed over the twins. Michelle smiled when she noticed the picture of Jennifer holding Chloe and Ben sitting on their side table.

"I want to ask you both something, and I felt it was too important to do over the phone."

"Yes, we'll babysit anytime." Jennifer beamed.

Michelle laughed. "No. I mean, yes, thank you. We will absolutely take you up on that. But I want to ask you both: Would you be the twin's Godparents?"

Tim's face brightened. "Absolutely. We'd be honored."

Jennifer's eyes shimmered with happy tears as she nodded.

Chloe and Ben would officially be a part of their lives. The privilege of being grandparents was ripped away from them, and Michelle was determined to fill that void. It was the one thing she could give them that Brad couldn't.

CHAPTER 21

Boston
2006

Aunt B's Bouquets became Shelby's second home. Only after a couple of years of ownership, she had updated the technology, increased the staff, and was well on her way to a record-breaking year of sales. She was content with her life, having her own apartment, a reliable car, and a successful business.

A few months after Aunt Becky's memorial, Sam apologized and admitted that she was grateful not to have the responsibility of owning a business that would take up so much of her time. They were back in each other's daily lives, and their friendship was stronger than ever.

Shelby was enjoying her single life and didn't have anyone demanding her time. Sam's boyfriend drama was reason enough to avoid blind dates and the dating scene altogether. She figured that when the right man came along, she'd know.

Shelby was stooped behind the counter and heard the bell jingle when the florist shop door opened. "Be right with you," she yelled. "Oh crap," she whispered to herself. She stood up from behind the counter, stared for a few seconds, and felt her cheeks burn. "Hi, how can I help you?"

The corner of his mouth lifted from behind a dark brown beard, and his brown eyes seemed to smile on their own as they stared back at her. "Hi. It looks like you might need my help."

She tilted her head. "I'm sorry?"

He pointed at her phone. "Your phone screen is cracked."

She wiped the screen with her fingers as if the crack would somehow disappear. "Oh, yeah." She scrunched her nose. "I just dropped it behind the counter."

"Um, anyway," she said, clearing her throat. "Are you picking up an order, or would you like to place one?"

"I need to place one."

She set her phone on the counter and turned to the computer. "What is the occasion?"

"Anniversary. You must be the new owner. Becky was my next-door neighbor growing up. I was sorry to hear that she had passed. She was a great lady."

Shelby looked at him curiously. She would have remembered him from the celebration of life memorial. "Yes, she was. I can't believe it has been two years already. I really miss her."

Shelby rattled off several options and glanced up from the computer. "How much would you like to spend?" This time, his eyes asked for help. "Fifty dollars?"

"If you'd like to follow me, I can show you a few arrangements in our cooler."

"Sure, sounds good."

As she walked around the counter, she felt his eyes scan her from head to toe, and now there was nothing between them. Her heart pounded as his nearly six-foot frame followed close behind her. He was tall, had dark hair, and was definitely handsome.

They looked through the floor-to-ceiling glass wall into the modest cooler room, filled with hundreds of flowers and greenery. Pedestals of different heights displayed a variety of arrangements. A large vase of multicolored roses caught his eye.

"That one looks great. I'll take it."

"Nice choice." She turned and met his gaze, causing her heart to race. "Would you like these delivered, or would you like to take them with you?"

"Delivered, please."

They walked back to the front, where Shelby took her position behind the safety of the counter. She hated feeling self-conscious as he watched her at the computer.

"Can I please have the name and address where you'd like them delivered?" She typed away, trying to ignore his gaze. "And what would you like the card to say?"

"Happy 30th Anniversary, Mom and Dad. Love Scott."

She glanced at him. "Oh, that's so nice of you."

"Well, I'm the lucky one. They are awesome parents." Scott handed her his credit card. "I work around the corner, so if you'd like to stop in, I can hook you up with a new screen."

"A new screen? Oh, my phone. Thank you, but that's alright."

"Are you sure?"

She scrunched her nose again. "Well, I probably should get it fixed sooner than later, huh?"

He lifted his brows. "Now that you know my name, can I ask your name?"

She gave him a shy smile and extended her hand. "It's Shelby Jones."

He took her hand and gave it a firm handshake. "It's nice to meet you, Shelby Jones, and thank you for your help."

"It was my pleasure." She released his hand and blushed, realizing it wasn't only her gaze that had lingered.

"Maybe I'll see you again?" he said, staring at her intensely. "You know, to get your screen fixed."

Her stomach fluttered. "Maybe you will."

His right eyebrow shot up. "Great, hope to see you soon."

Shelby bit her lower lip while watching him walk to the door and set off the bell.

He turned and gave her one last glance as he shut the door.

She found it hard not to carry a smile for the remainder of the day thinking about Mr. Tall, Dark, and Handsome.

A few hours later, Henry came to the front and slapped his hand on the counter. "Hey, boss lady," he said with a grin. Henry was a loyal employee and stayed on after Becky passed. Although he was old enough to be her father, he respected her authority and was quite impressed with her business acumen at her young age.

"Hey, Henry. What do you need?"

"The missus called, has a flat. She's stuck at the grocery store, and I need to go rescue her, as she put it," he said, shaking his head. "There's one more delivery I can take care of on my way there."

"No, no. You go. I can deliver it and close up. Which one is it?"

"It's the large multi-color rose arrangement in the cooler. It goes to the O'Donnell's, next to Becky's old house."

Her eyebrows lifted. *Mr. Tall, Dark, and Handsome's parents.* "Oh, okay, no problem. Thanks, Henry. Good luck with the rescue."

Shelby drove down the street slowly. She had never been to Aunt Becky's house with Sam, and if she had, she might have met a young Scott O'Donnell. Funny, Sam never mentioned him, especially with all her boy drama over the years.

Shelby pulled up to the O'Donnell's house, finding the driveway full of cars. She worried about seeing Scott and if he would think she was a stalker. Her heart pounded as she waited for the door to open, hoping Scott would answer. Then, the door handle turned, and she changed her mind. *Please don't let it be Scott.*

"Well hello, Shelby Jones," Scott said with a wide smile.

Shit, she said in her head, and felt her cheeks burn. Her eyes raked over Scott, finding him just as attractive in his casual attire of blue jeans and a T-shirt.

An older woman appeared in the doorway next to him. "Oh, those are gorgeous!"

"Mom, this is Shelby Jones. She's the owner of Aunt B's Bouquets."

Shelby smiled and handed her the vase. "Happy anniversary."

"Oh, thank you. Becky was such a sweet lady. Please come in."

"Thank you, but I should go."

Scott's mother handed the vase off to her son, took Shelby's arm, and pulled her into the foyer. "Nonsense. Have you eaten yet, honey?"

Scott gave Shelby a wink and shut the front door.

Their home was warm and inviting, smelling incredible with the aroma of barbeque wafting in from the backyard. From the narrow hallway, she saw a small group standing around a kitchen island, talking and laughing.

The chatter stopped when Scott's mother brought her into the kitchen. She smiled politely while being introduced to a room full of friendly strangers.

Scott waved his arm, gesturing for her to follow him. "Come on out back; I'll introduce you to my dad."

His father was standing in front of the grill with a spatula in one hand and a beer in the other. She saw where Scott got his height and good looks from, but he had his mother's dark brown eyes.

"Well, nice to meet you, Shelby."

"Nice to meet you too, Mr. O'Donnell, and happy anniversary."

"Thank you. How's the flower business treating you?"

"It's going really well."

She smiled and looked around, feeling awkward and out of place.

"What can I get you to drink?" Scott asked.

"A beer sounds good, thanks."

As dusk set in, string lights popped on in the backyard, and a small group gathered around the fire pit. She relaxed in an Adirondack chair and stared at the flames. Everyone had been so nice and welcoming, and she loved watching Scott interact with his family and friends, then wondered, *could he be the right man to come along?*

Eventually, they were the only two at the fire pit. She was mesmerized by the flames, and when she came out of her trance, she felt his eyes on her, making her blush. "I should get going. I have to be at the shop early tomorrow."

Scott walked her out to her car parked in the street, his parents' driveway now empty except for his white Toyota Tacoma. The front porch light reached across the front lawn, giving them just enough light to see each other in the darkness. "I'm glad you stayed and met my family. I hope you had fun."

She raised her eyebrows. "Well, your mother really didn't give me a choice."

"I'll have to thank her."

She glanced down, then looked up and met his gaze. "I had a nice time, thank you."

He raised an eyebrow. "Maybe we could grab lunch sometime?" Then he smiled. "And don't forget to get that phone screen fixed."

"That sounds nice, and I won't forget." She chuckled.

"Drive safe, and good night, Shelby Jones."

She gave him one last smile before opening her car door. "Good night, Scott O'Donnell."

Shelby told herself she would know when the right man came along, and Scott O'Donnell, Mr. Tall, Dark, and Handsome, was that man.

They sat down in a booth at Joey's bar and ordered two bottles of beer.

"Is this one of your hangouts?" Shelby asked.

"Yeah, I usually meet the guys from work here on the weekends and after golf. This must be your first time here because I know I would have noticed you," he grinned.

Shelby chuckled. "It is, actually. It's been a while since I've hit the bar scene." She scanned the room and noticed a couple sitting at the bar. "That looks like my friend, Sam."

"Do you want to go say hi to him?" Scott asked.

"Her. It's Samantha, but she hates it, so she goes by Sam. Come on, I'll introduce you."

They walked up to the bar, and Shelby leaned close to Sam. "Can I buy you a drink, miss?"

Sam whipped her head around and smiled at the sight of her best friend. "What the hell are you doing here? You finally tore yourself away from the shop?"

Shelby laughed, then noticed Sam's face sober as she looked at Scott.

Scott stared at Sam for a moment and started to speak, but she cut him off.

"Hi, I'm Sam. You must be *the* Mr. Tall, Dark, and Handsome Shelby has been talking about."

Scott extended his hand. "I guess so, but I go by Scott. Nice to meet you."

Sam leaned back on her bar stool. "This is Matt, and this is my best friend, Shelby, and Mr. Tall, I mean Scott."

Matt shook Shelby and Scott's hands and offered to buy them a drink.

"Thanks, but we just got our drinks." Shelby motioned with her thumb. "You guys want to join us at our booth?"

Sam stood. "Actually, we are getting ready to head out, right, Matt?"

Matt looked confused, but followed Sam's lead and stood up from his bar stool. "Um, yeah. Well, it was nice to meet you both."

"Oh, okay. Well, maybe another time." Shelby faked a smile, knowing Sam was lying. Then she thought maybe Sam didn't want to intrude on their date or used it as an excuse to end hers.

Scott was relieved when Sam said they had to leave. He wondered why she pretended not to know him. Sam had to have remembered him; he certainly remembered her. At least Shelby didn't notice. But would they continue with the charade if things became more serious between him and Shelby?

Over the next year, a casual lunch became weekly dinner dates, stay-in movie nights, and the much-anticipated sleepover.

Shelby lay under Scott's arm, her leg draped over his waist under the bedsheet.

"I can't believe it's been a year already," she said, running her finger in a circle on his chest. "You know our first date was technically at your parent's anniversary party."

Scott caressed Shelby's arm. "I wanted to kiss you, but we only met that afternoon, and I didn't want you to think I was being creepy."

She smiled and traced her fingers down his face. "I'm not a kiss-on-the-first date kind of girl, but I wanted to kiss you, too." She slid her leg over his waist and straddled him, resting her hands on his chest, and letting her hair cascade down her shoulders.

She watched his dark brown eyes follow her curves and meet her ocean eyes. He sat up, kissed her passionately, then put his forehead on hers and whispered, "I love you."

Her eyes lit up with affection. "I love you too."

CHAPTER 22

Milltown
June 2006

Liam's eyes lit up when Michelle finally walked out to the living room in a silky tea-length black dress that hugged her curves. "Wow."

She rolled her eyes and blushed.

They kissed seventeen-month-old Chloe and Ben goodbye and thanked Martha. Both of them felt guilt and relief at having time for themselves.

He wouldn't reveal where he was taking her, but an hour later, they pulled into the yacht club's parking lot.

Michelle raised her eyebrows. "When you said dinner, I had no idea we'd have dinner on your parent's yacht."

"Well, you deserve a special night for your birthday."

A staff member greeted them, walked them to a small table on the main deck, and poured them a glass of wine. He disappeared into the cabin and returned with their gourmet dishes.

"Mmm, that was amazing." She raised her eyebrows. "And look at that. I was able to finish my dinner before it got cold."

Liam smiled in agreement, then pulled her chair out and walked her to the bow.

She closed her eyes and breathed in the summer air. "It's a beautiful night."

He wrapped his arms around her. "*You* look beautiful."

She relaxed into his embrace and scoffed, "I don't have the figure I used to."

He turned her around. "You're right. You're even sexier."

She shook her head and rolled her eyes when he offered his hand. "Dance with me."

"Stop," she said, waving him off.

He tilted his head and took her hand, pulling her close. "Please?"

The song "Wonderful Tonight" played right on cue from the cabin.

Michelle gave him a look of surprise. "How did…"

He twirled her away and pulled her back into him, making her giggle. "You're such a romantic, Liam Grant."

"What can I say? You bring it out in me," he said, raising his eyebrow.

She smiled, then rested her chin on his shoulder as they swayed to the music.

When the song ended, his heart pounded in his chest. He stepped back, took her left hand, and got down on one knee.

Her eyes widened. "Liam, what are you doing?"

"Michelle Ann Carrington, you make me want to be a better man. You are an amazing mother, and I fall in love with you more every day. I want us to be an official family. Will you marry me?" He opened a small black velvet box, displaying a two-karat solitaire diamond ring. Her expression and hesitation filled him with a quiet panic.

"Liam. I—" She tilted her head. "Yes."

He stood and placed the ring on her finger. His racing heart slowed as relief replaced the anxiety.

She stared at her hand until he lifted her chin and kissed her softly, then he led her below deck.

Rose petals scattered on the bed, and lit candles throughout the room, assumed a successful proposal.

She raised her eyebrows. "What if I said no?"

"Well then, this would have been awkward." He grinned.

Michelle stared out the car window, knowing this was the best thing for Chloe and Ben. They shared his last name, and soon she would as well. She cared deeply for Liam and adored his interactions with the twins. He *was* a great father. She convinced herself that she could make this work, be his wife, and, in time, open her heart and give him the love he deserved.

He glanced at her. "You okay? You're awfully quiet."

"Hmm? Yes. I'm fine." She looked at her hand. "The ring is beautiful."

"I'm glad you like it."

"Did Martha know?"

"I told her I had a surprise for you, so she probably guessed it was a proposal."

The lake house was quiet and dimly lit when they walked in. Martha emerged from her room with anticipation covering her face. "They were perfect angels. How was your evening?"

They both smiled, then Michelle extended her left hand to display the sparkling diamond.

"Congratulations!" Martha said with a beaming smile. She wrapped her arms around Michelle and gave Liam a wink. "I'm so happy for the both of you."

September 29, 2006

Liam stood immersed in the romantic ambiance of the ballroom at the Brickville Inn. He was filled with anticipation as he waited at the end of the aisle. It seemed like a dream that he and Michelle would soon be husband and wife.

Michelle stared at herself in the full-length mirror. She had imagined herself and Brad on this day, but it was not meant to be. Liam was her future now.

Ann put her hand on her heart. "Oh, darling, you look lovely!"

"Thank you, Mom." She placed her hand on her stomach. *Breathe,* she repeated in her head.

The setting sun radiated a fiery glow through the window shades; that was their cue.

Ann smiled. "You ready, sweetheart?"

Seth stood in the doorway and extended his arm. "You are beautiful, darling." She took his arm, then they walked to the French doors. The guests stood while the quartet played "Canon in D," but her heartbeat was the only thing she heard as it pulsed in her ears.

Michelle glanced at Liam beside the officiant. He exuded confidence in his fitted Armani tux. This new five o'clock shadow made him more attractive, if that was even possible. She convinced herself that this would be the best thing for the twins. She opened her heart, allowing herself to love Liam more each day.

His breath caught, and he fought back tears as Michelle walked down the aisle toward him. He never imagined he would marry the woman who had held his heart for as long as he could remember.

Seth kissed Michelle's cheek and placed her trembling hand in Liam's. Then he took his seat beside Ann.

Liam's eyes followed the lacy, plunging neckline that accentuated her figure and whispered, "You are stunning."

She took a deep breath and gave him a nervous smile.

They widened their eyes at each other and tried not to laugh when the twenty-month-old twins squirmed in their grandparents' laps. Each one took turns trading the twins with Martha, which quickly became a game of toddler hot potato.

The officiant began the invocation, leading right into the declaration of intent. "Do you, Liam, take this woman to be your lawfully wedded wife, to live together in Holy matrimony, to love her, comfort her, honor and keep her, in sickness and in health, in sorrow and in joy, to have and to hold from this day forward, as long as you both shall live?"

His eyes were sincere and loving. "I do."

The officiant turned to Michelle. "Do you, Michelle..."

Her chest visibly rose and fell with each breath. Liam squeezed her hands to calm her as she stared into his eyes.

"As long as you both shall live?"

Michelle turned and looked at the officiant, whose raised eyebrows told her to answer. She looked back at Liam and said. "I do."

"Liam, as you place this ring on Michelle's finger, please repeat after me. With this ring, I thee wed and pledge you my love now and forever."

He repeated after the officiant, slid the ring on her finger, and met her eyes with a warm smile.

"Michelle, as you place this ring on Liam's finger, please repeat after me."

Liam squeezed her hand again as tears pooled in her eyes. Her voice cracked when she spoke. "With this ring." She cleared her throat and continued. "I thee wed and pledge you my love." She paused, finding it hard to say the last three words as she pictured Brad's face. "Now and forever." Then she placed the ring on Liam's finger and exhaled.

"By the authority vested in me by the State of New Jersey, I now pronounce you, Liam, and you, Michelle, husband and wife."

Conservative applause erupted from the small group of family members while the twins imitated the adults and clapped excitedly.

After a short reception, they returned to the lake house for a quick change and to say goodbye to Chloe and Ben.

Michelle hugged her mother. "Thank you for staying with Martha to help with the twins."

Liam placed his hand on Martha's shoulder. "Yes, thank you both."

"You two enjoy your honeymoon. We'll be just fine." Ann took Michelle's face in her hands. "We are so happy for you, my love."

As they drove to the airport, Liam couldn't suppress his smile. Only a few years ago, when he thought about his future, he never imagined having a wife and children so soon after college, but this was his reality, and he was incredibly happy.

He glanced at Michelle, looking relaxed and content. After she drank half a bottle of champagne at the reception, her nervousness seemed to disappear, or at least be masked. But he had noticed a change in her a few months before the wedding. They had more intimate moments than not. Maybe because the twins were on a manageable sleep schedule, or maybe the deep sadness had left her and was replaced with happiness about building a life together. Whatever it was, he finally felt content and hopeful about their future as a family.

They settled into the plush leather seats of the private jet when the pilot came into the main cabin. He was tall, groomed to perfection, and had a strong, confident presence.

"Congratulations, Mr. and Mrs. Grant. The flight to Nassau will take approximately four hours. Dominic will be taking care of you. Enjoy your flight."

As quickly as the pilot departed, Dominic appeared. "Congratulations, Mr. and Mrs. Grant. I hope you are comfortable. Shortly after we take off, I'll be happy to serve you."

Flying high above the clouds, Dominic returned to the cabin with champagne flutes and a bottle of Dom Perignon. As he poured the champagne, another steward rolled a small cart out with a beautifully displayed charcuterie board.

"Please feel free to move about the cabin. Can I get you anything else?" he asked.

Liam nodded. "Everything is perfect. Thank you, Dominic."

"Excellent, sir. Enjoy."

Michelle unbuckled her belt and walked over to the cart. "Interesting."

Liam walked up behind her and wrapped his arms around her waist. "What's interesting?"

"That I am the only woman on this plane." She turned around in his arms. "Don't you find that interesting?" she quipped, feeding him a grape and sliding her finger between his lips.

His eyes lit up. "Mmm," he moaned, guiding her hips into him.

He half expected her to be quiet as the champagne wore off and the realization of their marriage hit her. But she was flirty and affectionate. Maybe her feelings were growing stronger for him. Whatever it was, he liked it. Hell, he loved it.

"I requested an all-male crew just for you," he whispered, then kissed her ear. His shadow beard tickled her neck, making her giggle and squirm in his arms.

With a few hours still left in the air, they settled back into the plush leather seats. The cabin lights dimmed as the champagne and hum of the plane's engines eased them into a tranquil state, causing them both to drift off.

The cabin lights popped on, and the pilot announced their arrival and prepared to land. They glanced out the small oval windows, with a view of the runway lights welcoming them to paradise. A warm, salty ocean breeze greeted them as they walked down the jet stairs to the tarmac. An Escalade sat with the passenger door open, ready to whisk them away to their private villa.

"Welcome to the Bahamas. What brings you to our lovely island?" the chauffeur asked.

"Our honeymoon," Liam answered, kissing Michelle's hand.

"The plane is one thing; you can't keep all the women off the beach," she said, raising her eyebrow. "I heard there are many topless beaches here."

"We probably won't spend much time on the beach," he said confidently.

The limo pulled into a small driveway where the chauffeur handed their luggage off to the concierge, who welcomed them at the front door of the Blue Beach Villa.

"Wait." He scooped Michelle in his arms. "Welcome to the honeymoon suite, Mrs. Grant, where all your desires will be met," he whispered.

"Promise," she whispered back.

His eyebrow shot up, ready to make good on that promise.

The concierge placed their luggage in the room and quickly exited.

He laid her on the bed and leaned in, kissing her neck and collarbone. The white sheer curtains waved through the open French patio doors. The soothing sound of a waterfall flowed into the hot tub while lights illuminated a blue glow around the perimeter of the private pool.

She ran her fingers up and down his arm. "It's so beautiful here; it will be so hard to leave."

His crystal-blue eyes bore into hers. "We have three days of uninterrupted adult time. I want to take advantage of every second I have alone with my wife."

She rolled on top of him and ran her fingers down the side of his chin. "I like this new look, and I do like the sound of my wife." Then she repeated in her head, *Liam Grant's wife.*

His eyes glowed with affection. If she only knew what her words meant to him. "I love you, Chelle, more than you'll ever know."

She so badly wanted to say it back, but she had to be sure she meant it—not only for him but also for herself. All of their intimate moments had just been sex. Brad was the only man she had made love to. If her marriage to Liam had any hope of lasting, she would have to allow herself to be vulnerable and open her heart—not only to love him, but to be *in love* with him.

Michelle sat up in bed. "Oh my gosh, what time is it?"

Liam rolled over and looked at his Rolex. "It's noon."

"Does every second alone include sleeping half the day away?"

"Remember, we're on island time, babe. Getting to sleep until noon *is* paradise when you have twins."

Liam stayed in bed, enjoying the sound of the ocean waves while Michelle showered. He had never felt so close to her. He was truly happy and sensed she finally was too.

She came out of the bathroom wrapped in the complimentary resort robe, her long brown curls still wet. "The bathroom is all yours." Then she noticed the room service cart and grabbed a strawberry. "I'm famished. Adult time burns a lot of calories, you know," she said, giving Liam a sheepish grin while holding the strawberry between her lips.

"You don't say?" He got up from the bed, walked over to her, and tried to untie her robe until she grabbed his hands.

"We'll never leave this room if you don't get in the shower." As he turned to walk away, she slapped his bare backside.

He glanced over his shoulder and gave her a playful grin.

They spent the next two days exploring the island, snorkeling, sitting on the beach, and connecting as husband and wife. He showed her he was more than a player, proving he was the husband and father she and the twins needed. He was determined that Michelle would never regret marrying him.

They sat on the tarmac in the private jet, waiting to take off. Michelle looked out the window. "Goodbye, paradise."

Liam leaned toward her. "Here." He handed her a folded piece of paper.

"What's this?"

He raised an eyebrow and smiled. "Open it."

She unfolded the paper and read, *Real Estate Purchase Agreement of the Blue Beach Villa,* then looked at him, stunned.

"An early anniversary present for next year and every year after that."

"Liam. This must have cost a fortune. You didn't think we should have talked about it?"

"I was promoted and received a bonus. We'll be fine," he said proudly.

She appreciated the gesture and didn't want to appear ungrateful, but she worried about what other decisions Liam might make without her now that they were married.

CHAPTER 23

Boston
2008

Shelby took a deep breath, inhaling the scent of her light pink rose bouquet, courtesy of Henry. The French doors opened, cueing the guests to stand.

"Are you ready, kiddo?" Patrick cradled his daughter's arm as tears welled up in his eyes.

Shelby blinked rapidly and nodded. They walked down the aisle over a sea of rose petals, guiding them to the altar as the instrumental of "Canon in D" grew louder.

Her face brightened as she drew closer to Scott. *He's so handsome in his tux*, she thought to herself.

The minister asked, "Who gives this woman away?"

"Her mother and I do," Patrick said, then he kissed Shelby's cheek, placed her hand in Scott's, and sat beside Liza.

Shelby handed her bouquet to Sam, took Scott's other hand, and looked into his adoring brown eyes.

"Shel, you are stunning," he whispered.

Shelby smiled and whispered, "You're not so bad yourself, handsome."

Sam was truly happy for them, but a part of her hated that she and Scott kept up the charade of not knowing each other. It wasn't like they had some grand love affair; they were teenagers. It was a shared agreement to keep it between them, and she figured Scott fully understood that telling Shelby the truth now would make her feel betrayed and question whether she could ever trust either of them again.

Shelby admired the villas in the beautiful tropical Bahama landscape while the taxi drove them to their hotel.

"Boy, I wonder what it costs to stay in one of those for a week, let alone one night," she said, peering out the passenger window.

Scott leaned forward and looked at the villas. "Out of our price range, that's for sure."

Shelby's eyes brightened. "Oh wow, look at that one, *Blue Beach Villa*. It's beautiful!"

They finally settled into their hotel room and walked onto the balcony, amazed by the white sandy beach and crystal blue water.

Scott wrapped his arms around Shelby's waist. "One week in paradise, Mrs. O'Donnell."

Shelby rested her head back on Scott's shoulder. "We need to branch out and open an Aunt B's Bahamas Bouquets."

Scott laughed. "We've only been here an hour, and you're already planning to move?"

Shelby turned and placed her arms around his neck. "Winters here and summers in Boston. It's settled."

Scott kissed the tip of her nose, then lifted her, guiding her legs around his waist, and carried her back into the room. "How about we settle on this bed for now?" he said, raising his eyebrows.

"I would like that very much, Mr. O'Donnell."

Shelby sat in the lounge chair, soaking in the tropical sun, waiting for Scott to return from the poolside bar. He appeared next to her holding two tall glasses of bright yellow and red, fruit-garnished Bahama Mamas. "Care for a cocktail, miss?" he teased.

She bit her bottom lip and lowered her sunglasses. "Why, thank you, but what would I tell my husband if he caught me taking a drink from a tall, dark, handsome stranger?"

"That you've met the man of your dreams and are running away with him."

She stood up, took the cocktail, and kissed his smiling lips. "I'll go pack my bags."

They sat in the taxi and gave each other a sad smile. The taxi driver loaded their suitcases into the trunk and pulled away from the hotel, leaving the blue ocean and sandy beach in the rearview mirror.

Shelby stared out the small oval window of the plane. "Goodbye, paradise," she whined. "Back to reality."

"We'll be back someday."

"Promise?"

Scott gave her a convincing smile. "I promise."

CHAPTER 24

Milltown
July 2008

The twins buzzed around the driveway on their toddler scooters. Ben got off his, picked up a ball, and threw it at Liam.

"Nice throw, buddy," he smiled proudly.

Ben ran to him and reached out his arms. "Up, Daddy."

Liam laughed, picked Ben up, and tossed him in the air, catching him and saying, "Gotcha!"

Ben laughed excitedly. "Moe!"

Liam watched his son's face. *I know that expression.* A picture of Brad flashed before his eyes. He threw Ben in the air one more time, then set him down.

"Uppie," Ben begged, pulling on Liam's pant leg.

He pinched his brows as a sudden feeling of doubt distracted him. "All done, buddy. No more."

When Michelle told him she was pregnant, he didn't have the heart to ask her. At the time, he wondered if it was too much for her to handle after losing Brad and convinced herself the twins were his. Neither of them ever questioned the twins' paternity. It was an unspoken agreement between them. It wouldn't change anything— even if it were true; he was their father.

Michelle sat on the wooden frame of the sandbox, watching Chloe and Ben play. The public park held precious memories. She and Brad played here many times as young children.

A woman's voice called out. "Michelle?"

Michelle turned, squinted, and placed her hand on her forehead to block the bright sun. "Mom C!" She stood, brushed her hands on her jeans, and hugged Jennifer.

"Hello, honey. How are you?" she said, squeezing Michelle tight.

"We're good. Are you out for a walk?"

"I've been walking in the park for a few years, trying to get myself out of the house. Do you remember coming here with Brad? Your mother and I had to drag the two of you out of the playground, often bribing you both with ice cream." She chuckled.

"I do remember. That's why I bring the twins to this park. I feel close to him here," she said, giving Jennifer a sad smile.

"I can't believe our little Godchildren are three years old already." Jennifer shook her head. "Where has the time gone?"

Chloe climbed out of the sandbox and walked over to Jennifer. "Wook," she said, opening her tiny hand to reveal a black and orange caterpillar curled in her palm. Chloe wrinkled her nose and looked up at Jennifer. "Tickleth." She giggled.

The smile fell from Jennifer's lips, and she covered her mouth with her hand and stared at Chloe. *How had she not seen it before now?* She had looked into those blue eyes for over two decades. Chloe's wrinkled nose and smile carried the same expression she had seen on her own son's face.

Michelle noticed Jennifer's expression and placed her hand on her shoulder. "Mom, are you okay?"

"Oh, I'm sorry." Jennifer stooped to look closer. "That's a lovely caterpillar, sweetie."

Chloe returned to the sandbox, showed it to her brother, who studied it, then continued throwing sand on the grass.

Jennifer looked at Michelle. "Her eyes and that expression. I'm sorry I have to go, honey."

"Mom?" Michelle turned to check on the twins, and when she looked back, Jennifer was gone.

Liam sat in his office, staring at their family picture on his desk. He couldn't get the image of Ben's expression out of his head. *Had he seen it with Chloe, too, and not realized it?*

"Hello, this is Liam Grant. I'd like to schedule an appointment with Dr. Kennedy ... Yes, next Monday at 9:00 a.m. will work. Thank you ... you too."

The workweek finally ended, and as he drove home, his mind wandered. *He wouldn't tell Michelle about his appointment with the fertility specialist. What good would it do to ask her if she also saw Brad's resemblance in the twins? Brad was gone. Chloe and Ben were his world. He loved them more than he thought he could love anything.*

As soon as Liam walked in the front door of the lake house, the twins ran to him. He picked them both up and squeezed them as they wrapped their little arms around his neck.

Normally, he would chat with the twins during dinner, but tonight, he watched them, looking for Brad's features and mannerisms. They sat in their booster seats, playing with their peas and carrots more than eating them, unaware of their father's anxiety. But Michelle noticed.

"You're awfully quiet tonight. You okay?"

"Yeah. Just a lot going on at work," he lied.

Chloe kicked her legs excitedly. "More cheeken pease."

"Sure thing, honey," Liam said. "Ben, do you want more chicken?"

"No!" he shouted.

Michelle tilted her head. "No, thank you, Daddy."

"No, thane you, Daddy," he repeated.

An hour later, they bathed the twins, tucked them in for the night, and settled on the sectional. He opened a bottle of beer and took a long swig.

Michelle glanced at him. "Work stressing you out?"

"Yeah, a little. It's all good, though," he lied again.

They sat quietly, enjoying the peacefulness of the night. Martha retired to her room earlier than usual, and it wasn't long before Michelle drifted off to sleep. The glow of the TV hypnotized him, taking him back to a time of fear and uncertainty—remembering the sterile smell of the hospital, the pinch of the needles in his arms, and the nausea. God, he hated the nausea. He closed his eyes and cleared his mind, meditating as the oncology nurse had taught him all those years ago.

A few hours later, he awoke and realized they were still on the sectional. He placed a blanket over Michelle and made his way to their bedroom.

The alarm told him the weekend was over, so he dragged himself out of bed and started the shower. As he washed away the night's sleepiness, he grew anxious. Maybe he was being ridiculous and should cancel the appointment, but not knowing would be worse than knowing, he convinced himself.

Michelle was already out in the kitchen with Martha when he left their bedroom.

She poured him a mug of coffee and rested her hand on his shoulder. "Hey, are you sure you're okay? It seemed like your mind was somewhere else all weekend."

"I'm fine. Really. You guys have a good day. I'll see you tonight," he said and kissed her goodbye.

"Good morning, Liam Grant. I have an appointment with Dr. Kennedy," he told the receptionist.

"Okay, you are all checked in. Please have a seat in the waiting room."

A young, attractive woman opened the waiting room door. "Mr. Grant? Please follow me."

He read her name tag and, although wearing loose-fitting scrubs, noticed her curves and silky blonde waves that cascaded down her back. He was happily married, but still a charmer.

"Please have a seat. Dr. Kennedy will be right in."

Liam flashed a smile. "Thank you, Rachel."

Rachel blushed. "You have a nice day, Mr. Grant."

After a few minutes, the office door opened.

Dr. Kennedy extended his hand. "Hello, Mr. Grant."

Liam shook his hand. "Nice to meet you."

"What brings you in today?"

"Well, my wife and I are talking about having a baby, and as my medical records show, I had childhood leukemia, receiving chemo and radiation. I understand it can affect fertility," Liam explained.

"Yes, that is true. In some patients, treatments can cause infertility or low sperm count. We can check your count to understand better what we're looking at. The results will take a few days. We can get a sample today if that works for you. Then my office will call you for another appointment to discuss the results."

"Oh, okay. Yes, that sounds fine." He hadn't planned on giving a sample on such short notice, but imagining Rachel out of her scrubs would do the trick, along with whatever else they provide to get the job done.

Michelle leaped out of bed and ran to the bathroom, bent over the toilet, and vomited.

Liam stood outside the bathroom door. "Chelle, you okay?"

"Oh shit," she groaned, then vomited again. "I think I have a stomach bug."

"I can work from home if you need me to," he offered. Then he remembered that Dr. Kennedy's office had called with his results. He would have to make an excuse to leave or change the appointment, potentially waiting another week, which would be torture.

"Okay," she moaned.

Liam went to the kitchen and found Martha preparing breakfast. "Michelle woke up with a stomach bug, and I have a meeting I can't get out of. Would you be able to take the twins to preschool today?"

"Oh dear. You go to work. I'll handle things here."

"Thank you, Martha."

Liam knocked on the bathroom door and peeked his head in. "Chelle, Martha can take care of Chloe and Ben."

"Thank goodness for Martha," she whined, resting her head in her hands.

"You need anything, babe?"

"Ugh, just to stop throwing up."

"Sorry. I hope you feel better. Love you." He shut the door as Michelle started round two. He shuddered at the thought of it spreading throughout the household and the twins becoming human volcanoes.

Liam waited in Dr. Kennedy's office and glanced around the room at the framed accolades he hadn't noticed on his first visit. A few minutes later, the doctor walked in, sat at his desk, and opened a gray folder.

"How are you today, Liam?"

"Fine, thank you."

"First, I'll explain what the tests evaluate," Dr. Kennedy said, reeling off over half a dozen medical terms, then he ended with, "All these factor into your fertility."

He gave the doctor a disconcerted expression. "I didn't realize how involved it was. I thought the test would basically tell me my sperm count."

"Well, regarding sperm shape, a normal result is fifty percent or more. Your result was thirty percent. Sperm movement is rated on a scale of zero to four, zero being no movement; your result was a two." He paused for a few seconds. "Based on these results, there is a low chance of conception, but it's not zero."

"I see." All of the information swirled around in Liam's head. The only thing that he kept hearing was a low chance of conception.

"I understand this is not the result you were hoping for, but there are fertility options that have been successful in cases such as yours."

Liam stood and shook Dr. Kennedy's hand. "Thank you. I'll discuss this with my wife and let you know if we want to pursue anything further."

He had no intention of telling Michelle anything about the appointments. He was Chloe and Ben's father; nothing would change that. Lost in thought and staring at the lines on the road, he remembered his last conversation with Brad.

"Listen, if anything happens to me, promise me you'll take care of Michelle."

"What are you talking about? If anything happens to you?"

"I mean it, Liam. Promise me."

"Yes, of course I will. But nothing's going to happen to you, dude."

The blare of a car horn startled him from his daydream. "Shit," he said out loud as he swerved back into his lane.

CHAPTER 25

July 2008

Liam walked into the lake house to find Michelle sitting at the kitchen island, munching on saltines and drinking hot tea.

He rubbed the middle of her back. "How are you feeling?"

"Better."

Chloe and Ben ran to him with outstretched arms. "Were you good for Martha today?"

"Yes," Chloe answered.

Ben nodded his head yes.

He set them down, and as fast as they came to him, they disappeared back into their playroom. He was relieved that the twins were spared from the stomach bug, but he couldn't get the test results out of his head.

After reading *Goodnight Moon* twice, Liam went to the main bedroom and found Michelle asleep. He admired her attempt to help feed the twins dinner, as the look on her face told him she was struggling with the smell of their grilled chicken and broccoli.

He lay in bed watching her sleep, his mind returning to that night. The night she needed him to take her pain away. *Was it possible she was already pregnant?* He rolled onto his back and stared at the ceiling. Eventually, his eyelids became heavy, and he fell into a deep sleep.

He stood on the Short Hills football field. A long pass from Brad landed in his hands. Michelle, Chloe, and Ben watched and waved at him on the sideline.

"Dad, Dad," the twins yelled, running onto the field. He kneeled, opening his arms, waiting for them to fall into him. They turned and ran away from him, yelling Dad again, and jumped into Brad's arms. They laughed and screamed with delight as Brad picked them up and spun around.

He stood on the field, confused and hurt, watching Michelle run down the field and throw her arms around the three of them.

"Chelle? Chloe? Ben?"

The incessant sound of his alarm woke him from his dream. Michelle rolled over, sat on the side of the bed, and moaned.

"You okay?" Liam whispered.

"My stomach still feels off. I was hoping it was just a twenty-four-hour bug." She put her hand over her mouth and sprinted to the bathroom.

Liam stayed in their bed, replaying the dream in his head. *He kept his promise to take care of Michelle. He loved her and the twins. But could he be raising his best friend's children? Did Michelle suspect the same? Does she see Brad's resemblance in Chloe and Ben, too?*

Liam found it hard to concentrate at work and was relieved when the week was over. Thinking about the fertility test results and dreaming about Brad every night had left him exhausted.

He walked in the front door of the lake house to find Michelle placing her finger over her lips. She took his arm and led him to their bedroom. "They are watching a movie, so we have a few minutes."

He raised his eyebrows. "A few minutes, you say." Then he pulled her close. "You must be feeling better."

Michelle rolled her eyes and shook her head. She placed her hand on his cheek.

Her intense gaze worried him. "What is it?"

"Liam, I'm pregnant."

His eyes lit up. "Are you serious?"

"Yes. I took a test this morning. I have a doctor's appointment on Monday," she said, giving him a fearful expression.

"I can't believe it. You're sure?"

She nodded her head yes.

He hugged her tight, took her face in his hands, and kissed her. Hearing those two words filled him with utter joy this time.

"So, you're not freaked out?"

"It will be crazy for sure, but we can handle it," he said with a smile. "Did you tell Martha or anyone else?"

"No. I wanted to tell you first, although Martha probably suspected. She knew I was pregnant with the twins before I did. I think she knows me better than I know myself," she said, shaking her head. "We shouldn't say anything to the twins yet. Wait until I see the doctor, and I'm further along."

"Do you want me to go to your doctor's appointment with you?"

"You don't have to, but if you want to, okay. They may do an ultrasound to check how far along I am."

He was still in shock, but if what he feared was true—that Chloe and Ben were Brad's—this baby would be his, no question.

Liam sat in the waiting room while Michelle met with her obstetrician and recalled his appointment with Dr. Kennedy. *He beat the odds. He could father a child.*

A nurse appeared in the doorway. "Mr. Grant, can you come with me, please? I'll take you to the ultrasound room. Your wife is already in there."

Liam walked in with a wide smile. "Hey, babe."

She looked at him with a nervous expression.

"Good morning, I'm Stephanie. I'll be doing your ultrasound. How are you?"

"Good, thank you. This is my husband, Liam."

"Nice to meet you." He took Michelle's hand, his eyes lighting up with anticipation.

"This is going to feel warm," she said, squirting an excessive amount of gel onto Michelle's abdomen. She ran the probe in circles, searching and playing with the buttons on the keyboard. She turned the monitor toward them and pointed her finger at the screen. "There's your baby." She turned up the volume so they could hear the rapid whoosh of a heartbeat. "Looks like you are approximately six weeks along, according to the measurements. A good, strong heartbeat." She cleaned the gel off Michelle's stomach and handed her a strip of pictures. "Congratulations."

Liam couldn't hide his joy during the entire drive home.

"I've never seen you this excited about something, except when you guys won States in high school."

He laughed. "I just ... it's great news. I didn't think I could..." He caught himself. "I mean, I figured we wouldn't have any more kids."

Michelle sighed loudly, but smiled at him. "Yeah, me either."

CHAPTER 26

Less than four years ago, Liam was enjoying his bachelor lifestyle. The last thing he thought about was having a family. Now, he couldn't imagine his life without their three-and-a-half-year-old twins and how incredibly happy he was that Michelle was pregnant.

Michelle sat on the exam table, waiting for her doctor, while Liam stood behind her and rubbed her shoulders.

"Mmm, that feels good."

Dr. Allen entered the exam room with a cordial smile. "Good afternoon. How have you been feeling, Michelle?"

"The morning sickness has finally subsided, and I have my appetite back. Tired, but good."

Dr. Allen helped Michelle lay back on the exam table, then slid the fetal Doppler probe across her lower abdomen, searching for the heartbeat. She tilted her head. "Sometimes they like to hide," she said with a compassionate smile. She continued to search for the heartbeat for several minutes, then turned off the Doppler.

"What's wrong?" Michelle asked, glancing at Liam.

"I'd like to do an ultrasound. Sometimes, they can be in a spot where it's hard for the monitor to pick up the heartbeat."

"Okay, but we heard it last month."

Dr. Allen placed her hand on Michelle's arm. "Let's not worry yet."

Liam went to the exam table, helped Michelle sit up, and held her hand. When she squeezed his hand tight, he knew she was scared.

The sonographer came in a few minutes later and escorted them to the ultrasound room.

Liam wrapped his arm around Michelle's waist and whispered, "It's going to be okay, babe."

"I did your ultrasound a few months ago?" she asked.

Michelle nodded. "Yes, you did."

Stephanie stated her rehearsed, "Okay, this is going to feel warm." Then she squeezed the gel onto Michelle's stomach.

Liam gave Michelle a reassuring glance.

The probe slid around her lower abdomen, eventually stopping on the fetus. She turned the screen toward them.

At fourteen weeks, the apparent shape of a head, arms, and bent legs could be seen.

"I'm so sorry; there's no longer a heartbeat." She gently cleaned Michelle's stomach and turned the monitor back in front of her. "I'm going to step out and inform Dr. Allen. Take all the time you need," she said, and quietly closed the door behind her.

"Liam. I don't understand." A single tear rolled down her cheek.

He brought her hand to his lips and closed his eyes. "I'm so sorry, babe."

A short while later, a nurse took them to Dr. Allen's office. They sat in silence, trying to process that this was the end of the pregnancy.

Liam reached over and laid his hand on Michelle's. She looked at him and tried to hold back the tears that began to fill her eyes.

Dr. Allen entered her office, closed the door behind her, and sat at her desk. "I am very sorry. Many times, it's an indication that something is wrong with the fetus. We don't know exactly how long your body will hold the pregnancy, and you may miscarry on your own. However, you have the option of a D & C. After you are placed under anesthesia, your cervix is dilated, and then we surgically remove the contents of the uterus. You don't have to decide right now if you'd like to take some time to think about it."

"Yes, I want to schedule the procedure. I can't walk around waiting to miscarry," she said and wiped a tear from her cheek.

Liam was surprised at how quickly she decided, but deep down, he understood. *Why prolong the inevitable?*

"Okay, we'll schedule it as soon as possible. It will be an outpatient procedure, so barring any complications, you will be able to go home that day. Again, I'm sorry. If you have any questions, please don't hesitate to call me."

Liam stayed focused on the road. He couldn't look at her. *It was his fault. Dr. Kennedy was right.*

Michelle leaned her head against the seat. "I'm glad we didn't tell the twins. How would we explain something like this to them? They're too young to understand."

I know, was all he could offer.

When they walked into the lake house, Michelle's eyes filled with tears as soon as she saw Martha. "Dear, what is it?"

"They couldn't find a heartbeat," Michelle cried, melting into Martha's arms.

Martha saw Liam's eyes brimming with tears. "I'm so sorry."

"Chloe and Ben in their playroom?" he asked.

Martha nodded her head yes.

Liam stood in the playroom doorway, watching the twins working intently on a floor puzzle.

"Daddy!" Chloe jumped up and ran over to hug him.

Ben threw down the puzzle piece and ran over to them and wrapped himself around Liam's leg.

"Hi, guys. Can Daddy help you with your puzzle?"

Ben released Liam's leg and hopped around the room.

"Yeah!" Chloe took her father's hand. "Sit here, Daddy."

"Daddy, you do this one." Ben giggled as he set the puzzle piece on top of Liam's head.

Michelle watched them from the hallway. *Chloe and Ben loved their father. He was so good with them. But deep down inside, she knew what Brad's mother suspected that day in the park. She would never tell Liam what she felt could be true, so losing his baby made the loss even harder and broke her heart.*

After putting the twins to bed, Liam went to the main bedroom, lay down on the bed beside Michelle, and stroked her arm.

She rolled over, buried her face in his chest, and wept. "I know you were so excited about this baby." She sniffled. "I was too."

He tightened his arms around her and kissed her forehead. "I know. It's not fair." *For a moment, he contemplated telling her about his visit to the fertility clinic; then he put it out of his mind. It wouldn't change what had already been decided. A part of him no longer lived inside her, and soon it would no longer exist. If she only knew how unfair it truly was.*

CHAPTER 27

Boston
May 2009

The alarm went off, forcing Scott to crawl out of bed. He stood in the shower, trying to rinse the sleep from his eyes. He was taken aback when he heard the bathroom door fly open.

Shelby hit the floor with her knees, hunched over the toilet, and threw up.

Scott wrinkled his nose and peeked around the shower curtain. "Oh man, stomach bug?"

Shelby groaned and rested her head in her hands. "I don't know. Oh shit," she said and hunched over the toilet again.

Scott stood in the shower and talked himself out of throwing up as Shelby finally finished with a round of dry heaving. He heard her gargle with mouthwash, then the bathroom door shut.

A few minutes later, he came out of the bathroom and sat on Shelby's side of the bed. "I'll call Henry and let him know you won't be in today."

She lay curled in a ball, her pale face peeking from under the covers. She kept her eyes closed and held her hand to her forehead. "Thanks," she whispered.

"Do you need anything?"

She shook her head no.

"Okay, I'll text you later. Love you." He patted her shoulder, leery of kissing her and contracting the stomach bug himself.

Hours later, she made her way downstairs to the kitchen. She read Scott's text and told him she was feeling a little better and would try to drink some tea. She glanced at the calendar on the refrigerator. Each month displayed a picture from their wedding, a thoughtful gift from Scott's mother. It made her smile, but then she noticed the date. "Shit, I'm two weeks late."

January 2010

Shelby placed an extra set of keys on the counter. "Okay, Henry, the shop's in your capable hands for the next six weeks." Shelby looked down and rested her hand on her stomach. "This little one is two weeks past due and is being evicted tomorrow."

Henry chuckled. "My wife was two weeks past her due date with our first one, too." He shook his head. "Some of them just need a little coaxing, I guess."

Shelby rested her hand on Henry's shoulder. "I appreciate you taking over while I'm out, and I'll pop in when I can."

Henry raised his eyebrow. "The only reason for you to show up here, boss, is so I can hold that little stubborn bundle of joy."

Scott kissed Shelby's sweaty forehead, his fingers blue from her tight grip. "You're doing great, babe."

"Okay, Shelby, one more big push," said the doctor.

Scott supported Shelby's back as she leaned forward, squeezed her eyes shut while clenching her teeth, and pushed with everything she had.

The doctor glanced at the clock on the wall, noting that Shelby had been pushing for two hours with no progress. "Shelby, I need you to stop pushing. You're going to feel some pressure." A crease appeared between the doctor's brows. "Shelby, the baby is face-up instead of facing toward your back. It is harder for the baby to be delivered through the birth canal. I prefer not to use forceps when the baby is in this position." The doctor's eyes glanced between Shelby and Scott. "We'll need to prep you for a C-section."

Concern covered Shelby's face, and then her eyes filled with tears.

Scott wrapped his arm around her shoulder. "It will be okay, Shel."

After putting on the hospital top, trousers, and hat, Scott followed the nurses to the operating room. "Hey, Shel," he whispered.

Shelby looked up at him with concern in her eyes.

He concealed his anxiety and squeezed her shoulder.

The doctor requested a scalpel. "Okay, you'll feel some pressure, but no pain."

Scott kept his eyes on Shelby, fearing that if he looked over the sheet barrier that blocked her view, he might pass out.

Within minutes, a high-pitched cry carried throughout the operating room.

"Congratulations, Mom and Dad, you have a girl."

"Shel, we have a girl!"

"Dad, would you like to cut the cord?" the doctor asked.

His face sobered, and he walked over to the side of the operating table and reluctantly took the surgical scissors, telling himself he could do this. He took a deep breath, and after a few snips, his body relaxed. Then, the nurses whisked Rhylie away.

Scott returned to the head of the operating table, his eyes filled with tears, and kissed Shelby's forehead. "I love you, babe. Rhylie is perfect."

Shelby's voice cracked as a tear rolled down her cheek. "Can I see her?"

A nurse handed Rhylie, bundled in a hospital blanket and a pink beanie, to Scott. "Here you go, Dad. Congratulations, Mommy."

Scott held Rhylie next to Shelby's cheek.

She closed her eyes, feeling the warmth of her newborn daughter's face, and cried. "She *is* perfect."

With Rhylie's sweet disposition, she spoiled the first-time parents and had no shortage of sitters. Scott's mother would often tell them, "You have no idea how lucky you are; she is such an easy baby." Even Sam babysat for a few hours so they could have a date night. It wasn't long before Rhylie became a constant figure at Aunt B's Bouquets and had Henry wrapped around her tiny finger.

Rhylie had been sleeping through the night for months, allowing them to relish their uninterrupted slumber. They both handled their work-life balance, content and enjoying their family of three.

Shelby stood at the stove with Rhylie on her hip. Scott walked in the front door, went straight to the kitchen, and scooped his daughter in his arms. "How's my beautiful girl?"

"Um, I have something to show you. Follow me." Shelby led them to the half-bath and pointed at the bathroom sink.

Scott's eyes widened and shifted between Shelby and the pregnancy test. "Seriously?"

She nodded her head yes.

"But Rhylie is only nine months old."

Shelby wrinkled her nose and let out a loud sigh.

He kissed Shelby tenderly, rested his forehead on hers, and chuckled. Then he bounced his daughter in his arms. "Rhylie, you're going to be a big sister!"

CHAPTER 28

Milltown
2011

Michelle moved restlessly in her sleep and cried out, "No, no. Stop!"

Liam awoke with a start and rolled over. "Babe," he whispered, rubbing her shoulder.

"Brad! Don't go! Don't leave me!" she cried out.

Liam sat up, turned on the table lamp, and rubbed her shoulder harder, trying to wake her. "Chelle, wake up, you're dreaming."

She squinted her eyes from the harsh light, and looked at him, confused. "Liam, he kept walking. He wouldn't stop. There was so much blood." She laid her head on his chest and cried.

He held her tight and stroked her hair. "I know, I know. You're okay." *She hadn't had a nightmare in years,* he thought, then replayed the scene in his head. He couldn't unsee it; he would never forget.

He held her until she fell back to sleep, eventually dozing off himself. A few hours later, he was woken again, this time by his alarm.

When he came out of the en suite, Michelle had left their bed. He went to the kitchen, grabbed a mug of coffee, and noticed her curled up with a blanket in the plush armchair beside the fireplace, staring at the flames. Nearly six years ago, he found her in the same state. He went over, sat on the ottoman, and placed his hand on her leg. "Hey, you okay?"

She let out a heavy sigh. "I haven't had that nightmare in so long." Her eyes filled with tears. "Why now?"

He ran his hand down her arm. "Anything I can do?"

She shook her head no and returned her gaze to the flames.

"I was going to come home early today. I have a surprise for you and the kids; well, I guess Martha, too," he said, giving her a slight smile.

Michelle looked at him but said nothing.

He stood and kissed the top of her head. "Try to have a good day. Love you."

"I love you too," she whispered. She was content living at the lake house, being a mother of two kindergartners, and being a wife to Liam. He had put his playboy image aside and proved to be the man she could count on and build a life with.

She had fallen in love with him during their honeymoon. She didn't mean to and fought it for as long as possible. But he stole a piece of her heart. *Was it guilt over loving another man that brought on the nightmare?* she wondered.

Liam pulled into the driveway as Michelle unloaded the twins and their backpacks. They ran over and wrapped their arms around their father, excited to see him earlier than usual.

"Bring your bags inside and tell Martha I have a surprise for everyone."

"What is it, Daddy? Tell us, tell us," they said, jumping excitedly.

"I'm not going to spoil it now."

Chloe and Ben raced up the stairs and yelled to Martha, leaving the front door wide open.

"Hey," he said, and kissed Michelle's cheek. "Feeling better?"

"Yeah. So what's this surprise?"

He put his arm around her and raised his eyebrow. "You'll just have to wait and see."

The five of them piled into the SUV, with Martha sandwiched

between the twins in the back seat. Chloe loved surprises and could hardly contain herself. She talked Martha's ear off before they even left the driveway.

Ten minutes into their drive, Chloe leaned forward in her seat. "Where are we going, Daddy?"

Ben leaned forward as well. "Yeah, Dad, where are you taking us?"

Michelle looked at Liam and chuckled. "Yeah, Dad, where are you taking us?"

He grinned. "We're almost there."

"Martha, do you know where we're going?" Chloe asked.

Martha placed her hand on Chloe's knee. "I know as much as you do, dear."

Chloe looked at her and scrunched her nose.

Ben peered out of his window. "I only see houses and trees."

Liam slowed down and pulled over on the side of the road.

"What's wrong, Daddy?" Chloe asked.

Ben leaned forward in his seat. "Did we break down?"

Michelle looked over at Liam. "What are you doing?"

He stepped out of the SUV and made his way to the passenger side, opening the car doors for them. "Come on, everyone, follow me."

"Are we going on a hike, Dad?" Ben asked.

"Sorta, buddy." He led them through a small forest of trees, stopping at an open field. "Welcome home," he said, extending his arms out to his sides.

Michelle's eyes widened. "Did you buy this?"

Chloe's face lit up. "Are you building us a tree fort, Daddy?"

"No, not a tree fort, honey."

"Cool! Are we getting dirt bikes?" Ben asked, hopping in place.

"No." Michelle shook her head. "We're not getting dirt bikes."

Liam smiled proudly. "No, sorry, buddy. It's for our new house."

"Oh my," Martha said while swatting a fly from her face.

A crease appeared between Chloe's brows. "But I like our house, Daddy. What about our playroom and basketball hoop?"

He picked Chloe up. "You can have a bigger playroom, a basketball hoop, and how about a pool?"

Ben jumped up and down. "With a slide?"

"Yep, you can have a slide, buddy," he said, rubbing the top of Ben's head.

Michelle gave him a stunned look. "Liam, are you serious? Build a house?"

"I've thought about this for a few years now. The lake house is your parents'. We should have our own home, something we build together as a family."

Michelle tilted her head. "But..."

Liam rested his hands on her shoulders. "Design it however you want. This is for you and the kids. For all of us."

Martha had the patience of a saint, but the twins were so excited that Michelle spared her and took the back seat with them instead. This time, Ben joined Chloe as the two talked non-stop the entire ride home. Michelle zoned out and thought about the lake house. *It held so many memories of her and Brad. It was where they brought the twins home. She felt selfish for not being more excited about a new home. She knew Liam didn't want to be under her parents' roof forever. He was a proud and generous man who wanted to provide for his family. But she struggled with letting go of the lake house. The fact that he bought the land on his own irritated her the more she thought about it. This was just like when he bought the villa.*

Liam sat in their bed, flipping through TV channels, waiting for Michelle to come out of the en suite.

She settled into their bed, avoiding eye contact with him.

"What's going on? You hardly said two words during dinner and won't even look at me."

"I just wish you had told me about the land and at least asked me if I wanted to move or build a house."

His brows drew together. "Did you think we would live here at the lake house forever?"

"I don't know. I have so many memories here and..." she said as her shoulders dropped.

"You know, I gave up my apartment and moved in here because I wanted to help you, to take care of you and the twins, and to build a life together." He sighed. "I know you have memories of you and Brad here. I made a promise to him. He asked me to take care of you if anything happened to him. And then..."

"When did he ask you that?"

Liam sighed again. "The morning of the accident. He showed me the engagement ring and asked me to be his best man." He shook his head, wishing he had never brought it up.

"So you felt obligated," she snapped back.

Liam stood up from the bed. "Seriously, what the hell?"

She shook her head. "I knew you'd come to resent me for taking you away from your bachelor lifestyle."

"You didn't take me away from anything, dammit! I love you and the kids, despite being surrounded by his memory. He's dead, Michelle! I know you can't love me like you loved him, but I'm here! I've been here with you, Chloe, and Ben the whole time! Why can't that be enough?" His face grew red with anger.

"Liam." Her eyes narrowed, stunned by his reaction.

He closed his eyes and ran his hand through his hair. "Do you think I don't see it? His face or mannerisms when I look at Chloe and Ben? Jesus!"

Her eyes widened, and she inhaled a sharp breath.

"I'm done living in his shadow." He threw the remote onto the bed and left their bedroom, slamming the door behind him.

Michelle sat in bed with a sudden sickening feeling in the pit of her stomach. *Oh no, he saw it too.* Her heart sank. She covered her face with her hands and wept.

After hours of lying in the dark, she finally fell asleep until Liam's alarm woke her, and she realized that he never returned to their bed. She went to the kitchen and found him drinking his coffee. "Liam—"

"I have to go to the city for a couple of days," he said, turning away from her and setting his mug in the sink.

She placed her hand on his arm and looked him in the eyes. "Liam, I'm sorry. I've been selfish and unappreciative." She tilted her head. "I do love you."

He sighed, his mouth set in a hard line, staring back at her. "I'll call you later so I can say good night to the kids." Then he walked away.

She had a feeling it wasn't only work that drew him to the city. She knew it was a place he liked to escape to.

It felt like days had passed waiting for him to call later that night, and when the phone rang, her heart sank again, wishing she could talk to him face to face. "Hello? ... Hi, how are you? ... Yeah, I'll get them. Chloe, Ben! Daddy's on the phone."

They grabbed the receiver and placed it between their heads. "Hi Daddy, hi Dad ... Okay, we will. Love you, Daddy."

She watched the excitement in their eyes as he spoke to them and felt hurt that he was indifferent to her.

They handed the receiver back to her and ran off to their playroom.

"Hey."

"I'll call again tomorrow," he said, ending the call abruptly.

Michelle stood and stared, the receiver still in her hand. High-pitched beeps interrupted the silence on the other end. She hung up the phone and closed her eyes. She knew this would be hard for them to come back from. So much had been said, but she was determined to make it right. Liam deserved better.

CHAPTER 29

Boston
2011

Shelby was fortunate to be free from morning sickness with her second pregnancy, but she would have taken a few months of morning sickness over a colicky baby. Tyler was not the content baby his older sister had been. Their newborn son soon tested her confidence as a parent. Tyler's sleeping pattern of two to three hours at a time and crying when he was awake wore on them and often woke Rhylie. Lack of sleep and frustration tested their patience and relationship, as intimacy was nonexistent. Any rest they enjoyed was purely for survival. The vicious cycle of snapping at each other and apologizing became a daily ritual.

Eventually, Tyler's colic subsided, and he slept through the night, allowing the household to fall into a welcomed routine. Finally, sleeping in the same bed, Shelby and Scott began to chip away at the wall of tension built over the last six months. Feelings of disappointment, resentment, and guilt ran deep, but their love ran deeper, and both hoped they could reconnect.

Shelby struggled to keep her eyes open as she and Scott sat in their bed, flipping through the TV channels.

Scott glanced at her. "I asked my parents if they could babysit the kids tomorrow night so we can go out to dinner."

"That sounds nice. I don't remember the last time we had a date night." She yawned, then slid under the covers and closed her eyes.

Scott leaned over and kissed her forehead. "Good night."

"Night," Shelby whispered. She thought about the distance between them even as they lay beside each other. *When was the last time they had sex? When was the last time they kissed, for that matter?* She was too tired to think anymore and fell asleep.

Shelby hurried in the front door with Rhylie and Tyler, wanting to start dinner for them before Scott's parents arrived to babysit. Tyler began to fuss, and Rhylie emptied her backpack onto the kitchen floor.

Scott walked in a few minutes later and saw that Shelby was flustered and irritated. "Hey guys, how was your day?"

Rhylie dropped her bag and ran to her father. He picked her up and wrapped his arms around her. "Hi, sweetie."

Shelby didn't look at him as she bounced Tyler on her hip in the kitchen. His cry became higher-pitched and louder in anticipation of the warm bottle.

Scott set Rhylie down and went over to Shelby. "Here, I'll take him."

She handed Tyler off and continued to stare at the bottle warmer. She didn't want to start their date night by snapping at him as soon as he walked in the front door.

Scott rifled through the diaper bag, pulled out a pacifier, and popped it into Tyler's mouth.

She handed Scott the bottle and tilted her head. "Can you feed him so I can change?" she said on the verge of tears.

"Sure. Rhylie, come sit with Daddy, and we'll read a book."

Shelby disappeared up the stairs to their bedroom and rummaged through her closet, searching for something to wear.

She heard Scott greet his parents as she slid a dress over her head.

"Hi Mom, hey Dad. Shelby is changing."

She looked in the mirror and groaned, then pulled the dress off, throwing it on the bed.

Scott's father lifted Rhylie, and she wrapped her little arms around his neck and said, "Papa."

Scott's mother took Tyler and sat on the couch. A smile peeked out from around the bottle's nipple. "Oh, my goodness, you're such a good boy," she gushed.

"Thanks, Mom. I'm going to see if Shelby is ready."

Scott went upstairs to their bedroom. "Shel? Are you ready? My parents are here."

She came out of the en suite wearing a red dress that hugged her post-baby curves.

His eyes lit up. "Whoa."

Shelby frowned. "It's too tight, isn't it? I look ridiculous."

He took her in his arms. "Babe, no, you look smokin' hot."

"You don't have to be nice. I'm gonna change."

"Don't change. We'll miss our reservation. You look great."

Shelby sighed. "Okay."

They walked downstairs to the living room, where Scott's parents sat with Rhylie and Tyler.

"Oh, you look lovely, Shelby," Scott's mother said.

"Thank you. I'm sorry I didn't get to start dinner for Rhylie, but there's food in the fridge."

Scott's mother snuggled with Tyler. "No problem. You two should head out so you don't miss your reservation. We'll be just fine."

Scott's father waved them away. "Enjoy your dinner."

Shelby stared out the passenger window, asking herself why she was in such a lousy mood and feeling so sad when they finally had a few hours alone.

Tears pooled in Shelby's eyes. "What happened to us?"

"What do you mean?"

"We hardly kiss. I don't remember the last time we made love. We always end up arguing and becoming frustrated with each other. I hate it," she said as tears spilled down her cheeks.

He slowed the car and pulled into a parking lot. "Shel, don't cry." He wiped a tear from her cheek with his thumb. "The last six months have been tough. We've been sleep-deprived, so we're going to have short fuses. We need to find *us* again. That's why I wanted to go out tonight. Just you and me."

"I'm sorry I'm grouchy all the time. I miss *us*, the *us* before kids."

"I'm sorry, too." He took her face in his hands and kissed her passionately.

She placed her hand on his neck, kissing him back with a fierceness that reignited a fire in her that had burned out months ago.

"If we don't stop, we'll end up in the back seat," he grinned.

She bit her bottom lip. "Well, I guess we better make that dinner reservation and save dessert for home."

A few hours later, they walked in their front door smiling and laughing, feeling like a couple again.

"Well, it looks like you two had a nice time," Scott's mother said.

Shelby smiled. "We did. Thank you so much for watching the kids. How were they?"

Scott's mother began picking up books and toys. "They were perfect angels."

"Mom, don't worry about those; we'll get them."

"You ready, Grandma?" Scott's father was already at the front door.

Scott gathered an armful of toys. "Good night. Thanks again."

They finally settled into bed, eager to start dessert, when they heard a cry.

Shelby pinched her brows. "That sounds like Rhylie."

Scott threw the covers back. "I'll check on her." He slipped on a pair of shorts, and a minute later, he stood in the doorway of their bedroom holding Rhylie. "She has a fever," he said with a look of defeat. There would be no dessert tonight.

Shelby put on her oversized T-shirt, trekked to the kitchen, and pulled out a bottle of children's acetaminophen. Scott had Rhylie lying in the middle of their bed, holding a cool washcloth on her forehead.

Several hours later, the three of them finally drifted off and slept until Shelby was woken by Tyler's cries for his morning bottle.

She slid out of bed, careful not to wake Rhylie. Scott didn't move. *Was he asleep or pretending?* she wondered. They both had played the *I was out and didn't hear him crying* card. She could feel the irritation building inside her, so she tiptoed out and shut their bedroom door behind her.

For a second, she felt guilty for becoming irritated, remembering their kiss and date night. But as Tyler's cry became louder and more demanding, the guilt faded, and she resented that Scott lay fast asleep with Rhylie under his arm.

Shelby lay on the floor next to Tyler, her eyelids heavy, and desperately wanting to close them. He was swatting at the tiny zoo animals dangling above him, cooing and jerking his chubby legs, content with a full belly.

Scott walked out to the living room with Rhylie and sat down on the couch, and yawned. "It feels like her fever's gone."

Shelby's mind reeled. *Really, you're yawning. You just got an extra two hours of sleep. Yes, I'm counting.*

Shelby smiled at her daughter. "You feel better, sweetie?"

Rhylie nodded her head yes and snuggled into her father's shoulder.

Shelby closed her eyes and yawned. "I have to go into the flower shop today, but I'll be home before dinner."

Scott's shoulders slumped. "All day?"

"If I can leave early, I will," she snapped.

"Geez. Okay."

She got up from the floor and rested her hand on his shoulder. "I'm sorry. I'm just tired."

He ignored her apology and looked down at Rhylie. "Hey, sweetie, want some breakfast?"

Rhylie lifted her head from her father's shoulder and nodded yes.

Shelby walked into the bathroom and shut the door. Hopefully, a hot shower would wash away her foul mood.

The floral shop was a place of solace, an escape from the tension between her and Scott and the demands of the children. Maybe a few hours at work would lessen her frustration and resentment. She wouldn't let this be their new normal.

CHAPTER 30

New York City
2011

Liam held a glass of bourbon, staring out the high-rise windows of his suite. The streetlights popped on as the sun fell below the horizon, and the New York City sidewalks disappeared under the crowds of people. The bourbon went down smoothly and warmed his empty stomach. He replayed their fight in his head. Michelle's words stung, and he had never been so angry with her. He had promised her when Chloe and Ben were born that he'd never betray her again, yet here he was, retreating to the city.

A knock on the penthouse door took him out of his trance. He threw back the last ounce of his drink and set the glass on the cart next to the empty bottle of bourbon. He opened the penthouse door, irritated and stone-faced.

"Hey, handsome, I heard you were in town," she said with a flirty grin. She glanced at his hand that held the door open. "So, you're married now. Who's the lucky girl?"

He looked into her big brown eyes. If he were sober, he might have resisted. But the entire bottle of bourbon had him numb and reckless. *Fuck the promise*, his impulsive mind told him.

He pulled her into his room, shut the door, and pressed his body against her, moving her silky blonde hair off her shoulder.

"Trouble in paradise?" she smirked.

He kissed her neck, sliding his hand under her form-fitting mini dress and up her thigh, then kissed her with his bourbon-soaked tongue. He lifted her, guiding her legs around his waist, and carried her to the bed. "I don't want to talk."

Milltown

A month had passed since their fight, and with the new house under construction, Michelle felt their marriage was in a state of destruction. They remained cordial in front of the twins, but she couldn't stand the cold silence between them.

Liam sat on the sectional with a beer in his hand, watching a baseball game. His distance over the past month was his coping mechanism. He tried to convince himself that he was a different man and had left the playboy persona in the past, but he broke his promise, and his selfishness again filled him with remorse.

Michelle walked out of the twin's bedroom into the living room. "Chloe and Ben want a kiss good night."

She sat on the sectional and stared at the TV screen. *They needed to talk, and she had to initiate the conversation, starting with an apology.*

Liam returned, sat down, and took a swig of beer, not acknowledging her; it was hard to look at her and not have the guilt stir inside him.

Michelle turned to him when Martha walked into the room.

"Can I have a word with you both?"

Liam glanced at Michelle, giving her a slight smile. "Uh oh, looks like we're in trouble."

Her eyes brightened. It was only a smile, but for the first time in a month, it wasn't a look of disappointment or indifference.

Martha folded her hands. "I'll just come right out and say it." She looked at the two of them. "I don't know what has been going on between the two of you for the last month; it's none of my business, but you need to know that Chloe asked me this morning if Daddy is mad at Mommy and if you are getting a divorce. She can sense the tension between you two and is worried."

Liam ran his hand through his hair. "Shit."

Michelle sighed. "Thank you, Martha, for letting us know. We'll talk to her."

"Okay. I'll leave you two to talk. Good night." Martha walked away, then stopped. "The four of you mean the world to me. I hope you know that." She walked down the hall to her room and shut the door.

Michelle's heart pounded in her chest. "Does Chloe have a reason to worry?"

Liam looked at her, his brows drawn together. "No. Of course not."

She looked at him intensely. "Well, you can hardly look at me or touch me. I can't help but wonder if I have something to worry about, too."

Liam moved closer, placing his hand on her knee. His eyes were sincere. "Look, I'm sorry. I was hurt, and what I said about Brad wasn't fair."

"No, I'm sorry. I needed to hear it. I didn't realize you felt like you were living in his shadow and never meant to make you feel that way. I love you," she said as her eyes misted over. "You, Chloe, and Ben are my entire world. I know you were devastated when I miscarried. It broke my heart, too." She leaned toward him and wrapped her arms around him. "I hate the distance between us."

He released their embrace and rested his hands on her arms. "I never tried to replace Brad. I know I'm not a perfect husband, but I love you, Chelle." He looked down. "And what I said about Chloe and Ben..."

"No," she said, lifting his chin. "*You* are their father."

He didn't think he could love her more until she said those four words. But he was filled with guilt. How could he have betrayed her? Why couldn't he have kept his promise? He desperately wanted to undo what he had done in the city.

He sighed and set his hand on her cheek.

She closed her eyes and kissed the palm of his hand. "I've missed you," she whispered.

He caressed her cheek with his thumb and kissed her passionately, then slid his hands to the first button of her blouse.

She bit her lower lip, watching him open each button and finally revealing her lacy bra, loving how his crystal-blue eyes bore into her with love and lust. She lifted his shirt over his head and pushed him back onto the sectional, falling on top of him. "Let me show you just how much I've missed you."

He pushed the guilt down deep, surrendering to her seduction, and vowed to never betray her again.

CHAPTER 31

Boston
2011

Scott answered the front door. "Hey Sam, Shelby's not here. She's at the shop."

"Oh, okay. I'll give her a call later."

Rhylie appeared beside her father, wrapped her arms around his leg, and smiled at Sam.

"Hey, kiddo, how are you?"

Rhylie released her father's leg and took Sam's hand, pulling her into the living room.

Sam chuckled. "I guess I'm coming in."

Scott laughed and closed the front door. "You hungry? I was just about to start lunch."

She gave him a side-eye. "Depends on what you're making."

"Well, I make the best grilled cheese and tomato soup in all of Boston," he boasted.

Sam rolled her eyes. "We'll have to see about that." She settled on the couch with Rhylie and opened a book.

Tyler's cry sang out on the monitor.

"Sounds like someone is awake from his nap," Scott said. "I'll be right back."

The monitor downstairs broadcast his conversation with Tyler, making Sam laugh to herself.

"Wow, dude, we might have to cut back on the pureed meats."

Scott stood at the top of the stairs and yelled down to Sam. "Hey, I gotta give Tyler a bath. He had a major blowout."

Sam looked at Rhylie and wrinkled her nose. "Eww." She got up from the couch and stood at the bottom of the stairs. "Have fun with that. I've got Rhylie."

"Thanks," Scott yelled back.

A short while later, Scott came downstairs with Tyler to find Rhylie and Sam eating at the dining table. "You didn't have to make lunch."

"Well, Rhylie and I were *starrrving*," she teased, then pointed toward the kitchen. "Tyler's bottle is warmed up over on the counter."

"Geez, when did you become so domesticated?" he joked, settling on the couch with Tyler.

"Well, there's a lot about me that might surprise you," Sam said, raising her eyebrows. "Like these grilled cheese sandwiches and tomato soup. I believe you'll find them cooked to perfection."

Scott shook his head and laughed. "Well, thank you."

Tyler finished his bottle, so Scott went over and sat at the dining table.

"Here, I can take the big guy while you eat," she offered, lifting Tyler from Scott's lap.

Tyler grinned at Sam, then let out a loud burp.

Sam wrinkled her nose. "Pew, milk breath. Gee, thank you for that, sir."

Scott laughed. "Are you sure you can handle all this domestication?"

"Listen, I can handle milk breath over a blowout any day." She cringed.

Sam set Tyler in his walker and went to the kitchen to wash the dishes.

Scott helped Rhylie out of her booster seat and settled her at the toddler play table.

"Hey, I'll clean up. You did enough."

Sam slapped the wet sponge into Scott's hand. "Okay, don't have to tell me twice."

He chuckled and looked at her with an adoring expression. "Ya know, you've changed a lot since we first met at your Aunt Becky's."

"We were young and stupid then," she said, giving him a side-eye. "Why are you bringing that up all these years later?"

Scott shrugged his shoulders. "I don't know. I guess just reminiscing."

"Well, I never told Shelby about it. I was too embarrassed. Man, it was so awkward." Her freckles disappeared behind her bright pink cheeks.

He nodded to himself. "I figured that's why you pretended not to know me at Joey's, and I never told her either." Then he glanced at Sam. "Yeah, it was awkward. I guess your first time usually is."

"Well, that's a secret best kept between us and no one else."

He raised his eyebrows. "Absolutely."

"Listen, I'm gonna head out."

Scott dried his hands and walked Sam to the front door. "Hey, thanks for helping out. I really appreciate it."

"No problem," she said and waved her hand in the air. "Bye, munchkins."

Rhylie ran over and hugged Sam's leg. Sam smiled and looked at Scott. Their gazes lingered long enough to become awkward, making them both look away.

The front door opened, startling them.

"Oh, hey Sam, what are you doing here?" Shelby said with a wide grin.

Sam blushed again, uncomfortable with the exchange between her and her best friend's husband. "Hey. I stopped by to see you, but obviously, you weren't home."

"Sam came to the rescue just in time. Tyler had a major blowout, so she made Rhylie lunch while I gave him a quick bath." Scott glanced at Sam, giving her a warm smile.

"Wow!" Shelby widened her eyes. "I'm impressed." Then she gave Sam a light punch on the arm. "Suzy Homemaker."

Sam rolled her eyes. "Okay, I'm outta here."

"Thanks again, Sam," Scott yelled from the front door.

Shelby went over to Rhylie and kissed the top of her head. "Who knew Sam could handle the craziness that is our life?"

Scott watched Sam walk to her car. "Yeah, who knew?"

Sam stopped and looked back at the front door and met Scott's eyes. He smiled and closed the door. She hated to admit it. The domesticated life wasn't so bad.

CHAPTER 32

Milltown and Short Hills, New Jersey
December 2011

"Okay, I think that was the last box." Michelle rested her hands on her hips. "How did we accumulate so much stuff?"

"Twins," Martha replied. Then she gathered the children, settled in the SUV, and became a victim of fifty questions.

Michelle stood in the doorway for one last look, ready to say goodbye.

"We'll be back here in the summer before you know it," Liam said, shutting the door behind them.

A thirty-minute drive took them to their new home, where the movers filled the garage with the last of their boxes. It took eight months, but the construction was finally complete. Liam made sure their new home was move-in ready, hoping to make the transition as smooth as possible for Michelle, Martha, and the twins.

Chloe and Ben ran up the stairs to admire their newly furnished bedrooms while Michelle helped Martha settle in her private quarters off the kitchen.

After a late dinner, Liam started the fireplace while Chloe and Ben settled on the large, plush sectional.

Martha placed a bowl of popcorn between them and handed each one a drink. "Be careful not to spill on the new couch," she instructed.

Michelle came up behind them and placed her arms around their shoulders. "It's our first movie night in our new house!"

She glanced out the picture window at the snowflakes swirling around and thought of Brad holding one of her snow globes. It became easier to remember him without losing herself in grief, but she shook her head to erase the memory.

"Maybe we can get a Christmas tree tomorrow. What do you say, Daddy?" Michelle asked, giving Liam a hopeful look.

"Yeah, can we, Dad?" the twins said in unison.

"Already had it on my list of things to do tomorrow." He chuckled.

"Yay!" they shouted.

Michelle and Liam sandwiched the twins between them, continuing their Friday night family ritual.

"Hey, you gonna share some of that popcorn before it's gone?" Liam teased. "The movie hasn't even started yet." He took a handful, causing the twins to giggle.

Michelle watched the three of them. She was so grateful for the twins, Liam, and the beautiful home he built for their family. She let go of the guilt of loving a man other than Brad. Liam wasn't the player he used to be, and maybe a part of him missed that life, but he seemed happy and content. Brad would always have a piece of her heart, but now he belonged in her memories and a treasured box of pictures. She was fully committed to leaving the past behind her. This was a new beginning for her and Liam—for all of them.

The twins passed out before the end of the movie. Liam took Chloe to her room, then returned for Ben.

Michelle turned off the TV and brought the empty popcorn bowl and cups to the kitchen, hearing Liam come down the stairs for the third time.

He came up behind her and swept her hair over her shoulder. "Welcome home, Mrs. Grant," he whispered, kissing her ear.

She turned around, rested her arms on his shoulders, and smiled. "Welcome home, Mr. Grant."

He lifted her, set her on the kitchen island, and unbuttoned her blouse. He pressed his hips between her legs and cupped her breast.

She closed her eyes and tilted her head to the side as he kissed her collarbone.

He raised his eyebrow. "Let's take this upstairs."

When he lifted her off the island, she wrapped her legs around his waist and her arms around his neck. She sat in his hands as he carried her up the long staircase.

He stopped in front of their bedroom and set her down, then wove his fingers between hers and raised her arms above her head. As he pressed his body into her, he kissed her neck, causing the corner of her lips to curve into a smile. He released her hands, whisked her up in his arms, and pushed the door open.

"I didn't carry you over the threshold of our front door, so this will have to do," he said playfully.

The morning sun warmed the bedroom and woke her from her slumber. She reached across the sheets, opened her eyes, and found herself alone in the bed. She got up and walked to their en suite and opened the door, seeing his reflection in the mirror as steam swirled around his muscular physique. She opened the glass door, wrapped her arms around his waist, and kissed his back. "So, how was your first night in the new house?" he asked her, then turned around. Michelle's eyes widened. "Brad?" He took her face in his hands and kissed her deeply.

Michelle awoke with a start, relieved that she was alone in the bed, realizing it had only been a dream. She wouldn't have to lie to

Liam about dreaming of Brad again, and she hoped she hadn't talked in her sleep.

She left their room and found Liam in the hallway outside Chloe's bedroom door.

He turned and put his finger up to his mouth. "Shhh." Then he waved her over. "He wasn't in his room when I checked on him," Liam whispered.

She peeked in to see Ben sleeping beside Chloe and a flashlight illuminating the floor beside the bed.

Michelle shut the door and whispered, "He must have gotten scared in his room."

Liam wrapped his arms around Michelle's waist and kissed the back of her head. "So, how was your first night in the new house?"

Her eyebrows arched. "Well, someone kept me up late."

The twins' Christmas school break felt longer than usual, and Michelle's patience was wearing thin with the twins bickering every day, so she planned separate lunch dates with them, and today was Ben's turn.

They exited the elevator to Liam's office and were greeted by his secretary.

"Well, hello there, Mr. Benjamin. Did you bring me lunch today?" she teased.

Ben blushed and shook his head no. "Hi, Mrs. Clark."

Michelle chuckled. "Hello, Beverly."

Ben gave her a shy smile. "We're surprising Dad with lunch."

"How nice of you," she smiled, then picked up the phone receiver. "You have a couple of special visitors here to see you, Mr. Grant."

Liam opened his office door, and Ben ran to him and hugged him.

"Surprise! Me and Mom brought you lunch, Dad!"

"Hi, buddy!"

"Hi, babe," he said and kissed Michelle's cheek.

Ben ran over to Liam's desk chair and spun around several times.

Michelle placed the food and drinks on the round glass table. "Okay, Ben, let's eat so Dad can get back to work."

Liam and Michelle finished eating while Ben nosed around his father's office, then he sat in the desk chair again.

"Benjamin, stop spinning in the chair. You'll throw up your lunch," she said, shaking her head.

A few minutes later, Liam walked them to the door. "This was an awesome surprise. Thank you, buddy," he said, hugging Ben, then kissed Michelle goodbye. "Thanks, babe. See you guys at home."

Mrs. Clark glanced at them in the doorway and answered her phone. "Yes, I'll put you through to Mr. Grant."

"Okay, I gotta go. See you later," he said, shutting his office door.

Michelle leaned toward Beverly and whispered, "Ben spilled some of his drink on Liam's table. I cleaned it, but it still might be a little sticky." She wrinkled her nose. "Sorry, Beverly."

"No problem. I'll take care of it. You two have a lovely afternoon. Goodbye, Mr. Benjamin. Next time, sneak me a cookie, okay?" She gave him a wink, then disappeared down the hallway.

The elevator doors opened, and a shapely blonde wearing a faux fur coat and stiletto knee-high boots started to exit the elevator just as Ben tried to enter.

Michelle placed her hands on Ben's shoulders. "Let her out first, buddy. I'm so sorry," she said, offering an apologetic smile.

The woman glanced down at Ben and walked out of the elevator. "No worries, honey."

Ben looked up at her as they entered the elevator. "Geez, she's really tall, Mom."

"Anybody would be tall in those boots. Can you push the letter L, please?"

Before the elevator doors shut, Michelle noticed that 'Miss Stilettos' walked past Beverly's desk straight to Liam's office. If Beverly were there, she wouldn't just let her walk right in. Michelle scowled, wanting to exit the elevator, but the doors closed. *What would she say? She forgot her purse? It was in her hand. Besides, she had Ben with her. A fur coat and stilettos were hardly business attire. Who was she, and why did she want to see Liam?*

Michelle saw her reflection in the metal elevator doors—her hair in a ponytail, a puffy winter coat, and UGG boots. *She felt plain and unattractive and imagined herself trying to keep up with the twins in such heels. Although beautiful and sexy, stilettos were impractical footwear in any season, let alone winter. 'Miss Stilettos' looked familiar, but she couldn't place where she would have seen her.*

"Hey buddy, want to do some window shopping?" she asked Ben. She thought if they killed enough time, they might run into this woman leaving the office building, allowing her to have a brief conversation and figure out where she knew her from, and more importantly, why she was there to see Liam.

"What's window shopping? What do we need windows for?" Ben asked.

Michelle chuckled. "Window shopping is looking at things for sale through the store windows. Remember that time we visited New York City for the day, and you noticed the sneakers you liked in a window, but we didn't go inside to see them?"

He scrunched his face. "But that's no fun."

"We'll look for a little while," she said, taking his hand. "Then we'll stop at the bakery before we head home, okay?"

Ben shrugged his shoulders and nodded his head yes.

"Yes, come in," Liam said, expecting Mrs. Clark to peek around the door. Instead, the shapely blonde entered and sauntered toward his desk. "Didn't my secretary see you?" he asked, immediately walking over to shut the door and noticed that Mrs. Clark was MIA.

"I got off the elevator, and she wasn't at her desk, so I helped myself in." She walked over to the floor-to-ceiling windows. "Nice view," she said, admiring the towering buildings from Liam's ninth-floor office. She turned to his desk and picked up the picture of Michelle, Chloe, and Ben. "Cute twins. You didn't tell me you had kids." She gave Liam an artificial smile, then placed the picture back.

Liam sat in his desk chair. "What are you doing here?" he asked in an irritated tone while trying to remain cordial.

"Well, Gabe is having an epic New Year's Eve party in the city at his penthouse." She hopped onto his desk, crossed her legs, and took his tie in her hand. "And I thought you'd like to join me and ring in the new year. Ya know, for old time's sake."

He took his tie out of her hand. "Look, Staci, I appreciate the invite, but you can't just show up here at my office. My wife and I are in a good place. Last time..." He glanced down, shame covering his face, then he looked up at her. "It shouldn't have happened. I can't see you again."

"Last time..." Staci smirked. "Actually, it didn't happen."

His expression showed disbelief. "What do you mean, didn't happen?"

"Honey, you passed out on me. You didn't find it odd that you still had your slacks on under the covers the next morning?" she quipped, raising an eyebrow. "Must have been one hell of a hangover."

He thought back to that morning, feeling like a truck had hit him, remembering very little of the night before. *A moment of relief passed through him, now knowing he hadn't cheated on Michelle. But he had intended to, so he wasn't completely innocent.*

"No worries, hun. I didn't take it personally."

Liam helped her off his desk and walked her to the door.

She turned and faced him, straightened his tie, and placed her hands on his chest. "Lucky girl," she said, staring into his eyes. "Well, if there's ever trouble in paradise again, you know where to find me." She winked at him as he opened the door.

Beverly stood up from her desk, perplexed. "Mr. Grant, I apologize. I stepped away for just a moment."

"It's fine, Beverly. Take care, Miss Moore." He shut his door, let out a heavy sigh, thankful Michelle and Ben hadn't run into her.

Staci's swaying hips led her to the elevator doors. As she pressed the button, she looked over her shoulder at Beverly and gave her a smirk and a wave.

Beverly gave her the once-over. "Hmm."

Michelle tried not to be suspicious, but this was Liam. Her intuition told her Miss Stiletto's visit had nothing to do with business.

Ben's patience only lasted twenty minutes, so they trekked back to the parking garage in Liam's office building.

They came around the corner of the bakery. *Bingo, there she is,* Michelle said in her head.

As Staci walked toward them, Michelle smiled politely and paused. "Excuse me, but you look so familiar. Have we met before? I mean, other than the elevator earlier."

Staci stopped and scanned Michelle from head to toe. "I don't think so," she said, then glanced down at Ben. "Oh, hi there, cutie. Blue eyes like your father."

The politeness fell from Michelle's face, and her eyes narrowed. "How do you know Liam?"

'Miss Stilettos' looked her dead in the eyes and smirked.

Michelle knew that look. The look that tells a woman: *not only do I know your husband, but I've had your husband.*

"We go way back. I'm Staci."

Michelle's mind reeled. *The picture on Lucy's phone popped into her head. Staci was one of the girls with Liam in New York City on New Year's Eve years ago.*

"You must be his wife? And you have twins. That's so sweet," she said, tilting her head and pouting her bottom lip.

Michelle glared at her. *She knew Ben had a twin? What the hell?*

"Mom, can we go?" Ben begged.

Staci faked a smile. "Bye, little cutie." She ran her hand over Ben's head, then strutted away.

In an instant, Michelle's blood boiled. *Who did she think she was, waltzing into Liam's office, and what the hell did she want with him?*

CHAPTER 33

Boston
December 2011

"The guys asked me to meet them at Joey's bar tonight."

Shelby glared at Scott from across the living room, her face revealing she was pissed.

"I don't have to go," he said with a sigh, his face showing his disappointment.

"No. Go. It's fine." Shelby went to the kitchen to make them breakfast.

Scott walked up behind her, placed his hands on her hips, and kissed her cheek. "I won't be too late. Then maybe we can have dessert?"

Shelby shrugged her shoulders. "Sure."

He sighed and removed his hands from her hips, then went to the living room and sat on the floor next to Tyler.

She glanced his way and felt guilty for being cold.

After a quick shower, she kissed Scott and the kids and left for the flower shop. Once again, hoping that a few hours away would erase her irritated mood.

She locked the door of the shop and saw Sam behind her.

"Hey, Shel. I was in the neighborhood and thought I'd stop to see if you wanted to hang out tonight. I'm sure you could use a night out."

Shelby sighed. "Wish I could. Scott's going to Joey's with the guys tonight. You can come over and chill with me and the kids." She rolled her eyes. "I know you've been dying to."

"Um, sure, why not? See you at 7:30?"

Shelby smiled. "Sounds good."

She stared at the double yellow lines driving home. *At least she wouldn't be alone while Scott enjoyed his freedom and time with his friends.* She knew the resentment would build as the night went on, so having Sam over to distract her from her thoughts was a good plan.

When she walked in the front door, she found Scott flustered as Tyler cried in the background. Rhylie sat at her toddler table, coloring.

"He's in his crib. I just got him cleaned up. He was soaked from head to toe."

"Oh, geez."

Shelby went to Tyler's room and picked him up from his crib. "Did you give Daddy a hard time?"

He stopped crying and laid his head on her shoulder. She popped the pacifier in Tyler's mouth, then took him to the living room and sat on one of the mini chairs at the toddler table. She ran her hand over Rhylie's curly locks. "Hey, sweet girl, what are you coloring?"

Rhylie held up her paper of scribbles. "Fowers," she said proudly.

Shelby tilted her head and smiled. "The flowers are beautiful."

Scott walked into the living room in a change of clothes. "Hey, the guys are meeting at six, so I'll just eat there."

Disappointment covered her face. "Oh. Okay. I thought we were going to eat together before you went out."

"I shouldn't be late," he said.

"Sam stopped by the shop. She's coming over later, so I guess I'll eat dinner with her then."

"Tell her I said hi." He kissed the top of Rhylie's head, then leaned down and gave Shelby a quick peck on the lips.

Her jaw tightened. "Bye."

Rhylie and Tyler were fast asleep when Sam knocked and walked in the front door, carrying a six-pack and pizza.

"That smells so good," Shelby said, taking the pizza box from her.

"Beer?" Sam asked.

"Absolutely. I don't remember the last time I had a drink." Shelby twisted the cap and moaned as she took her first swig.

"The rugrats asleep?"

Shelby chuckled. "Yes, and let's hope it stays that way."

They settled on the couch with their beer and pizza, enjoying the peace and quiet.

"So, you gave Scott a guys' night out, huh?"

Shelby took another swig of beer and rolled her eyes. "He couldn't get out of here fast enough."

Sam noticed Shelby's eyes misting over. "Hey, you okay?"

Shelby tried to hold back the tears but couldn't stop them.

"Shel. What is it?"

Her voice squeaked. "Scott."

"What did he do? Do I need to kick his ass? Because you know I will."

Shelby had witnessed Sam's temper; she loved a good fight.

Sam kept her eyebrows raised, her body tense, waiting for permission.

Shelby laughed through her tears and shook her head no. "Things have changed between us. I feel like we're in survival mode. We get irritated with each other easily, and I don't even remember the last time we had sex."

Sam relaxed and grabbed a slice of pizza. "I don't know how you guys do anything with two kids so close together." She took a bite and washed it down with a sip of beer. "Sorry, but you always look exhausted."

"Great." Shelby rolled her eyes. "No wonder we don't have sex. It's hard to be attracted to a zombie." She laughed, then started to cry again.

"Shel, hasn't Tyler been sleeping through the night for a while now?"

"Yeah, but we had a date night a while ago, and the kids were asleep when we got home. We got into bed, and before we could even kiss, Rhylie woke up crying with a fever. She spent the rest of the night in our bed."

Sam wrinkled her nose. "Oh, buzzkill."

"I don't think he's happy. I know I'm not. Don't get me wrong, I love him and the kids; they are my world. We've just..."

"Just what?"

Shelby couldn't hide the pain in her eyes. "We've grown apart. I don't think we like each other anymore."

"Shel ... Look, you guys need to have sex. Hot, steamy sex and reconnect."

Shelby raised her eyebrows. "So, you're giving relationship advice now? If only it were that easy."

"Hey," Sam gave her a side eye. "It's true I don't have the best track record."

Shelby glanced at the TV, turned it on, flipped through the channels, and settled on a romcom.

A few hours later, Sam looked at her phone. "Wow, it's ten o'clock already."

"Really? Scott left at five-thirty." Shelby scowled. "He said he wouldn't be late."

"You okay if I head out?"

"Yes, I'll be fine."

"I know the rugrats will be up at the crack of dawn, and you need all the sleep you can get."

"Gee, thanks, but you're not wrong. Thanks for listening and for dinner." Shelby walked Sam to the door and hugged her goodbye.

She plopped back down on the couch and checked her phone. No texts from Scott. *What if he was in an accident? What if he's flirting with another girl who doesn't resemble a zombie?* She lay down and stared at the TV screen. The pizza and beer had filled her empty stomach, and within minutes, she relaxed into a welcomed slumber.

CHAPTER 34

Short Hills
December 2011

"Look, Chloe, me and Mom bought decorations for New Year's Eve," Ben said, showing off the bag of glittery decor.

Michelle rested her hands on Ben's shoulders. "Okay, let's put that away and wash up for dinner. Daddy will be home soon."

Liam walked through the mudroom to the kitchen and was greeted by an ear-piercing squeal of the party horn. "Wow, that's loud, buddy. Why don't we save that for New Year's Eve."

Chloe skipped to her father. "Martha made our favorite dinner, Daddy, chicken parquet."

Liam chuckled. "You mean Chicken Parmesan," he said, rubbing the top of her head.

"Yeah, that," she said, wrinkling her nose.

He walked over to Michelle and kissed her cheek. "Hey."

"Hi," she said in a matter-of-fact tone, not looking at him.

Michelle was quiet during dinner and debated whether to bring up 'Miss Stilettos' after the twins went to bed, but Ben beat her to it.

"Dad, me and Mom saw your friend today," Ben said, taking a mouthful of garlic bread.

"You did?"

"Yeah, she had a mink coat and tall, pointy boots."

"It was a fake fur, honey." Michelle glanced at Liam and blushed, feeling stupid for her petty clarification.

Liam looked at her, then back at Ben. "Oh yeah, buddy." He faked a smile as *shit* repeated in his head.

"I don't remember her name, but she was really tall, and she kept calling me cutie," he said, then gulped his milk, leaving a white mustache across his top lip.

"It was Staci," Michelle said, giving Liam a contrived smile, then looked down and moved her food around her plate.

His jaw tightened, and he readjusted himself in his chair. He knew that once the kids were in bed, Michelle would confront him.

As the night went on, his anxiety grew. Michelle wouldn't talk to him or make eye contact with him.

He went into their bedroom and closed the door, noticing the en suite door was open, anticipating an intense conversation. "The kids are asleep," he said, then sat on their bed, and eased into an offer to do something with the twins.

"I'm off tomorrow. Maybe I can take the kids to a matinee?" he suggested, but received no reply. He was ready to explain and assumed he'd be sleeping in the guest room.

Michelle turned off the en suite light and walked over to the bed wearing a red silk robe. Rather than grilling Liam about Staci, she chose to speak *his* language, making it clear what she expected from him.

His eyes lit up as she walked toward him, but he was confused. "Look, Chelle—"

She placed her finger on his lips and used his own line on him. "I don't want to talk."

She released her bun, letting her light brown waves fall onto her shoulders, then stood between his legs and untied her robe, revealing the only piece of clothing she wore: her lace panties. She ran her fingers through his hair, staring into his eyes.

He breathed in the scent of her and pulled her hips closer to him, then slid her panties off. He understood what this was. She was making it clear that his fidelity was to her and only her.

She pulled away, crawled onto the bed, and knelt behind him, pressing her breasts into his back, then wrapped her arm across his chest and traced his ear with her tongue. She slowly ran her other hand down his chest, then his abs, finally sliding her hand under his waistband.

Her seduction ignited a fire inside him. This *was* a language he spoke well. He stood and turned toward her.

She grabbed his waistband and rolled his boxer briefs down his thighs.

He slid them off, kicking them aside.

She stared at him, her eyes telling him what she wanted.

He took her in his arms, laid her on the bed, and pressed between her legs, then took her hair in his hand and pulled her head back and kissed her extended neck.

She arched her back and moaned. "Don't stop."

He placed his lips next to her ear while pulsing his hips and whispered, "There's only you."

She took his face in her hands and stared into his eyes.

He knew what her eyes were saying: *I trust you*, so he kissed her, expressing his total commitment to her.

Morning came too soon, as they were woken by Chloe and Ben rushing downstairs. Michelle got up, put on her silk robe, then sat on Liam's side of the bed and faced him.

"I'm glad we cleared that up last night."

Liam looked at her with understanding. It was clear. She would not tolerate his old behavior.

She walked to the en suite and locked the door behind her.

He sat in bed, filled with a range of emotions. He was relieved and grateful Michelle didn't want to talk about Staci. But, most of all, he was remorseful for his intended infidelity after their fight and prayed she would never find out.

Michelle stood in the shower, letting the hot water run down her face. It wasn't easy giving Liam her heart and fully trusting him. She made it known that she'd tolerate nothing less than his total commitment to her.

Liam went downstairs to find the twins sitting at the island, eating breakfast and talking with Martha.

Chloe danced around. "Dad, it's News Year's Eve!"

He chuckled. "Yes, it is!" Then he gave her a kiss on the top of her head. "Good morning, buddy. No party horns until tonight. Got it," he said, giving Ben a stern look.

"Aw," Ben whined.

He glanced at the handmade calendar hanging on the refrigerator door. In the center, a plastic number seven magnet held the calendar in place.

"Boy, something important is happening in January, and I can't remember what it is," he teased. "Martha, do you know?"

Martha shook her head and threw her hands in the air. "I can't think of a thing."

"Dad! Martha!" Chloe and Ben shouted. "It's our seventh birthday!"

He threw his head back. "Oh, that's right!"

Chloe jumped down from her stool and ran to the calendar. "Look right here," she said, pointing to January 10th. "It says Chloe and Ben, seven years old, in big letters. And do you see that?"

"What?" Liam looked closely at the picture of a crudely drawn dog. "I can't tell what that is."

"You need glasses, Dad?" Ben said in a sarcastic tone.

Liam went over and grabbed Ben from the bar stool, threw him over his shoulder, and tickled the back of his legs. "I need glasses, huh?"

Ben screamed and laughed, trying to escape his father's grip. "Stop, Dad, stop! I'm gonna barf!"

Michelle came downstairs and smiled. "What is all this commotion?"

"Mommy, do you remember what's on January 10th?" Chloe asked.

"Hmmm. Oh, we're picking Bear up, right?"

Finally freed, Ben ran to his mother. "And what else, Mom?"

"I don't know." The corner of her mouth quirked up. "What am I forgetting?"

"Mom!" the twins shouted.

Michelle grabbed them in her arms and laughed. "How could I ever forget my favorite day of the year?"

Liam watched Michelle with the twins. Tonight, they would ring in the new year in their new home. The three were his world, and he vowed to be the husband and father they deserved.

Michelle sat on the sectional with her arms wrapped around the drowsy twins. "Hey, Chloe, Ben," she said, rubbing their arms. "The ball is going to drop."

Martha sat in the plush armchair, fighting to stay awake.

They sat up, saw the descending glowing ball on the TV screen, and leaped off the couch.

The four of them shouted in unison with "Dick Clark's Rockin' New Year's Eve" hosts. "Ten, nine ... two, one! Happy New Year!"

Confetti covered the TV screen as Ben blared the party horn

around the room, making up for holding off the entire day.

Liam took Michelle in his arms and kissed her. "Happy New Year, babe."

Chloe hugged Martha. "Happiest News Years."

Martha chuckled, then covered her mouth and yawned. "Oh my goodness, way past my bedtime."

Liam kissed Martha on the cheek, and Michelle hugged her, then Martha began cleaning.

"I got this," Michelle said.

Martha yawned again. "Okay then, good night, all."

"Okay, you two, off to bed," Liam ordered, leading the twins up the stairs.

"I'll be right up. I'm just going to take care of some of this." Michelle gathered decorations, bowls, and cups, carrying them to the kitchen.

She heard a ding and looked around. It went off again, leading her to the mudroom. Liam's coat pocket glowed. She reached in and pulled out his work phone, planning to bring it upstairs to him. A text labeled S.M. appeared on the home screen. "*Happy New Year, Handsome. Missed you*" followed with a heart emoji. Michelle's heart raced, and her cheeks grew hot. "What the hell?"

Liam stood at the top of the stairs. "You coming, Chelle?"

She jumped and put his phone back in his coat pocket, and yelled, "Yeah, I'll be right there." She had to trust that he would also make it clear to Staci that he was not the same bachelor she enjoyed all those years ago, or the 'language' spoken between them would be much different from the night before.

CHAPTER 35

Boston

Christmas and the new year brought a time of reflection for Shelby and Scott and the hope for a renewed relationship. Shelby resolved to let go of her resentment, and Scott promised they would make time for each other, having a date night once a week.

By spring, Scott's golf league began again, and Shelby was busier than ever with Aunt B's Bouquets. Date nights dwindled to once a month and ended altogether by summer. Between Scott having drinks after golf and meeting the guys every weekend at Joey's bar, the distance was greater than before, and Shelby's resentment set in once again.

Sam became Shelby's Friday or Saturday night date, whichever night Scott decided he needed to escape.

With summer in full swing and Scott's golf league over, he continued the weekend ritual. Shelby no longer complained and accepted that Scott preferred to spend his time at the bar, not with his wife.

Shelby's face expressed a look of defeat. "I don't know Sam. We tried, but life keeps getting in the way."

Sam's eyes narrowed. "Shel, what are you saying?"

"I don't know how to fix it. I don't cry over it anymore. I just get more resentful."

"He loves you, Shel. I think guys just need their guy time."

"Well, he's at Joey's bar again. He can make a 'date night' with the guys every week, but not with his wife."

"Hey, are you sick of our date nights already?" Sam teased.

Shelby laughed. "At least I can count on *your* weekly commitment."

"Damn straight."

"By the way, whatever happened to Kenny?"

"Well, it wasn't workin' out. He was too clingy." Sam rolled her eyes.

Shelby placed her hand on Sam's. "Yeah, you're not good with clingy."

Sam nodded and laughed.

Shelby frowned. "Sorry, but I need to cut this date short. I have to be at the shop early tomorrow."

Sam made her way to the front door and turned to Shelby. "Listen, you guys will get through this. You did before; you will again."

Shelby shrugged her shoulders. "Thanks for the pizza and beer. See ya next weekend."

Sam made a stop on her way home. She was curious and walked into Joey's bar, glancing around until she heard a familiar voice yell, "Hey, it's Sam!"

Scott weaved his way across the bar toward her, holding a half-filled glass of beer, and hugged her.

"Looks like you need a ride home there, buddy," Sam said, pulling away from him.

"Come on, have a beer with us." His eyes were glassy, and his body swayed, trying to steady himself.

"No thanks. You should get home to Shelby."

"What time is it?"

Sam raised her eyebrows. "It's almost ten o'clock."

"Shit. Shelby's gonna kill me."

Sam took the glass out of his hand and set it on the bar. "Okay, wave goodbye to your friends."

Scott raised his arm and waved. "See you guys, heading home to the old ball and chain."

"Jesus Scott, you're an ass!" Sam grabbed his arm and led him out of the bar.

As she helped him into the passenger seat, he put his nose close to her and sniffed. "Your hair smells good."

She rolled her eyes and buckled his seatbelt, causing him to burp.

"Dammit, don't you puke in my car! I'll kill you before Shelby gets a chance to."

Sam got in the driver's seat, glanced at him, and shook her head.

Scott rested his head back on the seat, fighting to keep his eyes open.

Once Sam pulled out of the parking lot, Scott dropped his head forward and let it rock with the car's motion. "Shelby doesn't love me anymore, Sam."

"Yes, she does, you idiot."

"All we do is argue or ignore each other. She doesn't need me," he slurred.

"You guys just need to talk. Listen, sleep this off and talk to her tomorrow."

"You're a good friend, Sam," he slurred again while dozing on and off.

"Yeah, you owe me one, that's for damn sure."

She glanced at Scott as his head rocked and remembered their awkward sexual encounter as teens in Aunt Becky's basement. He had grown into Mr. Tall, Dark, and Handsome, as Shelby called him, but right now he was a drunken ass. Sam pulled into the driveway and unbuckled his seatbelt. The porch light was off, so she assumed it was Shelby's way of telling Scott that she was pissed. He opened the passenger door and almost fell out.

Sam ran around the front of the car. "Jesus, come on, big guy." She helped him out, then put his arm over her shoulder and wrapped her arm around his waist. She struggled to walk with him as they weaved across the front lawn and up a slight incline. The summer night air had cooled, making the grass wet with dew.

Scott slipped on the wet grass and tripped over Sam's foot, causing him to fall to the ground. He let out an "Oof" and landed on top of her.

"Dammit, Scott!"

He laid his head on her chest and laughed.

"What are you laughing about? Get off me, you idiot," she barked, trying to push him off.

He stopped laughing and stared at her with his glassy brown eyes.

Sam's heart raced as she stared back at him. Her lips parted, but she said nothing. Her mind raced. *Jesus, he's handsome. And drunk. And my best friend's husband. Dammit, Sam, what are you thinking?*

Scott pressed his lips onto her mouth and ran his hand over her breast.

She kissed him back, savoring his drunken lips, then yelled in her head, *What the hell are you doing!*

A beam of light stretched across the front lawn, startling them. They both looked toward the house to see Shelby standing at the front door. Her eyes were wide with confusion, then changed to anger.

"Oh, shit!" Scott said.

They watched Shelby disappear behind the front door, and the porch light shut off.

Sam pulled herself out from under Scott. "Shelby! No! Wait!"

CHAPTER 36

Short Hills
Monday, July 2, 2012

The city no longer served as an escape when life got hard. Liam understood what he would lose if Michelle learned about his indiscretions. He promised to be a better man for his family and himself, cutting all ties with Staci and avoiding the city.

The twins sat at the kitchen island, eating breakfast. Chloe was wide awake as usual, chatting away with Martha while she washed the dishes. Ben was slumped on the island, his head leaning on his extended arm, feeding himself a fork full of scrambled eggs.

Liam came up behind the twins and rubbed their backs. "Good morning. Excited for your vacation?"

"I am Daddy!" Chloe chirped.

Ben nodded, his head still resting on his arm.

"You guys behave for your grandparents and have an awesome time." He kissed them both on the head and said I love you.

Ben slid off the barstool and dragged himself up the stairs, meeting his mother at the top.

"Rough morning, buddy? Get dressed. We'll be leaving soon."

Liam turned around, saw Michelle coming down the stairs, and met her at the last step.

"Hey, I have to go to the city for a few days next week, and I figured since the kids will be with your parents, we could have a little vacation ourselves. What do you think?"

She glanced out the sliding glass doors at the rose garden. "Sure."

He kissed her cheek. "Great. See you after work."

He walked back through the kitchen and put his arm around Martha. "Have a safe trip and a wonderful time with your family."

"Thank you, Liam. I will."

"Mommy, I can't wait to go on vacation with Grandma and Grandpa Carrington," Chloe squealed.

Michelle's eyes softened, and she ran her hand across Chloe's head. "Well, go get your brother so we can finally leave."

Chloe rolled her eyes. "We're always waiting for Ben."

Michelle chuckled and watched Chloe run up the stairs. When she turned around, Martha was staring at her. "What?"

Martha's hands rested on her hips. "I can see that something is bothering you."

"I'm fine."

The corner of Martha's mouth turned down. "Hmm."

Michelle tilted her head. "I am. Anyway, maybe I'll visit Lucy this summer." She sighed. "College feels like a lifetime ago, and I haven't seen her since she visited when the twins were five."

"Well, I'm sure you'll have a pleasant time catching up with one another," Martha said in a matter-of-fact tone.

Michelle rested her hands on Martha's shoulders. "Really, don't worry about me. Enjoy this well-deserved vacation from the twins, from all of us."

Martha gave her a curious look. "What do you mean by all of you?"

Michelle rolled her eyes. "You do so much for all of us. You need a break, too." She was relieved when Chloe and Ben reappeared, ending Martha's interrogation.

"Alright, say goodbye to Martha."

They wrapped their arms around Martha's waist.

Ben looked up at her. "Have fun with your family."

Martha smiled. "Why thank you, Benjamin, I certainly will."

Chloe gave Martha an extra tight squeeze. "I love you, Martha."

"Goodbye, my loves. Promise you'll behave for your grandparents."

"We will," they replied.

Michelle wrapped her arm around Martha and walked her to the door. "Have a wonderful time. I'll see you when you get back."

After closing the door, Michelle released a heavy sigh. "Okay, let's get your bags in the car!"

Ann stood in the foyer with Chloe and Ben's arms wrapped around her until they heard Seth coming down the hallway. They released their grandmother and ran to their grandfather.

"Thanks, Mom, for taking them with you and Dad. I know they'll have a great time."

"Have a safe drive to Boston, dear, and give Lucy our regards."

Michelle hugged her mother. "I will. I love you."

Seth walked over to her with Chloe and Ben still hanging on him and kissed his daughter's cheek. "Safe travels. We'll take great care of the twins."

"Thank you, Dad. I know you will."

Michelle waved to the twins as she pulled out of her parents' driveway. Then she glanced over at the Coles' house, her second home growing up. How could it be almost a decade since Brad had died? She stared at the road as she descended into anger and heartbreak. One last stop. Home.

After months of putting Staci out of her mind, something told her to look into this "friend" of Liam's, and what she found confirmed her suspicions. She needed to leave him a message. One that couldn't be left in a voicemail.

Michelle walked upstairs to their bedroom, recalling her and Ben running into the arrogant tramp in December. She found out Staci's full name through Lucy's Facebook pictures only yesterday and scoured Staci's posts. She opened her laptop to her new screen-saver picture of Liam asleep behind Staci's pretentious selfie, dated May 2011, when he went to the city after their fight.

Leaving it on the screen, she tossed her laptop on the bed. She grabbed their wedding picture off Liam's dresser and shook her head. "I'm such a damn fool for giving you my heart," she said out loud. Heat stung her cheeks as the anger built inside her, throwing the picture across the room.

Tears pooled in her eyes as she sat on the edge of the bed. She removed her rings and set them on the nightstand. If the picture on her laptop and shattered picture frame didn't leave a clear message, her wedding rings would.

By the time she arrived in Boston, Liam would find his indiscretion displayed on her laptop. She was able to hide her deep sadness from her parents, but Martha knew her too well, and she was thankful the twins saved her from having to explain it all.

CHAPTER 37

Liam came home to a quiet house, and the only one to greet him this time was a solemn-looking Bear. He ran his hand over his silky head. "Hey, good boy. Do you miss Chloe and Ben already?" He opened the patio door, let Bear out, and stared at the rose garden.

It was one of Michelle's favorite places. Last spring, when their property was landscaped, she insisted on planting rose bushes of every color, especially pink ones, her favorite. A year later, the garden was lush and vibrant.

He released a satisfied breath and thought to himself, like his wife, the roses are beautiful and captivating, but if not handled with care and respect, the thorns serve as a painful reminder of their delicate strength. Michelle trusted him with her heart, and he would prove to her he'd do anything to protect it.

Bear ran back inside and watched Liam fill his food bowl. A string of saliva hung from the side of his mouth in anticipation, and within minutes, his dinner was gone. After leaving a water trail across the floor, he went to his dog bed, made three complete circles, and lay down. Liam grabbed a hand towel and shook his head. "I'm pretty sure you leave more on the floor than you actually drink, buddy."

Michelle would be home anytime with their takeout, so he loosened his tie and walked up the stairs to change, imagining all the places they would have sex in the empty house. With her agreeing to go to the city with him, he felt confident they had put Staci behind them. He opened their bedroom door, turned the light on, and found shards of glass scattered across the hardwood floor and a gouge in the wall revealing the impact of the picture frame. His heart raced as he looked around the room.

He called out to Michelle but received no response. Nothing else was out of place. Then he saw her laptop on their bed. He opened it, and staring back at him was a picture of Staci smiling, with him passed out in the bed behind her, frozen on the screen.

"Shit! What the hell, Staci!"

He called Michelle's cell phone, but it went straight to voicemail. "Chelle, please call me."

He ran his fingers through his hair. "Chelle, I didn't. Dammit, Staci!"

He walked over and picked the picture frame up off the floor, pulled out the remaining pieces of glass, and set it back on his dresser. He grabbed the hand vac from the closet, but when he turned it on, the motor's sound couldn't drown out the voice in his head. *You fuckin idiot, you have to fix this.*

He sat down on the side of the bed and hit redial. "Hi, this is Michelle. Leave a message." He had to let her know that, although it looked incriminating, he and Staci hadn't slept together. He didn't cheat on her, even though he had intended to.

"Chelle, please call me so I know you are okay. Please." He looked across the room and stared at the picture of Michelle with Chloe and Ben sitting on her dresser. She found out he was with Staci after their fight last year, and if she assumed also when the twins were born, she would be right. He glanced at his bedside table and saw Michelle's engagement ring and wedding band. Her message was clear.

CHAPTER 38

Boston
Tuesday, July 3, 2012

After a sleepless night at the Boston Harbor Hotel, Michelle finally left a message for her college roommate. A quick lunch with Lucy would suffice—just enough time to say hello and catch up, without getting into why she was really in Boston: to avoid Liam. She stared out the window, remembering Lucy's visit. If Lucy hadn't shown her the New Year's Eve pictures a few years ago, she never would have found out about Staci.

"Lucy!" Michelle blurted, then hugged her tight.

Lucy raised her eyebrows. "So, twins, huh? You've been busy."

"Yeah. They are a handful, but incredible."

"Are they here?"

"They're at the park with Martha. She wanted to give us some time alone so we could visit." She chuckled. "So, what are you doing now? Where are you living and working? Tell me everything."

"Remember that I graduated early in December of our senior year?"

Michelle nodded. "Yes."

"Well, I interned at an accounting firm in New York City, then was offered a job at their UK division. I loved it and met so many people. Now I work in Boston. My fiancé and I have a dog, Charlie." She pulled out her phone and scrolled through pages of pictures, stopping to show Michelle a few from the UK. "Oh, here she is." A goldendoodle was

sandwiched between her and another woman on a couch. "That's Dani, my fiancé."

Michelle smiled. "You two look really happy."

"Thanks, we are. But wedding planning, ugh," she said, rolling her eyes. "Oh, hey, I ran into Liam. Oh gosh, it had to be New Year's Eve when I was interning in New York City." She scrolled through her pictures again and showed Michelle her phone. "He had a girl on each arm." She pointed to the image. "I think she was Staci, and this one was Tanya? Anyway, we partied with them. It was a crazy night. I remember Liam being a player at UConn. I wonder what he's doing now. Do you ever talk to him?"

Michelle studied the picture, not surprised by the skintight mini dresses the blondes wore in the dead of winter while hanging off Liam. "Well, he's married now, has five-year-old twins, and I talk to him every day," she said, raising her eyebrows.

Lucy's jaw dropped. "Oh my gosh, Chelle. I didn't know you and Liam became a thing. Wow."

Michelle laughed. "Lucy, it's okay. He's grown up. Still a flirt, but he's a great father."

Michelle sighed, staring at the harbor as tears flooded her eyes. Holding her arms close to her, she ran her finger over the small heart-shaped scar on her right elbow, knowing that Liam never meant to hurt her that day on the ball field when they were kids, but he knew his infidelity would leave a scar on her heart.

She assumed he was with Staci in the City when she was in labor with Chloe and Ben. Granted, they weren't married or even a couple when the twins were born, but she expected his loyalty, unfair or not. Last year, though, that was purely selfish.

Liam left three voicemail messages. She listened to the first one and ignored the other two.

"You never would have done this to me, to our family. I still miss you so much," she said to herself, then closed her eyes, remembering when everything was right in the world, when Brad was her world.

He kissed her tenderly and stared at her intensely with his deep blue eyes. "Chel, our bond is too strong; nothing could ever change us. Remember, I love you a thousand times infinity."

She opened her eyes, still holding the image of Brad in her mind. "If only we had infinity." She wiped away her tears, called the front desk, and grabbed her purse. Right now, a trip to the liquor store was on the day's agenda.

Keeping her reservation open, she planned to stay at the hotel at least until the twins returned from their summer vacation with her parents. If anything, it would give her time to decide if she wanted to stay with Liam, but worried about how it would affect Chloe and Ben. After all, he was a great father, and they adored him.

The elevator doors opened to a sea of marble, towering white columns, and a chandelier the size of a Mini Cooper. The sliding glass lobby doors opened, and the warm air brushed her long, light brown hair across her face. Her Prada sunglasses dimmed the bright glare of the summer day. She watched as the red BMW growled to a stop under the canopy. A young valet jumped out of the sports car and held the door open for her, smiling from ear to ear.

"Beautiful car."

She glanced at the valet's name tag, smiled back, and handed him a twenty-dollar bill. "Thank you, Jeremy."

His eyes lit up. "Thank you!"

Driving had a way of sending her into a trance. Deep thoughts clouded her head as she replayed their fight, then pictured Liam's infidelity on her laptop.

The last place she wanted to be was New Jersey—in the house he built for their family and their future. *What would their future look like now?*

The blinking neon sign for City Wine and Spirits interrupted her thoughts, reminding her this was her destination. She convinced herself that a couple of bottles of wine would ease her anxiety, especially after the restless night in the hotel.

She browsed the wine section and settled on two bottles of Chardonnay, setting them on the counter, and reached into her purse for her wallet.

"Hey, Shelby. How's it going?" the clerk asked.

Michelle gave him a puzzled look. "Sorry, you must have me confused with someone else. I'm not from here; only visiting." Then she handed the clerk her license.

He put his glasses on and studied her license. "Oh, I'm sorry. You look just like a woman I know." He shook his head. "You two could be twins," he chuckled.

Michelle gave him a polite smile. "Well, I've always wanted a sister."

"Hope you enjoy your time in Boston," he said, handing her the license and bag of tomorrow's hangover.

"Thank you, I'll try."

As she walked out of City Wine and Spirits, she attempted to put her license and wallet back in her purse when her phone rang, startling her. She fumbled with her wallet, phone, and bag of wine bottles, finally settling in her car. She looked at her phone and sighed, leaned back on the headrest, and closed her eyes. "Damn you, Liam."

She opened the roof, allowing the sun to fill the inside of the convertible, drove to the parking lot exit and looked left, then right. As she pulled onto the three-lane roadway, she heard a woman yell her name. Wondering if it was Lucy, she lowered her sunglasses. A gasp escaped her lips as time paused, locking eyes with her mirror image. A sudden jolt sent the convertible into a tailspin. Her body slumped into the passenger seat as the car etched a trail through the small, quaint park toward the riverbank. She tried to open her eyes as visions of her life raced through her mind, then everything faded into a sea of darkness.

CHAPTER 39

Boston
Tuesday, July 3, 2012

Moving restlessly in her bed and finally settling on her back, Shelby stared into the abyss of her bedroom.

The vision of her husband and best friend kissing ran on a constant loop in her head. She glanced at her clock on the nightstand: 3:00 a.m. Maybe this was their breaking point. Maybe what had changed between her and Scott couldn't be repaired. Maybe she was overreacting. He *was* drunk. But Sam *wasn't*.

Shelby finally closed her eyes and drifted off to sleep, waking a few hours later to Tyler's cry. She looked over at the empty bed beside her, not knowing where Scott had slept last night. Still angry and exhausted, she told herself she didn't care. She sat on the side of her bed and stared at her hand, then removed her wedding rings and set them on the nightstand. For a second, she thought maybe it was an overreaction, but something compelled her to take them off.

After an unusually calm and cooperative morning with Rhylie and Tyler, she dropped them off at her parents, telling her mother she had to run into the floral shop for a few hours. But what she needed was time alone. Time to think about the kids' future, not just the future of her already strained marriage.

Having a two-and-a-half-year-old and a one-year-old while running her own business and trying to keep her marriage alive was becoming more than she could handle. Aunt B's Bouquets was her refuge, an escape from the craziness of her home life. Henry was opening the florist shop, so there was no need to rush to work.

She drove home and pulled into the driveway. After turning the car off, she released a heavy sigh and rested her hands and forehead on the steering wheel. Maybe Sam did her a favor. She wasn't happy and had a feeling Scott wasn't either. Her phone pinged—another voicemail from Scott. "Shel, I'm sorry. Please call me." She scoffed, threw her phone on the passenger seat, and looked out the window. It was a beautiful summer day in Boston, so she convinced herself that the two-block walk to the park would help her think more clearly.

She walked down the sidewalk and wondered what the hell Sam was doing kissing Scott. It seemed Sam didn't even like him, let alone be attracted to him. Shelby shook her head in disbelief.

She stood in front of City Wine and Spirits, waiting for the crossing signal to change. The quaint little park across the street that overlooked the river would be her calm before the storm of confronting Scott. The blinking neon sign caught her attention, and she contemplated drowning herself in a large bottle of wine. Out of the corner of her eye, she spotted a license on the sidewalk. She glanced around and picked it up. "Hmm, New Jersey, an out-of-towner." Her breath caught and her heart raced as she stared at the woman in the photo—a picture of herself. A deep crease formed between her brows as she scanned the license, *DOB: 06/30/1982.* "Holy shit, that's my birth date," she whispered, then read the name and address: *Michelle Ann Grant, Short Hills, NJ.*

Shelby's heart pounded in her chest, wondering if someone had stolen her identity. She ran down the sidewalk and stopped at the entrance of a large parking lot, searching for the woman with long, light brown hair—*her* hair. The woman, who also shared her birth date, height, and eye color.

Her mind reeled as she looked across the street at the park. The rumble of a motor startled her when a red convertible made its way out of the parking lot several feet in front of her.

"Michelle! Michelle!" Shelby yelled, running toward the convertible, waving the license in the air, unaware she was off the sidewalk and now in the road.

The driver turned, lowered her sunglasses, and looked in Shelby's direction while the car continued to roll into the roadway.

Shelby stood frozen as she locked eyes with her mirror image. Her face turned from disbelief to horror as the tires of a pickup truck screeched toward the red convertible. She watched Michelle's body jolt from the truck's impact, sending the convertible into a tailspin toward her and knocking her to the pavement. The smell of gasoline and burnt rubber filled her nostrils as she tried to open her eyes until the sounds and sunlight disappeared under a blanket of darkness.

CHAPTER 40

Short Hills
Tuesday Evening, July 3, 2012

Liam called to ask about Chloe and Ben, hoping to find out where Michelle had gone without his mother-in-law realizing he had no idea where his wife was. Ann eventually remarked that Boston was beautiful and hoped Michelle would have a delightful time visiting Lucy.

At least now he knew where she was. He would give her the space she needed, but eventually, he would go to her, apologize, and beg for her forgiveness.

When his phone vibrated, he grabbed it from his pocket, hoping to hear Michelle's voice.

"Hello ... Yes, this is Liam Grant ... Hello, Sergeant Phillips." His first thought was that a phone call from a state trooper rarely brought good news. "Yes, Michelle Grant is my wife." His heart pounded in his chest. "Yes, she is in Boston, visiting a friend. Is she okay? ... Boston Medical Center ICU," his voice wavered. "I will get there as soon as possible. Thank you."

Liam ended the call, ran his hand through his hair, and sat on their bed. He looked over at Michelle's wedding rings on the nightstand. Nausea washed over him. *This was all his fault.* He closed his eyes. "Please, God, let her be okay."

CHAPTER 41

New Jersey
August 6, 2012

"How are you feeling today, honey?" a gentle voice asked. "You'll be groggy for a few days with the pain medication, but you're out of the woods. You had quite a journey from Massachusetts to New Jersey," the nurse said. "You're a very loved young lady."

Her heavy eyelids only allowed her to see the room through tiny slits. She wanted to speak but couldn't open her mouth. She had no sense of time and struggled to keep her eyes open long enough to assess her surroundings. Sleep always won, sending her into a land of dreams and confusion.

Bound by the heaviness of her body, she drifted in and out of a semi-conscious state over the next few days. The various scents of men's cologne and perfume became familiar aromas. She welcomed the presence and warm touch of the blurry figures and muffled voices that would appear at her bedside.

At times, she felt as if her limbs were being pulled in every direction, so she concentrated on the humming of a soft melody that accompanied the torturous movements. Sometimes, the movements stopped abruptly; other times, they ended with a warm cloth across her face and gentle brush strokes through her hair.

Early one morning, the sun woke her. She blinked several times until she was able to keep her eyes open long enough to scan the room. The bed was inclined, and instead of blurry ceiling tiles, she saw the walls and windows and her reflection on the black TV screen next to her bed, but didn't recognize the stranger looking back at her. She lifted her hand to her face, sliding a finger across a small bandage, and recoiled at the tenderness of her cheek. Then she scowled at the tomb that bound her right leg and winced when she tried to move.

A nurse entered her room and smiled. "Well, good morning. I thought you might like a change of scenery. Are you comfortable sitting up a little?"

She nodded her head and whispered, "Yes."

"By the way, I'm Jade, one of your nurses. Dr. Hall will be in this morning. He'll be pleased to see you awake."

Her throat was sore and dry, but she managed to whisper again, "How ... long?"

"How long have you been in the hospital?" Jade asked.

She nodded.

"A little over a week here in New Jersey. You were transferred from Boston."

A straw was brought to her lips, and she took a sip, relishing the cool stream of water that flowed down the desert in her throat. "Where?" she said, but paused, having to clear her throat. "Am I?"

"You're at the MTC Hospital in New Jersey, honey."

She blinked several times as New Jersey repeated in her mind.

A tall, thin man with gray hair and a dark complexion appeared at the end of her bed and removed the stethoscope from around his neck. "Michelle, it's nice to see you awake and alert. How are you feeling this morning?" Dr. Hall asked.

She pinched her brows, *Michelle,* repeating it in her head, then answered. "Sore."

Dr. Hall approached the side of her bed and placed the stethoscope on her chest. After a few minutes, he placed his hand on her arm. "Your heart and lungs sound good, but you encountered some head trauma in the accident."

She cleared her throat again and whispered, "My name is Michelle?"

"Yes, Michelle Grant. It's not unusual to have some confusion with the level of pain medications you were given for your injuries."

"Accident?" she mumbled.

"According to your medical records from the Boston Medical Center, you were involved in a motor vehicle accident. Your husband had you transferred from Massachusetts to New Jersey. Do you remember any of that?"

"No, I ... I ... don't," she whined.

"All your scans have come back normal, but you may be experiencing temporary amnesia."

Her mind seemed incapable of forming rational thoughts as her eyes darted between the nurse and the doctor. The monitor beeped as her pulse rate flashed in bright red numbers.

Dr. Hall placed his hand on Michelle's arm again. "I realize this can be overwhelming. We have an excellent staff of psychotherapists if you would like to talk with one of them."

"How long?" she asked.

Dr. Hall tilted his head. "How long?"

"The amnesia," she whispered.

"I'm sorry; it's hard to say. It affects everyone differently."

Michelle glanced at Jade, who gave her a reassuring smile.

"I will check back with you tomorrow morning. Physically, you are healing as expected. In the meantime, let the nurses know if you want to talk with one of our psychotherapists." He nodded, then disappeared as quickly as he had appeared.

A tear rolled down her cheek as fear and anxiety overwhelmed her. The heaviness of her aching body paled in comparison to the weight of the unknown.

CHAPTER 42

Boston
August 2012

Scott walked into the police station with irritation written on his face. This time, he would make them listen. "Can I speak to Sergeant Greene?"

The officer behind the front desk stood stone-faced, his hand wrapped around his holster. "Your name."

"Scott O'Donnell. He's working on my wife's case."

Sergeant Greene walked down the hallway and spotted Scott at the front desk. "Mr. O'Donnell, what brings you in today?"

Scott glared at the sergeant. *What brings me in today? Are you fucking kidding me?* Then he took a deep breath. "Do you have any leads on my wife yet?"

"So, you haven't heard from her?"

"If I had, do you think I would be here? She's been missing for over a month now."

"Well, my guess is she's still pretty pissed."

Scott knew what he was doing; he wanted him to snap. The sergeant tried this tactic when the police came to the house after he had filed a missing person report. "She would not leave her two young children, no matter how pissed she was at me."

"Did you consider maybe she doesn't *want* to be found?"

Scott closed his eyes, took another deep breath, and exhaled.

The sergeant raised his eyebrow. "Or *can't* be found?"

Scott's eyes shot open. "I'm not stupid. I know the husband is always the first person in question."

"Do you have something you'd like to share?"

Scott clenched his jaw. "Dammit, if you won't do your job, then I will."

He stormed out of the police station and sat in his car for a moment, gripping the steering wheel until his knuckles were white. Once the anger passed, he drove to work, hoping it would distract him.

He sat at his desk and turned on his iMac. He stared at the blinking cursor on the computer screen as it waited for his keystrokes. Finally, he typed in, *how much does a private investigator cost?* "Holy shit, $150-$200 an hour?" He sat back in the chair and ran his hands through his hair. "Then there's a retainer?" He shook his head. "How the hell will I be able to do this?"

CHAPTER 43

New Jersey
August 2012

Dr. Hall left Michelle's room, but she could hear him talking with someone in the doorway.

"She doesn't appear to know who she is. In most cases, it is temporary amnesia. She may not recognize you. Physically though, I'm happy with her progress. I will keep you updated."

A woman's voice replied, "Thank you so much, doctor."

Michelle heard a knock on her door, then a radiant, middle-aged woman walked in and gave her an endearing smile. The woman's strawberry-blonde hair sat neatly on her shoulders and framed her delicate, attractive features. A few discrete wrinkles showed in the outer corners of her kind eyes.

"It's wonderful to see you, darling," she said in a maternal tone.

Michelle stared at her. She remembered that fragrance.

"Good morning, Mrs. Carrington."

"Good morning, Jade."

"I'm sorry, but who are you?" Michelle asked.

Ann glanced at Jade, then tilted her head with a tearful smile. "I'm your mother, Ann Carrington."

Michelle's cheeks grew warm. Not knowing her own mother made her head spin.

"It's okay, darling. We are all here for you. We will help you through this; help you remember," Ann said, placing her hand on Michelle's arm.

Michelle looked down. Her mother's touch was sincere, but she felt no comfort in it. Ann was still a stranger.

Ann pulled her hand away and looked at her daughter with a loving smile. "Would you like to talk?"

Michelle took a deep breath. "Okay."

Jade left the room to give them privacy, and when she returned a few hours later, Michelle was asleep, but the trail of tears that traced the contours of her face told Jade they were not happy tears. She finished taking Michelle's vitals and checked her IV.

Michelle turned her head, relieved to see Jade's familiar face.

"Did you have a nice visit with your mother?"

She returned her gaze to the window. "I don't remember her or anyone she was talking about."

"Well, your husband called the nurses' desk. He's coming tomorrow. Maybe that will trigger some memories, honey."

Worry covered Michelle's face. *The thought of her husband, another stranger, coming to visit terrified her. She couldn't remember her mother. Why did Jade think she would remember her husband? She had vague memories of a dark-haired figure standing at her bedside, but the pain medication made her sleepy and confused most of the time, so she wondered if he was really there or if she was dreaming.*

Jade handed her a cup of water and her medication, then patted her arm. "Your vitals have been stable, and your knee is healing nicely. If you continue on this path, you should be able to go home soon."

"But I still don't remember who I am." Michelle grasped the neck of her hospital gown, feeling vulnerable and unsure of everything.

"Jade, I feel so lost and broken. What do I say to the man—I mean, my husband—when he comes tomorrow?" Her eyes were wide with fear. "What will happen if I have to go home with him? Where else would I go?"

"Oh, honey, it will be alright." Jade tilted her head. "I can stay in the room when your husband comes tomorrow."

Michelle nodded. "Yes, thank you."

"Okay, my job here is done for today." Jade winked. "I'll see you in the morning."

"Bye, Jade, and thank you." Michelle watched her walk out of her room, relieved that she would not have to face her husband alone, but was still consumed with worry until the pain medications took over and lulled her to sleep once again.

Michelle awoke at sunrise to a warm glow filling her room. She felt calm and rested until remembering that her husband would visit in a few hours, also realizing she didn't even know what he looked like.

Jade breezed into her room, chipper as always. "Well, good morning. You look rested on this beautiful sunny day."

Michelle ran her fingers through her hair to smooth away her bedhead and looked down at her hospital gown. "I must look a mess." She didn't think about how she looked until now.

"Listen, I'll help you to the shower. I'll grab you a new hospital gown. Oh, and I have a cardigan you can wear. My other two patients are getting scans, so we'll do your hair, too. Okay?"

Jade helped her up from the hospital bed.

"Thank you, Jade. What would I do without you?"

After showering, she felt human again. At least she wouldn't repulse her husband.

She finished her breakfast and rested her head back on her pillow. *Just breathe,* she repeated in her head.

Jade breezed in again.

"Jade, do you know what my husband looks like?"

A knock interrupted Jade's answer. The scent of men's cologne entered the room first. It was familiar and alluring. As he walked into the room, his piercing blue eyes captivated her. *Is this what love at first sight feels like?* she wondered. But she's supposed to know him. She looked down and felt her cheeks burn.

"Michelle, hi, it's Liam," he said, standing at the foot of her bed. "How are you today? It's okay if you don't recognize me. I know you've been through a lot."

She looked up, and her heart skipped a beat. He looked as if he had just walked off the cover of GQ, nearly six feet tall and beyond handsome.

Her body trembled, then she felt Jade's hand on her shoulder.

"Hello, Mr. Grant. I'm Jade, one of Michelle's nurses. You've probably visited during my off shifts. It's nice to meet you."

Liam offered an appreciative smile. "Hello, Jade. Thank you for taking such excellent care of my wife."

Michelle found it hard to say anything, not recognizing the attractive man claiming to be her husband. His charisma made her feel uncomfortable and insecure.

"Would you like to talk?" he asked.

She glanced down again to avoid his dreamy blue eyes. "Sure."

Jade squeezed her shoulder, then turned to the computer.

Michelle watched Liam's eyes bounce between her and Jade, sensing he wanted to talk alone, but she needed Jade to safeguard her, no matter how handsome or polite he was. "I'm sorry, I don't recognize you."

"It's okay. Dr. Hall said it might take some time to regain your memory. We'll take it slow."

She released a nervous sigh and tucked her hair behind her ear. "Thank you."

"I spoke to your mother. She told me you had a nice visit."

"She was very kind and lovely, but I didn't recognize her either."

"I'm sure she understood. Is it okay if I come back later with some pictures? Maybe that will help?"

She glanced at Jade. "Um, I guess."

He gave her a polite smile. "Get some rest. We'll talk later."

After he left her room, Michelle let out a loud sigh and fell back onto her pillow. "Thank you for staying with me. That was so hard."

Jade looked at her and raised her eyebrows. "Well, at least he's not hideous."

Michelle laughed, then started to cry.

"Oh, honey." Jade sat on the side of the bed and placed her hand on Michelle's arm. "You'll get through this. You survived a terrible car accident, for goodness' sake. You are stronger than you think."

Michelle continued to cry. "What if I never remember him or my life before the accident?"

"Give it time, sweetie." Jade stood up from the bed. "I need to check on my other patients. If I'm able to, do you want me to be here when he comes back later?"

"No. I need to try this alone." She wiped the tears from her cheeks. "You tell me every day I'm strong, so now I need to be."

"Never stop believing that, honey. You get some rest."

Michelle stared at the ceiling. Remembered his cologne, piercing blue eyes, and how her stomach fluttered and heart raced when their eyes met. She knew nothing about him, and he knew everything about her.

A knock on the door woke her from her nap. She turned her head to see Liam standing at the foot of her bed again.

"Sorry to wake you. How are you feeling?"

"Okay, thanks." Heat flooded her cheeks as she sat up and tried to fix her disheveled hair.

Liam tilted his head and smiled. "You've always been beautiful."

Her eyes shifted as she fidgeted with the blanket. *Would her cheeks ever stop burning in his presence?* She questioned whether he was just being kind or if being a charmer was who he was.

"I thought these might help jog your memory." He handed her a small pile of pictures and pointed to the end of her hospital bed. "Do you mind if I sit?"

"Sure." Then she slowly flipped through the pictures, studying them intently.

"That one is of our wedding, and that one was of our trip to the Bahamas for a short honeymoon."

She looked at the pictures, hoping to recognize something; anything. Seeing herself in a little red bikini beside this stranger, her husband, made her uncomfortable. She stared at her smiling face, knowing it was her but remembering nothing of the trip.

"I'm so sorry," she said, trying not to cry.

Liam gathered the pile of pictures and put them back in his pocket. "It's okay. We'll try another time. I know it will come back to you."

He noticed a few pictures he had set on the bed and picked them up.

"Wait, what are those pictures of?" She was curious and didn't want him to keep anything from her.

"Why don't we wait for those? I'll show you another time, okay?"

"Can I please see them now? Maybe I'll recognize something."

"I'm not sure that's a good idea."

A flash of suspicion crossed her face. "Why?" She wondered if he was an honest man. He appeared to be a loving husband, but did he manipulate people with his charm and looks?

His face became solemn. "Okay."

"These are our children, Chloe and Ben, seven-year-old twins.

They really miss you. They've been asking every day to visit you, but I told them you needed your rest. It's been a long month and a half without you home."

Michelle stared at the pictures as their blue eyes stared back at her. They looked happy and cared for. She looked up at Liam as tears filled her eyes. She placed her hand over her mouth and studied the pictures again. These two beautiful souls were her children, and she felt nothing.

Liam placed his hand on her leg, causing her to flinch as tears spilled down her cheeks.

He pulled his hand back. "I'm sorry. I was afraid you wouldn't be ready. That's why I was reluctant to show you."

"I have children? This is too much. Please leave. I can't do this," she cried.

Liam's eyes widened, then his head lowered. "I'm sorry. I'll go."

She buried her face in her hands and wept. His disappointment in her was overwhelming. How could she not remember her own children? Carrying them, giving birth to them, the first seven years of their lives?

Her heart pounded in her chest, feeling no connection with Liam or anyone. Soon she would be released to her family—to strangers. Could she trust them to help her find a lifetime of lost memories?

CHAPTER 44

Short Hills

"Daddy! Dad!" Chloe and Ben yelled.

"Hi, guys," he said, pulling them close.

"How's Mommy? When can we go see her?" Chloe asked. "I miss her so much."

Ben's eyes brightened. "Yeah, Dad, can we see Mom?"

Liam didn't have the heart to tell them that their mother couldn't remember them and may not even want to see them. He knew not being able to visit their mother was torture because she was their world.

"Well, Mommy is still resting. She's getting stronger every day and should be able to come home soon." He glanced at Martha with a sad expression.

Martha read his face. "Come along now, loves, let's get ready for bed; we have a busy day of school shopping tomorrow."

"Aw," they whined.

"I'll be right up to tuck you in. Now listen to Martha."

Ben had been sleeping in Chloe's room since they returned home from their vacation with their grandparents and learned of their mother's accident. Chloe didn't mind. After all, they had spent the first nine months of their lives in close quarters.

Liam tucked the covers around them and gave them each a kiss.

"Dad?" Chloe asked.

"Yes."

"Me and Ben made Mommy get-well cards today. Can you bring them to her tomorrow?"

"Sure, sweetie. She'll really like that. Good night, I love you."

He switched off the light and closed the door. He had to lie to them as he wouldn't be visiting their mother tomorrow. His jaw tightened, remembering his visit with Michelle. He walked downstairs and sat at the kitchen table.

Martha glanced at him. "Liam, can I get you anything? A glass of wine or beer, perhaps?"

"No, thank you." He placed his head in his hand and sighed. "I'm not sure what to do. She doesn't remember me, or the kids. She's supposed to come home soon to a place she doesn't know, a family she doesn't remember. It will crush the kids when she doesn't recognize them."

"Liam, we will get through this." Martha placed her hand on his shoulder. "I've known Michelle her entire life. I remember the day the Carringtons brought her home. She was so tiny, but so strong. She will remember. I know it. I can feel it."

Michelle sat in the chair next to her hospital bed, staring out the window, holding the pictures of her children. She desperately tried to pull memories of them from the archives of her mind. Her attention was drawn away from the window as a new face appeared in her doorway. The woman's short stature was heightened by a salt and pepper bun that sat neatly on top of her head, and her soft features were as maternal as her demeanor.

"Michelle. Hello. I'm Martha Kirkwood. I'm Chloe and Ben's nanny."

Her eyes swept over Martha, then she smiled. "Hello."

"Do you mind if we visit for a bit?"

"Sure, that would be nice."

Martha pulled a chair beside her and settled in as if she would stay awhile.

"Ann—I mean—my mother told me you have been with our family my entire life."

"Yes, that's right. I was your nanny. Then, when you were expecting the twins, your parents insisted I stay with you." Martha glanced at the pictures Michelle held in her lap. "Chloe and Ben have been the light of our lives. They miss you dearly. I want you to know I am here for you and will help you however I can."

"Thank you." She looked at the pictures. "I've been trying to remember anything from my past, but it seems those memories want to stay hidden."

Michelle became more at ease with Martha's caring and nurturing manner. She listened, hoping any little detail would trigger a memory. She never questioned that Martha could have told her any-thing, and she wouldn't have known whether it was the truth or a lie.

"Thank you, dear, for letting me visit with you. We all love you and are so grateful to have you come home to us."

"I appreciate your support, but honestly, I'm terrified of leaving the hospital."

Martha patted Michelle's arm. "I truly believe that once you are back home with your family, everything will come back to you."

The week flew by as she anticipated her release into a world of unknowns.

"Jade, Dr. Hall is going to release me Friday."

"Yes, I heard." Jade glanced at the stand next to Michelle's bed. "Are those the cards from the twins?"

"Yes, Liam dropped them off at the nurses' station. I guess he didn't want to talk or couldn't stay." She wasn't sure who she was more upset with, Liam or herself, after the way things ended on his last visit. "The cards are so sweet, Jade. I can't disappoint them."

"You won't. When you see those little faces, your heart will melt, and you'll grab those babies into your arms, and deep down inside, you'll feel that connection."

Michelle released a heavy sigh. "For their sake, I hope I do."

CHAPTER 45

Michelle sat on the side of her hospital bed, staring at her knee brace. The brace had become a part of her identity. She only had it off during physical therapy, the doctor's evaluation, or a much welcomed shower.

She watched Jade type away at the computer while completing her discharge papers. Leaving the safety of her hospital room filled her with anxiety. Jade had become a friend in a world full of strangers.

"Remember, you are strong. You can handle this." Jade handed Michelle a small, folded piece of paper. "Here is my cell number. You can call me anytime. I mean it anytime."

Michelle's eyes filled with tears. "You literally are my only friend. Thank you so much for all you did for me. This is the only home I've known."

Jade hugged her tight. "Oh, honey, I will miss you. You were my daily dose of sunshine."

She could smell Liam's cologne and knew he was in her doorway. He knocked, then entered, carrying a designer bag on his shoulder and a bouquet of roses in his hand.

"Hi, Chelle. How are you feeling today?"

She looked at Liam and tilted her head. *Chelle*—she knew that name.

He handed her the flowers and looked at her curiously. "Is something wrong?"

"You called me Chelle."

"I'm sorry. I won't call you that if it bothers you."

"No, it's okay." She smiled. "It just sounded familiar."

He smiled back, pleased that he had said something familiar to her that eased her anxiety.

Jade turned around from her computer with a handful of papers. "Michelle will still need to attend physical therapy. They will contact you to set up her next session." Jade handed her the pile of papers and a pen. "Michelle, I need your signature. Then you are free to go."

"Um, I'm not sure how to sign my name. I mean, I know how to write," she blushed.

"Honey, it's fine. Just sign Michelle Grant. It's all good."

She tried to hold the pen steady as her hand trembled.

"Okay, if there are any issues, call the number on the discharge papers. Dr. Hall's office will call to schedule a follow-up appointment with you. Your wheelchair should be here shortly." Jade placed her hand on Michelle's shoulder and squeezed it. "Take care, honey."

Liam set the designer bag on the hospital bed. "I brought you some of your clothes."

"Thank you. But Jade gave me these to wear home."

He gave her the once-over and a polite smile. "That was nice of her."

"But thank you for bringing them," she said as guilt stirred inside her for not accepting his kind gesture. Then she changed the subject. "Will the twins be home?"

"No, I'm going to pick them up after school. I thought you might want a few hours to yourself."

A hospital aide knocked on the door and entered with a wheel-chair. "Ready to spring this joint?"

In her head, she said no, but she faked a smile and sat herself in the wheelchair.

"I'll meet you outside with the car," Liam said and grabbed the designer bag from the bed.

The hospital aide wheeled her to the sidewalk. She scanned the parking lot but was unsure of what he was driving. It was just another thing she didn't know about her husband. She closed her eyes and breathed in the fresh air.

A black Escalade pulled in front of them. "Looks like you're going home in style," the aide remarked.

Liam walked around the front of the Escalade and opened the passenger door and helped her up from the wheelchair. He lifted her in his arms and slid her onto the black leather seat. His touch was firm but gentle, and she savored the scent of his cologne up close.

"Martha is at the house and will help you settle in the first-floor guest room."

She sniffed the bouquet. "Thank you for the flowers. They're beautiful."

"You're welcome. Chloe and Ben helped me make the bouquet for you from our rose garden. They are very excited to see you."

She knew his small talk was to help ease her anxiety. But with each mile that drew them closer to home, the anxiety grew, and her mind raced. *What did home look like? Feel like?*

"Martha visited me. She was so kind. I wish I could say I remember her, but I don't."

"It's okay. Give it time."

"I'm sorry. I've only thought about how this is affecting me. I didn't even consider how it was affecting others." She looked down, her face burning with shame.

Liam placed his hand on her knee. "We're all here for you. We'll help you get through this."

His touch made her stomach flutter, and she gave him a slight smile, then stared out the passenger window.

He returned his hand to the steering wheel and glanced at her. "We're almost home."

Her eyes followed an impressive stone wall that looked as though it was a mile long.

They turned onto the brick-layered driveway, hugged by manicured walls of dark green shrubs. The house was like a chateau set back among a towering landscape of trees. It felt shielded from the outside world—private and safe. The stone facade and large oak door were a warm and inviting entrance to their home. It appeared they were well-off. Of course, her first inclination was the designer bag Liam brought to the hospital and the drive home in the Cadillac Escalade. But none of that mattered. Reclaiming her memory was her only desire.

Liam pulled into the three-car garage. "Welcome home," he said, giving her a warm smile. He went around to the passenger side, took her in his arms again, and gently lowered her out of the Escalade.

She winced at the stiffness of her body and wondered if she would ever be free of the pain.

He handed her the quad cane, then took her other arm. "You're doing great. Just take it slow."

Martha stood in the doorway. "Hello dear, wonderful to see you."

She kept her eyes on the ground and shuffled toward the door, entering a mudroom where little sweatshirts and hats hung in custom-built cubbies.

As they made their way to the kitchen, the aroma of freshly baked cookies became stronger.

Liam helped her to a chair at a quaint round table, where a large plate of chocolate chip cookies sat in the center.

"Would you like a glass of water?" he asked.

"Sure. Thank you." She looked around at the sleek white cabinets, granite countertops, and an island half the size of her hospital room.

"Martha can make you something to eat if you like," he offered, handing her the glass of water.

"Thank you. The water is fine for now." She took a sip and continued to take in the beauty of her home. "How long have you—I mean we—lived here?"

"We built this house last year. You designed nearly every inch. Does anything feel familiar to you?"

"No, I'm sorry." She tucked her hair behind her ear and sighed. *Yet another thing she didn't know about herself.* "If it's okay, I'd like to lie down before the children come home from school."

"Yes, of course," he said, helping her up from the chair and walking her down the hallway. "I hope this is okay for now. I told the kids that you will need to stay in the guest room downstairs until your knee heals."

"And what did you tell them about my amnesia?"

"I told them that the accident caused you to forget who you are, but that you love them very much. I heard them in Chloe's room last night talking about how they will help you remember all of us."

"I will do everything I can to not hurt or disappoint them. I hope you know that."

"I do. They're very happy to have you home. We all are." He helped her to the bed and placed her water on the nightstand. "Sleep well." He smiled and shut the bedroom door behind him.

She looked around. Staying in the guest room was appropriate, as she felt like a guest in her own home. It would be her new safe haven. Liam would eventually expect her to join him in their bedroom, but as charming and handsome as he was, the thought of sharing a bed with him was too much to think about, at least for now.

CHAPTER 46

Two hours had passed, and Michelle awoke and stared at the ceiling. The aroma of the lavender sheets and plush comforter was a stark contrast to the sterile, bleached hospital linens that she had become accustomed to.

A knock on the guest room door pulled her from her daydream.

A sweet maternal voice called out. "Michelle?"

"Yes, come in."

Martha peeked around the door. "I hope I didn't wake you."

"Oh no, I was just lying here thinking about the children," Michelle said, struggling to sit up.

"Let me help you, dear."

"Thank you. Can you tell me more about them?"

Martha sat on the bed and rested her hands on her lap.

"Chloe is a dear, very talkative and loving. Ben is quiet and thoughtful, and though he won't admit it, he adores his sister. They are quite close, and competitive. Even though they quarrel, they don't like to be without each other, so they are currently sharing Chloe's room, which has helped them with your absence."

"I'm glad they have each other."

"They are very smart. Sometimes too smart for their own good." Martha raised her eyebrows. "I'm sure they were distracted at school knowing you were coming home today. They will most likely talk Liam's ear off the entire ride home. He has been so patient with them."

"He seems like a good man and father. Speaking of fathers, when my mother visited, she came alone. I haven't seen or met my father. Do you know if he ever came to the hospital?"

"I know he visited you after you were transferred back home to New Jersey. It was very hard for him to see you unconscious with all your injuries. I believe they are coming here to visit you soon. Your mother is a realtor, and your father is a highly respected corporate lawyer, so his job takes him all around the world."

"Yes, Ann—I mean—my mother told me a little bit about that."

Martha put her hand on Michelle's arm and squeezed it. Can I make you something to eat now?

"Yes, thank you."

Michelle grabbed her cane and eased herself off the bed. She was grateful to have a female presence in the house. Short of Jade moving in—an impractical request she knew—Martha was the next best person, an ally. The fact that Martha had known her all her life gave her hope that she would remember who she was.

She closed her eyes as the warm broth soothed her throat. "Thank you, Martha. This is delicious. I guess I got used to the hospital cuisine."

Martha chuckled and glanced at the wall clock. Liam and the children will be here soon.

Michelle felt a knot in the pit of her stomach. She knew that meeting Chloe and Ben was inevitable. She didn't want to disappoint them, and the scrutiny of Martha and Liam hung heavily on her.

"Do I look like the mother they know?" she asked, straightening her shirt and running her fingers through her hair.

"You look like the Michelle I've always known. You may have a few bandages on that beautiful face, but they will know you as I do. Now, don't fret. You won't disappoint them."

From the kitchen, they heard the car doors slam, and the twins' high-pitched chatter became louder as they raced to the mudroom door.

Michelle heard Liam tell them to slow down. She looked at Martha, took a deep breath, and exhaled with her eyes closed. The door flew open, hitting the wall with a thud, making her jump and open her eyes.

"Mommy! Mom!" Chloe and Ben yelled simultaneously.

They raced to her and wrapped their outstretched arms around her neck, nearly knocking her out of her chair. She gained her balance and embraced them, breathing them in.

"Hey, now, careful, guys. Mom is still sore." He tilted his head and mouthed, sorry to her.

She smiled back at him. "I'm alright."

"Did you get our get-well cards?" Chloe asked.

Ben looked her over. "Do you have any really cool scars?"

"Are you okay, Mommy? Do you remember our house? Do you remember Bear?" Chloe asked excitedly.

Martha stepped in. "Okay, okay, let your mother breathe. How about one question at a time?"

They stepped back, stared at her, examined her face, then looked down at her knee brace.

Michelle noticed their resemblance, sharing her features, but had Liam's blue eyes. Both had light brown hair, but Chloe stood a few inches taller than her brother.

"Did you break your knee, Mommy? Does it hurt?" Chloe asked.

"Yes, I broke it in the accident. It still hurts a little." She placed her hand on the quad cane handle. "So, I use Fred here."

Ben wrinkled his nose. "Fred?"

"Yes, he's my walking buddy and helps me get around."

Ben tilted his head. "Why'd you name it Fred?"

"Since it's been by my side for quite a while, I decided to give it a name." She chuckled, feeling her cheeks warm.

Ben shrugged his shoulders and gave a little wave. "Hi, Fred."

Michelle giggled, then looked at Chloe. "You asked me if I remembered Bear. I guess not. Who's Bear?"

"Bear is our dog. He's a Bernice Mountain dog. Right, Dad?"

"Close. Bernese," he said, giving her a wink.

"He's five years old. He's a rescue. We saved him from the shelter," Chloe said, very proud of her detailed explanation. "He's getting a haircut right now. Dad, are you picking Bear up today?"

"Bear will be ready tomorrow. Thank you for reminding me." Liam placed his hands on her shoulders. "Chloe is our master scheduler. She keeps us organized and on our toes."

She looked up at her father, delighted with the recognition.

"Well, I'm excited to meet—I mean, see Bear again."

"Do you two have homework?" Liam asked.

Chloe smiled. "No, I finished it all at school."

"I have math." Ben scowled. "It's only the third day of school, and we have homework already."

"Alright, head upstairs and finish it."

"Aw, can't I work on it at the kitchen table, Dad?"

"No. You won't be able to concentrate. Now go upstairs. I want to talk with your mom."

"But Chloe gets to stay. That's not fair." Ben stomped.

"Ben, how about when you finish your homework, you bring it downstairs and show me? Let's see if I remember how to do the math, okay?" She smiled, hoping to connect with her son.

Ben stared at the floor.

"Ben. What do you say? That sounds like a good idea, right?"

"Yeah, I guess."

"Okay, go on now."

Michelle placed her hand on Ben's arm. "Thank you, Ben."

"Chloe, could you please help Martha?" Liam asked.

"Dad, can I..." Chloe paused when her father gave her a pleading glance. "Yes, I will."

Liam ran his hand down Chloe's head. "Thank you, honey."

Before Chloe walked away, Michelle took her hand. "I'll be right here. I'm not going anywhere."

Chloe hugged her and whispered in her ear. "I missed you so much, Mommy. I'm so happy you're home." She kissed her mother's cheek and skipped across the kitchen to where Martha stood waiting for her.

Michelle placed her elbow on the table, held her fingers over her lips, and looked at Liam. "I am trying so hard to remember, Liam." She glanced across the room, her eyes scaling the stone fireplace chimney to the ceiling, trying to hold back tears.

"Why don't we sit where it's more comfortable?" Liam walked her to the family room and helped her to the plush armchair facing a wall of windows. "Here, you can put your leg on the ottoman."

The windows showcased a garden of roses in every color. A manicured landscape surrounded a large brick patio that had taken many hands and many hours to lay. Various sizes of birds fluttered around a fountain in the backyard.

"It's beautiful."

"You would often sit here and stare out at the garden." He knew it was Brad who she often thought about, but that conversation was for another day. "Are you comfortable? Do you need a pillow?"

"No, I'm fine, thank you."

They continued to talk, trying to resurrect any memories of their life together. He made her laugh with stories of the children or Bear's mischief.

Ben hopped down the stairs and stood in front of them, holding out his math homework.

"Well, let's see how you did, sir."

Ben studied her face as she scanned the paper.

"Nice work, Ben," she said, giving him an approving smile.

"Thanks, Mom."

It warmed her heart to be called mom, even if she didn't feel like his mother.

"Ben, can you tell your mother what we do on Friday nights?"

"Oh yeah! Fridays are family movie nights. We make a big bowl of popcorn and take turns picking a movie. Do you want to pick the movie for tonight, Mom?"

"How about you surprise me?"

"Okay!" Ben ran to Chloe to inform her he was in charge of picking the night's feature. If he could one-up Chloe in anything, he took full advantage of the opportunity.

Her eyes filled with hope. "I think it's going okay so far."

Liam smiled and laid his hand on hers. "I think so, too."

His eyes seemed to penetrate her soul, forcing her to look away and blush. She hesitated to fall for a man she barely knew, even if he *was* her husband.

Liam started the movie and turned the lights off as the warm glow of the fire bounced shadows around the room.

Chloe and Ben sat under a large sherpa blanket on the plush sectional, with Michelle sandwiched between them. Her arms rested on their shoulders and shook as they laughed out loud.

Her own laughter surprised her and made her blush when she noticed Liam was watching the three of them.

An hour later, Chloe and Ben were asleep as the movie's last fifteen minutes played out.

Liam rubbed their legs. "Come on, sleepyheads, let's go to bed."

Michelle kissed them each on the head. "Good night."

"I'll be back down in a few minutes if you don't mind waiting?" he asked.

"Sure."

She eased herself off the couch, holding her cane in one hand and the cups and popcorn bowl in the other, and hobbled to the kitchen. She started washing the dishes when Liam walked over to her.

"I can take care of those. You sit and relax."

"I've been sitting all day. I don't mind. I like washing the dishes. It relaxes me."

He gave her a puzzled glance. "You've always hated doing dishes."

Her face turned bright red. "Oh, I'm sorry. I only wanted to help."

Liam placed his hand on her arm. "No. I'm sorry. Thank you for cleaning up after the kids. This is your home. I want you to be comfortable doing what feels natural. And I don't think Martha will have any issues with you washing dishes." He winked.

The sincerity in his blue eyes was seductive, making her heart race. She grabbed the towel and dried her hands. She hated becoming flustered so easily around him. "Well, I think movie night was a success. It was nice. Um, good night, Liam."

"Good night, Chelle."

She hobbled down the hallway to the guest room, feeling his eyes follow her. She shut the door to her safe haven, then settled onto the guest bed, grateful for the love and understanding she received. *Why was she so terrified? Liam was patient, kind, always a gentleman, and those damn dreamy blue eyes. The twins were as amazing as Martha and Liam had described. If this was her life, what was there to be afraid of?* She closed her eyes and replayed the night in her head. It was almost too good to be true.

Michelle awoke the next morning, unsure if what she saw was a dream or reality. It was her first night of uninterrupted sleep in weeks. It felt like paradise.

She sat up and grabbed the photo albums Martha had left on the nightstand for her. The pictures portrayed a happy, loving family— her family. She heard whispering on the other side of her door, then a knock. "Come in."

"Good morning," Martha said as she opened the door for Chloe, who was concentrating on balancing the tray she was carrying, her tongue peeking through her closed lips.

"Surprise, Mommy!" Chloe's eyes were wide with excitement. "We made you breakfast in bed. Martha made the food, but I set up the tray." She beamed.

"Oh, my goodness, what a surprise! Thank you, sweetheart."

"The pink roses are your favorite, and eggs Benjamin ... I mean." Chloe wrinkled her nose. "What are they called, Martha?"

Martha chuckled. "Eggs Benedict, dear."

"Oh yeah, that's what I mean. And your bacon is extra crispy, and French toast with powdered sugar and coffee with..."

Michelle looked at her with amazement as she continued to rattle off the entire contents of the tray.

"Slow down, dear." Martha smiled and helped Chloe place the tray on Michelle's lap.

"Come here, sweetie," Michelle said, patting the bed beside her.

Chloe walked to the other side of the bed, crawled up, careful not to tip the tray, and sat next to her mother.

Michelle read the handmade card, tilted her head, and placed her hand on Chloe's cheek.

"Mommy, look at the back." Chloe grabbed the card and flipped it over. "It says I love you a thousand times infinity. I added the heart.

Then you say, I love you a thousand more," she instructed.

"Thank you, Chloe. You are so thoughtful. I love it. I mean—I love you a thousand more."

Chloe grinned, quite pleased with herself.

Michelle placed the cloth napkin on her lap as Chloe stared at her in anticipation.

"Oh, my goodness, this is the best Eggs Benedict I've ever had."

Chloe beamed with pride as Martha left the room to give them time alone.

"Ben is still sleeping. He's a lazy bum on the weekends," Chloe said, rolling her eyes.

"It's alright. We can have girl time, just you and me." She wrapped her arm around Chloe and pulled her close.

"Were you looking at pictures of us, Mommy?" Chloe picked up the photo album and opened the cover. "Did it help you remember?"

Michelle didn't have the heart to tell Chloe she couldn't remember anything from the photos. The maternal instincts were there. Being a mother felt natural, but being Chloe and Ben's mother felt foreign.

"You know what? I would love for you to tell me all about the stories behind the pictures."

Chloe perked up. Michelle learned early on that Chloe loved to talk, so she spent the next hour laughing and bonding with her daughter, who revealed a life that Michelle saw play out in the various photos but had no memory of.

The bedroom door burst open. Ben ran in and jumped on the bed, causing the tray to tip. Michelle grabbed the coffee mug and flower vase while silverware clanked against her plate.

"Ben!" Chloe screamed.

"It's okay, it's okay," Michelle said calmly. "Good morning, sleepyhead." Michelle extended her arm, inviting Ben in for a hug. He slid off the bed and hugged her tight.

"Did you like the pink roses? Me and Dad picked them for you yesterday."

"Yes, they are my favorite," she said, giving Chloe a wink. "Thank you, honey."

Martha entered the guest room, took the tray, and passed Liam on her way out.

Michelle's eyes lit up, and she felt that familiar flutter at the sight of her husband.

"Good morning, everyone. Did someone forget to invite me to the party?"

The sound of paws galloping down the hall became louder. A large Bernese Mountain dog came trotting into the guest room. His long, wispy tail wagged behind him as he panted an enormous smile at the sight of his family.

Chloe and Ben yelled with excitement. "Bear!"

"Bear, sit," Liam instructed.

He looked up at Liam and sat, then sniffed Michelle's hand, resting his head on her lap, and whimpered.

Chloe stroked Bear's head. "Aww, he's sad that your leg is hurt, Mommy."

For a moment, Michelle's family wrapped her in comfort and love, but deep down, something felt wrong. She prayed her memory would return, making her and their family whole again.

CHAPTER 47

Three weeks later

Michelle awoke soaked in sweat. She sat up, trying to make sense of where she was, then looked over at the nightstand and stared at the family beach picture. Her hands trembled as a sudden rage built inside her. She picked up the picture frame and threw it across the room. It hit the wall with a loud thud, causing the glass to shatter to the floor.

A moment later, Martha knocked on the guest room door. "Michelle, are you okay? Michelle?"

Martha received no reply, so she cautiously opened the door. A beam of light from the hallway reached across the dark room, revealing Michelle sitting on the edge of the bed, rocking back and forth, sobbing, and whining, "Why? Why?"

Liam rushed into the guest room to find Martha sitting next to Michelle. He saw the broken frame and shards of glass and flashed back to the night Michelle left him, fearing that she remembered.

Martha took Michelle's face in her hands. "Michelle, look at me."

Her eyes were distant, in pain, off somewhere lost.

Liam left, and ten minutes later, returned to the room. "Martha, the doctor is on his way."

"I've never seen her like this, Liam, never. Trying to remember must be too much for her."

An hour later, the doctor arrived. Liam paced in the living room while Martha checked on the twins. He heard the guest room door open and met the doctor in the hallway.

"I gave Michelle a sedative. This should help her sleep. Has this happened before?" the doctor asked.

"No. She returned home three weeks ago, and this is the first time since then. We thought everything was going well."

"My office will contact you tomorrow morning to schedule an appointment with Dr. Kent. She's an excellent psychotherapist."

Liam pinched his brows. "A psychotherapist?"

"Yes. It's not uncommon for amnesia patients to seek therapy. I'll send in a prescription for an anti-anxiety medication as well."

Liam walked the doctor out, then took a seat at the kitchen island.

Martha left the twins' room and found Liam in the kitchen.

He looked at her and shook his head. "She's sleeping. The doctor gave her a sedative."

Martha rested her hand on Liam's shoulder. "The children stirred for a moment but fell right back to sleep. Thank goodness they did not see their mother in that state."

"I'll stay with Michelle for a while. Thank you for checking on the twins."

Liam went to the guest room, covered Michelle with a blanket, and sat in the chair by the window, watching her sleep. He knew this wouldn't be easy, but he wasn't prepared for a mental breakdown.

Liam glanced at Michelle as she stared out the car window and noticed her hands trembling. He reached over and laid his hand on her knee.

Michelle looked at him with shame draped over her face. "I'm so sorry."

"It's okay. I know all this is overwhelming." He stared at the road and, selfishly, was relieved that she didn't regain her memory. But it was only a matter of time before he would have to tell her the truth. He owed her that much.

When they pulled into the parking lot of the medical building, her heart pounded in her chest.

He helped her out, then walked behind her as she limped to the entrance of the building.

Liam approached the reception desk. "Good morning. Michelle Grant is here to see Dr. Kent."

"Hello, Michelle." The receptionist handed her a clipboard and pen. "Please fill out the new patient forms and bring them back up when you're finished. You can have a seat in the waiting room."

Michelle began to fill out the forms and paused.

"What's wrong?" Liam asked.

"I don't remember my birth date," she said, biting her bottom lip as her eyes misted over. "I think my license said June, maybe?"

"It's June 30, 1982. It's okay, I got it."

Liam took the clipboard from her, filled out the forms, had her sign them, and returned them to the front desk.

She stared at the floor until a nurse called her name.

Liam stood to help her up from the chair.

"It's okay, I can do it. Thank you."

"Mr. Grant, you're welcome to help yourself to the coffee while you wait."

Liam nodded and sat back down, then stared at the TV screen in the waiting room, lost in thought. *He was thankful Chloe and Ben hadn't woken last night. He truly wanted Michelle to remember the twins, but not why she went to Boston. He knew it was selfish, but he hoped she would only remember being in love with him and their life together. If only she had talked to him before her accident, maybe they wouldn't be here.*

A nurse approached him and interrupted his daydream.

"Mr. Grant, the doctor would like you to join them."

Dr. Kent stood and shook Liam's hand. "Please have a seat," she said, gesturing to the chair next to Michelle.

He sat in the plush armchair and gave Michelle a comforting smile.

"How are you, Mr. Grant?"

"Liam, please. I'm well, thank you."

"Liam, I asked you to join us because Michelle agreed she'd like to proceed with therapy. After talking with Michelle and reviewing her medical records, she has what is referred to as dissociative amnesia, which means she has difficulty recalling personal information about herself. Typically, it's not permanent, and I have seen success in other patients who have presented with this type of amnesia."

He glanced at Michelle. "That is encouraging."

The corner of Michelle's mouth lifted, then she looked away.

"To start, I'd like to meet with Michelle one-on-one and may ask you to join us periodically. Would you be willing to join our sessions?"

Liam put his hand on Michelle's and looked into her eyes. "I only want what's best for my wife." He looked back at Dr. Kent. "I believe Michelle would benefit from your sessions, and of course, I will be here whenever you need me to be."

Michelle blushed and lowered her eyes to the floor.

"Michelle, what are you feeling right now?" asked Dr. Kent.

"I don't want to disappoint Liam or the children," she said, keeping her eyes lowered.

"Yes, that is understandable. However, it will be difficult to be there for them if you don't take care of yourself first."

Michelle's eyes met Dr. Kent's impassive expression. "I know. I just want to remember so badly, especially for the children's sake."

"Okay. Well, why don't we start with twice a week? Liam, will there be any issues with Michelle making the appointments?"

"No, it won't be a problem."

"Okay. It was nice to meet you both. I'll see you soon, Michelle."

Liam stood, shook the doctor's hand, and helped Michelle from her chair. He felt the urge to kiss her on the cheek, but stopped himself. He was unsure how she would respond to his affection, especially in front of the doctor.

Their small talk in the car made the ride home bearable and less awkward. He was grateful Michelle had agreed to the sessions, but worried about what it would mean for them and their family if she remembered everything.

This time, pulling into their driveway brought her comfort. She felt safe in their home and appreciated Martha's companionship, but wondered why she had the sudden breakdown and prayed she wouldn't put them through that again.

Martha greeted them in the kitchen. "Good morning, Michelle. I hope you are feeling well today."

"I am, thank you."

Liam glanced at his phone, then placed it in his pocket. "I have to go to the office for a few hours. I won't be late."

He walked over to Michelle, and this time in the privacy of their own home, kissed her on the cheek, and whispered, "I hope you have a good day."

Michelle closed her eyes and breathed in his cologne, welcoming her husband's affection for the first time since leaving the hospital.

Michelle spent her next session with Dr. Kent describing her hospital stay, befriending Jade, and explaining that nothing was triggering her memories at home. Liam was being so patient, but he would eventually want his wife back in their bedroom. She expressed her anxiety about meeting her parents. They were supposed to visit the week she returned home. But thankfully, they had to reschedule. Then, with her breakdown, they thought it was best to give her some more time.

"Michelle, I'd like you to close your eyes for a moment. Take a deep breath through your nose and slowly release the air through your lips. Relax in the chair. One more time, breathe in through your nose and slowly out through your lips. Keeping your eyes closed, what do you see? What are you picturing in your mind?"

"I'm at a park. I'm pushing a child on a swing. Another child wraps their arms around my leg. Then I see a man waving and a black dog is running towards me. Their faces are blurry, but I know them. I feel love for them."

"Okay, open your eyes. Do you think you are remembering a time with Liam, Chloe, and Ben at this park?"

She closed her eyes and shrugged. "I don't know, maybe."

Dr. Kent set her pen on her desk, signaling the end of their session. "I believe that starting a journal would be helpful. Write down your feelings and any flashes of memories and dreams you have. Would you be willing to do that?"

"Yes." She agreed just to appease Dr. Kent, but wasn't convinced it would help.

CHAPTER 48

Michelle had been seeing Dr. Kent twice a week for the last month and was determined to do whatever it took to make her family whole again. She was more at ease and fell into the family's daily routines. Finally, being free of the knee brace, she felt confident she could handle the long staircase to explore the second floor.

She grabbed Fred, more out of habit than necessity, and made her way up the stairs using the quad cane and railing. Pictures of Chloe and Ben hung in the long hallway, displaying the first seven years of their lives. The guest room was stocked with her clothes and shoes, thanks to Martha, so there was no need to go to the main suite. Still, she was curious. She entered feeling as if she were invading Liam's privacy, but she told herself this was *her* bedroom, too.

She entered the walk-in closet and ran her hand over the crisp men's dress shirts. One of his suit jackets still carried his cologne. Her clothes were organized by season and color, except for a rack of formal dresses. She pulled out a shimmering blue strapless dress, held it up to her in front of the full-length mirror, and stared at the image of a stranger. She hung up the dress and walked around the bedroom. Her dresser displayed a picture of the twins at Pre-K graduation, holding their certificates, smiling from ear to ear.

She looked across the room and noticed a picture of Liam holding Chloe and Ben in the hospital sitting on his dresser. A vision flashed in her mind: the beeps of machines, the sterile aroma, and the feeling of wires all over her. *A flashback of the ICU?* She dismissed the vision and walked over to Liam's dresser.

Everything had its place. He appeared to be a perfectionist. Her stomach fluttered as she thought back to the first time she had seen him at the hospital. His crystal-blue eyes captivated her. He was handsome, polished, charismatic, and a gentleman, but a stranger.

She made her way downstairs and saw Martha in the kitchen. "Martha, Liam told me we were childhood friends and went to the same high school and college, but were we always a couple?"

Martha excused herself and returned with a decorative box. She placed it on the large granite island, looked at Michelle, and took her hand.

"I wondered if you had asked Liam, but I guess I have my answer. I needed to wait until we were alone."

Michelle's eyes sparked with curiosity.

Martha opened the box to reveal several rows of pictures that were thoughtfully organized and separated by colorful, labeled tabs. "We might as well start at the beginning." She smiled.

Martha explained that Ann and Seth had tried for years to have children, eventually deciding on adoption. She was their only child and grew up in a loving home, wanting for nothing.

"You're probably wondering why your parents needed a nanny for one child." She sighed and continued. "You were born pre- maturely and stayed in the Neonatal ICU for two months before you could come home."

Michelle tilted her head. "Earlier, I had a memory of being covered in wires. I thought it was when I was in the ICU after my accident."

Martha's expression sobered.

Michelle thought it odd that Martha became quiet and sensed she was holding something back.

"Are you okay, Martha?"

"Hmm? Oh, yes, dear," she said, patting Michelle's hand.

Michelle accepted her lie and didn't press her. "Were Chloe and Ben in the NICU?"

"Only for twenty-four hours after they were born." Martha hesitated for a moment. "Where was I? Oh yes. Your mother, poor dear, was terrified. She was so afraid she would do something wrong, so she hired a nanny. I moved to France with them for your father's job." Martha tilted her head. "Are the pictures helping at all? Does anything look familiar?"

"No, I'm sorry." She stared at the pictures of a happy young woman with a flawless complexion and ran her fingers across the small scars on her face.

"You're still beautiful. Those tiny scars are a testament to your strength, dear."

Michelle blushed, then leafed through the beginning tabs, looking at picture after picture of a boy who was a constant figure in her life.

"Martha, who is this boy? He's in almost every picture with me. Do I have a brother?"

"No, dear. His name is Bradley Cole; he was your next-door neighbor. You two were inseparable. You played together from the time you were both toddlers. Your parents and the Coles hoped you would end up together. But you two tortured your parents for years until late in your senior year." Tears formed in her eyes.

"Martha, what's wrong?"

"He's no longer with us. It was so heartbreaking; he was too young. He died in a tragic accident on the UConn campus a few weeks before your college graduation. You and Liam witnessed it."

Michelle's eyes also filled with tears, not because she mourned Brad or witnessed something so terrible, but because she couldn't remember someone so significant in her life and his tragic death. She held another picture and looked puzzled. "This is Liam, right?"

"Yes. You, Brad, and Liam were friends growing up. Liam took you to your senior prom. The story was that Brad waited too long to ask you, and Liam beat him to it. Brad's mother was so upset that he didn't ask you. Although I believe Liam had a crush on you throughout middle and high school."

"But I was in love with Brad the whole time?"

"Yes, dear. But after Brad died, you and Liam became close. Liam was there for you, just as he is now. He loves you very much." Martha looked down and sighed.

Michelle's brows drew together. "What is it, Martha?"

"I don't like to keep things from Liam, but Brad is a sensitive subject. He knew Brad was going to propose to you before he died."

"I believe Liam always felt like the second choice. So please keep that between us."

"Of course. I don't want to hurt him. He's been so kind, patient, and understanding with me. I suppose that's why he hasn't mentioned Brad."

"I imagine so, dear."

"Is it okay if I keep the box in the guest room? I promise to keep it hidden."

Martha hesitated, then smiled and handed her the box.

"Thank you, Martha. I truly appreciate your trust. I'm going to lie down for a little while."

She sat on the side of the guest bed and ran her fingers over the nine-inch scar on her right knee. A permanent reminder of the accident that stole her memories. She slid under the comforter and studied the pictures of a forgotten life. Her eyes grew heavy, and she eventually drifted into a deep sleep.

In a slow, deliberate move, she turned her head and felt the sun's warmth on her face. A little voice yelled, "Mommy, higher!" The high-pitched squeak of the chains became a methodical rhythm. Her arms extended out in front of her, pushing the child into the air. Little arms wrapped around her leg. She looked down, smiled, and ran her fingers through a pile of blonde curls. "Chelle, over here," a man's voice called out. He waved his hand above his head and smiled. His face was blurry, but familiar. Out of the corner of her eye, she could see a black figure lumbering toward her. A long pink tongue dangling from the side of its mouth rose and fell with every stride. The barking became louder and louder as the dog closed in on her. Before she could react, she hit the ground hard.

Her body jolted, and her eyes popped open to a black nose sniffing her face. A long pink tongue swept across her lips. "Yuck, Bear!" She wiped her mouth with the back of her hand and laughed at the mammoth lying beside her, panting, his hot breath in her face. Bear laid his head on her chest and whined.

"What is it, Bear? Something worrying you?"

She stroked his silky head as his wispy tail swept back and forth on the comforter.

Realizing that the box was still on the bed, she eased herself off and limped to the closet, hiding the box in the designer bag. She turned and placed her finger to her lips. "Shhh, our little secret, okay, buddy?"

CHAPTER 49

Michelle studied her face in the bathroom mirror, running her fingers over the scar above her right eye and left cheek. She would see her parents in a few hours. Dread reached the pit of her stomach, making her nauseous. She adjusted the fitted tea-length sapphire dress that highlighted her ocean eyes. Although it was months later, tonight they would be celebrating her June birthday. Liam told her June 30th was the day, but her license made it true. It was the only thing of hers that was found at the accident site. The only thing from her past that told her who she was.

She stared at herself in the mirror and pictured herself holding her license, feeling proud. A red-haired girl punched her arm. "I told you you'd pass!" She stared at herself in the mirror and rubbed her arm as if she recalled the impact of the strike. She shook her head, checked herself in the mirror again, and left the guest room.

Martha smiled. "Oh, you look lovely, dear," she said, handing Michelle a pile of folded cloth napkins. "Would you mind setting those on the dining table?"

She guessed Martha could sense her anxiety and welcomed the simple task to distract her.

"The children are so excited to finally celebrate your birthday. They had planned to do so when they returned from traveling with your parents."

"Where are Chloe and Ben?" she asked, trying to control her trembling hands while carefully placing each napkin.

"They are finishing their homework in their rooms, and Liam should be home any moment."

Martha walked over and took Michelle's hands in hers. "Look at me, dear. Take a deep breath."

She looked at Martha, took a deep breath, closed her eyes, and exhaled through puckered lips. The sound of little feet running down the stairs opened her eyes.

Chloe pushed her brother. "Mommy, Happy Beladeld Birthday!"

"Happy late birthday!" Ben shouted, pushing Chloe back.

"Thank you, thank you," she said, wrapping her arms around them.

Chloe smiled proudly. "I finished my homework first, Mommy."

Ben scowled at her. "No, you didn't, Chloe. I finished first!"

Martha shook her head. "It's not a race. You both finished, and that's all that matters. Your grandparents will be here shortly, so please wash up for dinner."

"Alright, but I get to sit next to Mommy," Chloe said, scrunching her nose at Ben.

"Aw," Ben groaned.

"You can both sit next to me. Now do as Martha asked."

She let out a long exhale again, trying to calm her nerves, when she heard a door open and close. Her eyes lit up when Liam entered the kitchen. He greeted Martha, then made his way to her and ran his hand down her arm, making her skin tingle, and kissed her cheek.

"Hello. You look beautiful." He handed her a bouquet and wished her a happy belated birthday.

Maybe he was only being kind, but she welcomed his affection. "Thank you, but don't you mean beladeld?" She chuckled.

Liam tilted his head, then realized. "Chloe," he laughed.

The twins raced each other again to greet their father.

"Hey, guys. How was your day?"

"Are Grandma and Grandpa Grant eating dinner with us too?" Chloe asked.

"No, not tonight, but soon."

Michelle hadn't even thought about Liam's parents until now. She was filled with anxiety again as she imagined meeting another set of strangers.

"I need to talk to Mommy. Please see if Martha needs help."

Liam extended his hand. "Can you follow me, please?"

She took his hand, his grip strong but gentle. Her heart raced as he led her up the stairs toward the main bedroom, wondering why he needed to talk to her alone.

Being in the main bedroom with him was intimidating, having no memory of intimate moments as husband and wife. She watched him reach into the bedside table and bring her a black velvet box.

She looked at him confused, then opened it.

"They are your engagement and wedding rings. You've probably been wondering where they were. I thought maybe you'd like to wear them tonight?"

"Oh. I hadn't thought about them while trying to remember everything else. They must have taken them off at the hospital."

His poker face concealed the unease that stirred inside him, and he reached for her left hand.

She watched as he cradled her hand, placed the rings on her finger, and caressed her knuckles with his thumb. A memory flashed in her mind of a wedding band being placed on her finger, but it wasn't Liam's hand holding hers.

She looked up and met his eyes, tempted to kiss him, but the doorbell chimed and made her jump.

He raised his eyebrows and smiled. "They're here."

She released a heavy sigh, then took his hand.

From the top of the stairs, she saw Chloe and Ben race to the front door and be immediately engulfed by her parents. When they reached the bottom of the stairs, Liam put his hand on the small of her back and whispered, "You can do this."

Liam also took a deep breath. If Michelle only knew the anxiety that plagued him daily. He knew he was taking a risk by giving her the rings. She could remember everything at any moment, and he had rehearsed what he'd say to her, but until that day, he would be the husband she deserved.

Michelle watched the loving interaction between her parents and the twins as she approached them.

"Oh, my darlings, you're growing so fast," Ann said.

Chloe leaned close to her grandmother and whispered. "It's Mommy's birthday party."

Ann whispered back. "Yes, it is."

Michelle greeted her mother, pretending she didn't hear their whispers.

Ann tilted her head with tears in her eyes and reached out her arms to hug her daughter. "You look well, darling. It's lovely to see you again."

Michelle hesitated, then wrapped her arms around her mother as a courtesy rather than a loving gesture. With her father, though, she extended her hand and offered a handshake.

Seth cupped both hands around hers. "We are so thankful you came home to us." He offered a contrived smile, sensing her uneasiness.

Liam ushered everyone into the living room. Chloe and Ben took their grandparents' hands, competing for each one's attention. Michelle could see that the twins and her parents were close and that they adored their grandchildren.

A few minutes later, Martha entered the room and informed them that dinner was ready to be served.

The children's chatter distracted Michelle and eased her anxiety while they ate. Liam asked Chloe and Ben to help Martha clear the table. They each made a face but said nothing in front of their grandparents and obeyed.

After a few minutes, the twins walked out of the kitchen carrying a birthday cake with lit candles, setting it on the dining table. "Happy Birthday, Mommy!" they shouted.

"Oh, my goodness!"

"Me and Ben made the cake. Martha helped, too," Chloe said proudly.

Ben bounced in place. "Hurry, Mom, make a wish and blow out the candles!"

Michelle extinguished the tiny flames in one breath, receiving a round of applause from the twins, and blushed with the attention.

After they finished dessert, Ben ran back to the kitchen and returned with a crudely wrapped object. "Here, Mom, I made it at school for you."

Michelle opened it carefully. "You made this?" She struggled to make out what the clay object was until Ben said, "It's a Huskie 'cause I know you like them from your college days."

"Oh, my college days, huh," she looked at Liam and laughed softly.

Liam rustled Ben's hair. "That's right. The UConn mascot is a Huskie. Good memory, Ben."

"Well, I love it," she said, giving Ben a side hug.

"Here, Mommy." Chloe handed her a large handmade card.

Michelle admired the artwork on the face of the card as Chloe watched in anticipation. When she opened the card, a large bouquet of paper flowers popped out, each petal labeled Pretty, Smart, Funny, Kind, Best Mom Ever, Love Chloe.

"This is beautiful Chloe. Thank you, honey," she said and kissed Chloe's cheek.

Ann signaled to Ben to come to her. "Ben darling, please give this to your mother."

Ben delivered the envelope and stood next to his mother.

A beautiful 'Happy Birthday Daughter' card with a personal note written inside forced Michelle to blink away tears. She opened a small envelope that held a spa gift card.

"You deserve a day of pampering, darling."

"Thank you. This is so thoughtful."

"Last one, Mommy." Chloe gave Michelle a beautifully wrapped rectangular box. "It's from Daddy."

She felt self-conscious as all eyes were on her again while opening Liam's gift. A delicate gold chain held a diamond and garnet pendant that sparkled as she lifted the necklace to admire it.

"Garnet is the twin's birthstone," Liam said.

"It's beautiful. Thank you."

"Put it on, Mommy," Chloe said excitedly.

Liam walked behind Michelle's chair and placed the necklace around her neck.

She traced the pendant with her fingers, feeling unworthy of such an expensive gift.

Liam set his hands on her shoulders and kissed her cheek.

She no longer shied away from his affection but felt comfort with his touch.

Chloe leaned in and admired the necklace up close. "Oh, it looks so pretty, Mommy!"

Ann smiled. "Yes, it's lovely on you, darling."

The twins helped Martha in the kitchen again while the adults settled in the living room. Michelle appreciated Liam's attempt to ease her anxiety by asking Ann about her real estate company and the housing market. He then asked Seth about his latest venture overseas.

She couldn't quite read her father. He was confident and somewhat arrogant. Maybe it was the lawyer in him.

"Darling, please know you are welcome anytime. Perhaps visiting your childhood home will help regain your memory. Don't you agree, Seth?"

"Yes, if Michelle feels up to it," Seth said, patting his wife's hand and looking at Michelle for acknowledgement.

"Um, yes, I suppose it wouldn't hurt," she said, appreciating her father's attempt to connect with her.

Her parents told her stories of her childhood and her life growing up with Brad, but they remained respectful of Liam. She smiled as the pictures Martha shared floated around in her head. She listened to her parents describe a life that sounded perfect, but deep down, did not feel like her own.

Without thinking, she blurted out. "So, I was adopted?" She immediately regretted it, as Ann could not hide the hurt on her face.

Michelle watched her father observe the look on his wife's face and retorted. "Yes, you were, and we've loved you as if you were our own flesh and blood."

"I'm so sorry. I didn't mean to..." Michelle looked down as heat rushed into her cheeks.

When she looked up at her mother, Ann blinked away her tears. "It's okay, darling. I'm fine."

Seth stood abruptly. "We'll be heading out now." Then he shouted across the room. "Chloe, Ben, we need hugs goodbye."

Ann walked over to Liam and hugged him. "Thank you so much for the lovely dinner."

She approached Michelle and placed her hand on Michelle's arm. "We love you, darling, and you have our full support, whatever you need."

"Thank you, and I'm so sorry." Heat crept into her cheeks again. "Maybe next week I can visit?"

Ann's face brightened. "Yes. That would be lovely."

Chloe and Ben wrapped their arms around their grandmother. She kissed the tops of their heads and walked to the front door with them still clinging to her.

Seth shook Liam's hand and hugged the twins. He didn't approach his daughter, but gave her a nod. "Michelle, I look forward to your visit. Take care."

Liam wrapped his arm around her waist after her father's cold goodbye. She welcomed Liam's affection, and as soon as the door closed, she felt relief and regret.

"I disappointed them." She sighed. "My father was…"

"Would you like me to go with you to your parents?"

She sensed Liam was irritated with her father and appreciated his chivalry, but she needed to be the one to make it right. "Thank you, but it's probably better if I go alone."

"If you change your mind, I'll be there; just say the word."

Liam couldn't comprehend the coldness Seth showed Michelle. *Where the hell was Seth's compassion for his only child, who could have died? He would continue to be cordial in front of Chloe and Ben, but his respect for his father-in-law was slipping away.*

CHAPTER 50

November 2012

Martha pulled into the circular driveway of the impressive, mani-cured Carrington estate. Michelle's heart raced as she stared at the grand entrance.

Martha placed her hand on Michelle's arm. "Are you okay?"

Ann stood in the doorway and waved.

"No, but I think I can handle this."

"Take all the time you need."

Michelle smiled as Ann welcomed her into their family home. Holiday décor was on full display, leading her eyes to the wrought-iron scrollwork on the impressive marble staircase to the second floor. A large crystal chandelier hung several feet above their heads. Fine art lined a long hall to the right, and on the left, a formal living room was filled with ornate furniture that appeared new and untouched.

"Would you like a tour?" Ann asked.

"Sure, that would be nice." She turned full circle, taking in the enormity of her childhood home.

After touring the main floor, they walked up the marble staircase to the second floor to her childhood bedroom, where a large curio cabinet displayed a collection of snow globes on the back wall.

"The snow globe collection is courtesy of your father. He traveled quite a bit when you were a child, and he would bring home a snow globe from every city he visited as a gift. It became a special tradition between the two of you."

"Martha told me we lived in France after you adopted me."

"Yes, that's right." Ann lowered her eyes, not offering any other details.

Michelle walked to the window seat covered in plush pillows that overlooked the Cole's house. A tree fort sat next to the fence that divided the properties. She remembered a picture of her and Brad in the tree fort from Martha's box of photos. "That's Brad's house?"

Ann's eyes sparked with hope. "Yes. You remember that?"

"No. Martha showed me some pictures of Brad and me in a tree fort, so I'm guessing that's the one in their yard."

Ann tried to hide the disappointment on her face. "Oh. Yes, it is."

Across the room, a desk displayed trophies and pictures of her accomplishments. She looked over her accolades, picking up photos, studying them, and noticing that she was athletic, accomplished, and, most of all, loved.

"Is anything familiar?"

She knew her mother was looking for the slightest sign of recognition on her face, and she could have lied, but all she could do was sigh. "I'm sorry, no."

Tears filled Ann's eyes. "You were in a terrible vehicle accident. I am so thankful that we did not lose you."

Michelle felt her anxiety build. "Well, thank you for letting me visit. This is all overwhelming. I don't want to disappoint any of you. I'm sorry, I just don't remember."

CHAPTER 51

Boston
November 2012

Scott walked into Aunt B's Bouquets and saw Sam behind the counter on the phone. She looked at him and raised her forefinger. He nodded and waited for her to finish the call.

Sam hung up the phone and walked around the counter. "Hey, any news?"

Scott closed his eyes and shook his head. "Shelby would never leave the kids this long, Sam."

Henry appeared from the back room. "Scott, do the police have any leads on our Shelby?"

"No, Henry," Scott sighed. "Besides accusing me of doing something to her, they have been no help. And the private detective I hired doesn't have any leads either."

Henry shook his head. "I'm sorry, Scott. We'll keep things running here for her, so don't you worry about the shop. Sam has been a big help." Henry placed his hand on Scott's shoulder, shook his head again, then turned around and disappeared into the back room.

Scott looked at Sam with heartbreak in his eyes. "Rhylie keeps asking where her mother is. I tell her that Mommy is lost and we're trying to find her. I don't know what else to say."

"Poor kid. She must be so confused. Would it be okay if I stopped by after I close up here?"

"Sure. They'll be excited to see you."

Sam rang the doorbell and glanced up the street. The gray sedan was in its usual spot, surveilling Scott's comings and goings or whomever visited the O'Donnell household.

After being questioned for three hours in July when Shelby was reported missing, Sam had only been to their house twice to help with the kids.

Scott answered the door and smiled. "Hey, Sam. Are Frick and Frack at their post?"

Sam rolled her eyes. "Yeah." Then she looked toward the gray sedan and gave them an exaggerated wave.

Scott grimaced. "Great, I'm sure that will be in their report tomorrow."

Rhylie ran to Sam and hugged her leg.

"Hey, kiddo," she said, running her hand over Rhylie's curls.

Tyler sat in his high chair, shoving Cheerios in his mouth, and smiled when he saw Sam.

"Want something to drink?" Scott asked.

"Sure." Sam sat on the couch, and Rhylie climbed up and snuggled into her. Sam wrapped her arm around Rhylie and kissed the top of her head.

"Mama lost."

Sam's eyes filled with tears. "We'll find Mommy, sweetie," she said and pulled Rhylie close.

Scott handed Sam a water bottle, then walked over and sat at the dining table beside Tyler. He placed his hand on his forehead, released a heavy sigh, and began to cry, then shook his head and sniffled.

Sam looked over her shoulder and saw Scott at the table. "Hey Rhylie, can you draw me a picture?"

Rhylie nodded, slid off the couch, and sat at her toddler table.

Sam walked over and put her hand on Scott's shoulder.

"I don't know what to do, Sam. I can't eat. I can't sleep. Where the hell is she?"

"I'm sorry. What can I do to help?"

"You're already helping with the flower shop."

"I mean here. For you and the kids."

"My parents and Shelby's parents have been taking Rhylie and Tyler a few times a week, but..." He glanced over at his daughter. "I can't keep asking them to do that. At some point..." He looked at Sam as tears pooled in his eyes again.

Sam stared at him until Tyler started whining and squirming in his high chair.

Scott stood to take Tyler out.

Sam put her hand on Scott's arm. "I've got him. Why don't you go throw some cold water on your face."

He nodded, walked to the half bath, and shut the door.

The thought of something happening to Shelby made Sam sick. It was all her fault. If she hadn't gone to the bar that night, none of this would be happening.

CHAPTER 52

Short Hills
February 2013

Being a mother felt natural; Chloe and Ben made it easy. But being Liam's wife was intimidating. His touch or charming smile sent a wave of emotions through her: attraction, insecurity, desire, and fear. She appreciated his reserved affection toward her, but he was still a stranger regarding their intimacy as husband and wife. She knew he wanted more, but he didn't pursue her beyond a kiss on the cheek or a gentle embrace.

After finishing her afternoon jog on the treadmill, she went to the kitchen for a glass of water. A crystal vase filled with a dozen red roses sat on the large granite island. A small white envelope labeled *Michelle* peeked out of the bouquet. She looked around and opened the envelope. *May I have the pleasure of your company this evening? Please go to the guest room. Liam.*

When she opened the guest room door, she was nervous but intrigued. A large white box with a red satin ribbon sat on the bed. She lifted the top off and separated the tissue paper to find a red shimmering strapless gown and sparkling strappy red heels. She held the gown up to herself, taking in its beauty. A gentle knock drew her attention to the door. "Yes, come in."

"I see you received Liam's gift." Martha smiled. "Oh, it's lovely, dear."

"Is Liam home?"

"No, he's sending a car for you in two hours. It's a surprise. He didn't even tell *me* where he's taking you. Now, let's get you ready!"

Michelle's heels clicked across the hardwood floor as she made her way to the kitchen. Martha looked up and placed her hand over her mouth, causing Chloe and Ben to jump down from their bar stools.

"Mommy, you look beautiful!" Chloe squealed.

Ben wrapped his arms around her. "You're all sparkly, Mom."

"Thank you," she said, carefully touching the light brown waves that flowed down her shoulders. "Martha, is my hair okay?"

"It's perfect, dear. You look lovely." Martha led her to the mudroom door. "The car is in the driveway, waiting for you. Have a wonderful time—you deserve it."

"Bye, Mommy. Bye!" The twins ran to her, hugging her one last time.

"Alright, let's finish your dinner, loves," Martha said, guiding them back to the island.

She walked out to the driveway and was greeted by an impeccably dressed chauffeur holding the limo door open for her. "Good evening, Mrs. Grant."

"Where are we going?"

"Mr. Grant has asked that I keep it a surprise," he responded politely.

Michelle stared out the tinted window and wondered what Liam's expectations would be tonight, but his attentiveness made her feel incredibly special.

As the limo pulled up to The Brickville Inn, nervous excitement filled her as she admired the restaurant's grandeur and beauty. Liam was sparing no expense. The chauffeur held the door, and when she exited the limo, she expected to find Liam waiting outside for her. Instead, the greeter stood before her, offered his hand, and helped her up the stone staircase.

"Good evening, Mrs. Grant. I'll take you to your table."

The pianist playing "Wonderful Tonight" drowned out conversations and small talk, adding to the romantic ambiance. She saw Liam standing by a private, quaint table with two high-back plush chairs on either side. He looked strong, confident, and dreamy.

She watched a smile grow across his lips as she walked toward him.

"Enjoy your evening," the host said, then disappeared into the sea of patrons.

Liam touched her waist, kissed her cheek, and whispered, "You are stunning."

She blushed as her stomach fluttered with his touch. "Thank you."

Liam held her chair, then sat down across from her.

He kept his eyes focused on her, causing her heart to race, feeling flattered and self-conscious.

"Do you like the dress?"

"Yes, thank you." She smiled and fidgeted with her cloth napkin. "It's beautiful."

"*You* make the dress beautiful."

Bright pink colored her cheeks as his charm engulfed her. Yet she was afraid to be vulnerable, but he was so damn handsome and alluring.

The sommelier approached their table. "Good evening, Mr. and Mrs. Grant."

"Good evening, Brent. Could you please bring us a Dom Pérignon Rose 2006?"

"Yes, excellent, sir. Celebrating a special occasion?"

"Yes. My wife."

She smiled self-consciously as heat crept into her cheeks again. Then she studied the dining room and other patrons, feeling out of place with the class and sophistication surrounding them.

"This restaurant is beautiful. Have we been here before?"

"Yes. We said our vows here. It was a small, private ceremony at sunset with our family."

"Oh, I'm so sorry, I don't remember."

"It's okay." He reached across the table and took her hand. "I proposed to you on your birthday." He smiled. "We married on September 29, 2006. Chloe and Ben were twenty months old."

Every touch by him sent an electric wave through her. She resisted giving in to his magnetism, but he made it nearly impossible.

The sommelier appeared again, holding the bottle with authority. In one fluid motion, he released the effervescence with a whisper, as if it were his art.

Michelle stared in amazement at his performance.

He filled their champagne flutes and rested the bottle on the ice stand.

"Thank you, Brent."

"You're welcome, sir. Enjoy your dinner."

Michelle took a sip and pulled her lips in as the bubbles tickled her nose.

She felt his eyes on her again.

"Do you like it?" he asked.

She met his gaze and bit her bottom lip. "Yes. I guess I do like champagne."

Liam began telling her stories of the twins. As she listened, she watched his mannerisms, the way his eyes lit up and the corner of his mouth quirked when he talked about Chloe and Ben. It warmed her heart and made her laugh, but she wished she remembered the stories, too.

They finished their four-course meal, and she wasn't sure if she was on her third or fourth glass of champagne, but a warmth coursed through her veins as the alcohol relaxed and intoxicated her. This was the most at ease she had felt with Liam. Maybe it was the champagne. Maybe she was falling for his charm. What she knew for sure was that she truly felt happy for the first time in months.

A few hours later, they pulled into the garage and quietly entered the mudroom. Liam removed her coat, then she bent down and attempted to take off her heels.

He helped her to the bench where the twins' coats and book bags hung on hooks. He kneeled in front of her and cradled her foot in his hand while unbuckling the strap of her heel.

She stared at him, taking care of her, still feeling the effects of the champagne. Her heart pounded as a fire ignited inside her. Her thoughts played out like a fast-forward movie: how his cologne announced him before he entered a room; the first time she saw him in her hospital room with those dreamy crystal-blue eyes; and the way her name left his lips.

When his caring eyes looked up, his masculine features captivated her. She placed her hand on his cheek, leaned forward, and kissed him.

He guided her up from the bench and pulled her close, then slid her hair over her shoulder and kissed her neck. He stopped and looked at her. "Chelle, are you—?"

She devoured his lips, pressing her body into his, and slid his suit coat down his arms, letting it fall to the floor.

He watched her loosen the knot of his black silk tie until they locked eyes. He grabbed the tie and pulled it over his head, discarding it like a piece of trash. In one fluid motion, he turned her to the side, whisked her up in his arms, and carried her down the hall toward the guest room.

She placed her hand on his cheek. "No."

He stopped and looked at her, confused.

"Take me to *our* room."

His eyes lit with desire. He kissed her softly, then carried her upstairs to their bedroom.

A thrill ran through her entire body. She had only imagined making love to a man she couldn't remember, but now a thirst to explore every inch of her husband replaced her fear of intimacy.

He set her down in their bedroom and dimmed the lights. This was his second chance to have her first time with him be an experience of love, not regret. He would surrender to her desires, restraining the fire that surged through him after months of celibacy and sleeping alone.

He turned her around and swept her hair over her shoulder, kissing the back of her neck as he unzipped her red shimmering dress and slid it down her body.

A tingle ran up her spine as he kissed her shoulder blade and traced his lips down to the small of her back.

He stood and turned her to face him, his eyes tracing the curves of her body.

"I've missed you," he whispered.

Her heart raced as her hands rested on his taut chest while unbuttoning his crisp, white dress shirt. She unbuckled his belt and bit her lower lip at his arousal while unzipping his fitted, tailored slacks.

He took her face in his hands and kissed her passionately, then guided her onto the king-size bed. They pressed their bodies into one another, intertwining their legs. He traced her collarbone with his lips, kissing her chest, and the fullness of her breasts. His warm hand traced down her torso and slid into her lace panties, causing her body to tighten.

He stood up from the bed and slid her panties down her toned legs, then removed his slacks and ran his hands along her inner thighs.

Her eyes smoldered with desire, telling him how much she wanted him, needed him. As he pressed his hips between her legs, euphoria coursed through her entire body; he was intoxicating. She may have forgotten what it was like to make love to her husband, but this night she would never forget.

She lay under his arm, her head resting on his chest. He caressed her arm, then kissed her forehead, and whispered, "I love you."

His words did not fall upon deaf ears as she pretended to sleep. This was a step to reconnecting with her husband, but she wasn't ready to say those three words.

Liam shut his eyes but could not shut off his thoughts. *If her memory came back tomorrow, at least they had tonight. He felt guilty about Staci and hoped she wouldn't remember that part of her past. He knew it was wrong, but the fear of losing Michelle again was worth the risk of his self-serving silence.*

"Good morning." Liam smiled and placed a coffee mug on the bedside table before sitting on the side of the bed.

Michelle sat up, holding the sheet to her chest. She combed her fingers through her hair and smiled back. "Good morning, and thank you for last night."

"You're welcome, and thank *you*," he said, and kissed her tenderly. "You mean the world to me and the kids. I don't know what we would do without you. We are so grateful you came back to us."

She noticed his eyes misting over and placed her hand on his cheek. "I'm grateful, too."

"Well, the kids will be up soon. Would you like to shower in our en suite or downstairs in your room?" he asked.

She hesitated for a moment, realizing that he didn't assume she would vacate the guest room only after one night together; he truly was a gentleman. At that moment, she decided to share their bedroom because she wanted to, not because she was expected to.

"I'll shower in our bathroom," she said with a flirty smirk. "It's time to give the guest room back to the guests."

His mouth curved into a smile. He disappeared into the walk-in closet, then went to the en suite and started the shower. He placed a plush cotton robe on the bed and kissed her cheek. "I'll see you downstairs."

She sat in the bed, flattered that he was so thoughtful. The last person to start a shower for her was dressed in scrubs, hospital gloves, and Crocs.

When Chloe saw her coming down the stairs, she jumped off the bar stool, stopped at the last step, and wrapped her arms around her.

"Mommy!"

Michelle squeezed her daughter. "Good morning, sweetheart."

Chloe rolled her eyes. "Ben is still sleeping."

She walked over to Liam in the kitchen with Chloe still clinging to her and heard him whisper to Martha. "Thank you for taking care of things this morning."

She saw a sly smile on Martha's face. "I assume you had a lovely dinner last night," she said, giving Michelle a wink.

Her cheeks warmed. "Yes, we did. Thank you."

Martha took Chloe's hand. "Come along, love. Let's go wake Mr. Benjamin."

Michelle put her arms around Liam's neck. "Thank you for being patient with me. I know it's been hard for you."

He wrapped his arms around her waist. "I'll do whatever it takes to help you feel whole again." The pang of guilt hit the pit of his stomach. Holding back the truth wasn't doing everything. He pulled her close and shut his eyes, putting the thought out of his mind.

Michelle rested her head on his shoulder. "Well, you're making it very easy."

CHAPTER 53

Boston
April 2013

Scott answered the front door. "Hey, Sam."

"Hey."

He took her duffel bag and led her to the guest room. "I hope this is okay. I really appreciate you doing this."

Sam nodded. "It's only temporary. She's coming home."

Scott faked a smile. "Well, at least Frick and Frack moved on to their next surveillance case."

Sam tilted her head. "Just when I was getting used to my new friends."

Scott rolled his eyes. "Hey, I'm picking up Rhylie and Tyler from my parents soon. They'll be excited to see you."

"Yeah, the munchkins have kinda grown on me."

"Listen, I haven't told Shelby's parents you're staying here during the week."

Sam gave him a side-eye. "Do you want me to talk to them?"

"No, I'll do it. They only know Shelby and I had a fight. They don't know the details."

Sam sighed. "Oh."

"It's not that I'm trying to hide anything from them. It's that this whole thing is a nightmare, and I'm trying to keep things as normal as possible for the kids."

"I know, Scott. We'll get through this; we have to."

Scott released a heavy sigh, then rang his in-laws' doorbell.

Patrick opened the front door with a solemn expression. "Come in, Scott."

He offered a polite smile. "Thanks."

Liza greeted Scott with a hug and led him to the living room. "Would you like something to drink?"

"No, thank you." He sat on the couch, leaned forward, resting his forearms on his knees, and began rubbing his hands together nervously.

"Are Rhylie and Tyler okay?" Liza asked.

"Yes, yes. They are fine. I mean, Rhylie still asks where Mommy is, but..." He sighed.

Patrick glanced at his wife, sensing Scott's uneasiness.

"I just wanted to let you know that, um." He looked down and gripped his hands tightly, trying to calm his nerves.

Liza tilted her head. "Scott, what is it?"

"I want to thank you both for helping me with Rhylie and Tyler. Sam has been a big help too, and..."

Liza glanced at her husband. "Of course, we'd do anything for our grandchildren, and we are thankful that you have been able to rely on Sam as well."

"You both know how much I love Shelby and want to find her. But you need to know that for many months before she went missing, we were struggling as a couple, were growing apart, and we weren't happy."

"The investigators asked us if we knew of any issues between you and Shelby. We obviously told them no," Patrick said, then looked at his wife. "I guess she hid it well."

"I need to tell you what happened the night before Shelby disappeared." He rubbed his hands together again. "I was at Joey's bar.

I had quite a bit to drink. Sam showed up, saw that I was drunk, and drove me home." He looked down and cleared his throat. "Sam tried to help me to the house when I tripped, causing us both to fall in the front yard. I don't know what came over me, but..." He hesitated and glanced up at his in-laws. "I kissed Sam. Shelby saw us from the front door."

Liza placed her hand over her mouth.

"Please don't be angry with Sam. It was my poor judgment that caused all this." He looked down again and cleared his throat. "Shelby may have wanted to leave me, but she would never leave Rhylie and Tyler."

Tears formed in Liza's eyes. "She never said anything that morning when she dropped them off with us."

"I know my daughter must have been hurt and felt betrayed by you and Sam." Patrick sighed. "But she wouldn't walk away from her children; that's one thing we agree on."

"I'm so sorry." He looked at his in-laws with sincerity. "Please know that Rhylie and Tyler have always been and continue to be my priority. We pray every night for Shelby to come home to us."

Patrick stared stone-faced at Scott.

"Um, I wanted to let you both know that nothing is going on between me and Sam. But she has moved into the guest room to help with the kids during the week. Then she'll go back to her apartment on the weekends. The kids love her, and she's stepped in at the florist shop, too."

Liza glanced at Patrick. "I see."

"It's only temporary," he said, but deep down, he knew. After nine months, the hope that Shelby would return home was fading into an unanswered prayer.

CHAPTER 54

Short Hills
June 2013

"My parents invited us to spend the day on the lake with them. What do you think? I haven't said anything to the kids yet in case you weren't up for it," Liam said, giving Michelle a hopeful look.

"Sure. The kids will have fun." She convinced herself it wouldn't be as bad as when her parents visited. Even so, they were strangers who knew more about her than she did herself.

He kissed her cheek. "Great. I'll tell the kids."

She watched him walk upstairs and call to the twins, "Hey, Chloe, Ben..." He disappeared down the hallway, and she heard the squeals of excitement and laughed to herself.

Ben leaned forward in his seat. "Dad, Dad, can we fish?"

"Sure, bud."

"Mommy, do you remember Legacy?" Chloe asked.

"Legacy?"

"It's the boat's name."

Michelle turned in her seat and faced Chloe. "Well, that's a cool name for a boat."

"Grandpa Grant told me he named it Legacy because one day he will pass it down to Daddy, and Daddy will pass it down to me," she said proudly.

"And me too, Chloe!" Ben shouted.

Liam glanced in the rearview mirror. "Yes, Ben, you too."

The twins squirmed in their seats as Liam pulled into the yacht club.

Liam's father waved from the bow as the four walked down the long dock.

The Grants enjoyed an affluent lifestyle. Legacy was a fifty-foot yacht of luxury, complete with a captain.

Michelle knew Liam came from a wealthy family, but she was in awe of the luxury vessel they would spend the day on and hoped that the children would distract her from the nervousness she felt walking onto their "boat."

Liam's mother invited her to sit on the leather bench in the shade.

Laura offered a polite smile. "It's so beautiful on the water, isn't it?"

"Yes, it is. Thank you for having us." Michelle smiled shyly, intimidated by her mother-in-law's class and sophistication.

"You are looking well, dear."

"Thank you. I'm getting better every day and grateful to be rid of Fred."

"Fred?" Laura gave Michelle a puzzled glance. "Was he your physical therapist?"

Michelle's cheeks burned with embarrassment, feeling stupid and common. "No, I'm sorry. It was a silly name I gave my cane."

"Oh, I see. Well, we're thrilled you, Liam, and the children could spend the day with us."

They awkwardly engaged in small talk until Chloe yelled, "Yay, Ben!"

"Mom, look!" Ben squealed. "I caught a fish!" The fish wiggled on the hook, jerking Ben's arm back and forth.

Liam smiled proudly. "Nice job, bud! That's a big one."

Michelle was grateful for an excuse to leave the bench, so she walked over to inspect Ben's prized catch. "Wow! That *is* a big fish."

Liam's father walked over to them. "Okay, let's get a picture, then throw him back."

Liam wrapped his arm around Ben, who grinned from ear to ear as he held the dangling fish high for the picture.

She loved watching Liam with the twins. He continued to prove that he was a great father and a loving husband.

Chloe disappeared into the cabin, and a few minutes later, reappeared in her bathing suit. "Mommy, want to go swimming?"

"Oh, I didn't bring a bathing suit, honey."

"I grabbed one for you," Liam yelled. He looked at his father. "Dad, do you mind taking over?"

Charles walked over and placed his hand on Ben's shoulder. Ben looked up and gave his grandfather a big grin, making Michelle smile with their sweet interaction.

Liam led her to the cabin, careful not to touch her with his "slimy fish hands," as Chloe put it, and from the bathroom, he yelled, "The bag with our suits is on the bed."

She reached into the bag and pulled out a red bikini.

"Um, is this all there is to this bathing suit?" she said, holding a handful of material and a pile of strings.

Liam laughed and pulled her close. "You look hot in this. I remember."

Her eyes lit up with his touch. The smell of his cologne and bronze muscular physique had her wishing they could stay below deck.

His eyes told her he sensed her arousal. He lifted her shirt over her head and unsnapped her shorts, sliding them down her warm legs. She ran her fingers through his hair as he kissed her stomach.

"Mommy! Are you ready to go swimming?" Chloe yelled.

"Mmph." Michelle sighed, throwing her head back.

Liam stood and kissed her. "To be continued."

"Be right there, honey," she yelled back.

Liam quickly changed into his bathing suit, returned to the deck, and took over his post next to Ben.

Michelle emerged from the cabin wrapped in a towel, uncomfortable, wearing the tiny bright red bikini in front of her in-laws. *Did she not own a one-piece suit?*

Chloe ran over to her. "You ready, Mommy? Do you want to jump in together?"

"I'm going to sit on the edge and slide in, okay?" she said, fearing a wardrobe malfunction.

"Can I show you my backflip?" Chloe asked.

"No backflips, Chloe," Liam said sternly.

"Aw!" Chloe stomped and turned away, causing her to slip, hit the deck hard, and fall into the water.

"Chloe!" Liam yelled.

Laura gasped. "Charles!"

Within seconds, Michelle was in the water with her daughter under her arm, guiding them both to the yacht.

Chloe was coughing and gasping.

Liam jumped in the water and helped put Chloe on the deck.

Charles wrapped his granddaughter in a towel and patted her back.

Liam hopped onto the swim deck, took Michelle's arm to help her out of the water, and looked at her right elbow.

"What's wrong?" she asked.

"Your elbow is bleeding."

"I'll be fine." She dismissed his concern and knelt beside Chloe.

Under the canopy, Ben wrapped his arms around his grandmother's waist, watching his sister with wide eyes.

Michelle rubbed Chloe's back. "That's it, honey, keep coughing, get the water out."

Chloe was shaking and sobbing while coughing and gagging.

"I'm glad all that swimming and lifeguarding in college paid off."

Liam looked at her, confused. "Chelle, you played basketball in high school and college—you didn't swim."

"No, I didn't. I swam at UConn."

A deep crease formed between his brows. "Chelle."

Images of her in a basketball uniform from the box of pictures floated around in her head. *How could that be? Swimming felt second nature to her. She searched her mind for an answer.*

Ben came over, stood next to Chloe, and asked if she was okay.

Michelle noticed the incident had shaken Ben and gave him a hug.

She stood and pulled Liam aside. "I want to take her to the ER to have her checked out. We should make sure she got all the water out of her lungs."

"She'll be okay. It scared her more than anything."

"Liam, maybe you think I'm overreacting, but children have died from water in their lungs. Remember that's how Sarah died."

"Sarah?" Liam gave her another confused look.

"My best friend in elementary school." She looked at him as if he should know who Sarah was. "Sarah fell in her pool and died that night in her sleep. She had water in her lungs. We're taking Chloe."

He placed his hand on her arm. "Okay. We'll get her checked out."

His concerned expression appeared to be more about her than Chloe, making her question what she thought was true.

Michelle sat in the back seat between the twins with her arms wrapped around them. She saw Liam glance at them in the rearview mirror, questioning whether he was checking on her or Chloe.

When they arrived home, they left Ben with Martha and took Chloe to the ER. Six hours later; they were exhausted and back home in the wee hours of the morning. Michelle insisted Chloe sleep with them, placing her in the middle of the king-size bed.

Chloe settled in the crook of her mother's arm, and soon they both were asleep. Liam lay on his side, watching them. He glanced at Michelle's elbow. The minor cut looked red and raised, yet the scar she had had for over two decades was barely visible. He thought it strange, but that wasn't the only odd thing. Who was Sarah? He didn't remember her from school, but he was young and going through his own hell. After everything that happened at the lake, what mattered was that Chloe was fine, Michelle was home, and his family was whole again.

At 10:00 a.m. Ben flung open their bedroom door and vaulted onto the bed.

"Ben!" Chloe shouted.

Liam propped his pillow behind him and sat up. "Good morning, buddy."

Ben scanned his sister. "Are you okay, Chloe?"

She nodded her head yes.

Michelle kissed Chloe on the head. "The doctor gave her a clean bill of health."

Ben crawled onto the bed to lie between his father and sister. "Mom saved your life."

Liam gave Michelle a wink. "Mom sure did, buddy. Let's head downstairs and get something to eat."

"I ate breakfast already!" Ben said excitedly. "I was the first one awake this morning!"

Chloe rolled her eyes. "First time ever."

Ben wrinkled his nose at his sister. "Hey! I beat you!"

"Come on, let's go." Liam lifted Ben off the bed and threw him over his shoulder.

Ben squealed and laughed, kicking his legs in the air. Chloe got up from the bed, followed close behind, and laughed along with her brother.

"I'm going to hop in the shower first. I'll be down in a bit," Michelle shouted over the twins' laughter.

She stood in the shower, letting the hot water run down her face. She recounted diving into the water after Chloe. The ability to dive in and retrieve her daughter was instinctual. She remembered swimming laps, her body's smooth, effortless motion through the water, and the smell of chlorine. But there were no pictures of her as a swimmer, and no one in her family told her she swam in high school or college. And what about Sarah? She recalled the details of her death, and Liam knew nothing about her.

She closed her eyes and remembered the night with Liam, a much better memory than the confusion that filled her head. A warm hand on her shoulder made her jump.

"Sorry I scared you," he whispered. He kissed her shoulder while tracing the contours of her body with his warm hands.

She turned around and grazed her warm, wet lips across his mouth, teasing a kiss.

The corner of his mouth curved up, and he leaned down and lifted her, guiding her legs around him, then pinned her against the warm tile wall with his body. He eased into her, causing her to moan.

Their eyes met as steam swirled around them. The chemistry was undeniable, and she questioned whether it was lust or love. That night in February, after a few glasses of champagne, she fell for his charm and his piercing blue eyes. Damn those eyes. Damn, every inch of him that now held her body and heart captive.

She placed her lips on his and whispered, "I love you." Her eyes widened, surprised that the words flowed so easily, since she had found them hard to say only a short time ago.

His eyes sparked with desire as they stared into her soul. He placed his hand on her face and sucked the water from her lips while pulsing his hips, sending her body into spiraling pleasure. *Yes. Oh, yes. It was love.*

Dr. Kent took a seat in her leather chair across from the couch. "How have you been, Michelle?"

"I feel great about things." She smiled. "Liam and I are closer than ever. I told him I loved him."

"Has your memory returned since we last spoke?"

"No, not really," she said, tucking her hair behind her ear. "I mean, I recalled being a swimmer and lifeguard in college after Chloe fell in the lake. I dove in after her; it was like instinct. I knew what to do. But Liam said I played college basketball and didn't swim."

"Is it possible you swam earlier in your life and played basketball in college and confused the two?"

"I guess it's possible. But I don't remember ever picking up a basketball, let alone playing in high school or college."

"You said that you and Liam are closer than ever. Does that mean you remember your love for him or your relationship with him?"

"Well, we have become intimate lately. I am attracted to him, and his relationship with the twins is endearing."

"You also said you told him you loved him. How did he respond?"

"He kissed me. I could see it in his eyes, and I felt it. He told me he loved me the first night we made love, but I pretended to be asleep. I wasn't ready to say it then."

"What happened that allows you to say it now?"

"I just think … He's a loving father, husband, and man. I trust him, and my attraction to him has grown."

"Would you say you remember being in love with him?"

"I don't know. I don't remember being in love with him." Michelle scowled.

She hated that Dr. Kent carried the same expression, whether she was making a statement or asking a question.

"Do you feel you have fallen in love with him again?"

"I guess. I mean, I love my husband, and it shouldn't matter whether it's rekindled love or new love," she snapped back.

"I'm not trying to upset you, Michelle. It's a positive step in your relationship with Liam."

Michelle's cheeks warmed, embarrassed that she had been short in her response, and nodded in agreement.

How would you describe your relationship with the children?

Her mood shifted, and her face lit up with the thought of the twins. "Good. I know their routines. I'm noticing their little quirks and personalities." She chuckled.

"Do you have any memories of them as infants or toddlers?"

"No, I've looked through their baby albums and feel like a mother; the instincts are there. I just..."

"Just what?"

"I love them, I do. How can I not remember being pregnant with twins, giving birth to them, caring for them?" Tears filled her eyes.

"What's important is that you are building a connection with them. Children can be quite intuitive. I believe the memories will come."

A tear rolled down Michelle's cheek. "Next month, it will be a year since my accident. Maybe I have to accept that I may never remember." She looked at Dr. Kent for an answer, but all the doctor offered was a tissue. She looked down. "I'm sorry."

"Don't apologize. Crying is a healthy release."

"Is it possible that not remembering who you were in the past allows you to be who you are today?"

Michelle stared at her. *She already had everything she had ever wanted and needed. Would remembering the past change any of it? Maybe Dr. Kent was right. Being who she is now has made their family whole again, and she wouldn't let anything change that.*

CHAPTER 55

Short Hills
August 2013

"Are you ready, kiddo?" he said, cradling her arm.

She inhaled the scent of fresh flowers as "Canon in D" swirled around them, growing louder. The French doors opened; the guests stood smiling, awe-struck by her beauty. Slowly, they walked arm in arm over a sea of rose petals, guiding them to the altar. A wave of affection came over her as she drew closer to him.

"Who gives this woman away? Her mother and I do."

She felt the warmth of his kiss on her cheek, then he placed her hand in the hand of an outstretched black tux arm. She took her place at the altar, taking his other hand in hers. His dark beard shaped his strong jawline, and his perfectly groomed hair accentuated his dark brown eyes that stared lovingly at her. She stared back at him, confused.

"Chelle?" the groom said.

Another man's voice called out. "Chelle!"

She turned and saw Liam standing at the end of the aisle, his face drawn with pain and confusion.

"Chelle?" She turned her head back to the groom in front of her.

"Mommy! Mom!" She turned her head again as Chloe and Ben called out, running down the aisle toward her.

Her heart pounded in her chest as she looked back and forth between the groom, who held her hands, and down the aisle at Liam and the twins.

"What is happening?" the groom said.

She released his hands and backed away from him.

Liam yelled to her again. "Chelle!"

"Liam!" she cried.

Michelle felt the warmth of a hand on her arm. "Chelle. Babe."

"What?" she whispered, blinking rapidly, trying to open her eyes.

"You were having a nightmare. You okay?"

She sat up. "It was so real."

"Did you have a dream about your car accident?"

She looked at him, her brows pinched. *Was this other man in her dream, Brad?* she wondered. "No, it was just a bad dream."

He got up from the bed and put on his jacket. "I have back-to-back meetings all day, so I may be late for dinner. Are you sure you're okay?"

She nodded. "Yes. I'll see you tonight."

Liam leaned down and kissed her forehead. "Love you."

"Liam?"

"Yeah?"

"I love you too," she said with a smile.

"I'll see you later." He closed the bedroom door behind him and released a heavy sigh. Each dream or nightmare Michelle had sent a wave of anxiety through him. He told himself he should tell her the truth and hope she would forgive him. He turned the door handle and released it when Chloe skipped down the hallway toward him.

"Hi, Daddy!"

"Good morning, sweetheart." He couldn't do it. He couldn't tear his family apart, not when they were finally back together.

Michelle inclined the treadmill and ran at a steady pace, losing herself in a playlist of songs. Flashes of the groom's face haunted her.

Was she marrying someone else? Who was he? She tried to remember his name.

Breathing heavily from her run, she lowered her tired arms and hit the safety string with her hand, causing her to stop abruptly. She stepped off the treadmill, wiped the sweat from her forehead, and remembered the box of pictures.

She went to the guest room and flipped through the box of photos, looking for the bearded man, but found nothing. Confused and frustrated, she hid the box and bag back in the closet.

Her cell phone rang, and an unknown number appeared on the screen. She ignored the call and checked her voicemail.

"Hey Michelle, it's Lucy. I hope you are well. Liam told me about your car accident. I'm so sorry. Listen, I'd love to catch up if you want to talk. Take care."

Michelle wandered through the house and called out to Martha.

"I'm in the laundry room, dear."

Martha was pulling clothes from the dryer and folding them neatly into four stacks. Michelle grabbed a shirt, folded it, and placed it on Ben's pile.

"Martha, do you know who Lucy is? I got a call from her saying Liam told her about my accident and wants to catch up."

"Lucy was your college roommate. Lovely girl. Smart as a whip. You may have a picture of her in the box I gave you."

She returned to the guest room and pulled the box out again. Finding the UConn tab, she pulled out several pictures with names written on the back. One of Lucy and her in their dorm room, another of them at a football game, and the last one of Brad, her, Lucy, and Liam at a party. Maybe talking with Lucy would help her recall something from her time at UConn.

"Hi Lucy? It's Michelle."

"Michelle! I'm so glad you called back. How are you?"

"Good, umm. You said Liam told you about my accident, but did he mention that I have amnesia? So, forgive me, but I don't remember you. I hoped that talking with you might trigger a memory from my past," she rambled.

"Yes, I'm so sorry. Well, while you were in Boston, I missed your phone call. When you didn't return any of my calls, I reached out to Liam. He told me you had been in a car accident. He gave me your new number, so I thought I'd give you a call."

"A nurse in New Jersey told me I was transferred from a Boston hospital. But why was I in Boston?"

You only mentioned being in town and wanting to meet up.

"Liam never said why I was there. I didn't think to ask while trying to remember everything else."

"Well, I'd like to say it was just to see me," Lucy laughed.

"Lucy, this might be a silly question, but did I swim in college or play basketball?"

"You played basketball, and you were pretty good, too. But you tore your ACL and had to have surgery."

She looked down and ran her fingers over the scar on her right knee.

"Oh. So, Brad Cole and I were a couple in college?"

"Yes, you and Brad were inseparable."

"So, I never dated Liam?"

"I don't think so. At least you never said you did, but you told me he took you to your senior prom."

After a few seconds of awkward silence, Lucy asked, "How are the twins?"

"Oh, they're great. I wish I could remember their first eight years or any of the years before my accident."

"Well, the twins were super cute when I met them. They may have been five years old. You were living at the lake house. Do you remember me visiting?"

Michelle sighed, "No, I'm sorry, I don't."

"Listen, if there's anything else I can do to help, please let me know, but I've gotta run. Thank you again for calling me back. It was nice to hear your voice. Bye, Chelle."

"Bye, Lucy."

Her mind raced. Why would Liam not tell her why she was in Boston, and did it even matter anymore?

She put the box of pictures back in the guest room closet, noticed the sweater Jade gave her at the hospital, and wrapped it around herself, finding it comforting and familiar. She reached into the bedside table, opened the folded paper with Jade's number, and felt guilty for not reaching out to her sooner. Her call went straight to voicemail, so she left a message.

"Martha, we're off to the park," Michelle yelled from the mudroom.

"Enjoy your visit, dear."

Michelle saw Jade sitting on a park bench enjoying the sun, a luxury she guessed, as Jade most likely only saw the sun's rays through a patient's window or on her breaks.

Bear greeted Jade first, resting his head on her lap for a pet. "Well, hello there," Jade laughed.

Michelle stood in front of her, smiling, with tears in her eyes.

Jade stood up from the bench and reached her arms out. "Oh, my goodness, you look wonderful!" she said, squeezing Michelle.

"I've missed you." Michelle tilted her head. "I'm so sorry I never called you."

"Listen, I understand. You had a lot going on."

They sat on the bench while Bear took his place at Michelle's feet and watched the birds flutter and squirrels dart around the park.

"So, how have you been?" Jade asked.

"Well, honestly, I still haven't regained my memory from before the accident, but I am really happy. The kids are incredible, and Liam," she sighed. "I swear I fall in love with him more every day. He certainly has mesmerized me with his charm, but..."

"But what, honey?"

"I've had a couple of dreams of another family; a bearded man, other children, and maybe even another dog? There's this feeling in my gut that I can't explain. I'm happy and can't imagine my life without Liam and the twins. A lot of times, I just bury it."

"Well, you were in pretty bad shape from the accident. When you were transferred from Boston to New Jersey, you were still on pain meds, so it could just be a dream that you're remembering."

"I hope so." Michelle looked at Bear and ran her hand over his head.

Bear's ears perked up as a squirrel hopped nearby. "Bear, leave it."

The squirrel darted past them, causing Bear to jolt upright. He yanked the leash hard and broke free, chasing after the squirrel toward the road.

"Bear! No!" Michelle yelled, running after him. "Bear, stop!"

The sound of tires screeching to a halt caused Michelle to scream, fall to her knees on the sidewalk, and cover her head.

"Michelle!" Jade yelled and ran to her.

The sedan driver got out of his car and grabbed Bear by the collar. He approached Michelle and Jade, who were still on the sidewalk.

Jade took Bear from the driver. "Thank you so much."

"No problem. I'm glad I missed him." The driver glanced at Michelle. "Is she okay?"

"We'll be fine." Jade smiled. "Thank you again."

Michelle was still on her knees, trembling and crying. Jade took the leash from Michelle's grip and clipped it onto Bear's collar. He sniffed at Michelle, whining and wagging his tail.

Jade kneeled next to her. "Michelle, honey, talk to me."

She looked up; the fear in her eyes told Jade this wasn't about Bear, so Jade helped her back to the bench.

"Honey, Bear is fine. What happened to you back there?"

"Jade, that red car—it was like the car that hit me. I remember a red car coming at me, then everything went dark."

She placed her arm around Michelle's shoulder. "I'm so sorry, honey. Maybe your memory is coming back?"

"Maybe."

Jade kept her arm wrapped around Michelle. "Let's just sit here for a while, okay?"

Michelle nodded. That was one memory she wished she hadn't remembered. If her memory was returning, would she finally know who the bearded man was that plagued her dreams?

CHAPTER 56

Boston
August 2013

Sam was fully immersed in the routine of the O'Donnell household. Rhylie and Tyler looked to her as a mother figure and became accustomed to seeing her every morning upon waking and again when being tucked in at night.

It wasn't the only role Sam took over in her best friend's absence. Last October, she filled in for Shelby at Aunt B's Bouquets. With the holiday season being one of their busiest times, Sam helped the staff navigate the business and life without Shelby.

Scott came downstairs, plopped on the couch, and turned on the TV. "They both were out in minutes. Did you make them walk home from the park?" he joked.

Sam dried the last plate and placed it in the cabinet. She grabbed two bottles of beer from the fridge and sat on the couch beside him. "You're welcome," she said, handing him a beer.

"Thanks." He took a long swig from the bottle and stared at Sam as tears filled his eyes. "It's been three hundred and ninety-two days. I don't think she's coming back."

Sam stared at him, and her eyes filled with tears. "I don't accept that. She has to be out there. Somewhere."

"The private investigator hasn't found anything. Sam, what if she's...?"

Sam stood up from the couch. "Don't you say it!" she yelled, pointing her finger at him, her voice strained. "No! She's not—"

Scott stood and wrapped his arms around her. "I won't, okay, I won't." He felt her pain as she broke down in his arms. But at some point, they would have to accept that Shelby may never come home.

A month had passed, and Scott never spoke again of the possibility that Shelby could be dead. Putting it out of his mind allowed him to continue to hope she would walk in the front door safe and sound.

He sat at the dining table, opening the mail, finding a letter from the bank that made him furrow his brow. "Shit, how'd I miss two mortgage payments? Possible foreclosure?" He went to the computer and logged into his bank account. "Dammit."

Sam sat in Joey's bar at a booth by herself. She never imagined her life would take such a turn, then wondered why she had come to Joey's. This is where it all began—where her stupid, selfish actions set this terrible nightmare into motion. Yes, Scott kissed her. But she didn't stop him or push him away. Instead, she embraced it and enjoyed it. She hated herself for that more than anything.

After finishing her burger, she drove home to the peace and quiet of her apartment. She looked in the bathroom mirror and frowned at the dark circles under her eyes. Staying with Scott and the kids on the weekdays and working at the flower shop took a toll on her. She sympathized with her best friend and, for a split second, wondered if Shelby had left because she had had enough. Then she told herself Shelby would never leave Rhylie and Tyler.

After brushing her teeth, she threw on an extra-large T-shirt, settled on the couch, and began flipping through TV channels.

A knock on her door startled her. "Who the heck could that be?" She looked through the peephole and saw Scott outside her door.

"Hey, is everything okay? Something happen to one of the kids?"

"Hi. No, no. Everyone is fine." Scott looked down at Sam's bare legs. "Oh, sorry, were you heading to bed?"

Sam glanced down at her legs and blushed. "Sorry. Come in. I'll be right back." She ran to her bedroom and returned, having added a pair of shorts under her oversized T-shirt.

"I know the raccoon eyes are a dead giveaway, but it's still light out; I don't go to bed that early."

Scott chuckled. "I was driving back from dropping the kids off at my parents' and … I don't know. I just didn't want to go back to an empty house."

Sam stared at him for a second. "You want a beer?"

"Yeah, sure." He sat on the couch and sighed.

Sam handed him the bottle and sat down, leaving a full seat cushion between them.

"Thanks. I'll drink the beer, then leave. I know you need a break from me and the kids. You see enough of me during the week."

"Yeah, you're pretty hard to look at," she teased.

Scott laughed. "Ya know, I really appreciate all you've done to help us out. You're a lifesaver."

"I wouldn't do it for anyone else."

Scott raised his eyebrows. "Believe me, I know."

Sam punched his arm, making him laugh again. She looked at him with sincerity. "It's nice to hear you laugh."

He rested his head back against the couch and stared at her with a content smile, making her stomach flutter.

His gaze lingered, and his breathing quickened. "Sam, I…"

As she stared back at him, the outside world disappeared. She set her beer on the coffee table and climbed onto his lap.

He took her face in his hands and pulled her close, kissing her with an unwavering passion.

Sam allowed herself to be free and in the moment. She needed intimacy as much as she imagined Scott did.

After months of being consumed by guilt, worry, and the craziness of navigating life together, they found an intense connection and comfort in each other's arms. There was no turning back now.

CHAPTER 57

Short Hills
September 2013

Michelle walked upstairs to the main bedroom and entered the walk-in closet. She sat on the velvet tufted bench and looked around. Everything was thoughtfully placed, as if on display at a high-end boutique. Her eyes filled with tears. Is this what her life would be, waiting for the twins and Liam to come home? She was grateful for this privileged life, but deep down, she knew something else gave her purpose and passion.

She wiped the tears from her cheeks. "Enough of the pity party." Finding her identity again would be up to her. With no memory of her former self, she would create a new version of Michelle Grant.

With the new school year starting, the calm morning routine of sleeping in on sunny summer mornings was over. The alarm woke Michelle at the crack of dawn and sent her to the twins' rooms to draw them out of their beds. She rested her arms on their shoulders and trudged downstairs to the kitchen. Ben groaned and rubbed his eyes. Chloe yawned and gave her mother a sleepy smile.

The twins settled at the kitchen island while Martha placed their breakfast plates in front of them and Michelle filled their glasses with juice.

Her attention was drawn to Liam as he walked down the staircase. She had seen him in his work attire every morning, but he

looked incredibly handsome today. He oozed power and sophistication in his perfectly pressed GQ attire. His confidence mesmerized
her as he walked toward her, sending a warm sensation throughout
her entire body.

"Good morning, babe." He kissed her cheek, then turned his
attention to Chloe and Ben. "Who's ready for school?"

"I am Daddy!" Chloe jumped off the bar stool and hugged him.
After finishing her breakfast in record time, she ran upstairs to her
room.

He rubbed Ben's back. "Moving slow this morning, buddy?"

He walked over to the coffee bar and filled two mugs. "You excited
for your first day?" he asked, handing Michelle a mug.

She widened her eyes. "Yes. And nervous."

"You'll be great. Look at all the bouquets you've created from our
garden alone." He raised his mug. "You'll be running the place before
you know it."

Her eyebrow raised as she took a sip of coffee. Liam was
confident in her abilities; she'd give him that. And being hired on the
spot for what felt like her first job interview ever, made her believe
she could handle the job and was on the right path to realizing her
purpose and passion.

Michelle walked to the entrance, took a deep breath, and opened the
door to the florist shop, causing a gold bell above her head to ring.
The floral aroma was so familiar and oddly comforting.

"Good morning, Michelle. We're going to put you right to work.
We have five orders already this morning. Come with me."

Her eyes widened as the owner ushered her to the back room.

Nora introduced Michelle to her co-workers as they passed by the
register. She slapped a small pile of handwritten orders onto the six-
foot-long metal table. "The single stems are in the cooler behind us.

To your left are ribbons on rolling racks; to your right, vases and baskets are organized by size," Nora rattled off. "Shout if you have questions." Then she disappeared into her office.

Michelle looked around and smiled as if she belonged. She hummed as she created her artwork, not at all intimidated by working alone on her first day.

A short while later, Nora walked into the backroom. "Wow, are you sure you've never worked at a florist shop? These are spectacular!"

Michelle blushed and chuckled. "Not that I remember."

She finished the last order and helped Nora load the arrangements into the delivery van.

"I could use an extra pair of hands with the deliveries. Would you mind riding along?" Nora asked.

"Sure, I'd love to."

"Kat, Charlie! Michelle's going with me. Hold down the fort."

An hour later, they were on their way to the last delivery. Nora glanced at Michelle. "You have quite a gift. I'm very impressed with your arrangements."

"Thank you. It's calming for some reason."

"Listen, I know this is your first day, and you're not scheduled for Saturdays, but I have a wedding in a couple of weeks and would like your help with the arrangements, delivery, and set up. What do you think? You up for the challenge?"

"Well, I just have to check the kid's calendar, but I should be able to. Are you sure you want *me*, though?"

"Absolutely."

Nora pulled into the driveway of a well-kept, two-story home. "Okay, last delivery."

"I got this." Michelle hopped out of the van and grabbed a rainbow of roses in a crystal vase from the back.

She rang the doorbell, admiring the welcoming entrance to the home, and didn't notice that her childhood home was on the other side of the tall wooden fence.

Jennifer opened the front door with a wide smile.

"Hello, delivery for Jennifer Co—"

"Michelle! How are you, honey?"

"I didn't realize." She paused. "These are for you," she said, handing Jennifer the vase. "Today's my first day. Um, happy anniversary. I have to go, but it was nice to see you," she rambled, then jogged to the van.

"Thank you," Jennifer yelled.

Michelle hopped back into the van. "I recognized that woman," she said, watching Jennifer wave as they drove away. Pictures of Brad's mother floated around in her head.

"Friend of yours?" Nora asked.

"Um, sorta. She knows me, but I don't remember much about her since my car accident."

"Oh, I'm sorry. Well, I appreciate your help today. I think you've found your gift. I look forward to working with you."

"You're welcome. And I think I have, too."

"I should be home around dinnertime."

"Bye, Mommy, bye, Mom," the twins yelled from the living room.

Liam pulled her close and kissed her goodbye. "Have a great day, babe."

Michelle pulled into the parking lot and met Nora and Charlie at the back door.

"We're off to the church, Kat," Nora yelled.

Michelle hopped in the back seat and breathed in the sweet floral aroma of the ceremonial and reception arrangements that filled the delivery van. She was happy to play a minor role on someone's wedding day, not remembering her own to Liam. She put the nightmare of marrying another man out of her head, telling herself it was just a crazy dream.

"We only have an hour and a half to set up the church. They wouldn't allow us to come any earlier," Nora said in an annoyed tone. "So, we'll have to hustle."

The church was serene and calm. Large dark beams provided support, intense beauty, and enveloping comfort.

The organist waved and approached Nora, Michelle, and Charlie. "I'm going to be practicing while you set up the arrangements. Just wanted to let you know so you aren't startled." She smiled and trotted off to the organ.

A few warm-up keystrokes still made Michelle jump until "Canon in D's" romantic tone sang from the organ pipes. Michelle hummed while perfecting the position of the floral arrangements on the pews. Visions of walking down the aisle made her smile. She looked at the altar and pictured the bearded man from her dream, who was smiling and waiting for her. She stood frozen, her eyes wide with wonder and confusion.

"Michelle? Are you alright?" Nora asked, placing her hand on Michelle's arm.

Michelle jumped with Nora's touch. "Oh, sorry. What do you think?"

"I think you look like you've seen a ghost. If you're going to see one, I guess a church is the best place," Nora teased.

"I mean the flowers. How do the arrangements look?"

"They look great. You, on the other hand, are as white as a sheet. Are you okay with finishing?"

The color came back into her cheeks as she blushed. "Yes. Of course, I'm fine."

Michelle sat in the back seat of the delivery van again on their way to the venue, listening to Charlie and Nora talk about everything from the weather to gas prices. She tuned them out when her mind wandered off. *Who was this bearded man who kept appearing in her head? Was he a memory, or was he from her dream? Still, she felt like she should know him.*

When they arrived at the venue, the van came to an abrupt stop. The Hilton hotel manager directed them to the reception hall, where employees buzzed around, setting up tables and laying linens.

"Each table gets a centerpiece, and the head table will have a large arrangement that drapes over the front of it," Nora instructed. "Once those are placed, we'll go over the finishing touches."

Two hours later, the final floral arrangements were placed. The three stood back and admired their work as the hotel employees hustled to lay the last place setting. A canopy of lights came to life, creating a romantic glow.

Michelle gasped. "Oh, it's stunning."

"Our work here is complete." Nora smiled.

Charlie patted Nora on the shoulder. "Another job well done."

Michelle sat in the front seat on the ride back to the flower shop, staring out the passenger window.

"Not to pry, but what happened at the church earlier today?" Nora asked.

Michelle felt her cheeks burn, looked down at her hand, and played with her wedding rings. "I had a memory from before my accident. I think."

"Well, that's a good thing, right? That you're remembering."

Michelle looked at Nora, then returned her gaze out the passenger window. "Yes," she lied. *Was it a good thing that a man other than her husband kept appearing in her thoughts and dreams?*

Nora pulled into the florist shop parking lot and relaxed her shoulders. "Phew."

The three filed out of the van, relieved the long day was over.

"Nice work today, Michelle. Thank you for your help. We'll see you Tuesday," Nora said. "Thank you, Charlie."

Charlie shot his arm in the air without looking back and waved as he walked to his car.

Michelle pulled into the garage, turned the car off, and leaned back on the headrest, contemplating whether to tell Liam what she remembered at the church, but he had told her they married at Brickville Inn, not in a church. This was the third time she had seen the bearded man's face and the second time she had seen herself marrying him. She convinced herself it had to be from her dreams.

Liam greeted her in the mudroom. "Hey, babe. How'd it go?"

Michelle hung her purse and jacket on the cabinet hook and plopped down on the bench. "I'm exhausted. Who knew hauling flowers around would be so tiring? It was beautiful, though. The reception hall looked straight out of a fairytale." She smiled proudly.

Liam kneeled, removed her sneakers, and massaged her feet.

She closed her eyes. "Mmm, that feels so good." *How was it he always knew exactly what she needed? His attentiveness was so damn attractive. He was almost too good to be true.*

"Martha took the kids for dinner and a movie, so we have the house to ourselves."

She opened her eyes to his crystal blues staring back at her. As exhausted as she was, he had her at, *hey, babe.*

"First, follow me," he said, taking her hand and leading her to their bedroom. He stood behind her, placed his hands over her eyes, and guided her to the en suite.

She leaned into him and giggled. "What are you doing?"

He removed his hands and kissed her neck as she looked around, taking in the thoughtful, romantic gesture. A drawn bubble bath, lit candles, a glass of wine, and a sensual instrumental soundtrack played in the background.

"Liam," she whispered.

He ran his fingers through her hair, tied it into a loose bun, turned her around, and slowly removed her clothes. Then, he took her hand and helped her into the bath.

The bubbles swallowed her as she settled into the soothing water. She rested her head on the plush bath pillow and closed her eyes.

He kneeled next to the tub. "Take as long as you like. I'll have dinner waiting for you." He kissed her cheek, then left the room, shutting the door behind him.

The flickering candles, music, and lavender scent lulled her into a trance. How could she have no memory of him—his seductive eyes, or the way his touch made her body drunk with desire? The wine warmed her empty stomach, and she closed her eyes, imagining Liam in the bath with her. Twenty minutes later, the sudden thought of the kids and Martha coming home to them making love popped into her head, drawing her out of her fantasy and the bath.

She wrapped herself in the white plush robe he had laid out for her and made her way to the dining room with her glass of wine. The lit candles placed in the center of the table gave the room a romantic amber glow, bringing a smile to her lips.

Liam came up behind her and kissed her neck. "Feeling relaxed now?"

She smiled and rested her head back on his shoulder. "You spoil me."

"It's easy to." He pulled out the dining chair and topped off her glass of wine. "Be right back."

She stared at the flickering candles; the effects of the wine made her lightheaded and flirty. The bearded man flashed in her mind. She widened her eyes and told herself he didn't matter; he was only a dream. Liam was here, and he was real.

Liam walked into the dining room with two plates and set them on the table.

She bit her lower lip as her eyes swept over him, noticing the short sleeves of his black T-shirt stretched tight around his biceps and his jeans fitting him perfectly in all the right places.

How was it he looked just as handsome in blue jeans and a T-shirt? This wasn't the first time she'd seen him in casual clothes. It had to be the wine on an empty stomach; she had to eat something before she embarrassed herself.

She stared at him while sliding the fork slowly from her lips. "Who knew you were such a good cook?"

He smirked and took a drink of his beer. "I made us dessert, too."

"I thought *you* were dessert," she said, biting the tip of her fork.

His eyebrow shot up, and his mouth curved into a slight smile. "I think you've had enough wine."

"This is only my third glass. I'm fine." She waved her hand at him. "I'm relaxed and all tingly." She giggled.

He shook his head and chuckled.

The smile fell from her lips. Then she looked down, cleared her throat, and moved the food around her plate. *So much for not embarrassing herself.*

Liam left the dining room and returned, setting a glass in front of her. "Here, drink some water; you'll thank me in the morning."

Michelle took a sip of water, stood up, and put her arms around his neck. "Can I thank you now?"

He removed her hair tie, allowing her light brown waves to fall around her face and onto her shoulders. "Finish your water, and you can thank me all night long."

She expected a kiss when he leaned into her, but he reached past her for the glass and placed it next to her lips. She rolled her eyes, took the glass from his hand, and took another sip.

He grabbed the plates off the table and carried them to the kitchen. She followed behind him, holding the wine bottle, her glass, and his empty beer bottle close to her chest.

"Martha should be back with the kids in about an hour. I'll finish cleaning up while you change," he said, placing the plates in the sink. He looked up to find Michelle sitting on a bar stool at the island with her legs crossed and her robe draped open.

She looked at him intensely. "An hour, you say?"

He dried his hands as he walked over to her and threw the towel on the counter. He stood in front of her and ran his hand up her thigh. "Are you flirting with me, Mrs. Grant?"

She looked over her shoulder at an empty glass. "All hydrated," she smirked. She pulled his fitted black T-shirt over his head and opened his jeans. Her eyebrow shot up. "Going commando, I see."

She stared into his eyes as he uncrossed her legs and slid her to the edge of the stool.

He eased into her, weaving his fingers through her hair, then placed his lips next to her ear and whispered, "God, you're beautiful."

She was drunk with a fierce desire, pulling him closer. He was the only man she wanted, even if another plagued her dreams.

They had changed their clothes only minutes before Martha and the twins arrived home.

"Hey guys, how was your dinner and the movie?" Liam asked while loading the dishwasher.

Ben hopped in place. "Good! We had spaghetti and meatballs."

"The movie was really funny, Dad," Chloe said. "Martha even laughed."

"Oh, it must have been a good one then."

Michelle lay on the sectional, hearing their conversation, trying to stay awake, but her eyelids refused to stay open.

She heard Chloe and Ben run toward the living room and woke up when they hopped on the sectional.

"Hey, Mom."

"Ben!" Chloe said sternly. "Mommy is sleeping."

"It's okay, honey. I'm awake." She reached out her arms to invite them in for a hug.

She released a drawn-out yawn. "Did you tell Martha thank you?"

"Thank you, Martha," they yelled.

Liam walked over to the sectional. "Time for bed, you two."

Michelle continued to yawn as she trekked up the stairs behind the twins. After tucking them in, she went to the en suite and struggled to keep her eyes open while brushing her teeth. Liam came in, hugged her from behind, and chuckled.

She turned around in his arms and smiled. "Thank you for tonight. I especially enjoyed dessert."

"It was my pleasure in more ways than one," he said with a grin.

As soon as her head hit the pillow, she fell asleep. *Visions swirled around in her mind, playing out like scenes in a movie, jumping from laughing with a red-headed girl to placing flowers in a vase at the flower shop, then to holding a crying baby while standing in the middle of a busy road. Someone was shaking her, trying to wake her. When she opened her eyes, the bearded man held her arms and shook her. "I'm sorry, Chelle. It meant nothing. You have to come home!"*

Her heart pounded as she stared into the darkness. *Was she awake now?* She reached across the bed and felt Liam lying beside her. She rolled close to him and draped her arm across his chest. It must have been the wine causing these crazy dreams, but she knew the man's voice and his brown eyes were familiar. He wasn't Brad—that she was sure of—but he wasn't Liam either.

CHAPTER 58

Short Hills
April 2015

Michelle came out of the en suite in her robe, her hair wrapped in a towel. The bearded man occasionally appeared in her dreams, but she dismissed him. Two years and eight months—a thousand days—had passed since being thrown into a world of strangers. Now, these strangers were her entire life, and she couldn't imagine it without them. Her life was better than complete. It was perfect.

She opened the top drawer of her dresser and heard the crinkling of paper. In the back of the drawer, she saw a small black velvet box and folded papers under the assorted colors of Victoria's Secret panties. She thought it odd that she had opened this drawer several times since moving back into the main bedroom and only now exposed the hidden treasures.

In crude letters, *Chelle* covered the front of a handmade card, undoubtedly written by a child. On the inside, *Happy Birthday love you 1,000 X infnte Bradley* was written in a rainbow of crayon colors. She smiled to herself, remembering Chloe sharing this term of endearment with her. Now she knew who it came from. Behind the card was a funeral program, *In Loving Memory, Bradley James Cole 1/10/1982 - 5/10/2004.* Her heart sank as she remembered her conversation with Martha and how Brad had died. She ran a finger across the picture. "I'm sorry, I don't remember you."

Then she realized. "January 10th—that's the twin's birthday too! Oh, Liam," she whispered.

Inside the funeral program was a folded paper and a handwritten note to Brad.

Brad,

My heart has shattered into a thousand pieces. You are my heart and soul. I've never known a day without you. You are the one who makes me whole, my missing puzzle piece, fitting me perfectly, completely, and forever. I don't know how to go on without you. I will never give my heart to another. It belongs only to you. I love you a thousand times infinity, Bradley James Cole. I can still hear your voice telling me- I love you a thousand more.

Chelle

A tear fell from her cheek and soaked into the lined paper. *It was so clear now. This is why Liam felt he was her second choice. Did she ever really love him? Was he hoping her memories would never return and that she would fall in love with him, never remembering her love for Brad?*

She pulled out the small black velvet box and opened it. A large solitaire diamond ring sparkled back at her. She was supposed to be with Brad for the rest of her life until she wasn't.

As the day went on, she imagined her conversation with Liam, reciting the right words in her head.

She stood in the doorway of their en suite. "The kids are all tucked in and waiting for you."

Liam left their bedroom and, a few minutes later, reappeared, shutting the door behind him.

She looked at him with a serious expression.

"You okay?" he asked.

"Why was I in Boston when I had my accident?"

He averted his gaze and adjusted his pillow. "You went to Boston to visit your college roommate, Lucy." *Had the time finally come? Would he be able to tell her the truth?*

"Well, Lucy called me a while ago, and I wasn't sure if I should call her back because I couldn't remember her, but then I thought talking to her might help me remember something."

"Well, I'm sure she was happy to hear from you," he said with an apprehensive smile. "Are you coming to bed?" A twinge of panic hit the pit of his stomach as he toyed with telling her the truth of why she was in Boston or just letting it go. He let it go.

She felt Liam wanted to end their conversation, but she didn't. "Also, I never told you that when I met Jade at the park with Bear last year, he got off his leash and was almost hit by a car. I remembered the car accident I was in. A red car hit me, knocking me to the ground."

"I'm sorry, babe. Remembering that must have been jarring."

"It was. I was pretty shaken and glad Jade was with me. I didn't tell you because I didn't want you to think I was having another breakdown."

"Chelle, I wish you had told me."

She went over to her dresser, pulled out the birthday card, funeral program, and ring—leaving the handwritten note in the drawer—then crawled into the bed beside him.

"I want to show you some things I found earlier." She placed the birthday card on his lap. "Chloe taught me this my first morning home."

He read the card and looked at her with a warm smile.

She tilted her head. "I didn't realize the saying came from Brad. Did you?"

"No. Not until now," he said.

Then she placed the funeral program and engagement ring on his lap.

He gave her a questioning expression.

"I found these hidden in my dresser drawer. I know they should mean something to me, but they don't. That sounds cold, but it's true. I'm not showing them to you to hurt you. I'm showing you because I love you. I realize Brad was your best friend and that he and I loved each other, but I don't remember that part of my life. I don't remember knowing him, loving him, or even grieving him."

Liam tilted his head. "Chelle."

"Maybe one day I will remember. But all I know is what I feel now, and it's not from a memory. I love you, Liam. You are the only one who holds my heart."

His piercing blue eyes misted over.

She placed her hand on his cheek, kissed him deeply, and whispered, "Make love to me."

He took her in his arms. He wasn't a second choice or a backup plan. Michelle loved him and only him. All he ever wanted was to be the one. Her one.

They undressed and settled under the covers, intertwining their bodies. Their eyes locked, surrendering their minds, bodies, and souls. Lost inside each other, they connected on a level beyond their control.

Before sunrise, they were still in each other's arms and finally fell into a deep sleep.

Her jaw tightened as anger built inside her. She stood at her front door, watching her husband and best friend kiss on their lawn; slamming the door, then watched her entire life play out in a blur. She heard someone call her name in the distance as a warmth ran up and down her arm. They called out to her again, but this time, they were close.

"Chelle, you're dreaming."

CHAPTER 59

Shelby woke with a start, turned her head, and tried to focus her eyes.

"You okay, babe?" Liam asked. "Were you having another nightmare?"

She sat up and stared at him for a moment as nausea washed over her. Her heart pounded in her chest and pulsed in her ears as tears pooled in her eyes. "I know why I left."

His heart raced, but he kept his voice calm and soft. "Chelle, I can explain."

She saw the anguish in his eyes when he took her hand.

"Chelle, please. I love you so much. Staci meant nothing to me."

She shook her head as tears spilled down her cheeks. "No, Liam." The tightness in her chest tried to suffocate her, causing her to take quick breaths and straining her voice. "You don't understand!"

Liam's eyes widened. "Chelle."

She pulled her hand away and stood up from the bed, holding the duvet to her chest. Her entire body trembled. "No, Liam," she cried, "you're not my husband!"

Her eyes rolled back, and her body collapsed.

Liam called out to her as he jumped up from the bed to grab her, but she fell to the floor with a thud.

Shelby tried to focus her eyes as she woke. "Martha?"

Martha looked at her with compassion, holding a cold pack against the side of her head.

"You fainted, dear. How are you feeling?"

She looked around the room. "Where's Liam?"

"He took the children to school and should be back anytime. He told them you were still sleeping."

As she sat up, the throbbing in her head caused her to place her hand on the protruding goose egg. "Martha." Her voice cracked as her eyes filled with tears. "I remembered who I am."

"Liam told me you were dreaming, and that you said —"

"My name is Shelby O'Donnell, not Michelle Grant."

Martha's face told Shelby that she was concerned more than confused.

"Dear, you hit your head when you fell. Maybe you're still disoriented?"

"No, Martha. I know who I am. My husband is Scott O'Donnell, and Rhylie and Tyler, my children. My parents. They all must think I left them, or that I'm dead." She buried her face in her hands and wept.

Martha wrapped her arms around her. "You seem quite certain about this."

Shelby nodded her head yes.

Martha released a heavy sigh. "I've had this feeling deep down that something was different about you. I believe I just refused to see it." She sat back and took Shelby's hand. "Dear, I need to tell you something."

Shelby trusted Martha. She had been her ally, confidante, and a mother figure for the past two years and seven months. But what could Martha say that would be more surreal than her not being Michelle?

Martha looked away, and her hands trembled. "It's unbelievable, but there's no other explanation."

Shelby could sense Martha was tormented by what she was going to divulge.

"It really is not my place to tell you this, but considering what has happened, you deserve to know the truth."

Shelby's heart raced. "The truth about what?"

"In 1982, you and your identical twin, Michelle, were born two months early to teenage parents and placed for adoption."

Shelby tilted her head. "I knew I was adopted. My parents told me, but they said nothing about having a twin. Why were we separated?"

Martha took a deep breath and shook her head. "Ann and Seth were the adoptive parents. They named you Danielle. About three months after you two were born, Michelle went home, but you were so fragile and had to remain in the neonatal intensive care unit. It was touch and go for you after your heart surgery." Martha squeezed her hand.

Shelby placed her other hand on her chest. *What else did her parents keep from her? Was her entire life a lie?*

Martha's eyes misted over, finding it hard to look at Shelby. "Seth was offered a job in France, and that's when they made the heart-wrenching decision to withdraw their adoption of you and move overseas."

Shelby stared at Martha with wide eyes, unable to process all the emotions swirling around in her head. "Do you think my parents knew about Michelle? Did they know I was a twin?"

"I don't know, dear, and Liam knows nothing of this."

"I felt like something was missing in my life and couldn't explain it. I was happy growing up and had a good life, but..."

Martha looked at her curiously.

"The dream I was having. It wasn't about the accident; it was about Scott and my best friend. They betrayed me." Her anger turned to disappointment, then sadness.

"It was only a kiss, as far as I know, but Scott and I weren't happy.

We had grown apart, and having two kids in eighteen months was so hard. I do remember that." A look of dismay appeared on her face as the realization came to her.

"What is it, dear?"

"Martha, I saw Michelle in Boston. I found her license on the sidewalk." Shelby's eyes darted back and forth as if replaying the scene in her mind. "It's all coming back. I remember looking at her license. I was looking at a picture of myself with the same birth date, height, and eye color. I was in shock and looked around frantically. Michelle was pulling out of a parking lot, and I yelled to her. I tried to stop her. She heard me, Martha. We stared at each other for a moment until…"

Martha placed her hand over her heart, her voice desperate. "What happened, dear? What happened to Michelle?"

"A truck." She shook her head. "It tried to stop, but it hit her car." She sniffled and took a deep breath. "Her car spun around. It came right at me, knocking me to the pavement, then I blacked out."

Liam stood in the bedroom doorway; the color drained from his face.

"Liam," Shelby said softly. She got up from the bed, walked over to him, and placed her hand on his arm. "How much did you hear?"

"That you saw Michelle in Boston and that her car was hit?"

He stared at Martha until she stood up from the bed, looking forlorn. "I'll leave you two to talk."

"Chelle, what did you mean I'm not your husband?"

"Liam, my memory came back." She lowered her gaze, then met his eyes. "You're not my husband because I am Michelle's identical twin sister, Shelby. I'm married to Scott O'Donnell, and we have two children, Rhylie and Tyler."

The look of concern on his face told her he questioned her sanity.

She took his hand, led him to the end of the bed, and sat down.

"Liam, you need to know what Martha told me. Ann and Seth held a dark secret and kept the truth from Michelle."

His face carried so much pain and confusion. "What is happening? I loved you as my wife, Chloe, and Ben's mother."

For a moment, she felt like that scared stranger he had brought home nearly three years ago.

Liam saw the anguish in her eyes and placed his hand on her cheek. "I love you."

She stared back at him. His eyes were honest and caring. Then he kissed her and wrapped his arms around her.

She felt comforted by his embrace, but wondered if he would ever see her as anyone but Michelle.

It still seemed unbelievable to her after telling Liam everything Martha had revealed. "I know Martha found it hard to tell me about what happened when Michelle and I were born." She sighed. "Did Ann and Seth even care, or was I just an inconvenience, and that's why they abandoned me?"

"I can't believe they made that decision easily. But when I think of Chloe and Ben, it's unimaginable." He stared at the floor. "I'm so sorry that happened to you, but Shel, I'm not completely innocent in all this either. I need you to know what happened and why you—I mean Michelle—were really in Boston."

"Before I fainted, you said some woman meant nothing to you. Who is she?"

He couldn't hide the shame that covered his face. "Staci is someone I met in New York City back in college. I had a reputation. I was the proverbial playboy. It was how I dealt with my feelings for Michelle. Throughout middle and high school, I had a crush on her and hoped she would see me, but she and Brad were soulmates, and I couldn't compete with that. Not even after his death. Michelle and I were together one night shortly after he died. Then she found out she was pregnant."

Shelby placed her hand on his knee.

He glanced up with a sad smile.

"Don't get me wrong, we were happy together raising the twins, and I think she grew to love me, but it wasn't enough. Deep down, I resented that she would never love me the way she loved him. And..."

"What? Please don't keep anything from me, Liam."

"After we had a miscarriage, Michelle never admitted it, but I think she felt that Chloe and Ben were Brad's."

Shelby's eyes widened.

"We fought over building this house, and it spiraled into all these pent-up feelings. We both said hurtful things. It ate away at me. I know that's not an excuse, and I'm not proud of it, but after our fight, I went to the city. Staci showed up at my hotel suite. I was drunk, and we started something that I later learned had never happened." He shook his head. "Staci took a picture of herself with me passed out in the bed behind her, making it appear we had slept together. Michelle eventually found the picture, and that's why she was in Boston. She left me." He continued staring at the floor.

"Liam." Shelby sighed and placed her hand on his.

He looked up and met her eyes. "From the moment I brought you home, I knew something was different. I kept telling myself it was because of the accident. It wasn't just that you didn't remember me, the kids, your past with Brad, and why you left—it was also little things like the scar on your elbow and when you said you swam in college."

Shelby ran her fingers over her elbow, searching for a scar that wasn't there.

"Selfishly, part of me never wanted you to remember. We were rebuilding our life." He released a heavy sigh. "The memories I was so worried about weren't even yours to remember."

She rested her hand on his cheek. "You are a good man."

He wanted to believe it, but his eyes were still heavy with guilt.

"I only know the man you are now, the one I fell deeply in love with. I've never known a love like the one I have with you and don't want to leave Liam, but I can't stay either."

He looked deep into her eyes. "Shel, the connection we shared last night, I've never had anything like that with anyone."

"I felt it, too, but..." Shelby closed her eyes and sighed. "You loved me as Michelle, and I imagine you were trying to make things right between us."

He nodded. "I needed you, I mean Michelle, to know that nothing matters more to me than our family."

"Liam, God knows I love you so much it hurts ..." She wiped a tear from her cheek. "But I have a husband and children. I have to go to them. They need to know I'm alive and didn't leave them."

"This whole thing is a nightmare come true." He closed his eyes and shook his head. "Michelle wouldn't stay away from Chloe and Ben this long. What happened to her? Is there any chance she's still alive?"

"I don't know, Liam."

He stood and ran his hand through his hair. "Chloe and Ben will be devastated with their mother missing and you leaving."

"You know how much I love them," Shelby said, then realized their true connection. "Liam, they are my niece and nephew."

A slight smile rolled across his lips. "They love you too. So much." His face sobered, and his jaw tightened. "I have to talk to Ann and Seth. They need to know."

"I think it's best if you and Martha go without me. I have so many questions for them, but I need to call Scott."

Shelby stood and wrapped her arms around him.

He held her close, kissed her cheek, and whispered, "I love you." Hearing Shelby say her husband and children were like a dagger to his heart, and that Michelle was still missing, made him sick and hurt for Chloe and Ben. Now that Shelby would be ripped away from them, too, it made him desperate to hold on to her.

Shelby watched Liam leave the bedroom and close the door behind him. She sat back on the bed, took her phone off the nightstand, and stared at the screen. *What would she say? Hi Scott, I've been living in New Jersey with amnesia, believing I was my long-lost twin. Oh, and by the way, I'm madly in love with my sister's husband.*

Every detail was slowly coming back to her, but at what cost? She typed in Scott's phone number and quickly deleted it, unsure if it was correct. She closed her eyes and pictured his number, then typed it in again slowly. Her heart pounded in her chest as his phone rang.

CHAPTER 60

Martha sat in the passenger seat of Liam's Escalade, quiet and heartbroken. She never imagined that she would expose the Carrington's secret, at least not in this way. It brought her great shame, and the thought of Michelle missing all this time broke her heart.

Liam pulled into the circular driveway and sat for a moment. *How would they even start the conversation with Ann and Seth? The woman you've known for the last two years and seven months is not your daughter, Michelle. She's her identical twin, who you abandoned as an infant. Oh, and Martha confessed your sins.*

Liam opened Martha's car door. "Are you sure you're okay with this?"

"Yes. They need to know that I told Shelby everything. It has to come from me. I suppose it's my penance for keeping such a terrible secret all these years."

He placed his hand on her arm. "I'll never understand it, Martha, but you have been a godsend to me, the twins, all of us. We all love you very much."

Martha tilted her head. Their love warmed her heart, but it couldn't erase the guilt and shame that she carried.

The Carrington's housekeeper greeted them at the front door and led them to the formal living room. Ann sat beside Martha on the ornate couch with a concerned look. Seth stood next to the bar cart, one hand on his hip and the other draped over his glass of scotch.

Liam walked over and stood by the fireplace. His ego wouldn't allow him to show inferiority to Seth, especially after learning of his unforgivable abandonment of Shelby.

"Liam, is Michelle not feeling well?" Ann asked.

"Ann, Seth." Martha paused, searching for the right words, sweeping her hands over her lap as if pressing her skirt.

"Martha, would you like me to tell them?" Liam asked.

"For goodness' sake, what is it?" Seth snapped.

Ann shot Seth a disapproving glance.

"It's alright, Liam." Martha straightened in her seat and clasped her hands.

"I'm afraid our past has come back to haunt us."

Seth's eyes narrowed. "What do you mean, Martha, by our past?"

Martha looked at Ann. "Our Michelle is still missing."

Ann took Martha's hand. "Michelle has amnesia, so maybe it feels like she's missing."

"No, Ann. I'm afraid it's more complicated than that."

Seth shifted his stance, took his hand off his glass, and placed it on his hip, clearly irritated.

"The woman Liam brought home from the hospital is not Michelle. She is Danielle, Michelle's twin."

Ann's face drained of color as she glanced at Liam, then at her husband, whose expression was now hardened and defensive.

Liam crossed his arms and glared at Seth. "Shelby O'Donnell, that's her name now, is Michelle's identical twin—the woman I brought home from the hospital nearly three years ago. She remembered who she was just this morning."

Ann placed her hand over her mouth and looked at Martha. "Where is our Michelle then?"

Martha wrapped her arm around Ann's shoulder and looked at Liam.

Liam relaxed his arms, walked over and knelt in front of Ann, taking her hand. "We don't know, but we will find her, I promise."

Martha took a deep breath and lifted her chin, justified in her decision. "I'm sorry, but I had to tell Shelby the truth. She had to know what happened when she and Michelle were born."

"What she must think of us?" Ann's cheeks burned with shame. "But what of Michelle?"

A deep crease appeared between Seth's brows. "We will find our daughter, Ann, that I am sure of. In the meantime, I want to know more about this Shelby O'Donnell." He took his phone from his pocket and left the room. His authoritative voice trailed up the staircase and disappeared behind the door of his study.

Liam helped Ann up from the sofa and hugged her. "Please know I'll do whatever it takes to find Michelle."

Ann placed her hand on Liam's shoulder. "I know you will, Liam. But how will you explain things to Chloe and Ben? And what of Shelby?" Her hand fell from his shoulder. "You two lived as husband and wife these past few years."

As he took a few steps back from her, his face reddened. "Shelby and I will talk to Chloe and Ben today after school. I will reassure them that their mother loves them and would never leave them." He looked at his mother-in-law with sincerity in his eyes. "Ann, I'm so sorry about all this."

"Liam, none of this is your fault. Just please find my daughter."

He hugged Ann again, and his heart sank. *It was his fault. He couldn't bring himself to tell them why Michelle had really left.*

Their ride back home was painfully silent. Martha stared out the passenger window, and Liam replayed the scene in his head the day Michelle left him. He pulled into the driveway as an incoming call appeared on the car's dashboard screen, making his body tense.

"Hello, Seth."

"Liam, I've learned that Shelby is who she says she is."

Liam glanced at Martha. *That was fast*, he mouthed. He knew Seth had connections in various forms, but it was frightening how quickly he had the information about Shelby.

"My source confirmed Shelby O'Donnell is, in fact, Michelle's identical twin sister. The NICU nurse and her husband adopted her and moved to Boston, where they raised her. Shelby's husband reported her missing while Michelle was in Boston. I have assembled a team to find my daughter. I will take care of this mess," he said arrogantly, and continued. "I also have someone looking into Shelby and her husband, Scott. I'll find out if they were involved in Michelle's disappearance."

Martha's eyes widened, and she covered her mouth.

Liam tightened his jaw. "You seriously believe that Shelby stole Michelle's identity and did something to her? Is that what you are implying, Seth? You saw her at the hospital in Boston—she almost died!"

There was a moment of silence, then Seth spoke again. "I assume you will talk to the children today. Reassure them that their mother loves them and that we will find her," he commanded.

"Yes, we are. Chloe and Ben are always my priority." He ended the call and shook his head.

Learning that Seth revoked Shelby's adoption, and now his accusation of her harming Michelle, caused him to lose all respect for his father-in-law. He couldn't hide the anger and slammed his hand on the steering wheel, causing Martha to jump. He looked at her, and his face softened, seeing tears form in her eyes. "I'm sorry, Martha."

"I'll be fine, Liam, but Michelle?"

An unspoken fear passed between them. After all this time, she couldn't just be missing.

Seth stood in the sitting room of their spacious main suite, staring out the window while finishing his glass of scotch.

"Seth, do you believe Shelby is posing as Michelle? Is this our punishment for abandoning her?"

"We did not abandon her. She was ill, and even the doctors were unsure if she would survive, Ann. We were in an impossible situation," he said defensively.

"I should have stayed here and waited, cared for her. Instead, we left her to fight alone and ripped her sister away from her." Ann broke down. "How could I have been so selfish?"

Seth walked over to her and wrapped his arms around her. "You are not selfish. We did what we thought was right." He took her face in his hands. "You are a wonderful, loving mother." He kissed her cheek. "We'll find our daughter, I promise."

CHAPTER 61

Boston

Scott pulled his phone from his jeans pocket. "Hello?" There was silence on the other end, so he said hello again.

"Scott. It's Shelby." She paused. "It's me. I'm okay."

His voice was tinged with shock. "Shelby? What happened to you? Where are you? Are you safe?"

"Yes, I'm safe. I'm in New Jersey."

He pinched his brows. "New Jersey? How did you end up there? Have you been there all this time?"

"I was in an accident back home and taken to the hospital."

He ran his hand through his hair and paced. "Shel, no one contacted me."

"I didn't have my phone or any ID on me. Well, not my own anyway."

"I know. I found your phone and purse in the car in our driveway."

"I'm sorry, but I found a license on the sidewalk." She sighed. "Scott, they thought I was someone else."

A crease appeared between his brows. "Who did they think you were?"

"They thought I was a woman from New Jersey. I know it all sounds unbelievable, but I remembered who I was this morning."

"What?"

"I was transferred from the Boston hospital to one in New Jersey, where I woke up with amnesia." There was a moment of silence. "Scott?"

"I'm still here. It's just..." He paused and thought to himself, *Amnesia? What the hell?*

Her voice became higher as she talked through her tears. "I want to come home. I need to see you and my children." She cleared her throat. "How are Rhylie and Tyler?"

Scott hesitated for a moment. "They're good. I can't believe you called after all this time. Shelby, I never stopped looking for you. I prayed every day that you were alive, but it's been almost three years." His voice cracked. "I thought you were..."

Shelby put her hand over her mouth, hearing the pain in his voice. "I have someone who can bring me home. His name is Liam Grant."

"Shelby, I want you to come home, but I think we should meet first without the kids." He knew they wouldn't remember her and questioned if she truly had amnesia all this time.

Her heart pounded in her chest, and she scowled. "Do you not believe me?"

"I have to consider the children, you understand?"

"Yes. I do." She knew that Rhylie and Tyler were too young to remember.

"Shel," he said, and paused.

"Yes?"

"I never stopped."

"I know."

"I'll call you when we figure out a place to meet. Bye, Shel."

"Bye, Scott."

He walked to the backyard, where Rhylie and Tyler were playing on their swing set, and sat on the edge of the deck next to Sam, his eyes glossy with tears.

"Scott, what is it?"

"That was Shelby on the phone. She's alive, Sam. She said she was okay and in New Jersey." He shook his head. "I can't believe it." He stared at Sam in disbelief. "She wants to come home."

"What? You're sure it was her? I mean, how? What happened to her?"

"She mentioned being in an accident and somehow finding herself in New Jersey with amnesia for all this time." He shook his head again.

"Seriously? Do you believe her?"

"I don't know. But I told her we should meet before she came home. I just need to be sure."

"That's a good idea. You don't know what's really going on with her. I mean, after all this time."

"She said that a Liam Grant can bring her home."

"Liam Grant?" Sam gave Scott a side eye. "I'm looking into this guy." She pulled her phone from her back pocket and searched for his name. "Hmm."

Scott leaned closer and glanced at her phone. "What?"

"If this is the guy, he's a VP at his family's marketing company. Look at his net worth." Her eyes widened. "Do you think she's been living with this guy?"

"I don't know. She didn't say."

"I'm going with you," Sam insisted. "Are you going to call her parents?"

"No. Not until I see her for myself."

CHAPTER 62

Short Hills

Shelby lay on the bed, replaying her conversation with Scott, sensing his disbelief. She recalled her love for him, but so much had happened that she wondered if her passion for him was gone or masked by her love for Liam.

She wondered what Rhylie and Tyler looked like now, and remembered rocking them to sleep, and their little personalities. Her love for them came flooding back, and she wanted desperately to feel them in her arms again. She reached across the bed and pulled Liam's pillow close, breathing in his scent, then closed her eyes, hoping she would wake from this unbelievable nightmare.

Liam walked into the bedroom and lay down next to her. He traced his finger over the contours of her face, resting his thumb on her chin, and kissed her softly.

"Liam," she whispered, leaning her body into him.

He held her tight and closed his eyes, trying to hold back his own tears as she cried in his arms.

She sniffled and wiped her cheek. "Why did this happen? Please tell me this is all just a terrible dream."

"I don't know. I wish it were."

"Part of me wants to stay right here and never leave. But Rhylie and Tyler." Her heart sank. "They won't even know me."

"I'm so sorry, Shel." He ran his hand through her hair and looked at her with deep sadness. "We have to tell Chloe and Ben today. Martha will be picking them up from school in a few hours."

"I know." She closed her eyes and buried her face in his chest. "What did Ann and Seth say? Honestly, I have so many mixed feelings about them." She scoffed. "Ironically, I came to love the people who abandoned me."

"They obviously want to find Michelle; we all do." He didn't have the heart to tell her what Seth had implied.

They held each other as the minutes turned into hours. Their unspoken grief and confusion drew them closer, both not wanting anything to change but knowing it had to.

Liam glanced at his watch. Martha would be home at any moment with the twins.

They got up from the bed and stood in the doorway, both dreading what had to be done. Shelby took his hand. "How do we do this? How do we tell them I'm not their mother?"

Martha pulled into the driveway, struggling to hold back her tears as she exited the car.

Ben squirmed in his seat. "I can't wait to see Bear!"

Chloe noticed Martha's expression. "Martha, why do you look so sad?"

"Come along, love," she said, taking Chloe's hand.

Ben sprinted out of the car.

"Benjamin, please take your backpack inside."

He spun around, pulled it from the back seat, and ran inside.

Chloe stared at Martha until she saw her father.

Liam greeted them in the mudroom and wrapped his arms around them. They spotted Bear and ran to the living room. His entire body wiggled as he showered them with kisses.

Martha placed her hand on Liam's arm and composed herself, and whispered, "When is Shelby returning to Boston?"

"She called her husband when we were with Ann and Seth." His heart broke with the words 'her husband.' "We are meeting with him tomorrow afternoon in Connecticut, then we'll know when she's leaving." He glanced over at Chloe and Ben. "The kids will get extra time with her, at least."

Chloe ran up to her father. "Where's Mommy?"

"She'll be downstairs in a minute."

Ben came over and stood next to his sister.

"Listen, we have something important to talk to you about, so I need you both to have a seat in the living room."

Worry covered Ben's face. "Are we in trouble, Dad?"

Liam ran his hand down the side of Ben's head. "No, buddy."

Martha stayed close by and watched Shelby walk down the stairs, noticing the dread on her face.

Shelby's heart was in her throat, and she prayed for the nausea to pass. She took a deep breath and counted to ten in her head.

"Mommy, Mom," Chloe and Ben yelled as they ran to her.

"Hello, my loves." She looked at Liam and struggled to hold herself together.

"Dad said he has something important to tell us and that we aren't in trouble or anything," Chloe rattled off.

Ben ran over and bounced on the sectional, then sat next to his father.

Liam looked at them, concealing the heaviness in his heart. "Okay, so you remember how Mommy was in a car accident and couldn't remember us?"

Chloe nodded. "Yeah, she had ambrosia."

Liam smiled. Chloe never failed to amuse him with her malapropism. "It's amnesia, honey."

"Oh yeah, amnesha."

"So, you know that you two are twins but not identical twins? You don't look exactly alike, right?"

Chloe and Ben nodded their heads yes.

"Well, we just found out that Mommy has an identical twin sister, meaning they look exactly alike."

Chloe tilted her head. "Where is she?"

Liam tried to explain honestly and plainly. "Well, first, they were adopted by different parents when they were babies, so they didn't grow up together or know about each other."

Chloe pinched her brows. "They were in their mommy's belly at the same time, then they split them up?"

"Yes." Liam nodded.

"Sometimes babies are born early and need to stay in a special room at the hospital until they are strong enough to go home," Shelby explained.

Liam smiled at her, then looked back at the twins. "Mommy was able to go home first with Grandma and Grandpa Carrington, but her twin sister needed more time to get stronger and couldn't move to France with them." Liam looked at Shelby, thinking that it was going well so far. "When Mommy's twin sister was strong enough to leave the hospital, she went home with her new parents and moved to Boston."

"But why didn't they keep them together, like me and Chloe?" Ben asked.

Chloe gave her father a questioning glance. "Why didn't Grandma and Grandpa wait for her to get better?"

"I don't know. Sometimes things happen we don't understand or have an answer for." He couldn't find the words to explain a decision he couldn't comprehend himself. "Remember when you were on vacation with Grandma and Grandpa Carrington a few summers ago?"

Chloe nodded. "Yes, I do."

"We had a lot of fun," Ben added.

"Well, Mommy went to Boston to visit her friend Lucy, and that's when she had her car accident. We didn't know at the time, but her twin sister was in the same accident."

Chloe and Ben looked at Liam, confused.

"When I brought Mommy home from the hospital…" He paused. Chloe and Ben looked at their mother for an answer.

She spoke in a tender tone. "Remember, I lost my memory."

They both nodded their heads yes.

"Well, it came back this morning." She glanced at Liam.

"So, you remember us?" Ben said excitedly.

"Um, no, honey. I remembered who I was. My name is Shelby. I'm your mother's twin sister."

Chloe pinched her brows. "But you look just like Mommy."

Liam put his hand on Chloe's arm. "Right, honey, because they are identical twins, they look exactly alike."

"Daddy, why didn't you know Shelby wasn't Mommy?" Chloe asked.

Liam looked at Shelby. He had asked himself that very question and felt his cheeks burn.

"Shelby looks exactly like Mommy, and after her accident, I thought she was confused and trying to remember us."

Ben tilted his head. "So, you're Mom's twin sister?"

"Yes, Ben."

"But you said you were our mother?" Chloe snapped as tears filled her eyes.

"Sweetie, I didn't know until this morning who I really was. I didn't even know I had a twin sister."

Chloe stood up from the sectional. "Where's Mommy then?" she cried.

"Is Mommy still in Boston?" Ben asked, watching Chloe's reaction.

"We don't know where Mommy is, but we will find her. I promise," Liam said, taking Chloe in his arms.

Ben pulled his knees close to his chest and rocked back and forth on the sectional with tears in his eyes.

Shelby went over and sat next to him. "Ben, honey, I'm so sorry. I love you both so much. I know this is so confusing and scary. I want your mother to come back home, too."

"Your mother loves you guys more than anything in this world." Liam assured them. "She did not leave you; she's just lost."

Shelby tilted her head. "Maybe she has amnesia too and will remember her family like I did."

Chloe let go of her father and wiped a tear from her cheek. "You remember your family?"

"Yes. They live in Boston. I have a daughter and a son. Their names are Rhylie and Tyler. They would be your cousins."

"How old are they?" Ben asked, wiping his cheek with the back of his hand.

"Um, Rhylie must be five, and Tyler would be three and a half," Shelby said, trying to blink away her tears.

"Are they going to come live with us?" Ben asked.

"No, buddy. They live with their father in Boston." Liam glanced between Chloe and Ben. "Shelby is going back to Boston, too."

The thought of her leaving broke his heart. He knew it was selfish and wanted Michelle back, especially for them, but he couldn't just turn off his feelings for Shelby.

Ben looked at his father. "But she's kinda like our mom, too."

"No! Michelle is our mom, Ben!" Chloe yelled.

Ben's eyes filled with tears again.

"Chloe, I would never try to replace your mother."

"When do you have to go?" Ben asked.

"In a few days."

Liam looked at the twins. "So, we are going to make the next couple of days special, okay?"

Chloe glanced at Shelby with sadness in her eyes. "I'm going to my room."

Shelby hated what this was doing to them, and Chloe took the news harder than Ben.

Liam looked at Shelby. "I'll go talk to her."

She leaned toward Ben. "How about we throw Bear some tennis balls?"

Ben shrugged his shoulders and sniffled his runny nose. "Okay."

Liam ran his hand down Shelby's arm. "Thank you."

She nodded, then led Ben and Bear outside.

Liam went upstairs, sat on Chloe's bed, and rubbed her shoulder. "Hey, kiddo, I know this is confusing and hard to understand. We will find Mommy."

"Dad? Why did Shelby pretend to be Mommy?" she asked, blinking her eyes rapidly.

"Honey, Shelby didn't pretend. Remember, she lost her memory and didn't know who she was. She looked exactly like your mom, and when Shelby saw the pictures of us together, she thought she was in the right place, but couldn't remember. We all thought she was Mom."

"Mommy doesn't know she has a twin sister?"

"I don't think so. She'll be just as surprised as we are." He wiped a tear from her cheek and kissed her forehead. "I love you, sweetie."

Shelby gathered some clothes from their bedroom to take to the guest room. Now that the twins knew, she didn't feel right sleeping in the main bedroom.

Chloe and Ben appeared in the doorway.

"Can we sleep in your bed tonight, Daddy?" Chloe asked.

Liam glanced at Shelby. "Sure, come on." He pulled the covers open, adjusted the pillows, and lay next to them.

Shelby stared at the twins cuddling with their father. A space left for their mother saddened her and, selfishly, one she wanted to fill.

"Well, good night."

"Mom ... I mean, Shelby, can you stay until we fall asleep?" Chloe asked.

Her request surprised Shelby, and then Liam gave her a welcoming smile.

"Yes, of course, honey." She settled on top of the duvet beside Ben and looked at Liam, her eyes expressing her love for all of them and how much she cherished this moment as a family.

Shelby stared at the garden, watching the sun rise behind the tall trees. "It's a beautiful morning, isn't it?" she said as she felt Martha's arm wrap around her.

"Come, dear, please sit with me," she said, leading Shelby to the sectional. Martha folded her hands in her lap. "I'm not proud of the fact that I kept such a secret." Heat crept into her cheeks. "I often thought of you and wondered what had happened to you. I'm so grateful that you grew up with a loving family."

Shelby gave Martha a sincere smile. "My parents were wonderful." She sighed, then her face hardened. "And deceitful."

Martha's cheeks warmed again, unable to hide her shame at sharing the same trait. She heard Liam and the twins upstairs, so she excused herself and went to the kitchen to prepare their breakfast.

Liam rested his hands on the twins' shoulders as the three walked downstairs. He knew they wouldn't be able to concentrate at school, so he allowed them to miss a day and planned to take them to his parents.

Shelby stood up from the sectional and smiled. "Good morning."

Chloe and Ben glanced at her and said nothing.

Liam tilted his head. "Good morning." His eyes apologized for the twin's silence.

Shelby mouthed, *it's okay*. She retreated to the guest room, turned on the shower, and fought the urge to burst into tears.

When she came out of the guest room, Liam and the twins were gone, but she noticed Martha was still in the kitchen.

"Are you hungry, dear?"

"Not really, but I should probably eat before we head to Connecticut." Shelby poured herself a mug of coffee and threw a bagel in the toaster.

Martha started toward her room. "Have a safe trip."

"Martha, wait, please. I'll be right back." She disappeared down the hall to the guest room and returned holding the box of pictures. She set it on the island, lifted the lid, and took out a high school graduation picture of Brad, Michelle, and Liam. "Do you mind if I keep this one?"

"Of course not, dear."

She placed her hand on Martha's arm. "Please give this to Ann; she should have it. Thank you for being here for me and allowing me to be part of this family when I was lost and trying to find my way. I've grown to love you as much as, I believe my sister did." She hugged Martha, then asked, "Can you do one last favor for me?"

"Yes, of course. What is it?"

"Can you take me to the florist shop? I need to say goodbye to Nora and, I guess, quit my job."

CHAPTER 63

Martha pulled into the parking lot and parked the car.

Shelby sighed. "So that's how I became a floral shop owner."

Martha smiled. "No wonder working here felt so right. You were in your element."

"Yeah, I was."

Martha placed her hand on Shelby's arm. "I'll wait in the car for you. Take your time, dear."

Shelby walked in the front door, and the aroma of fresh flowers reminded her why she had been drawn here. Aunt B's Bouquets was her pride and joy back in Boston. Her smile turned to a hard line when she saw Kat and Charlie.

Kat was behind the counter, placing a card in the center of a bouquet, and glanced at the entrance. "Hey. We missed you yesterday."

"Michelle, how ya doing?" Charlie asked as he walked up to her.

"Okay. Is Nora here?"

"Yep, she's in the back. Hey, Nora, Michelle's here," Kat yelled.

Nora appeared from the back room. "Hey there, feeling better? Ready to get to work?"

Shelby smiled awkwardly. "Um, so you know that I have—well, had—amnesia."

Nora glanced at Kat and Charlie, then back at Shelby. "Yes."

Shelby found it hard to articulate her words and rattled off, "Well, recently, I regained my memory, and I'm not Michelle Grant. I'm actually Shelby O'Donnell from Boston, Massachusetts. I have a husband and two kids there. And..." She was unable to finish and broke down.

Nora's wide eyes swept from Kat and Charlie to Shelby. "Oh, honey," she said as she wrapped her arms around Shelby.

Charlie handed Shelby a tissue and patted her shoulder.

"Thank you," she said, wiping her nose. "I'm going home to Boston. I'm going to miss you all. I loved working here." Her voice squeaked. "I'm so sorry, Nora," Shelby said, giving her one last hug.

The bell jingled, and the glass door shut behind Shelby. The three stood shocked for a moment before Kat blurted out, "Holy cow. That's like something out of a movie."

After dropping Chloe and Ben off and explaining everything to his parents, he drove back home, lost in his thoughts. *Where are you, Chelle? Why did all this have to happen?*

It was too quiet when he entered the house, making his heart race. "Shel?" He checked the guest room, then the other bedrooms. He stood at the top of the stairs, heard light chatter, and saw Martha and Shelby enter the kitchen. A worried expression covered his face. "Where did you go?"

"I asked Martha to take me to the flower shop to quit my job and say goodbye. Are you okay?"

"Yes. I thought for a moment; never mind."

She walked over and hugged him. "Liam, I wouldn't just leave you."

The doorbell rang, causing them to glance at the front door.

He released a heavy sigh. "That's probably Seth. He called and said he's coming over." Liam placed his hand on the door handle and paused, reluctant to invite his father-in-law in after their last phone conversation.

"Hello, Seth."

Seth tightened his jaw when he saw Shelby, then looked at Liam.

"I want to talk to you privately."

Liam led Seth to the living room, leaving Martha and Shelby in the kitchen.

"I told you I had someone looking into this, Shelby O'Donnell."

Liam looked at him with disgust and tried to keep his voice low as he leaned toward his father-in-law. "You can stop referring to her as 'this Shelby O'Donnell.' Wasn't it only a few days ago you loved her as your daughter?"

Shelby looked at Martha with concern, then walked toward the living room and noticed the tension between them after overhearing some of their conversation.

They turned and saw Shelby staring at them.

"Do you seriously believe, Seth, that I would harm another person and steal their identity for some sick revenge?" She glanced at Liam as tears flooded her eyes. "Liam, you don't believe I would do that, do you?"

He went to her and rested his hands on her arms. "No, absolutely not." His eyes reassured her.

"So, you don't know Michelle or anything about her?" Seth questioned.

Shelby felt anger surge through her. "No. Of course not. I didn't even know I had a twin. YOU made sure of that," she snapped. "Why would I leave my children and husband? I lay in a hospital bed for months. Then I was handed over to strangers, and you think it was part of some elaborate scheme?" Her face turned scarlet red. "I don't know Michelle, and I didn't do anything to her!"

Seth crossed his arms and glared at her.

Shelby was breathing heavily and tried to speak through her tears. "I've lost nearly three years of MY life! My children were babies. They won't even remember me!" She fell back onto the sectional and cried into her hands.

Liam placed his hand on her shoulder and glared at Seth. "Are you finished?"

Seth's jaw tightened. "We'll need to discuss how to handle this regarding the children. Chloe and Ben must not be collateral damage in this situation."

She looked at Seth with contempt. "I have no intention of hurting Chloe and Ben. I love them as if they were my own. I believed I was their mother all this time. They are, in fact, MY flesh and blood." Pointing her finger at her chest.

Her comment took Liam aback as a sick feeling crept through him, recalling his fertility results and the likelihood that Chloe and Ben were Brad's.

Seth's eyes widened, then he scowled and retorted. "Protecting my grandchildren and finding my daughter is my top priority."

Liam glared at Seth. "Chloe and Ben have always been the priority. I think it's time for you to leave." He walked to the front door and opened it.

Seth narrowed his eyes at Liam and said nothing as he left.

Liam shut the front door and returned to the living room to find Shelby standing by the fireplace.

"I'm sorry I let Seth get to me. You know how much I love Chloe and Ben."

He wrapped his arms around her. "It's okay. I know you do." He held her tighter. "I'm so sorry that arrogant bastard talked to you like that." He kissed her cheek and whispered, "I love you."

CHAPTER 64

Liam held Shelby's hand as she stared out the passenger window. The next few hours, until they reached the halfway point to meet Scott, filled her with anxiety and anticipation. *Would he look the same? Would he be happy to see her? She imagined their embrace, but would she feel the same love for him as she once did? That day in July— the day of the accident—had changed their lives forever.*

"How are you doing?"

Shelby glanced at Liam and gave him a slight smile. "Okay."

The silence was deafening, so he turned the radio on. When the song "Imagine" played, Shelby's eyes filled with tears.

Liam became caught up in the moment and pulled the Escalade over to the side of the road. "I can turn around right now. Bring you home where you belong. We'll figure this out," he pleaded.

"Liam. I have to see Scott. I owe it to him. It's the only way he'll let me see my children. I need to hold them. I know you understand that as a father."

He turned off the radio. "I do. I'm sorry." He gripped the steering wheel and looked straight ahead. After releasing a heavy sigh, he pulled back onto the road.

Shelby stared at his stone face. She hated what this was doing to him.

He finally glanced at her and placed his hand on her leg. She slipped her fingers between his and held his hand tight.

"Do you remember everything now? Like your childhood?"

"It's been coming back in flashes."

He squeezed her hand. "So, tell me about Shelby Jones O'Donnell."

She smiled at him, but her eyes were sad. "Well, one of my first memories was the death of my friend Sarah."

"I'm sorry."

"Looking back, I know you thought I was crazy when I brought her up after Chloe fell in the lake."

"Not crazy, just confused."

"What's crazy is that we were at UConn for four years and we never ran into each other." She released a heavy sigh. "Michelle was so close, and neither of us knew."

He shook his head. "It is unbelievable that you both ended up at the same college."

After telling him bits and pieces of her life, she told him about finding Scott and Sam.

Liam raised his eyebrows. "So, you caught them on your front lawn."

"Yes." She stared at him for a moment. "It wasn't a picture like Michelle found, but I guess things aren't always as they seem."

His expression sobered. "I guess not."

Shelby turned her gaze to the side window. "Hmm."

Their conversation ended in awkward silence, and a few minutes later, they pulled into the park.

Liam scanned the parking lot. "Did Scott say what kind of car he was driving?"

"If he has the same one, it's a white Toyota Tacoma. There he is." She pointed. Her heart raced, and she placed her hand on her stomach as the anxiety churned inside her. She released a long breath from her puckered lips as Liam parked.

He walked around the front of the Escalade to open her door. "Are you okay?"

Shelby nodded, got out of the car, and froze when she saw Scott. He still sported a full beard that framed his face and drew out his dark brown eyes just as she remembered. He was the man from her dreams.

"Are you sure you're okay?" Liam asked again.

"Hmmm?" She glanced at him and back at Scott. "Yes."

Scott stared back at her, then walked over and wrapped his arms around her. "Shel." He took her face in his hands, and his eyes filled with tears. "I can't believe you're really here."

Liam stood with his hands in his jeans pockets. His fitted black T-shirt hugged his chiseled physique, showcasing his biceps. Seeing her in Scott's arms sent a wave of adrenaline through him. It was in his DNA to be the dominant male. He tightened his jaw, took a deep breath through his nose, and looked down.

Tears formed in Shelby's eyes as she recalled her love for her husband, but his touch didn't give her the same comfort as it once did, filling her with guilt and anxiety. Movement in the passenger seat of Scott's truck caught her eye. A red-haired woman stared at her and opened the passenger door. Shelby pulled away from Scott, shocked and piqued at the sight of her best friend.

Sam slid out of the truck and stared at her.

Shelby's body tensed, feeling more irritated than her tone revealed. "Sam, you came with Scott?"

"Hey Shel, I'm so glad you are safe. We had no idea what happened to you." Sam reached out her arms and hugged her.

Shelby gave Sam a contrived embrace, as her best friend's betrayal still ran deep.

Liam walked up to Scott and extended his hand. "Liam Grant," he said, shaking Scott's hand tightly.

Shelby watched her husband and the love of her life stand in front of her, tolerating a handshake. She closed her eyes for a split second and prayed she would wake from this nightmare, but when she opened her eyes, both of them were staring at her.

"Do you want to sit at a picnic table so we can talk?" Scott asked.

Shelby gave him a sincere smile. "Sure."

Sam followed Scott to the picnic table while Liam walked close behind Shelby, placing his hand on the small of her back. His touch made her stomach flutter, causing her to blush in the presence of her husband.

Scott and Sam sat down on the same bench at the table, forcing Shelby to sit across from them. She suspected they might have become a couple after almost three years.

A deep crease appeared between Scott's brows. "Shel, what happened to you? You said you found a license belonging to someone resembling you?"

Shelby looked up at Liam, who stood beside her with his arms crossed, then back at Scott.

"Yes. I just found out that Michelle Grant, Liam's wife, is my identical twin."

"You have an identical twin? Did your parents know?" Scott asked.

"Yes, I do. And I don't know."

Sam shook her head. "Shelby, that's crazy."

She gave Sam a look of indifference. "Anyway, the morning after I saw you and Sam on our front lawn, I dropped the kids off at my parents, drove back home, and walked to the park to think."

Scott glanced down, then up at her. "I'm sorry, Shel."

"I know," she said.

Sam looked away. "We're both sorry."

"I know!" Shelby said sharply and cleared her throat. "Michelle happened to be in Boston and must have dropped her license. I found it on the sidewalk and couldn't believe what I was looking at. I saw her pulling out of a parking lot and yelled to her." Shelby sighed. "And for a moment, we stared at each other. It all happened so fast." She closed her eyes and took a deep breath. "A truck hit her car, and before I knew it, I was on the pavement and lost consciousness." She looked up at Liam. "We don't know what happened to Michelle. They assumed she had been thrown from her convertible, but it was actually me. Her license was on the road next to me, so they assumed I was Michelle."

A deep crease appeared between Scott's brows. "Jesus."

Sam's eyes widened.

"I know it all sounds like a crazy story, but I promise you, Scott, I didn't leave you and the kids. I would never leave Rhylie and Tyler."

Shelby felt Liam place his hand on her shoulder. "The state police contacted me and told me my wife had been in a car accident. When I got to the hospital, she was in the ICU; she was injured pretty badly. After I had her transferred back to New Jersey, she finally woke up but had no idea who she was."

"I'm so sorry to put all of you through this." Shelby put her hair behind her ear and nervously played with a twig she picked up from the table. "I had amnesia, and my memory came back the day I called you."

Sam cleared her throat and looked at Liam. "So, your wife has been missing this whole time?"

He removed his hand from Shelby's shoulder and slid both hands into the front pockets of his jeans. "I'm afraid so. She wasn't in her vehicle when it was pulled from the river. As Shelby said, they assumed she was ejected from her convertible during the accident."

Sam's gaze softened. "That's crazy. I'm so sorry."

"Thank you. Our family has been through so much already, and we are just looking for answers as to what happened to her."

Scott gave Shelby a sympathetic look. "I'm sorry I asked you to drive here to meet with me, but I had to be sure who I was bringing home to my—I mean our—children."

Shelby placed her hand on Scott's. "I know. It's been a long time."

Liam looked away, telling himself to get a grip. He had to let her go; after all, she was Scott's wife.

Sam noticed Liam's reaction and wasn't surprised. She, too, felt a sharp pang of jealousy with Shelby and Scott's mutual affection.

"I knew you weren't planning on bringing me home today. I get it." Shelby played with the twig again.

"Shel, I show Rhylie and Tyler your picture every night before bed, and we say a prayer."

Shelby tilted her head. "How are they? I know they won't remember me. They were too little."

"They're good. Rhylie is in kindergarten now, and Tyler's doing well in preschool."

Scott smiled and put his hand on Sam's. "Sam here has been a big help." Sam smiled back, embracing his touch.

Shelby looked at his hand on Sam's, then met Scott's eyes. Jealousy stirred in her for a second until she felt Liam's hand return to her shoulder.

Scott quickly removed his hand from Sam's and looked up at Liam. "Do you have children?"

"Yes, we have ten-year-old twins, Chloe and Ben."

Shelby knew it was out of habit for him to say 'we.' For a moment, she felt Liam was referring to her, not Michelle, and felt selfish thinking such a thing.

"I bet your children found this situation very confusing." Scott shifted his gaze from Liam to Shelby. "I'm confused by it all. I mean,

I'm so grateful you're alive and safe. And to find out you have an identical twin—it's unbelievable," he said, shaking his head.

In a moment of awkward silence, Shelby noticed Sam squirming. She knew her well enough to know that she spoke her mind.

Sam sat up straight. "So, I'm just going to come out and say it."

Scott looked at her, unsure of where she was going with her comment.

Sam stared at Liam. "Shelby had amnesia and was brought to your home and told that she was your wife, Michelle. So here we are, over two and a half years later. I can't imagine she was sleeping in the guest room the entire time."

Scott scowled at her. "Sam! What the hell?"

Liam squeezed Shelby's shoulder and took a deep breath. He started to respond when Shelby placed her hand on his and interrupted him.

"And I suppose my children were not the only ones you tucked into bed at night, my dear friend." Shelby glared at Sam. "I didn't know who I was. You two knew exactly who you were sleeping with."

Scott shot her an intense look. "Shelby, that's not fair. I never stopped thinking about you, looking for you. Sam also helped at the flower shop, and I nearly lost the house paying for a private detective!"

Her heart sank thinking of her staff at Aunt B's Bouquets and that Scott and the kids almost lost their home.

"Jesus, I was questioned by the police. They thought I did something to you. It wasn't like Sam and I were having some great love affair the whole time!"

Shelby sighed and broke the twig in half. "So, you consoled each other like you did on our front lawn?"

Sam looked down as shame covered her face.

Scott's eyes grew wide, and a vein appeared along his temple. His face was bright red, and he got up from the bench.

Liam tensed, placing both hands on Shelby's shoulders, and leaned his body into her.

"Sam was there when I needed someone to talk to. She understood my pain; she was in pain, too. We both lost you!"

Shelby took a deep breath. "I think we should talk alone."

They walked to another table as Liam and Sam waited awkwardly, not speaking a word to each other.

"Shel, I've been carrying a lot of guilt from that night. I was drunk, and I know that's not an excuse, but I never meant to hurt you. I loved you."

"Scott, we were growing apart and unhappy. I know you felt it too. And now, so much has happened."

"Shel, I have to ask. Do you really want to come home?"

Tears filled her eyes. "Yes, of course I do."

"I mean, you show up here looking perfectly fine and living quite the life," he said, nodding his head toward Liam, "with GQ over there."

"What were you expecting me to look like? And that's not fair. I didn't know who I was, Scott. And I would never intentionally leave my children."

Scott shook his head. "It's just unbelievable, all of this."

"Are you and Sam together now? Do *you* want me to come home?"

Scott looked away. "Shel..."

"I knew things had changed between us after having Tyler, but I never thought you and ... Sam."

"We didn't plan it."

Shelby tilted her head as tears pooled in her eyes. "Do you want to put our family back together?"

Scott placed his hand on Shelby's cheek. "I think we should try,

Shel. We owe it to Rhylie and Tyler and ourselves."

"I think so, too." She wasn't sure if she believed the words coming out of her mouth, but she told herself it was the right thing to do. "Did you tell my parents I'm okay, and that you were meeting me?"

He removed his hand from her cheek. "No. I wanted to see you for myself first."

"That's probably for the better. I want to talk to them and ask them why they kept the truth from me."

They returned to the picnic table where Shelby stood next to Liam, and Scott sat beside Sam again.

"I know this is a lot to ask of you, Liam, but would you be willing to bring Shelby to Boston? I need to talk to the kids," Scott said, giving Shelby a sincere smile. "I'll text you the park address where we can meet, and I'll bring Rhylie and Tyler with me."

"Shel, they are awesome kids. Rhylie is so kind and smart, and we have Tyler completely potty trained." Sam smiled proudly.

Shelby scowled at Sam. "Yes, *my* children are awesome."

Liam crossed his arms. "I'll need a couple of days to make arrangements. Will Saturday work?"

Shelby looked at him. She knew he was lying. He could have her in Boston by nightfall.

"Yes, Saturday is good," Scott said.

"Scott, please give Rhylie and Tyler a hug and kiss for me. And tell them I love them very much and that their prayers worked."

He nodded. "I will."

The four walked to the parking lot and stopped by Scott's truck. Shelby placed her hands on Scott's arms. "Thank you." Then she hugged him, feeling love for him as a friend, not as her husband, and hoped in time that would change.

Liam nodded. "Scott."

Scott nodded back. "Liam."

Liam held the car door open for Shelby. After shutting it, he glanced back at the Toyota Tacoma and made eye contact with Scott. They stared at each other for a moment, then Scott turned to Sam.

Shelby placed her hand on Liam's leg as they drove out of the parking lot. "Thank you, and I'm sorry it got so intense." She looked in the side-view mirror and saw Scott and Sam embrace, then kiss.

Liam glanced at her. "Are you okay?"

"Yes." She noticed Liam glance at the rearview mirror; his face hardened as he undoubtedly also witnessed Scott and Sam's affection. "I'm not naïve. I saw their body language, and Scott basically admitted they were together when we talked alone."

Liam stopped and put the Escalade in park. His tone expressed his frustration. "Then what are we doing here?"

Shelby scowled. "What do you mean?"

"I won't let him hurt you, Shel. I don't think you realize what it did to me seeing you in his arms."

"Liam, you and I are married to other people. I won't lose my children. I've already lost so much time with them. I don't want to argue with you."

"So you're going back to him even though he's in love with your best friend?"

Her eyes narrowed, and heat rushed into her cheeks.

He glared at her, unwilling to lose her without a fight.

Shelby released an irritated sigh. "I know a part of you still loves Michelle. If she came home today, would you leave her for me, her sister? What would that do to Chloe and Ben?"

He closed his eyes and gripped the steering wheel. "I just…"

"Liam, it's not your job to protect me. I don't know if Scott and I will be able to reconnect, but we have to try for Rhylie and Tyler's sake. And, God willing, when Michelle comes back, you need to try to put your family back together, too."

He drew his eyes to the windshield and clenched his jaw, releasing a heavy sigh through his nose, then pulled out of the parking lot.

She stared at him for a moment, then returned her gaze to the passenger window. "I know this is hard. It's hard on all of us."

CHAPTER 65

They walked into the mudroom and found Martha in the kitchen.

"I'm glad you had a safe trip. The children are upstairs getting ready for bed."

Liam nodded. "Thank you, Martha."

Since the news of their mother missing and Shelby leaving soon, Ben took up residence in Chloe's room. It continued to be his safe place when something upset him or he was scared.

Shelby glanced at Liam as she walked toward the guest room. "I'm going to change," she said, still irritated by their argument.

A few minutes later, there was a knock on the guest room door. "Shel?"

She opened the door and looked into his seductive crystal-blue eyes, causing the predictable flutter in her stomach. She loved and hated that he had that effect on her.

"Chloe and Ben asked if you would say good night to them."

"Of course."

Shelby knocked and peeked into Chloe's room. "Hey, you two, can I give you a hug?" They both nodded their heads. She kneeled on the bed and grabbed them in her arms. "Sweet dreams, my loves," she said, hugging them tightly. "I love you both so much; never forget that."

Ben hopped off Chloe's bed, settled on the trundle, and smiled at Shelby as she turned off the lights and shut the door.

When she walked down the stairs, she noticed Liam sitting on the sectional, staring at the fireplace. She sat next to him and released a heavy sigh. "I'm going to miss tucking them in at night."

He put his arm around her and pulled her close. "They will miss it, too. Look, I'm sorry about earlier."

"I know." Shelby relaxed in his arms, not wanting their last days together to be filled with anger and frustration. After a few minutes, she stood up, reached for his hand, and led him to the guest room. She shut and locked the door behind them. Nearly three years ago, the guest room kept her safe from her husband, a stranger. Now, it would be her haven with the love of her life.

She looked into his eyes. "I know we just came from seeing Scott, but—"

Before she could finish, Liam took her face in his hands and kissed her deeply. He released her bun, allowing her light brown waves to fall onto her shoulders.

They undressed each other, studying one another as if they were locking the images in their minds. As they lay on the bed, Shelby pulled him close, guiding his hips between her legs.

His eyes glowed with affection. "You have my heart and every part of me."

She stared at him intensely. "For one last night, you're mine," she whispered.

He kissed her neck and rested his lips next to her ear. "Tell me there's no one but me."

"Liam," she purred as he pressed deeper into her, causing her breath to catch.

"Tell me," he whispered.

She took his face in her hands. "There's no one but you."

The sunrise peeked through the guest room window. They would only have a few hours before Chloe and Ben wandered downstairs.

Shelby lay tucked under Liam's arm, running her finger over the contour of his abs.

He kissed her forehead and sighed.

She rolled on top of him, resting her hand and chin on his chest, and stared into those damn eyes, the ones that held her heart captive.

He brushed a strand of hair from her face and rested his thumb on her cheekbone. "When you lie next to him, I want you to think of me."

She tilted her head. "Every time I close my eyes; I think of you. I can feel your touch, the warmth of your body on mine, and your scent." Tears pooled in her eyes. "You are seared into my memory, Liam Taylor Grant."

A single tear spilled down her cheek and fell onto his chest. He rolled over on top of her and wiped the trail left by her tear with his thumb, then kissed her passionately, holding her as if he would never let go.

A warm breeze rocked the anchored Legacy on the shimmering water. Shelby watched Liam help Ben cast his line; it would be the last time for her.

Chloe sat between Shelby and Martha, trying to enjoy the day, but struggled with longing for her mother and not wanting Shelby to leave.

Shelby placed her hand on Chloe's knee. "Chloe, you are the smartest, kindest, and strongest young lady I've ever had the privilege to know and love. Your mother lives inside you and Ben, and I know she is so proud of both of you."

Chloe glanced at Shelby, then drew her eyes away. "I don't want Mom to be sad because I don't want you to go," she said, looking down and playing with the decorative string on her blouse.

Shelby tilted her head and glanced at Martha.

Martha wrapped her arm around Chloe. "Honey, your mother would never be upset with you for loving Shelby and not wanting her to leave."

"Dad! Dad! I got one!" Ben yelled.

Liam helped reel in the fish while Ben beamed excitedly.

"Good job, Ben!" Shelby yelled. Then, the three of them walked over to admire the prized catch.

"He can't breathe; throw him back, Daddy," Chloe shouted.

"It's okay, honey. We will."

Chloe's reaction didn't surprise Shelby. She had become more sensitive to the world around her after learning that her mother was still missing. But Ben kept his emotions hidden, acting as if nothing would change.

As the sun lowered, they left Legacy floating at the dock and piled into the Escalade. Shelby sat in the back seat between the twins. Both sat quietly and stared out their windows in a daze from the fresh air and sunshine.

Tonight would be their last dinner together as a family. Shelby had asked Martha to make the twins' favorite dish of spaghetti and meatballs. She knew a day on the water, a family dinner, and a movie night were planned for her, but Chloe and Ben needed the distraction just as much as she did. She was so torn, wanting to protect them from heartbreak but wanting to go home to Rhylie and Tyler, who had also lost their mother.

Ben swirled the fork in his spaghetti, raised it high above his head, opened his mouth wide, and attempted to lower the sauce-covered strands into his mouth. As Ben slurped, the noodles bounced between his chin and the tip of his nose, leaving streaks of red on his face.

Chloe scrunched her nose, disgusted by her brother's table manners.

"Hey, Ben, you got a little something..." Shelby circled her finger in front of her face and handed him a napkin. She looked at Liam and chuckled.

When he smiled back, she noticed the deep sadness had left him for a moment.

Martha cleaned the dishes, dimmed the kitchen lights, and walked to the sectional. "Thank you for a lovely day, everyone. It was truly special. I'm going to retire to my room. Enjoy the movie. Good night."

Shelby got up from the sectional. "Martha, thank you for all you've done for me. I will always treasure your kindness and friendship."

Martha wrapped her arms around her. "I truly hope you find peace, dear. We all care deeply for you. I know it was with the belief that you were Michelle, but you hold a special place in my heart." She gave Shelby a sincere smile as tears filled her eyes. "Fate has a peculiar way of coming full circle. Good night, dear."

Liam walked into the living room holding a large bowl of popcorn. "Okay, who's ready for the movie?"

"We are Dad," the twins said, as they settled on the sectional.

She would miss this family ritual, then imagined herself holding Rhylie and Tyler in her arms.

Shelby looked over at Liam. He had been watching her daydream. Her heart broke with the heaviness of this last night together. In less than twenty-four hours, she would have to say goodbye to them.

As usual, Chloe and Ben were half asleep before the movie's end. Liam picked up Chloe and started toward the stairs when she awoke. "Can we sleep in your bed again, Dad? With you and Shelby?"

Liam tilted his head and glanced at Shelby.

She smiled and nodded.

He rubbed Chloe's back as she laid her head on his shoulder. "Sure, honey."

Shelby completed her ritual of cleaning up and turning the movie off for the last time. She went to the guest room and stared at herself in the mirror as she brushed her teeth. Then, she rested her hands on the sink. "Just keep it together one more night."

Liam was in bed with the twins, who were already fast asleep.

She crawled under the covers and lay on her side, facing him.

He reached his arm across the top of the pillows, waiting for her to slide her fingers between his.

She held his hand, losing herself in his gaze as he mouthed, *I love you.*

CHAPTER 66

Shelby was filled with guilt, heartache, and gratitude after literally walking in her sister's shoes and loving her sister's children and husband. She sat on the guest room bed, holding the picture of Michelle, Chloe, and Ben. "Thank you for letting me live in your world. Two years and eight months; a thousand days. If only we had a thousand more times infinity."

When she came out of the guest room, Chloe and Ben greeted her. They took her hands and walked her to the kitchen island, which was covered with a breakfast spread, a bouquet, and handmade cards.

"We made you a special breakfast," Chloe said, trying to hide her sadness.

"Thank you, sweetie."

Shelby sat on the bar stool and admired the bouquet of roses.

Ben smiled proudly. "Me and Dad picked the flowers from our garden for you."

"They are beautiful. Thank you, honey," she said and picked up the card he made.

She smiled at her stick figure throwing a tennis ball to Bear, whose round body looked more like a turtle than a dog. On the inside, he wrote in large letters, *Thank you for taking care of us and being our Mom. Love, Ben.*

She pulled him into her arms while wiping a tear from her cheek. "I love this. Thank you, Ben."

Chloe handed Shelby her card, which displayed colorful hand-drawn flowers. Inside, Chloe taped a picture of the four of them with

Bear, who looked like he was smiling while sitting proudly between the twins. On the opposite page, a large heart surrounded the words, *I love you 1,000 X infinity.* Shelby held the card to her chest, struggled to speak, and wrapped her arms around Chloe. "I love you a thousand more, sweetie," she whispered.

Bear came over to Shelby and rested his head on her lap. He wagged his tail and looked at her with his big brown eyes. "Oh, I'm going to miss you too, Bear," she said, running her hand over his silky head. "You're such a good boy."

Shelby looked up when she heard Liam walk into the kitchen. She resisted the urge to place her arms around him and kiss him as she had done every morning.

"This was very nice, guys. Please go get ready; we need to leave for the airport in an hour," he said, ushering them out of the kitchen.

When the twins were out of sight, he took her hand and led her to the mudroom. "I need to feel you in my arms," he said, pulling her close.

She kissed him tenderly and melted into his embrace. "It's not fair. Fate can be so cruel."

They sat quietly while eating the special breakfast from the twins, which was more out of consideration than hunger. When they finished, Liam took her hand and led her upstairs to the main bedroom. A suitcase sat on the bed, open, waiting to be filled.

"Please take whatever you need or want."

Shelby looked at him and tilted her head. "Liam."

He turned to walk out of the bedroom when she grabbed his arm and pulled him close.

"I need to hold my babies, but I don't want to leave you." Her breathing quickened as panic set in. "I can't make my heart slow down."

Liam took her face in his hands. "Look at me." She stared into his eyes. "Take a deep breath and let it out." He took a breath with her. "Again."

A single tear rolled down her cheek as they rested their heads together. "Please. Stay with me until you take me to Sc—"

Liam kissed her, stopping her from saying *his* name.

He walked over and stared out the bedroom window while she carefully placed Jade's sweater and every card and gift from the twins into the suitcase.

Liam walked back over to the bed as Shelby zipped the suitcase closed.

She took his hand and placed the birthstone necklace in his palm. "Michelle should have this."

He looked at his hand and closed his fingers around the necklace.

She sat on the side of the bed, her hand trembling as she looked at the rings on her finger.

He set the necklace on the nightstand and kneeled in front of her, resting his hands on her lap.

She slid the rings off and laid them next to the necklace.

They had been placed there nearly three years ago by her sister. But for Shelby, it wasn't because she wanted to leave Liam; it was because she had to.

He stared at the rings for a moment, then looked up at her, placed his hand on her cheek, and whispered, "Once again, the woman who holds my heart loves another man." He closed his eyes and laid his head in her lap and broke down.

Tears streamed down her face as she ran her fingers through his hair. Her chest tightened as she fought the urge to sob.

He lifted his head from her lap, his eyes carrying so much sadness. "Not only are Chloe and Ben losing their mother again, I'm losing the love of my life."

As the private jet flew high above the clouds, Chloe and Ben sat quietly, looking out the small oval windows. They were usually chatty and excited to fly, but their deep sadness kept them seated. The short flight spared them from four torturous hours on the road, agonizing over the heart-wrenching goodbye they would endure when reaching their destination.

Shelby stared out the plane window, remembering how Tyler would fall asleep in her arms as she ran her finger down the side of his chubby little cheeks while rocking him. Then she wondered if Rhylie still wrinkled her nose at anything she disliked. When she glanced at Liam, she realized he had been watching her, so she gave him a smile and then returned her gaze to the window. Her eyes filled with tears at the thought of saying goodbye to him, to all of them.

They pulled into the parking lot across from the park and walked to the crosswalk. Shelby looked back toward the parking lot entrance, the first and last place she saw her sister.

"You okay?" Liam asked.

"Hmm?" She shifted her eyes to him. "Yeah, this is where the accident happened."

He took her hand and squeezed it, then pressed the little silver button on the tall black pole. A bright orange hand held them in place on the sidewalk in front of Boston's City Wine and Spirits. This is where one life ended and a new one began. A bright white walker appeared on the crossing signal and started the countdown. The five of them crossed the three-lane roadway and stopped at the entrance to the park.

Liam placed his arm around Martha as tears filled their eyes.

Shelby looked back at Liam, smiling with love and heartbreak. She held tight the little hands not by birth but of blood, surrendering a life that for only a moment belonged to her.

"Mom, I mean..." Chloe paused and looked up at Shelby. "Can we go meet them now?"

With a bittersweet smile, she replied, "Yes, my love. Yes."

CHAPTER 67

Boston

From a distance, Shelby saw Scott. He looked in their direction and waved. Rhylie and Tyler chased each other around a park bench, screaming and laughing. Rhylie's hair was darker and longer, and she stood almost a foot taller than when Shelby saw her last. But Tyler was now a little boy with curly blonde hair. She wanted to run to her children, but knew it would frighten them.

Scott gathered Rhylie and Tyler and rested his hands on their shoulders, watching Shelby approach them.

Her eyes filled with tears, wanting to grab them into her arms, but she saw they were unsure as they clung to their father.

Shelby knelt in front of them. "Hi Rhylie, hi Tyler. I missed you so much. You're so big now."

Rhylie offered a shy smile, but stayed close to her father.

"See, I told you all our prayers worked. Mommy came home to us," Scott said, rubbing their shoulders.

Shelby tilted her head. "I want you to meet Chloe and Ben; they are your cousins."

Chloe smiled. "Hi."

Ben gave them a slight wave.

Rhylie smiled and waved back.

Tyler, bored with standing still, approached Ben and touched his arm. "Tag!" he shouted and ran away.

Scott laughed as Ben tilted his head and shrugged his shoulders, then ran after Tyler.

Chloe followed Martha and her father to a picnic table, as running around the park was something a young lady such as herself was much too mature for.

Shelby followed Scott and Rhylie to the park bench and sat with them. "I know, honey, that you don't remember me, and that's okay. I was gone for a long time."

"Where did you go?" Rhylie asked, sitting close to her father.

"I was in a bad accident, and when I hit my head, it made my memory go away. I didn't know who I was and couldn't remember Daddy, you, or Tyler for a long time. But now I do. And I'm so happy to see you."

"Oh." Rhylie looked up at her father.

"Remember, we talked about this? Mommy is coming home with us today." Scott smiled at Shelby.

Rhylie nodded her head yes. "Is Sam coming too?"

The smile fell from Shelby's lips when she looked at Scott.

His eyes said sorry. "No. Sam is going to her apartment, honey."

Rhylie frowned. "Sam isn't going to live with us anymore?"

Before Scott could answer, Shelby put her hand on Rhylie's knee. "You'll still get to see Sam," she said, giving her daughter a reassuring smile.

Scott knew it was incredibly hard for Shelby to say that, but he was grateful.

Before the accident, Rhylie was only starting to string words together at two and a half, and now she could hold a conversation. The three talked as Shelby learned more about her daughter.

After a while, Liam, Chloe, and Martha walked over to them. Liam placed his hand on Shelby's shoulder and squeezed it. "I'll get your suitcase from the car."

His touch brought her comfort and heartache. "I'll go with you, Liam." Then she glanced at Scott.

He knew Shelby wanted to say goodbye to Liam privately, so he gave her a nod, and wrapped his arm around Rhylie. He understood, as he had said goodbye to Sam just this morning and helped her take her belongings from their house back to her apartment.

Chloe stood in front of Scott and Rhylie and smiled.

"Hi Chloe, I'm Scott, Rhylie and Tyler's dad."

"Hi," she said, then looked at Rhylie.

"What grade are you in?"

"Kindagaden," Rhylie said shyly.

Chloe smiled proudly. "I'm in fourth grade."

Tyler and Ben finally came over to Scott, Martha, and the girls and flopped down on the picnic table bench, panting. Their hair was sweaty and pasted to their foreheads.

Shelby walked close to Liam, their hands brushing every few steps. She desperately wanted to take hold of his hand, but resisted the urge.

They reached the rental car in the parking lot, which was out of view of the others.

Liam opened the back hatch door, grabbed the suitcase handle, and paused. His eyes were glossy with tears.

Shelby wrapped her arms around him and began to cry. "If I had never met you, I wouldn't have known who I really was. I thank God every day for you. I love you, Liam; never forget that."

He closed his eyes, buried his face in her hair, and breathed in her scent as he held her in his arms for the last time. He took her face in his hands and kissed her forehead. If he had kissed her lips, he wouldn't have been able to let her go.

"If you need anything, no questions asked. I'll be here in less than two hours."

She tilted her head and ran her hand down his arm. "I know."

They returned to the park bench, where Martha stood talking with Scott and the children.

Shelby looked at Martha; both of them trying to hold back their tears. They held each other tight for a moment, then said goodbye.

Liam looked at the twins. "It's time to go, guys."

They ran to Shelby and wrapped their arms around her.

She squeezed them and kissed the tops of their heads. "I love you both so much."

"When will we see you again?" Chloe asked, trying not to cry.

Shelby glanced at Liam, then met Chloe's tear-filled eyes. "I don't know, honey. But we're family, so I'll always be here for you."

Shelby watched Liam walk over to Scott and extend his hand.

Scott tightened his jaw and reluctantly accepted his gesture.

Liam looked him straight in the eye, tightening his grip. "Don't hurt her."

Scott glared back and squeezed Liam's hand tighter. "I have no intention of hurting *my* wife."

CHAPTER 68

Scott carried Shelby's suitcase into their house and set it in the foyer. Rhylie and Tyler ran to the couch and turned on the TV. Within minutes, the cartoon mesmerized them, and they were unfazed by their mother's presence.

Shelby looked around. Everything was exactly as it had been nearly three years ago. She remembered every room and the warmth of her home, but she felt like a guest.

"All your clothes are still in our room. I couldn't bring myself to do anything with them."

"Thank you."

"Are you hungry? I'm going to make the kids some lunch."

"I can make it for them, Scott."

He looked at her. "Sure. Okay," he said, and pulled items from the refrigerator to make sandwiches, placing them on the modest island.

Shelby grabbed a paper plate and paused.

Scott looked at her. "What's wrong?"

She sighed. "I don't even know what they like."

"It's okay. I'll talk you through it," he teased and bumped his shoulder lightly into her.

The four of them finished their lunch, and the kids retreated to the couch again and, within a short time, fell victim to an afternoon nap.

They sat awkwardly at the dining table until Scott placed his hand on Shelby's.

"Look, Shel, I'm sorry. All this was my fault. If I hadn't gotten drunk. You wouldn't have left and gotten into the accident and…"

Shelby placed her hand on his. "Things were strained between us, and I think our feelings for each other were changing. But I should have talked to you."

"I found your rings on the nightstand that night. The police didn't consider you a missing person—well, not until your parents convinced them you wouldn't leave your children. Shel, they investigated me. They thought I did something to you."

"I'm so sorry, Scott."

"I called the detective after we met in Connecticut, but he may still want to see you for himself."

"Yes, of course."

"I told my parents this morning. They are so happy you are home."

"Did you talk to my parents?"

"No. You said at the park you wanted to talk to them yourself."

"Yes, I remember. I should probably call them now."

Shelby went outside on their back porch and noticed the addition of a swing set in the small fenced-in yard. She smiled, thinking Scott was a great father and the kids must love it.

Shelby felt guilty for not calling her parents when her memory returned, but she knew they would come to New Jersey, so she waited until she was back home in Boston. Her heart raced as she dialed her mother's number.

"Hello?"

"Mom. Mom, it's Shelby."

"…Shelby?"

"I'm safe. I'm home."

There was silence, then quiet crying. After a few seconds, Liza tried to speak. "Shel … by."

"Mom," she cried as tears rolled down her cheeks. "Scott is

bringing me to see you and Dad, okay?"

"Yes, oh, Shelby, honey."

"I'll see you soon, Mom. I love you."

Scott pulled into the Joneses' driveway and placed his hand on her knee. "Call me when you want me to pick you up."

"Thank you." She glanced behind her. "Bye Rhylie, bye Tyler," she said and blew them a kiss.

Rhylie leaned forward in her seat. "Can we see Mimi and Papa?"

Scott looked in the rearview mirror. "We will later, honey."

Shelby walked to the front steps of her childhood home when the front door flew open. Liza pulled her daughter close, and Patrick wrapped his arms around them both. The three stood in the doorway, crying in each other's arms.

They went inside and sat at the dining table, where Shelby explained why she had dropped the kids off with them that morning in July and told them not to blame Scott for her being gone.

Liza tilted her head. "Scott told us what happened with Sam, but honey, where were you all this time? I understand being upset with Scott, but to leave the children?"

"I didn't leave Scott or the children, Mom. Most of the morning was a blur, but I remember walking to the park. I found a license on the sidewalk of a woman who looked just like me. When I finally spotted her pulling out of a parking lot, I yelled to her and looked into the eyes of my identical twin sister, Michelle Carrington."

Liza's eyes widened, and she placed her hand over her mouth.

"Her convertible was the car that hit me." Shelby's expression hardened as she stared at her parents.

Patrick's jaw tightened, and he looked down. "Shelby, there's something we never wanted you to know, but —"

"I already know what the Carringtons did, Dad."

Liza reached her hand across the table. "Shelby, honey."

She ignored her mother's gesture. "What I don't know…" She sighed. "Is how you became my parents."

Liza glanced at Patrick, then her eyes lowered. "I was your nurse in the neonatal care unit in Virginia, where you were born. You were so fragile, but you were a fighter. You were there for five months. I couldn't let you go into the foster system." Liza looked at Patrick again. "We wouldn't let that happen."

Her father's face hardened. "The Carringtons didn't deserve you."

Liza placed her hand on Patrick's. "Once the adoption was finalized, we moved to Boston, believing there would be no chance that the two of you would ever cross paths."

Shelby looked down. "Hmph." Then, she looked up at her parents again. "Michelle also attended UConn. As well as her husband, Liam."

An expression of disbelief passed between her parents.

"I didn't have my ID with me that day. A lot was assumed after the accident."

"What do you mean, honey?" Liza asked.

"Everyone thought Michelle had been thrown from her convertible. I had her driver's license in my hand. I guess it was lying on the road next to me. Obviously, I matched everything on her ID, being her identical twin."

Patrick closed his eyes and sighed. "You didn't leave us; you were taken from us."

"For over two years, I had amnesia and lived my sister's life. Loving her children. And falling in love with her husband." Her eyes filled with tears. "It all feels like a cruel joke. Leaving them was so hard."

Liza took Shelby's hand. "I'm so sorry you went through all this, honey, but we are so thankful to have you back with us." Her face was full of gratitude. "Rhylie and Tyler finally have their mother back."

CHAPTER 69

Short Hills

The drive to the airport and flight back to New Jersey left the four quiet and lost.

They would have to find a new normal without Shelby. If Michelle were found alive, it would be a miracle. Liam hated the thought of Chloe and Ben being told anything else.

Bear greeted them when they walked into the mudroom, bringing a moment of happiness to the twins' somber mood.

Martha placed her hands on their shoulders. "Come, shall we make chocolate chip or snickerdoodles?"

Ben looked up at Martha and smiled. "Chocolate chip!"

The twins were fast asleep on the sectional, so Liam turned off the TV and carried them up to bed one at a time. He returned downstairs, went to the guest room, and sat on the side of the bed in the dark, replaying their last night alone in his head. He turned on the nightstand lamp and picked up the picture of Michelle, Chloe, and Ben. "I'm so sorry, Chelle. Where are you? Is this my punishment?"

He set the picture back down and noticed a small red ribbon sticking out of the nightstand drawer. When he opened it, he found a black leather journal that appeared unused until he turned a few pages and saw several had been written on.

Okay, Dr. Kent, I'm starting a journal. I don't know if this will help me regain my memory, but I'll give it a shot.

Liam shut the journal, as if he was invading Shelby's privacy, but besides his memories, this was all he had of her, so he opened it again. He read a few pages of her describing their daily activities, and still, nothing was familiar to her, but she had already felt the love a mother has for her children. She knew he wanted more from her, but she was afraid and unsure. It was too soon.

He turned the page and smiled as he read her description of the night he surprised her with the dress and dinner. How her stomach fluttered with his touch. How his crystal-blue eyes captivated her, and when they made love for the first time since coming home.

He closed his eyes and sighed. The journal slipped from his hands onto the floor, opening to the last page. He stared at it for a moment, then picked it up.

Liam,

If you are reading this, I have left you with my deepest personal thoughts as I tried to find my way as Chloe and Ben's mother and your wife. I love the sound of your wife.

Little did you all know, you brought a stranger into your world, cared for her, made her feel safe, and loved her like no other.

Chloe and Ben are my family, my flesh and blood, and I fear all I have of my sister. Because I had the privilege of living her life, but only for a moment, I knew the woman she was—a woman of strength, integrity, faith, and loved as deeply as she was loved.

Liam, you will always have a piece of my heart. I love you a thousand times infinity.

He closed the journal and pinched the bridge of his nose to stop his tears. "How do I do this without you?" He opened Shelby's text feed, and the indicator bubble pulsed on his screen. He stared at it anxiously, waiting to hear from her, but it disappeared, and his heart sank.

CHAPTER 70

Boston

Shelby closed the book and kissed Tyler on the forehead. "I love you, my big boy. Sweet dreams." Tyler smiled and rolled onto his side. His eyelids were heavy, and sleep found him quickly.

She went to Rhylie's room and sat on the side of her bed. "I'm so happy to be home with you, Tyler, and Daddy. I'm sorry I was gone so long."

Rhylie nodded, then asked, "Can I call Sam and say goodnight?"

Shelby's smile concealed the sting of her daughter's words. "Sure, honey. I'll get Daddy." She kissed Rhylie on the cheek. "I love you."

She left Rhylie's room and stood in the hallway with her hand over her mouth, fighting back tears. She gathered herself and went to the living room. "Rhylie wants to say good night to Sam."

Scott tilted his head. "I'm sorry, Shel."

She stood in the hallway while Scott called Sam. As much as it hurt her, she stayed and listened.

"Hey, Rhylie wants to say goodnight."

"Night, Sam, I love you. Okay. Bye," Rhylie said and handed the phone to her father.

"Thank you. I will." He ended the call and kissed Rhylie on the forehead. "Sweet dreams, honey." Scott shut the bedroom door and found Shelby standing in the hallway. "I'm sorry. They really became attached to her. I know that hurts you. Just give them time." He hugged her and sighed. "We'll all get through this."

She ended their embrace and put her hands in her back pockets. "Um, I think I should sleep in the guest room. I'm sorry, but I can't sleep in the bed where you and…"

Scott nodded. "Okay. I get it."

He took a set of sheets from the hall closet upstairs and brought them to the guest room downstairs. "I'm sorry, it's kinda a mess in here." He moved a few baby items out of the way and pulled back the comforter on the twin-size bed.

"I can do it, Scott."

"I don't mind, Shel."

"Really, it's okay. Can you get my suitcase, though?"

He handed her the bedsheets and returned with her suitcase, setting it by the door. He watched her pull the comforter over the sheets and wondered how long she would stay in the guest room.

"I'm so grateful you are safe and home." He hugged her again and kissed her cheek. "Good night."

She brushed her teeth in the half bath and looked at herself in the mirror. *How long would the awkwardness last between them? Would she ever be able to sleep in their bed again? And how long would it take her to stop longing for Liam?*

She quietly closed the guest room door and lay on the twin bed. *It felt so small compared to their king-size bed at home.* She sighed. *It wasn't her bed or her home anymore.* She looked at her phone; the screen displayed a picture of her, Liam, Martha, the twins, and Bear in front of the fireplace, courtesy of none other than Ann Carrington. For almost three years, Ann had been her mother, but now she only felt contempt towards her.

She couldn't bring herself to change her home screen, so she opened her texts, scrolled to Liam's name, and typed goodnight, but quickly deleted it. *Don't send it,* she told herself. *It will just make all of this harder.* She closed her eyes, remembering the feel of him, the scent of him, his crystal-blue eyes, and cried herself to sleep.

CHAPTER 71

Short Hills

The weekend was over, forcing Liam, Martha, and the twins to return to some type of normalcy. Liam dropped the twins off at school, hoping that seeing their friends would distract them. He pulled Beverly into his office and explained everything.

She found it all unbelievable and heartbreaking, gave him a hug, and kept his phone quiet. He stood looking out of his office window, daydreaming, when a knock on his door made him turn around.

"Liam, I'm sorry to disturb you, but I have the elementary school on hold for you."

He gave her a worried look. "Thank you, Beverly."

"Hello?"

"Hello, Mr. Grant, this is Principal Smith. I'm calling because we had an incident with Benjamin this morning."

A crease formed between his brows. "What happened?"

"Well, it appears he had an outburst in Mrs. Whitmore's classroom. Do you know what may have caused this behavior? Mrs. Whitmore said, he's always been a wonderful, helpful student."

Liam sighed. "Yes, I know what this is about. We recently had some troubling news about his mother." He just couldn't explain it all again. "I'm sorry he acted out in this way. I will talk to him."

"Benjamin is currently in our main office. It would be best if you came and brought him home. There will be no disciplinary action."

"Okay, I will leave now. Thank you, Principal Smith."

Liam went to Beverly's desk. "Beverly, please cancel my afternoon meeting. I need to pick Ben up at school, and I won't be returning to the office today."

"Yes, no problem. I hope Ben feels better soon."

Liam knew this would be hard for the twins, but he never expected Ben to act out, especially in school. He wondered how long it would be before Chloe could no longer hide her sadness. He refused to let this be their new normal.

When he entered the elementary school's main office, he saw Ben sitting in a chair, looking forlorn. "Hello, Liam Grant. I'm here to take Benjamin Grant home."

"Hello, Mr. Grant. Please fill in the sign-out sheet."

He went over and squatted in front of Ben, placing his hand on his knee. "Let's go home, buddy."

Ben sat in the back seat and stared out the window. Liam glanced at him in the rearview mirror. It broke his heart that his son was struggling and acting out uncharacteristically.

As soon as they walked into the mudroom, Ben dropped his book bag and ran upstairs to his room.

Martha came out of the laundry room holding a basket of clothes, surprised to see Liam.

"Hi, Martha. Ben had an incident at school, so we're home for the rest of the day."

"Oh dear. Let me know if I can do anything."

Liam knocked on Ben's door and opened it, finding him on his bed with his face buried in his pillow.

He sat on the side of the bed and rubbed Ben's back. "Can you tell me what happened today, buddy?"

Ben shook his head no and sniffled his runny nose.

"Look, bud, I'm not mad. I only want to know what happened."

Ben rolled over, showing his tear-soaked eyes. "Tommy was bragging about his mom, and I got really mad because I don't have a mom anymore. I want Mom and Shelby to come home."

Liam pulled Ben up and held him tight. "I know, buddy. We all do."

He set Ben down. "Can you do me a favor?"

Ben nodded.

"The next time you get mad, I want you to take a deep breath and slowly count to ten."

Ben looked away.

"I know it sounds silly, but it works. Why don't you lie down for a little while, okay?"

Ben buried his face in his pillow again.

Liam shut the bedroom door and stood in the hallway. *Where are you, Chelle? They need you.*

Liam picked Chloe up after school, planning to talk to her about Ben. Before he had his seat belt fastened, Chloe told him she had heard about Ben being sent to the principal's office. He reassured her that Ben was okay, not in trouble, and that she should be nice to him.

He entered the garage and turned off the car. "Chloe, it's okay to cry or be mad. You can talk to me, honey."

"I don't want to make you sad, Daddy," she said, blinking her eyes rapidly.

Liam opened the passenger door, helped Chloe out, and hugged her. "Honey, you won't make me sad. You and Ben can always talk to me. I love you, sweetie."

Ben brushed his teeth, ran to Chloe's room with his pillow, and pulled the trundle out. Chloe laid a blanket over her brother and hopped onto her bed.

"Good night, I love you guys." Liam turned off the light and shut the bedroom door. He could hear them whispering, grateful they had each other. Then he thought of Michelle and Shelby, having their connection cruelly stolen.

He went downstairs to let Bear outside and stood on the back patio, looking up at the night sky. He hoped the fresh air would calm the anger that brewed inside him as he thought of Shelby making love to Scott. *Why was he torturing himself?* He called Bear inside, went to the butler's pantry, and poured himself a bourbon. As he stood at the kitchen island, his jaw tightened, then he drank the entire glass in one swallow. He closed his eyes and tried to count to ten like he told Ben, but his fist tightened. He gritted his teeth and threw the glass across the kitchen, shattering it against a cabinet.

Bear jumped out of his bed with his ears flat against his head and ran behind a chair.

Martha walked out of her room and saw Liam squatting next to several shards of glass. "Liam, are you alright?"

He looked over his shoulder and raised his hand to stop her from walking toward him. "I'm sorry to startle you. The glass slipped out of my hand."

She accepted his lie and went back to her room.

His anger turned to self-reproach as he cleaned the shattered pieces of his heart. He coaxed Bear back to his bed, reassuring him everything was okay, even though nothing was.

He lay in the king-size bed alone. He wouldn't let the emptiness consume him. In the past, he would have run off to New York City to distract himself from his pain, but that immature, selfish behavior was behind him, and it had cost him so much. Because of Shelby, he was a different man, a better man. Chloe and Ben needed him now more than ever. His needs were no longer important to him. The twins were his only priority.

CHAPTER 72

Boston
June 2015

Tomorrow, Shelby would go to Aunt B's Bouquets and see Henry and the rest of her staff, including Sam. She hoped to return to work a few days a week while continuing to bond with Rhylie and Tyler as their mother again. Sam had replaced her in nearly every aspect of her life—at work, as a mother, and as Scott's lover. She was determined to reclaim her life with her husband and children; she owed them that much.

Two months had passed, and she still couldn't bring herself to sleep in the main bedroom. A warm embrace or kiss on the cheek was the only affection she and Scott shared. They both struggled to reconnect; Scott felt guilty about missing Sam, and she still felt loyalty to Liam.

She sat on the couch folding laundry and glanced at the TV as the morning news aired.

"A fisherman made a gruesome discovery while fishing over the weekend. State police say that partial skeletal remains were found in the Charles River. There are no further details as local officials continue to check reports of missing persons. This is a developing story."

A chill ran down her spine and made her shudder as she listened to the news reporter. A vision of Michelle slumped in the seat of the red convertible and plunging into the river flashed before her eyes. She gasped and shook her head, trying to erase the image from her mind. Then she grabbed her phone and debated whether to call Liam, but decided against it, not wanting to worry him. She continued folding clothes but carried a sick feeling in the pit of her stomach for several minutes. "Please, God, don't let it be Michelle," she whispered.

CHAPTER 73

Short Hills

"Martha, I need to run an errand. Can you please make sure the kids get settled into bed?"

"Yes, of course."

Liam would have told Martha he was meeting with Seth, but Seth had sounded so ominous on the phone, and he didn't want to worry her.

He wasn't looking forward to talking with his father-in-law, as their last conversation ended with him telling Seth to leave. He rang the doorbell and glanced over at the Cole's house. *Brad had been gone for over a decade. How could that be?*

Ida opened the door, greeted Liam, and walked him to the formal living room.

A few minutes later, Seth walked in holding a glass of scotch, ashen-faced with bloodshot eyes. "Please have a seat, Liam."

Liam's eyes narrowed. "I'll stand." He had never seen Seth like this.

Seth gave him an irritated glance. "Suit yourself."

"Why did you summon me, Seth?"

Seth drank the last of his scotch and set the glass down abruptly on the bar cart, tightened his jaw, and glared at Liam. "I summoned you here because I have news about Michelle."

Liam's heart raced. "What did you find out?"

"Partial skeletal remains were found in a river in Boston. A DNA test confirmed they were Michelle's." Seth lifted his chin and inhaled through his nose, trying to remain stoic.

Liam fell back onto the ornate sofa. He had feared the worst, but hearing it confirmed put him in a state of shock.

He glanced at Seth. "Does Ann know?"

"Yes. I just told her. She obviously is devastated. We will hold a private family service. I will call you with the details."

Liam stood up slowly, walked over to his father-in-law, and placed his hand on Seth's arm. "Please give Ann my love."

Seth closed his eyes and nodded.

Liam drove home in a daze. *This was all his fault. Michelle would still be alive if he hadn't been so selfish and hadn't driven her away. How was he going to tell Chloe and Ben?*

He pulled over before their driveway, rushed out of the car, and threw up on the shoulder of the road. "Oh my God, Chelle, if I would have known." He fell to his knees and sobbed. "I'm so sorry. Please forgive me."

A car sped by and blared its horn, startling him. He stood up and brushed the dirt from his knees, climbed back into his car, and pulled into the driveway.

He quietly walked in through the mudroom and went to the half bath, where he cupped his hands under a stream of cold water and buried his face in them to wash away his tears. He rinsed his mouth of the sour taste, then went to the butler's pantry and grabbed a glass, filling it halfway with bourbon. He threw it down his throat and filled it, this time to the brim.

Martha came out of her room and stared at him. His face was pale, and dirt covered the knees of his slacks. "Liam, what happened?"

He sighed and looked at her, his eyes glassy and tired. "Martha." He looked down. "Martha. Michelle is gone." His voice strained as he spoke again. "Michelle's dead." His head tilted to the side as he looked at her, unable to hold back his tears.

Martha's lips parted, but she couldn't speak. She wrapped her arms around him and buried her face in his chest and wept.

He embraced her, knowing that losing Michelle was like losing her own daughter. They held each other for several minutes, then went to the living room and sat on the sectional. He took Martha's hand. "Seth said the skeletal remains found in a river in Boston were Michelle's." He closed his eyes and covered his face with his other hand. "Martha, she must have died in the river."

"Oh, Liam, no," she whispered as she held a tissue to her lips.

"There will be a private memorial. Seth will call with the details." He ran his hand through his hair. "How am I going to tell Chloe and Ben?"

"I will be there with you, whatever you need, Liam." She squeezed his hand and cleared her throat. "I'm going to retire to my room. I'll see you in the morning."

Liam stood and hugged her again. "You have been our rock. We love you so much."

Martha nodded and retreated to her room.

He returned to the butler's pantry and pulled out another bottle of bourbon. His heart broke even more, hearing Martha quietly sob in her room. He grabbed his empty glass and the bourbon bottle and sat back down on the sectional, filling his glass to the rim. He didn't know if he would ever be free of the guilt and the shame. Each sip brought back another memory of Michelle. She was in his life longer than she wasn't. He finished the bottle and went to the guest bedroom. He had to be the one to tell Shelby about her sister.

CHAPTER 74

Boston

Shelby shut Tyler's door after reading *If You Give A Mouse A Cookie* three times. Rhylie was already fast asleep, tired from her school field trip. She picked up the cyclone of toys in the living room and saw Scott's sweatshirt hanging over one of the dining room chairs. She walked up the stairs to the main bedroom and stopped halfway when she heard Scott on the phone.

"I'm sorry. I know. This is hard for me, too. We're trying. It's just. Listen, I have to go. Bye. Me too."

Shelby walked back downstairs to the living room and sat on the couch, holding Scott's sweatshirt in her arms. She pulled it close, closed her eyes, and breathed in his familiar scent.

He came downstairs and saw Shelby sitting alone, staring out the window. He walked over and sat next to her. "Hey, you okay?"

She turned to face him, placed her hand on his cheek, and kissed him.

He pulled her close and kissed her deeply, only stopping to lift her T-shirt off and lay her on the couch.

She needed to know if her desire for Scott was still there. She had to find it again. As he lay on top of her, she pulled his shirt up his torso, welcoming the warmth of his abs and running her hands over the contours of his body.

He stared at her, and for a second, she remembered how his brown eyes used to make her stomach flutter. She stared back at him, and her heart told her what she knew deep down. "Do you love her?"

"Shel." He laid his head on her shoulder.

"Do you love Sam?"

He sighed and sat up. "Shel, we became close this last year."

"But are you in love with her, Scott?"

"That's not fair. Can you tell me you're not in love with Liam? Shel, it's been two months since you came home, and we still don't sleep in the same bed." He glanced at her hand. "And your rings are still on the nightstand."

A line was etched between her brows. She couldn't deny that she was still in love with Liam because he was all she dreamt of while sleeping alone in the guest room.

She started to respond when her phone rang on the kitchen island. Unknown to Scott, it was Liam's ringtone. "I should get that." She got up from the couch, grabbed her T-shirt off the floor and pulled it over her head, then answered her phone while walking to the guest room.

"Liam?" Her answer sounded desperate, having longed to hear his voice.

"Shel."

"Yes, I'm here. Are you okay?"

"Shel," his voice cracked. "She's gone. She's dead."

"Liam, who's dead?"

She heard him catch his breath. "Michelle. Michelle is dead."

Shelby held her hand over her mouth. *Was Michelle the gruesome discovery made by the fisherman on the news?* Her voice strained. "I'm so sorry."

"It's my fault. She'd still be here if I didn't … I never got to tell her that nothing happened that night with Staci."

"Liam, no."

"Shit. Chloe and Ben. How do I tell them? I can't break their hearts."

"I'm sorry. I wish I could be there with you. I love you."

"Don't say that. Don't love me. I only hurt the people I love. Michelle died thinking I cheated on her."

Shelby had never heard him talk like this and knew he'd been drinking. "Are you home?"

"Yes."

"Is Martha there?"

"Yes, why?"

"Can I talk to her?"

"She's sleeping. Michelle was like her daughter."

"I know she was. Liam, promise me you'll go to bed now."

"I'm so tired. I miss you, Shel. I love you so much. I'm sorry," he slurred, and ended the call.

Shelby threw her phone on the bed and covered her face with her hands; her mind was reeling. *Chloe and Ben. I have to go to them.* She wiped her cheeks, and when she opened the door, Scott was standing in the hallway.

"Michelle is dead. My sister is dead, Scott."

He pulled her into his arms and kissed the top of her head. "I'm so sorry, Shel."

"I have to go to them."

He held her tight and sighed. "I know. Chloe and Ben need you. *He* needs you."

CHAPTER 75

Short Hills

Liam woke up, finding a glass of water and ibuprofen on the nightstand. He knew Martha must have found him in the guest room.

Chloe, as usual, was up before Ben and sat at the kitchen island while Martha prepared breakfast.

Liam opened the guest room door and made eye contact with Martha.

"Chloe, can you please let Bear out?" Martha asked.

Chloe jumped down from the bar stool and ran over to Bear, lying by the sliding glass door. He swept the floor with his tail and popped up when Chloe opened the door.

Liam mouthed thank you as he quickly made his way up the stairs. He stood in the shower, washing off his intemperance of bourbon from the night before, but he couldn't wash away the deep sadness that ran through his veins. Dread hung heavily on him as the conversation he would have with Chloe and Ben was inevitable. He would need every ounce of emotional strength to help the twins with their heartbreak.

Two days after Liam's call, Shelby received his text with the details of Michelle's memorial service. She asked how Chloe and Ben were doing, and all he texted was *devastated*. Texting felt so cold, but she knew he would have called her if he had wanted to talk, and he didn't.

Liza offered to attend the service with her, and as much as Shelby thought she should go alone, she feared Seth's reaction to her presence and welcomed her mother's support.

The black Escalade pulled under the Hilton Hotel canopy. The driver exited and helped Shelby and Liza with their suitcases. They approached the front desk and were welcomed by the concierge. He typed away at his computer. "Yes, I have your reservation right here. Two king suites."

Shelby gave him a puzzled expression. "Oh, I only reserved one room with two doubles."

"It appears the reservation was updated. Both rooms have been taken care of."

It wasn't enough that Liam had the private jet fly to Boston and back to New Jersey; he paid for their rooms, too. With all he was going through, he was still taking care of her.

Liza raised her eyebrows. "He certainly knows how to treat his guests."

They went to their suites and agreed to meet in an hour. Shelby felt a sense of being home when she walked in and noticed a stunning bouquet on the large round table, recognizing the roses from their garden. She sat on the king-size bed and texted Liam that she and her mother were in New Jersey. She thanked him for the flight, car, rooms, and flowers, telling him it was all too much.

He immediately texted back. "I'm glad you could make it. Chloe and Ben have been asking about you. They miss you. We'll see you in a few hours."

His text was so unadorned, which saddened her, but she understood. Today would be an unbelievably difficult day for all of them.

They stopped at the front desk and requested a taxi to take them to the funeral home.

The desk clerk smiled. "Mrs. O'Donnell, a limo is waiting out front for you and Mrs. Jones."

"Oh, thank you."

Liza glanced at her daughter while shaking her head.

"I know, Mom. I already told him it was too much."

They entered the limo, sitting across from each other. As Liza watched Shelby stare out the window, she saw the toll everything was taking on her daughter. The tragedy of the accident. Learning about her twin, then her twin's death. Wanting to be the wife to Scott and mother to Rhylie and Tyler that they all deserved. And what seemed to be the most significant toll on her, leaving Liam and the twins. "You still love him, don't you?"

Shelby looked at her mother; her eyes flooded with tears. "He will always have a piece of my heart, Mom." A single tear escaped and rolled down her cheek as she turned back to look out the window.

"Chloe and Ben are your family. You will forever be connected to him. What you need to decide is what type of connection you want that to be."

Shelby turned her head back to her mother. "I won't leave my children again."

"Shelby, I'm not telling you to leave your children. People co-parent every day, even long distance, and make it work." Liza sighed and gave her daughter a questioning look. "Do you love Scott?"

"I will always love Scott."

"Do you love him enough to let him go? To allow both of you to be happy?"

Shelby closed her eyes. "Mom, I…"

The limo came to a stop. She wiped her tears and composed herself as the chauffeur opened the door.

Shelby felt a wave of nausea wash over her as she stepped out of the limo.

Liza followed behind her daughter, then slid her arm around

Shelby's. They both took a deep breath and walked into the funeral home.

The funeral director walked them through the wide hallway to a private, lavish room adorned with floral arrangements and pictures of Michelle at various ages.

Ann and Seth stood next to a large pedestal that held an ornate urn, a picture of Michelle with Chloe and Ben, and handmade cards from the twins.

Brad's parents sat on a plush loveseat, holding each other's hands. The Carringtons and Coles now shared a common loss—the loss of their only child.

Chloe and Ben stood beside their father, unsure what to do with themselves.

Liam looked up and locked eyes with Shelby.

Her body ached to hold him, to comfort him. Those crystal-blue eyes that once held so much love and passion were lost and distant. He was now a widower. He looked so broken and alone.

The twins spotted Shelby and ran to her. She hugged them tight as they wept in her arms.

Several people stared at them, taken aback by Michelle's identical twin.

Liam walked over and introduced himself to Liza. He slid his hand down Shelby's arm, both of them fighting back the urge to grab ahold of one another. He rested his hands on the twins' shoulders as they let go of Shelby and wiped their tears.

She looked at them lovingly. Her sister's children, at one time her children, standing right in front of her, yet so far out of reach.

Martha came over and hugged Shelby. "I'm so glad you came, dear."

Shelby introduced Martha to her mother, and the two shared an embrace.

Seth appeared and told the twins that their grandmother wanted them. They hugged Shelby one more time, then walked away with Martha.

Seth gave Shelby and Liza the once-over and placed his hand on Liam's arm to make it appear he was having a cordial conversation. "This is a private service. Who told you to come?"

Shelby's eyes widened and misted over. Seth's coldness took her aback. She looked at her mother, who was now glaring at him.

Liam discreetly pulled his arm away and tightened his jaw. "I did. She's Michelle's sister." A crease formed between his brows. "For God's sake, Seth, have some compassion and an ounce of decency."

Seth narrowed his cold, dark eyes, not expecting Liam's response.

Liam turned his back to Seth, extended his arm, and guided Shelby and Liza to a row of chairs. He placed his hand on the small of Shelby's back and whispered, "I'm so sorry."

She could smell bourbon on his breath and knew he needed it this time to calm his nerves and get him through the memorial.

They sat down, and Liza patted her daughter's leg. "I thank God that awful man did not raise you."

"Mom," Shelby whispered, and thought she might have known him to be a different man, a loving father, had they not abandoned her.

Shelby watched Ann comfort Chloe and Ben and wanted to embrace her, but with Seth so close, she didn't dare risk another confrontation.

Ann glanced at Shelby and gave her a sincere smile.

Shelby welcomed Ann's reserved compassion and felt it was a quality Seth should try to emulate from his wife.

Brad's mother went over and took a seat next to Shelby. "Hello, Shelby. I'm so sorry for all you have been through. Your sister was like a daughter to me. When we lost Brad, Michelle was my saving grace." Jennifer paused. "Now they are together." She placed her hand on Shelby's and squeezed it. "I want you to know you hold a special place in my heart."

"Thank you, Jennifer; you don't know how much that means to me."

Jennifer nodded and glanced at Liza.

Shelby placed her hand on her mother's knee. "This is my mother, Liza Jones."

Jennifer extended her hand. "I'm sorry we have to meet under these circumstances."

Liza cupped Jennifer's hand between her own. "Yes, me too."

The funeral director asked everyone to take their seats. Ann, Seth, Liam, the twins, and Martha sat in the first row. Liam's parents, the Coles, Shelby, and her mother were directly behind them. A few close family friends and business associates filled the remaining rows.

The minister who performed Liam and Michelle's wedding ceremony gave the eulogy. He described a life of love and joy, stories from Michelle's childhood, Brad, college, marrying Liam, and her precious children.

Shelby listened as a series of pictures floated through her head. Michelle and Liam on their wedding day, their honeymoon, holding Chloe and Ben in the hospital when they were born, and pictures of the four of them over the years; a happy, loving family. For a time, she believed those were her pictures, her family, her life. It broke her heart knowing her sister would never see Chloe and Ben grow up.

Only the minister spoke. Shelby knew it would be too difficult for Chloe and Ben, and Liam still carried so much guilt and shame. The minister said a last prayer and thanked everyone for attending Michelle's memorial.

Ann hugged Brad's parents goodbye and stood alone, looking at Michelle's picture.

Seth was talking in the back of the room, so Shelby and Liza approached Ann.

Shelby placed her hand on Ann's arm. "I'm so sorry, Ann. My sister was deeply loved, and her family was everything to her. I want you to know how grateful I am to you for showing me love and compassion after the accident, believing I was your daughter."

Ann placed her hand on Shelby's cheek and looked at her endearingly. "I realize this is your loss, too." Ann tilted her head. "It was easy to love you."

Shelby smiled. "Ann, I'd like you to meet my mother, Liza Jones."

Ann blushed as Liza was the beneficiary of her shameful decision all those years ago. "Hello, Liza."

"Hello, Ann. I'm so sorry for your loss, but I must thank you."

"Thank me?"

Shelby tensed, wondering what would leave her mother's lips.

"Yes. For loving and caring for my daughter as if she were your own."

Ann looked at Liza, unable to reply.

Shelby felt her cheeks burn. "Ann, I never got to speak to you before returning to Boston, but I hope you know how much I love Chloe and Ben."

Ann nodded. "I do." Then she hugged Shelby and whispered, "He needs you."

Shelby pulled her head back and stared at Ann, who gave her an approving smile.

Seth appeared next to his wife. His eyes were just as cold as before. "Is everything alright here?"

Ann placed her hand on Seth's arm. "Everything is fine, darling."

"I am sorry for your loss, Seth. Take care, Ann." Shelby took her mother's arm and walked over to Chloe and Ben, who had moved to the loveseat. She kneeled and placed her hands on their knees, hating to see such deep sadness on their little faces. "I'm so sorry about your mother. I love you both so much and will always be here for you."

Liam walked over, and Shelby stood up. He ran his hand down her arm again, making her stomach flutter and her body ache to hold him.

"Daddy, can Shelby and her mom come over for a little while?" Chloe asked.

Shelby looked at him, not expecting the invitation.

"Yes, if they can. When are you leaving for Boston?"

"Tomorrow morning."

CHAPTER 76

They entered the limo, where Chloe and Ben were sandwiched between Liam and Shelby.

Martha and Liza sat across from them and watched a semblance of happiness stir in the twins.

Shelby smiled as the limo approached the house. She watched her mother admire the stone fence that bordered the property, and the finely manicured shrubs that lined the driveway, just as she had done when Liam brought her home from the hospital.

Liam held the mudroom door and told the twins they could change, knowing they were desperate to get out of their formal wear. Martha excused herself to her room while Liam took Liza's coat, then helped Shelby with hers.

As he stood close behind her, she closed her eyes, breathed in his cologne, and remembered what Ann had whispered to her.

Liza's eyes sparked in amazement as she looked around, then her eyes followed the stone fireplace up to the ceiling.

Shelby watched her mother's face. "It's beautiful, isn't it?"

Liza nodded as they walked to the living room and sat on the large sectional.

Liam came into the living room. "Can I get you something to drink?"

"Just water, thank you," Liza replied.

Shelby stood up. "I can get it, Liam."

He followed her to the kitchen and leaned against the island.

"Would you and your mother like to stay for dinner?"

"That would be nice, thank you." She placed her hand on his arm.

"How are you doing? I was so worried about you when you called me."

He looked away. "I'm sorry I worried you and you heard me like that."

Shelby grabbed a bottle of water from the refrigerator. "It's okay." She raised her eyebrow while tapping the bottle against his chest. "Just don't let it happen again."

He laughed and opened the bottle for her.

She tilted her head. "It's nice to see you smile."

She walked to the living room, where Chloe and Ben were already sitting on the sectional, talking with her mother.

"Did Rhylie and Tyler come too?" Chloe asked.

"No, honey, they didn't."

Chloe frowned. "Oh."

Liam came over and stood next to the sectional behind the twins. "Hey guys, Shelby and her mother are staying for dinner; then Martha will bring you to Grandma and Grandpa Carrington's, okay?"

Chloe and Ben smiled at them.

Liza glanced at her daughter. "We are?"

"Sorry, Mom, I didn't think you'd mind."

Martha walked into the kitchen, and the clicking of toenails danced across the floor behind her. Bear lumbered toward the twins, and when he saw Shelby and Liza, he wiggled his body over to them.

Chloe and Ben giggled as Bear licked Shelby's hands and face.

"Oh. Bear. I missed you too." Shelby laughed.

Liza went to the kitchen and chatted with Martha and helped her prepare dinner.

Liam corralled Bear and sat between the twins and Shelby. He loosened his tie and drank his water.

The corner of Shelby's mouth curved up, acknowledging his drink of choice. She listened as the twins, mainly Chloe, updated her about school and Bear's antics. She missed knowing what was going on in their daily lives.

As they all gathered at the dining table, Shelby remembered the life they used to share, like she had never left. For a while at least, her presence would distract the twins from their deep sadness.

Shelby helped Liam clean the dishes while the twins ran upstairs and packed their overnight bags, leaving Liza and Martha to relax and chat at the table.

"This was nice. Thank you. Thank you for everything: the flight, the hotel, the limo."

"I will always take care of you, Shel," he said, handing her a rinsed pot.

As she dried it, she looked at him. "Liam. You don't need to."

He glanced at her. "I want to."

Chloe and Ben dragged their bags down the stairs to the mudroom.

Martha and Liza walked into the kitchen, appearing as a united front.

Shelby slipped Liam a curious glance.

"Ben, please be a dear and grab my bag from my room. Chloe, would you please let Bear outside?" Martha looked at Liam and Shelby. "I'm going to drop Liza off at the hotel on our way to Ann and Seth's. Liam, can you give Shelby a ride back to the hotel?"

He drew his brows together. "Sure."

The twins returned to the kitchen.

"When will we see you again?" Chloe asked Shelby.

She looked at Liam. "I don't know, honey, but this isn't goodbye, it's see you until next time, okay? You can call me anytime." She reached her arms out and pulled them close. "I love you both so much."

Ben released his hug, but Chloe hung on and whispered in Shelby's ear, "I miss you so much."

She squeezed Chloe and whispered back, "I miss you too."

She stood and hugged Martha. "Goodbye and thank you."

Martha smiled. "Take care, dear."

Shelby rubbed her mother's shoulder. "Goodnight, Mom. I'll see you later at the hotel."

Liza hugged Liam. "Thank you for your hospitality."

The mudroom door shut, and the house was quiet. "Looks like it's just you, me, and Bear." He raised an eyebrow. "Care for a real drink? I promise I'll stick to water."

She smiled. "I guess I could use a glass of wine."

He turned off the lights, leaving only the fireplace to illuminate the living room. Finally, after a formal day of hell, he felt he could breathe. He opened the top button of his shirt and removed his tie, relaxing into the sectional. He rested his head back and watched Shelby take off her heels, kneel on the couch next to him, and tuck her legs underneath her.

She sipped her wine, closed her eyes, and breathed in his cologne.

He couldn't take his eyes off her. He loved how her lashes lay on her rosy cheeks and her soft pink lips were wet with wine. Her hair was pulled back neatly into a bun, and her black dress hugged her curves. Besides the small scars on her face from the accident, she was identical to Michelle. But he no longer saw her as the woman he had loved nearly his entire life; he saw her as the love of his life.

She opened her eyes, and his crystal-blues stared back at her. She had longed to be this close to him again and nervously blurted, "I'm still sleeping in the guest room."

His gaze lingered, then he took the glass of wine from her hand and helped her up from the sectional.

She looked at him, confused. *They just sat down. Was he taking her back to the hotel already?*

He placed his hand on her cheek. "You deserve so much better than me."

"Liam, don't say that."

"Michelle would be alive if it weren't for my selfishness."

Tears formed in her eyes. "She chose to leave."

His hand fell from her cheek, and he clenched his jaw, then turned away from her.

"Look at me." She placed her hand on his cheek, turning his head to face her. "You're not the reason she died."

"But I am the reason she left."

"You have to stop blaming yourself. It was the accident that took her life, Liam, not you."

His eyes narrowed. "Chloe and Ben have to grow up without their mother. They deserve better."

"You are their entire world and a loving father. Liam, you are a good man and deserve happiness and love, too." She wrapped her arms around him, wanting to take his pain away. Then she felt the weight of his mournfulness as he melted into her arms.

"I love you. You are *my* world, too." She brushed her cheek against his tear-stained face, then placed her lips next to his.

"Shel…" he whispered. "If I kiss you, I won't be able to stop. I won't be able to let you go this time."

She placed her hand on his cheek and looked deep into his eyes. "Then kiss me."

He pulled her close, savoring the sweet taste of wine on her lips, then whispered in her ear, "Jesus, do you know what you do to me?"

She pressed her body into his and bit her bottom lip. "I think I do."

His eyes followed her hands as she unbuttoned his shirt and opened his slacks.

He turned her around and unzipped her dress, letting it slide down her body to the floor.

She turned back around and released her bun, shaking her hair loose.

He grabbed the large plush blanket from the sectional, placed it in front of the fireplace, then guided her on top, and leaned his body into her. "You don't know how much I've needed you. I've dreamt of holding you again and making love to you."

She ran her fingers through his hair, studying his face. "I've missed you so much." Her eyes filled with tears. "Leaving you was the hardest thing I've ever done."

He kissed her deeply, filling him with a peace he thought he'd never feel again.

Hours later, she woke up in his arms and smiled. "Have you been watching me sleep?"

"I was afraid that if I fell asleep, I would wake up and find you were only a dream."

She placed her hand on his cheek and kissed him. "It wasn't a dream. I'm right here."

"Shel, I'll do whatever I have to do. I don't want to do life without you."

She released a heavy sigh. "If I've learned anything from all of this, it's that life can change in an instant, and I can't pretend to be happy. It's not fair to Scott or our children."

Liam traced her face with his finger, resting his hand on her cheek. "We'll figure this out, I promise."

She smiled, knowing he would keep that promise, and glanced at the window; it was well into the night. "How long was I asleep?"

"Not long, but I suppose I should take you back to the hotel."

Shelby wrinkled her nose and nodded.

He stood behind her, clasped her bra, and slid her dress onto her shoulders. He swept her hair to the side and kissed her neck while zipping up her dress. "I prefer taking your clothes off to putting them back on."

She turned around, rested her arms around his neck, and smiled. "I do, too."

At 3:00 a.m., the roads were deserted and dimly lit by street-lights. Liam interlaced his fingers with Shelby's while they drove back to the hotel. Much of the heaviness left him, and he felt alive again.

He walked her to her hotel room and stood in the open doorway. "Sleep well."

His crystal-blue eyes showed love and passion again, making her heart full. "I will."

Shelby's phone pinged, waking her up after only a few hours of sleep. A text from her mother led to a knock on her door a few minutes later.

The corner of Liza's mouth lifted. "Well, good morning. You look like you've had little sleep."

Shelby rolled her eyes. "Come in, Mom."

Liza took a seat on the couch in the large suite. "So?"

Shelby yawned and sat next to her mother. "I have to let Scott go. He's in love with Sam, Mom. He deserves to be happy, and Sam makes him happy."

Liza placed her hand on Shelby's leg. "And Liam?"

Her eyes glistened with tears. "He's the love of my life."

Liam waited in the hotel lobby for Shelby and her mother. He had to see her again before driving them to the airport to return to Boston, and he wanted to talk to Liza.

Liam pulled out Liza's chair, then Shelby's. He sat down between them and grasped Shelby's hand. "Liza, thank you for coming with Shelby to Michelle's memorial. This whole situation is unbelievable, but I want you to know how much I love your daughter."

Liza's eyes filled with tears as she tilted her head. "I see a light in my daughter that shines so brightly when she's with you. That is the kind of love and happiness every parent wishes for their child."

Liam kissed Shelby's hand. "I will do whatever it takes to make her happy."

The three stood on the tarmac by the Grant's private jet. Liam hugged Liza goodbye and held her hand as she walked up the steps to the plane. He went over to Shelby and wrapped his arms around her. This time, he knew she would come back to him, and he fully understood that ending her marriage to Scott was not easy for her. "This isn't goodbye; it's see you until next time," he said.

Shelby smiled and rested her forehead on his. "See you until next time." She kissed him passionately, then took his hand and walked to the steps. "I love you."

"I love you too. Have a safe flight."

Liza sat comfortably in the leather seat, noticing that her daughter was no longer conflicted. Liam could provide her daughter with a privileged life, but it was Shelby's heart he would protect for the rest of his, and for that, Liza was grateful.

CHAPTER 77

Boston

The Escalade pulled up to Shelby's childhood home. The driver opened Liza's door, pulled her bag from the trunk, and carried it to the front steps, where Patrick stood waiting to greet his wife.

Shelby walked her mother to the front door. "Thank you, Mom. Your support means the world to me. I love you." She hugged her father and returned to the Escalade, rehearsing what she wanted to say to Scott. But her mind went blank when she saw him in the doorway of their home.

Scott took her suitcase and hugged her. "How are you?"

"It was a lovely memorial, but seeing Chloe and Ben heartbroken was so hard. They're too young to lose their mother."

"I'm sorry, Shel."

She took a deep breath. "Scott, let's sit down."

Shelby looked around at the home they had created for their family and smiled, then looked at Scott. "We both know this isn't working. Neither of us is happy."

Scott sighed. "I knew it wouldn't be easy, and honestly, I didn't think we would have such a hard time reconnecting. But so much has happened, and so much has changed."

"We're in love with other people. I know Sam makes you happy and that you, Rhylie, and Tyler love her."

Scott looked down. "Shel, I'll always love you." His eyes misted over. "We made two incredible little humans, didn't we?"

A tear ran down her cheek. "Yes, we did."

He wiped her tear with his thumb and hugged her.

Scott's mother walked in the front door with Rhylie and Tyler, and when they saw their mother, they ran to her.

She pulled them close and hugged them tight. "I missed you, my loves."

Scott took the kid's bags from his mother and set them aside, then placed his hand on her arm and smiled.

Shelby walked over to Scott's mother and hugged her. Their embrace expressed their unspoken words.

She placed her hand on Shelby's cheek. "Be happy, Shelby, and know that we love you."

Shelby sat on the park bench, watching Rhylie and Tyler kick a soccer ball to each other.

Sam walked up and sat on the bench. "Hey."

"Hi, Sam. Thank you for meeting me."

"Sure."

Shelby turned and faced her best friend. "Do you truly love him?"

Sam glanced at Rhylie and Tyler, then back at Shelby. "I do, Shel. I didn't mean for it to happen; it just did. I love those little rugrats, too."

Shelby looked back at Rhylie and Tyler and gave Sam a side-eye, knowing she was sincere.

Tears formed in Sam's eyes. "I never got to tell you how sorry I was about that night. You are my best friend. I thought you were dead."

"I know. It's okay, Sam. I forgive you. Both of you."

Sam tilted her head. "Thank you."

"I shouldn't have reacted the way I did, but it led us here." Shelby glanced at Sam. "Rhylie and Tyler miss you."

"I miss them so much, Shel."

"Scott loves you, Sam."

Sam's mouth parted, but she didn't speak.

"He deserves to be happy, too. We all do." Shelby no longer felt animosity toward Sam, and if anyone were to co-parent her children, she was grateful it would be her best friend.

Rhylie and Tyler saw Sam sitting with their mother and ran to her.

She opened her arms and hugged them. "Hey, kiddos."

Rhylie squeezed her. "I miss you, Sam."

"I miss you and Tyler too, sweetie."

Tyler grabbed Sam's hand. "Come play."

"You too, Mommy," Rhylie said, grabbing her mother's hand.

Shelby gave Sam a sincere smile. "Sure you can keep up?"

Sam raised her eyebrow. "Just watch."

Scott loaded the large suitcase into the back seat of his truck and walked back into the house.

Shelby sat on the couch with Rhylie and Tyler at her sides. "Mommy will come back in a few days to bring you to New Jersey to visit Chloe and Ben, okay?"

Rhylie's face carried a worried expression. "Are we staying there forever?"

"No, honey. You and Tyler will live with me part of the time and with Daddy and Sam the other time."

Rhylie's face lit up. "Sam is coming home?"

"Yes, honey, she is."

As if on cue, Sam walked in the front door and was greeted by Rhylie and Tyler. "Sam!" they shouted.

Shelby walked over to them and kneeled. "Can I have a hug and kiss goodbye?" She held them tight, grateful to still be in their lives.

"I will see you in a few days. Be good for Sam and Daddy. I love you." She stood up, then looked at Sam and gave her a hug. "Thank you for being there for them and loving them. I am eternally grateful. I love you, Sam."

"Ditto." Sam ended their embrace and wiped a tear from her cheek. "Okay, enough sappy talk. I can't handle any more tears."

Shelby laughed. She had missed her snarky friend. "Oh, one more thing." She pulled out a set of keys from her pants pocket. "Aunt B's Bouquets is all yours. Well, not quite yet, but the papers are with the lawyer."

Sam's eyes widened. "Shel?"

"Aunt Becky would be so proud of how you stepped up and took over for me. I'm proud of you, too."

Sam tilted her head. "Thank you, Shel."

Scott stood by the front door, waiting for Shelby. "All set?"

Tyler hopped over to his dad. "Sam's home!"

Scott smiled at Shelby. "Yes, she is, buddy."

The drive to the airport this time didn't leave them wondering or worrying about what their life would be when Shelby returned from New Jersey. Their love for one another allowed them to let go of what was. They were grateful for the time they shared and truly happy for one another. They would blend the two families with forgiveness, honesty, and love.

Scott walked Shelby to her gate and tried to hold back the tears that pooled in his eyes. He held her and kissed her forehead. "Be happy, Shel."

She held him tight as tears rolled down her cheeks. "You too, Scott."

Short Hills

The sun slid below the horizon as her plane landed. She hailed a taxi and settled in the back seat, smiling as she imagined Liam's reaction to her coming home a few days early. Thirty minutes later, the long brick fence came into view. She was home.

The taxi pulled into the driveway, and Shelby asked the driver to stop halfway so she could walk up to the house without alerting Bear. He took her suitcase from the trunk and set it next to her. "Thank you so much," she said, handing him a tip.

Her heart pounded with excitement as she rolled her suitcase up the driveway. Large raindrops began to pelt her. The faster she walked, the harder the rain fell. She followed the rows of lights that hugged the edges of the concrete path, leaving her suitcase at the bottom of the stone steps, and ran up to the front door, finally safe from the deluge. She tried to wipe the rain from her face, but every inch of her was soaked. "Great, I must look like a drowned rat." She pulled her phone from her purse and texted Liam to come to the front door.

In less than ten seconds, Liam opened the door and stared at her. His eyes sparked with amazement.

She raised her arms out to her sides. "I'm home," she said, giving him a silly grin.

He tried not to laugh at the sight of her and grabbed her in his arms and kissed her wet lips. "I thought you weren't coming for a few days."

She set her soaking-wet arms on his shoulders and smiled. "I wanted to surprise you." Then she scrunched her nose. "Um, my suitcase is outside."

He ran down the stairs barefoot in the pouring rain and returned with her suitcase, ran his fingers through his wet hair and shook his head at her.

She scrunched her nose again. "Sorry."

He smiled and kissed her. "We'll deal with that tomorrow." Then he picked her up in his arms and carried her upstairs to their en suite.

"Where are Chloe and Ben?" she whispered.

He set her down and locked the en suite door. "Field trip day. They were wiped out and fell asleep early."

She raised her eyebrows. "Lucky us."

He started the shower, then pulled his T-shirt over his head.

She ran her hands down his chest, wet from his rain-soaked shirt.

He unbuttoned her blouse and rolled it down her arms. Tiny bumps covered her skin as a chill ran through her body. The soaked blouse slapped onto the tile floor, making her giggle. He gazed lovingly into her eyes as he finished undressing her.

She unzipped his jeans and ran her finger along his waistband, her eyes playful and filled with desire.

He slid his remaining clothes off, then picked her up and kissed her passionately while guiding her legs around his warm body. He walked them into the shower under a waterfall of hot water, causing the chill to leave her in his arms.

She ran her fingers through his wet hair, staring into those crystal-blue eyes, the ones that would now be hers to wake up to every morning.

He leaned her against the shower wall and pressed his body into hers, staring back into her ocean eyes with deep passion and love. "Welcome home, Shel. Welcome home."

EPILOGUE

July 3, 2012
Boston

Michelle looked around as images of her life flashed before her in rapid motion. She turned her head slowly and saw a figure reaching out to her. The voice was familiar and brought her a sense of peace and serenity.

"Chelle, take my hand. You're safe now," the angelic voice said.

With a curious expression, she reached her hand out through a sea of blue and white. "Brad?"

"We've been waiting for you, Chelle."

Brad extended his hand while a young girl with crystal-blue eyes stood close to him and whispered, "Mama."

As she took Brad's hand, she tilted her head and smiled at the daughter she and Liam had lost. Her heart was full, and a peacefulness washed over her.

Brad smiled. "You're home, Chelle. You're home."

December 2015
Short Hills

Ann closed her suitcase and turned around to find Seth standing in their bedroom doorway. "I hope you have reconsidered and will apologize to Liam and Shelby. She and her children are a part of our lives now."

Seth walked over to her and placed his hand on her arm. "Ann, I refuse to argue about this again."

"Seth, I won't be isolated from my grandchildren."

"I would never allow that," he said arrogantly.

"When was the last time Liam allowed you to see Chloe and Ben?"

Seth's jaw tightened, knowing it was the night of Michelle's memorial months ago.

"I said nothing all these years while you dictated my life, but no longer."

"What are you saying, Ann?"

"I'm going to Charleston to help Martha settle into her new home. She has cared for our family for over thirty years. Martha deserves a peaceful retirement; it's my turn to take care of her."

He propped his hands on his hips. "Well, how long will you be gone?"

"I don't know, Seth. But I hope my time away allows you to reflect on all the bridges you have burned. Otherwise, I fear you will live out the rest of your life as a lonely, bitter man."

His eyes widened. Ann had never spoken to him so boldly.

She placed her hand on his cheek and looked into his eyes, hoping to see the man she fell in love with, but all she saw was arrogance. "Goodbye, Seth."

Charleston, South Carolina

Nearing eight decades, Martha would retire to her quaint cottage in Charleston. She was thankful for Liam's generous gift and was content to live out the rest of her days in the leisurely community of southern hospitality and warm coastal weather.

She walked out to the piazza and settled in her rocking chair with a cup of tea. The Carringtons and Grants had provided her with a privileged life, for which she was grateful.

A smile crossed her lips as she reminisced. Rearing children filled her life with many cherished memories, but it was Michelle and Shelby who held a special place in her heart.

She was free from the guilt of harboring the Carrington's secret, but it came with a terrible loss. Michelle was like a daughter, and it broke her heart that Chloe and Ben would grow up without their mother. She was grateful, though, that Shelby had come into her life and that she could build a relationship with the premature baby the Carringtons had abandoned all those years ago. She felt contentment and peace, knowing that Chloe and Ben would be surrounded by their new family.

Nassau, Bahamas

A beam of light flashed into the twins' room. Ben grabbed his flashlight from under his pillow and hopped onto his knees. He peered out of the window and sent two quick flashes, signifying 'hi,' to the neighboring villa.

Four quick flashes answered back.

Chloe kneeled next to her brother. "Awake."

Ben nodded in agreement.

The sound of footsteps made them flop onto their beds and close their eyes. Once the coast was clear, Chloe whispered, "Tomorrow we have to teach Rhylie and Tyler the signal for parent alert."

"Yeah, that was close," Ben whispered back.

Shelby and Sam relaxed under a large umbrella, enjoying the warm ocean breeze and sipping their virgin margaritas.

Ben and Tyler carried buckets of water up the beach, where they built a giant sandcastle while Chloe and Rhylie tied flowers together to make a wreath.

Sam gave Shelby her signature side-eye. "Who would have thought the two of us would be sitting on a beach in our bikinis in the Bahamas?"

Shelby lowered her sunglasses and glanced at Sam. "Not me."

Sam rolled her eyes. "I still can't believe you talked me into wearing a bikini looking like this."

Shelby chuckled and took another sip of her drink.

Scott picked up the soccer ball and yelled to the boys.

The girls finished their wreath and set it on the empty chaise beside Shelby. "Oh, it's beautiful girls."

They both smiled proudly, then ran off to join the boys.

Liam came up behind Shelby and started rubbing her shoulders.

She closed her eyes. "Mmm, that feels so good."

Sam set her drink down and eased herself off the lounge chair. "I'm one drink in, and this is my second trip to the restroom. Seriously, how are you doing this a third time?"

Shelby laughed. "Wait until your ninth month."

"Ugh," Sam replied as she waddled away.

Liam sat on the chaise and glanced at the wreath. "Looks like the girls finished; you ready?"

He helped Shelby up, carefully picked up the wreath, and called out to Chloe and Ben. The four of them walked to the water's edge, said a prayer for Michelle, and then laid the wreath in the water.

Chloe yelled, "I love you a thousand times infinity, Mommy!"

Not to be outdone by his sister, Ben shouted, "I love you a thousand more, Mom!"

Shelby rested her hands on Chloe and Ben's shoulders as they watched the wreath float into the vast blue water.

Liam stood behind Shelby and wrapped his arms around her, laying his hands on her protruding stomach, and kissed her cheek. "How's our little guy doing?"

She placed her hands on top of Liam's and smiled. "Michael can't wait to meet his family."

AUTHOR'S NOTE:

Thank you so much for reading *A Thousand More*. I loved sharing Michelle and Shelby's journey with you, and I hope their story stayed with you long after the last page. If you enjoyed this story, please consider leaving a brief, honest review on your favorite retailer's website. Your feedback not only brightens my day but helps other readers discover the book.

Want to know the story behind Michelle and Shelby's adoption? Join my newsletter and get a special bonus prologue that tells it all.

Website: www.kslynn.com
TikTok: @author_kslynn
Instagram: @author_kslynn
Facebook: K. S. Lynn Author

ACKNOWLEDGEMENTS

I would like to express my deepest gratitude to my family for their support throughout this journey, especially my husband for his encouragement, patience, and belief in me. To my parents, for showing me what true love and marriage can be. Special thanks to Nicole and Keegan Evans for their technical support and beautiful book cover.

Heartfelt thanks to my beta readers, Nicole Evans, Lisa King, Tami Folkenflik — my soul sister, Debby Evans, Jane Clear, Kathy Rathbun, Teresa Falkenberg, and The Cottages Book Club, especially Cheryl Regan, Cindi Baker, Judy Welti, and Hannah Cole, who I think of fondly with a "closed smile." Thank you all for your time and effort. Your honest, thoughtful, constructive critiques helped strengthen the story.

Thank you to Joe Bunting, founder of The Write Practice, and his team for providing tools, guidance, and expertise, encouraging aspiring authors to realize their potential. Many thanks to my fellow 100 Day Book authors for their honest, thorough feedback and for becoming dear friends: Debi Miller Bonds, Sue Muller Hacking, Cathy Graham, Tjitske Duiker, and Terry Thurk Angell.

Special thanks to John S. Malnor, my book coach, mentor, and cheerleader. Your guidance, knowledge, and expertise are invaluable.

I am forever grateful for the roles each of you played. Without you, this book would be an unrealized dream.

Finally, I would like to thank Speak Up Talk Radio International Firebird Book Awards, the Outstanding Creator Awards, and Reader's Favorite Book Reviews for recognizing my book—it is an honor to be included among such talented and inspiring authors.

ABOUT THE AUTHOR

K. S. Lynn lives in Upstate New York, married to her high school sweetheart of forty-one years and their rescue Labrador mix, Bailey. Their three adult children are a source of inspiration, pride, and joy. She enjoys traveling, spending time with family and friends, and losing herself in a good book.

A Thousand More, her award-winning debut novel, was born from a dream in 2005. While her three young children attended elementary and preschool, she spent a few hours a day writing a story that ultimately was lost to the demise of her hard drive.

Losing the first twenty-five pages made her believe she wasn't meant to write a novel. She abandoned the story until 2019, when her desire to write returned. Twenty years later, her fictional characters' stories are finally being told.

www.ingramcontent.com/pod-product-compliance
Lightning Source LLC
Chambersburg PA
CBHW030537260626
47157CB00006B/2069